Ben Blackshaw Novels
by
Robert Blake Whitehill

DEADRISE

NITRO EXPRESS

TAP RACK BANG

GERONIMO HOTSHOT

DOG & BITCH ISLAND

BLAST

Blackshaw Short Fiction

SLUDGE
with
Taylor Griffith

PARDON ME
with
Erin Blake

AWOL
with
Erin Blake

TOUGH LUCK KID
with
Charles Ta

APACHE 8
with
Deanna Reynolds

BLAST

A Ben Blackshaw Novel

by

Robert Blake Whitehill

TELEMACHUS PRESS

Cover Designed by Carol Castelluccio www.studio042.com/

Cover Art by Buffalo Gouge www.Facebook.com/BuffaloGougeArt

Publishing services by Telemachus Press, LLC
7652 Sawmill Road
Suite 304
Dublin, Ohio 43016
http://www.telemachuspress.com
and
Calaveras Media. LLC
www.calaverasmedia.com

Visit the author website:
www.RobertBlakeWhitehill.com

ISBN: 978-1-956867-54-1 (eBook)
ISBN: 978-1-956867-55-8 (Paperback)

FICTION / Thrillers / Suspense

Version 2022.11.21

PRAISE FOR BLAST

With *BLAST* we get the return of Ben Blackshaw, a man dealing with the past while trying to make sense of the events unfolding around him. Strap in tight. This is one wild, enjoyable adventure that was well worth the wait.
Cyrus Webb
Media Personality/Top 100 Amazon Reviewer
Editor-in-Chief of CONVERSATIONS Magazine
www.cyruswebbshow.live

In the latest Ben Blackshaw thriller, *BLAST*, Robert Blake Whitehill brings to bear all his deep and varied knowledge of Smith Island and the Chesapeake Bay. Ben, his wife Luanna, and his compatriot Knocker Ellis Hogan, are up against Faction, a group hellbent on cashing in on the bounty of the bay by destroying it. amid all the mayhem, Whitehill doesn't neglect the human side of the drama. Ben and Luanna are driven not only by the goal of averting disaster, but of surviving the ordeal to return home to baby Callum. Whitehill follows another new mother's return from maternity leave to her dangerous job, where she must weigh the thrill of the chase with her responsibilities to her family.
Matty Dalrymple
Author of The Ann Kinnear Suspense Novels and Lizzy Ballard Thrillers
www.mattydalrymple.com

Five Stars ☆☆☆☆☆
Robert Blake Whitehill has once again taken each of his characters on an adventurous and wild ride with his pen. *BLAST* is a masterful mixture of

today's technology, espionage, greed, and a believable plot that is in the same league with Patricia Cornwell, Michael Crichton, Alafair Burke, Rollins, Tom Clancy, Lawrence Block, and Lee Child, in it's thrilling ride through dangerous waters. His characters always stay true to themselves, yet he manages to keep both them and the plots fresh in each book. A must read for every suspense and adventure reader.

Marta Moran Bishop
Critically Acclaimed, Award-Winning Author, Poet, Goodreads Author, Radio Show Host, Video Producer.
www.martamoranbishop
https://tinyurl.com/2kj3c32e

BLAST by Robert Blake Whitehill is an intriguing, thrilling, and thought provoking yet cautionary tale of what ifs: of home-grown terrorism, power and control. The character driven premise is dramatic, detailed and intense; the characters are animated and unconventional-the camaraderie between the Smith Island residents is dynamic and incredible-they work together like the proverbial 'well-oiled machine'.

Sandy
www.thereadingcafe.com

It's always a good day when a new Ben Blackshaw book comes out. This sixth installment has all of the action and thrills we have come to expect. When bodies start showing up in the ice, Blackshaw and the other Smith Islanders need to figure out what is happening. There are plenty of bad guys, explosions, and suspense along the way. I love the humor that is sprinkled in, just a touch to lighten things up, and the fact that the women in this series are just as tough as the men. As always, I finished this book already looking forward to the next.

Brinda Glatczak
WiLoveBooks - The United States (2,922 books) (goodreads.com)

CONTENTS

For My Family

BLAST

PART I
SNOW ANGEL

CHAPTER 1

BEN BLACKSHAW HAD been out for a walk to clear his head in the frigid breeze and failing light, but the corpse was not helping at all. This snow angel was definitely dead, frozen as it was few inches below the icy surface of the Chesapeake Bay on this December afternoon.

Blackshaw shifted to get the last searing orange light of the setting sun out of his eyes. Then he turned and looked back north toward Smith Island to get his bearings, to see how far he'd walked, and to fix where the corpse lay relative to his saltbox house on the shore. He could see a few of his neighbors who were also out strolling on the ice and marveling at this cold gloaming view of their little archipelago, which was almost never possible to see like this, not without a deadrise workboat's deck underfoot. The breeze freshened. A little twister spun powdery snow into the air like a spirit departing, or perhaps touching down with things to say.

In the distance, Sonny and Mary Wright whooped with delight as they whirled donuts on the ice in Wade Joyce's old golf cart. Mary, who was Wade Joyce's widow since the moment Sonny killed him, had wed her husband's murderer in the spirit of true love, and with maybe a squidge of gratitude at being set free from the beatings the cantankerous Wade doled out. In addition to her charm and wisdom, Mary brought a beautiful deadrise to the marriage, the *Mary Todd*, as well as the golf cart.

Blackshaw crouched to examine the body as best he might under the circumstances. The snowfall on top of the ice had melted into the familiar heavenly pattern every kid loves to lie down and flap and scrape into the white stuff. On closer inspection, Blackshaw thought perhaps the shape in the snow was more like da Vinci's splayed Vitruvian Man, with narrower limbs, and with less of the full outline of an angel's flowing robes. He figured the dark clothing on the corpse must have drawn in the sun's warmth to thin the snow like this.

It was damn creepy, Blackshaw admitted to himself. As a former SEAL in the United States Navy, he had seen death in many forms—many of his own making. He wondered if a flooded old grave in some sunken Chesapeake island burial ground had released her to drift away until this Arctic blast said stop, hold still, make an angel of yourself, and be known again to the living. *Her.* Blackshaw noticed that's how he was thinking of the corpse, once a woman.

She was face down, but her long hair fanned into an arc of dark stiff tendrils. The long, loose hair, the narrow waist, cinched in what looked to be a short white apron, its sash ties wrapped around her once and probably knotted at the front, the denim jeans, these weren't the signs of old burial, which would have included a hair ribbon and Sunday best. This was the Reaper's latest stook in his winter harvest, a harvest likely just beginning.

Blackshaw stood and turned, on the verge of giving a yell for Sonny and Mary to quit fooling, drive over, and have a gander and a ponder with him. Instead, he saw his friend, Knocker Ellis Hogan, slowly homing in on him across the ice in his Bugatti Veyron.

Ellis was older, without being the least elderly. He had served in Vietnam as MACV-SOG with Blackshaw's father, Dick. After narrowly escaping death at the hands of superior officers for whom they'd been volun-*told* to carry out illegal, clandestine missions, Ellis and Dick Blackshaw had staggered back to Smith Island to work the Chesapeake Bay in peace on *Miss Dotsy*, the family's deadrise workboat. They had enjoyed fifteen quiet years. Then, Dick Blackshaw had been forced to abandon Smith Island to lead longtime nemeses away from his loved ones and neighbors. Ellis had stayed behind, working for Ben now, culling oysters, and helping with crabbing in their seasons. Then, after that decade and a half gone without a word, Dick Blackshaw had made his return to Smith Island hauling hundreds of millions of dollars of stolen government gold bullion, but with a pack of savage black bag operatives nipping at his heels. Bloody business followed. In the end,

Ben Blackshaw divided his half of the fortune among his Smith Island neighbors.

Ellis, steward of the other half of the gold by rights of salvage and partnership, had made no such civic contribution to the other folks on Smith. Instead, he bought the two-million-dollar supercar in a fit of grandiosity underwritten by the new and spectacular wealth he had earned with his new captain. But he'd penned up the car, a sleek, snarling beast made for open roads like the Autobahn, or closed tracks like the Nürburgring, in a catawampus old shed with only thirty feet of dirt driveway leading to down to the water surrounding the tiny hummock his house occupied. Then, in a more poetic moment tinged with boredom, he had cut the roof off the fantastic car, filled the cockpit with potting soil, and planted geraniums. Ellis was *that* kind of rich.

As Ellis drew the big car to a stop on the ice next to Blackshaw, it was clear the geraniums were dead now, and the driver's seat, foot well, and pedals had been carefully excavated of topsoil. Earth strewn with old brown flower stems still buried the passenger seat up to the dashboard. It looked like Ellis was driving a poorly tended, recently opened grave.

Ellis shut the rumbling engine down. The quieter sounds of distant laughter on the breeze returned while he cast an eye over the woman in the ice. He turned his deep brown, care-lined face to Blackshaw and said, "I looked out my window, and thought you were out here kneeling to pray. I told myself, *that can't be right.* I had to come out here and see."

"Hey Ellis. Merry Christmas."

"Merry Christmas. Any idea who our popsicle is?"

Blackshaw glanced west toward the distant container ships silhouetted in the channel; they too were frozen in place—at least until a thaw, an ice breaker, or both reopened Baltimore Harbor for business.

"Reckon she's not from around here, Ellis. But we're going to need some tools, some chain, and a few strong backs to bring her home."

CHAPTER 2

CHOAD LAGLEET WATCHED the black site for three weeks before he struck. NSA operatives posing as graduate students at the nearby Universidad de Cantabria in Santander, Spain, manned the rundown second floor apartment across the street from the flat where LaGleet kept his vigil. He had counted a total of six operatives on overwatch inside and out. He wondered if the dons in Spanish Intelligence, the Centro Nacional de Inteligencia, even knew a United States OGA, or Other Government Agency, was interrogating an American detainee over there at the place they'd code named Franco Station like a not-so-funny inside joke. It did not matter to LaGleet. Faction knew what was up, and Faction was paying LaGleet's bills.

LaGleet saw one of the NSA guys, whom he called Stubby because of his disarmingly short stature and ovoid girth, shuffling down the sidewalk to Franco Station with a bag from a local pharmacy in hand. LaGleet grabbed a pen, made a tick-mark on a pad beside two other slashes, and noted the time. That made three NSA operators inside, plus the target. He knew that right now, the other three spooks were actually attending classes at the university to shore up their cover stories.

Krill, LaGleet's second in command who had short, dark hair, blue eyes, and a gymnast's compact yet powerful frame, stood on the sidewalk near the target apartment building finishing a cigarette; she was making sure no other operatives hit the street needing a surveillance tail. After a few minutes, Krill was satisfied. She ground the cigarette butt into the sidewalk.

Less than two minutes later, she stepped through the apartment door and joined LaGleet and the four other teammates. The others were watching a Spanish soap opera while tearing their weapons down and reassembling them in advance of the work to come.

LaGleet asked, "What was in Stubby's bag?"

"More bandages and dressings," said Krill.

"Christ, what the hell are they doing to him?" LaGleet mused.

Krill sat down at the little dining table in front of her wafer-thin tablet and warmed up its encryption protocols.

She added, "Also an antibiotic. It's over the counter here. Did you know that?"

"That I did not," said LaGleet. "Maybe we should stock up."

"The stuff Stubby bought is pretty heavy duty, like Screed's got fucking MRSA. In Madrid they've got two statues of the guy who discovered penicillin. Dr. Fleming. Anyway, one statue's right by the bull ring. Getting gored in the ring used to mean major infection—a death sentence. Penicillin changed that."

LaGleet asked, "And Fleming's other statue—let me guess. The red light district?"

"Bingo," said Krill.

"All kinds of ways *horny* can ruin your day," said LaGleet.

LaGleet decided to push the strike back ten minutes until Bonamy Screed's interrogators had done whatever was necessary to patch up the disgraced ex-Deputy Director of the FBI. One less thing to handle in transit. LaGleet told his team about the slight delay, and then asked, "Everybody ready to dance?"

He got casual nods and *yup*s from the crew. No steely-eyed, grim-faced, cinematic *affirmative*s or *lock-and-load*s or dramatic yanking and spanking of gun parts that clacked, rattled, and snapped. The team looked like a little group of ordinary tourist moms and dads about to head out for drinks. One of his guys even went to the can for a last pee before the gig. The sheer banality of their appearances, and their utter calm before this snatch-and-grab job, a mission on which they might be wounded or even killed within the next eleven minutes, inspired pride and awe in LaGleet.

Krill said, "I'm ready to send the follow-up."

"Do it," LaGleet ordered. He stood and moved next to the window peering across the way toward Franco Station.

Krill tapped the tablet once, and said, "Bombs away." Then she drew her pistol, made a quick check of its magazine, and holstered it again. She slipped the tablet into her messenger bag and looped the strap over her shoulder.

From a spoofed account that appeared to belong to the bursar's office at the University of Cantabria, she had just sent an email to each of the NSA operatives across the street. It said that there was a problem with their tuition payments, and if they did not show up on campus in person within the hour to address the issue (i.e. rectify their accounts), their Schengen student visa applications would be revoked, and the entire matter would be referred to the Ministerio de Asuntos Exteriores y de Cooperacion, whereupon deportation proceedings would be initiated. Just the kind of shit to terrify a kid on his postbac' year abroad. The wording of the email, in Krill's excellent Spanish, made it clear that this was the third and final notification the students would receive. Though Krill had referred to the email as a follow-up, neither a first, nor a second email had ever been sent.

Then, as if on cue, came the expected phone call. The team had temporarily hacked the bursar office's line over to Krill's phone. Krill waited to answer after a several rings because a bursar's office is a busy place. For two minutes, she explained to one of the operatives across the street in her most patient yet officious Castilian Spanish that yes, their tuition was in fact past due.

LaGleet didn't expect the entire NSA team at Franco Station to bug out like a fire drill, but if even one operative went back to campus to see what the hell was going on, it would thin the opposition ranks, and make the take-down that much easier.

"Holy shit," muttered LaGleet at the window. Stubby and one more spook he'd dubbed Tybalt, because he was actor-handsome and looked like a total strapped-on hothead, emerged from the apartment building and made an overly casual retreat down the street, glancing over their shoulders at odd times like rank amateurs.

LaGleet moved back to the pad, grabbed the pen, and crossed off two tick-marks, and noted the time. Bonamy Screed had been left in the care of just one spook, dubbed Grendel because of his monstrously ugly face. Stubby and Tybalt would be gone for thirty minutes at least, depending on whether they grabbed a taxi or walked. They would be busting ass to get back to Franco Station once the baffled university bursar explained their tuition payments were current.

"Any warnings back to Franco Station about the decoy—anything?" asked LaGleet almost incredulously.

Krill checked an application on her phone and looked up grinning. "Nothing."

"Emails? Cell phone? Sat-phone? Smoke signal?"

"Not even a carrier pigeon," Krill said.

LaGleet shrugged with smug incomprehension. He said, "Shall we?"

His team, which earlier that morning had voided the flat of all personal effects, and scrubbed out all fingerprints except for a few here and there from preserved anonymous cadaver hands they had brought along for the purpose, got to their feet and headed for the door.

CHAPTER 3

MOVING THE BODY was a tough go. The bitter cold sapped Sonny's electric chainsaw battery; it barely had enough juice to carve the ice close around the body to cut it loose from the rest of the Chesapeake. A length of chain connected the death-berg to the back of Ellis's Veyron. At least they had managed to invert the ice slab so now the cadaver faced the sky, which felt more dignified and respectful. The snow angel's face seemed young, but it was hard to get a clear look through the ice that still masked it. Blackshaw walked beside the strange block during the slow tow all the way to shore to help free it from snags in the ice field's surface. Sonny and Mary led off in the golf cart. Curious neighbors followed the odd cortege. Such a weird procession had never before been seen on the bay.

Blackshaw decided that Ruke's Café and Grocery Store made a good impromptu mortuary. It had been boarded up for over a year, but it still had big dining tables. In fact, it still looked pretty much the way it did the day it closed, with a platoon of salt and pepper shakers waiting on the counter to be set out on the tables for the next day's burgers and fries. Ruke's owner had suddenly taken sick. He was now lodged in a nursing home on the Eastern Shore in Crisfield puffing oxygen and dreaming of a buyer for the old store. Any hope of reopening the old place himself had faded with the second stroke.

Sonny Wright had managed to restart the furnace, but a tenacious chill inside had as much to do with the body on the table as with the weather.

Blackshaw and his wife LuAnna, who carried their baby Callum bundled in her arms, made slow circles around the table supporting the macabre block of ice. The Blackshaws' orbits looked paced-off and respectful, like sentries at the Tomb of the Unknown Soldier.

Ellis sat comfortably in a chair nearby, content to let Blackshaw and LuAnna, who had keen cop eyes from her time as a Corporal in the Maryland Natural Resources Police, examine the evidence. LuAnna had wanted to bring her hair dryer from home to speed up the thawing, but the power in the store had been shut off ages ago, and even with power, the cranky old fuse box would likely have blown from the high wattage strain.

Here in the store, with friends peering in through the dirty windows, Blackshaw asked his bride, "Any thoughts?"

After a moment, LuAnna said in complete seriousness, "Reckon she's still dead."

The watchful baby Cal warbled his agreement.

"You got the smart of that," said Blackshaw. "What else? Think she came off one of those ships?"

"Might-could be," said LuAnna. "Did Bob Crockett say anyone was missing off Tangier Island?"

"Everybody's accounted for," said Blackshaw. "Even the folks from south of the border with the seasonal worker type visas—they're all present and correct."

Ellis piped up, "What if there's a pestilence on one of those ships, and she tried to walk away on the ice before she got sick, but she's a carrier, and we're about to thaw out the Andromeda Strain so it can go buck wild on our asses right here."

Blackshaw and LuAnna stared at Ellis. Blackshaw said, "Isn't there a Christmas party you're supposed to be at? Like in Monaco, or Biarritz?"

"Bet this cold snap's got your jet airplane's tires a little soft," said LuAnna. "Can't be too careful."

Ellis grinned. "I got people for that. And who'd want to miss getting frozen-in with you all."

Like a crystal opera glove, the ice encasing the cadaver's left arm slid free and shattered on the floor. Everyone caught their breath and waited for their hearts to quit hammering.

Blackshaw said, "Look at her forearm. She was tortured."

"Idiot," LuAnna said with a smile. "Those are burns."

"Like I said. Putting cigarettes out on her like she was a damn ashtray."

"Bless your heart, Ben. See that apron on her?" LuAnna passed Cal over to Ellis, shucked her own coat off one arm, and rolled up her shirt sleeve. Little red marks, and a few thicker red lines marred her skin. "She wasn't tortured. That's hot oil spatter. And here, she was likely in a rush pulling a hot pan from the oven, and grazed the door, or the wire rack, or some such. She's a cook."

"She's still dead," Blackshaw said. "And some ship's crew is going hungry."

Ellis said, "If she came off a ship. You think they called her in missing?"

"Depends on why she went over the side. Somebody might want her missing," said Blackshaw.

LuAnna said, "Well, she wasn't peeing off the fantail."

Blackshaw and Ellis waited for her to say more. She obliged with, "Ladies don't do that. You guys, on the other hand, when you fetch up drowned, your flies are most always down, and you aren't wearing your life preservers. You go to pee over the side, catch a wave the wrong way, and bye-bye, you're gone."

"The voice of experience," said Ellis with approval. "But that's little boats. Not big ships with indoor heads and stabilizers and such."

"Exactly my point," said LuAnna.

Blackshaw said, "So maybe she was on deck for a smoke or something. Remember, she died before the bay froze, so she could still drift all this way from the channel. How long do you figure the Chesapeake's been locked-up?"

LuAnna said, "It was a big slushy ten days ago. Packing solid between five and eight inches in the shallows a week ago. Maybe two weeks since the deep channel ran all free and clear of ice."

Ellis shook his head. "Bet the ship she came from has already off-loaded, or reloaded and got the hell out of the bay before the freeze."

Sonny and Mary Wright came through the door. Sonny held his electric chainsaw up and said, "Let's get this show on the road!"

"You charged her up that quick?" LuAnna asked.

Mary grinned and said, "Hell no. I bought him extra batteries with that thing so he couldn't sit on his butt with a job half done when a tree comes down. You know how men are. They think it's nagging if you remind them of a chore every six months."

It was LuAnna's turn to say, "Voice of experience." She was smiling right at Blackshaw when she said it.

CHAPTER 4

LAGLEET AND KRILL gave one of their teammates time to wrangle a van around from its garage to stage at the end of the block. At the driver's cell phone signal, the five remaining members of the insertion crew left their own building's vestibule and crossed the street to Franco Station.

Krill pressed several of the doorbells arrayed by the mailboxes— doorbells for top floor flats. She made sure to avoid the one for the target flat. Though the building was older and built with solid old-world materials, she couldn't be sure of the acoustics. Nothing would spook the lone Franco Station operative faster than a chorus of doorbells going off all at once in adjacent apartments. An upstairs resident was lazy enough to buzz them all in without a challenge over the intercom. Krill put away the lock-picking tools she had in hand just in case, and rammed the door open before the buzz let up.

LaGleet led the way up one flight of steps to a short, dim corridor that strobed with a single flickering fluorescent bulb. He pointed at the target door, and made sure everyone else had seen it, too.

At a nod from LaGleet, Cowpers, the team's bang man, stole forward and quietly prepped the entire door with shaped breaching charges. Then he rejoined the crew halfway down the stairs, where everyone opened their mouths, shut their eyes, and covered their ears.

The detonation was like a loud crack of thunder. Door splinters and plaster dust flew down the hall. The shockwave was barely passed before Cowpers knuckleballed two flash-crash grenades through the shattered entry.

The bomblets double-thumped the air hard, and LaGleet's team blew into the Franco Station flat with guns up and ready.

Grendel, the lone spook on duty, had a dazed look on his ugly mug as he stumbled into the sitting room, firing his pistol without aiming as he came on. LaGleet cut his knees out from under him with a short burst from his FN P90 submachine gun. The babysitter collapsed through the second burst, which LaGleet had purposely held low, and took three more rounds in his gut. Krill two-tapped the operative in the head, and while the other teammates cleared the kitchen, she and LaGleet penetrated the little hall to the only bedroom. Empty.

Together they smashed their way in through the bathroom door and found their target, Bonamy Screed, cowering low in the iron claw-foot tub. The man needed a shave, a haircut, and a few days in direct sunlight. He asked, "Do you speak English?"

"Fuck no!" said LaGleet. "We're the cavalry. We talk American."

"Let's go!" shouted Krill, dragging Screed from the tub. Screed yelped at Krill's manhandling. She'd latched onto one of his two heavily bandaged hands.

"Take it easy dammit!" Screed shouted.

LaGleet was about to tell Screed to sack-up and move out, when more shooting erupted out in the sitting room.

One of their guys yelled, "They're back!" before his head jetted blood from a hefty bullet hole in his temple. Stubby and Tybalt hadn't fallen for the fake email after all, but they'd waited too far down the street to make their surprise return really count for something.

"Fire escape!" shouted LaGleet, as he snatched up the pharmacy bag from a side table next to a tattered loveseat.

Cowpers hucked a grenade out the door into the hall, and yelled, "Frag out!"

The grenade blasted dust and a forearm back into the living room, but one of the bastards was still shooting into the apartment from the stairwell.

There was a momentary lull in the gunfire during their remaining attacker's magazine change. LaGleet and Krill shoved Screed out the window to the fire escape and kicked him down the ladder. LaGleet fired back through the window, hoping Cowpers had the good sense not to block his shots toward the door.

With his messed-up hands unable to grip properly, Screed's descent was a barely controlled fall. The van skidded to a stop in front of the building. Screed hobbled to it, but just stood fidgeting by the sliding door without opening it. He held up his bandaged hands in front of Krill to explain his uselessness.

The driver stomped on the gas just as the last of their team, everyone except their squadie who'd been shot in the head, dived through the sliding door.

Cowpers pulled two radio detonator units from his pockets and looked at LaGleet, who nodded. Cowpers gave the units a squeeze. Everyone watched out the van's rear windows.

Franco Station blew splinters, shards, and one corpse out into the street below. An instant later, LaGleet's observation flat across this street answered with a *thrump*, and gouts of flame roaring from all the windows. The apartment buildings resembled ships of the line trading fiery broadsides of brick and blood.

"Jesus Christ!" shouted Screed. "What the hell!"

"Covering our exfil'," LaGleet said. He took stock of his team as they panted in exhaustion; they were wiped out, though the job had taken less than a hundred seconds, start to finish. LaGleet turned to give Cowpers a congratulatory sock in the shoulder and said, "Damn near turned both buildings to dust!"

The bang man rolled over onto the van's floor, dead at last from a bullet that had snuck under his arm past his rifle plate carrier.

CHAPTER 5

LUANNA STARED AT her husband and said, "You can't be serious."

"As a heart attack," Blackshaw said. "We call the cops. We send this nice dead lady on her way with them."

Sonny had masterfully wielded his chain saw to shave the ice around the body's front and sides to a thin glaze. The furnace in the store was running hot now, especially with the thermostat maxed out. A puddle of melt water expanded beneath the mortuary table.

Ellis had shucked his coat, scarf, and gloves. His upper half was now down to his flannel shirt and a watch cap. He said, "I agree with Ben. We've done everything we could. Saved the law a big hassle bringing the body indoors. If we poke around Miss Doe any more than we have, we're tampering with physical evidence. You should know this."

"And who do you think's going to come out here to fuss over a corpse?" LuAnna was riled. "It's Christmastime. The bay's locked-up solid."

"The new ice breaker will come by before too long. And the Coast Guard will chopper in prescriptions, food, and mail likewise soon enough, if some third-grader still hasn't figured out how to deliver the stuff by drone. She could hitch a ride with any one of them. If we call it in now," Blackshaw went on, "at least they'll know what's happening. We can report it, and nobody's lying."

LuAnna said nothing.

Blackshaw knew better than to believe her silence meant she was persuaded.

He continued, "We don't need the police looking squint-eyed at us. You said it. It's Christmas. She had a mishap and she drowned. She's a stranger, she's dead, and there's nothing we can do. Nothing we're beholden to do."

LuAnna dandled Cal in her arms where she stood. Blackshaw had seen her bounce on the balls of her feet even when she was not holding their baby. By now it was the reflex of an exhausted new mother.

"Sonny? Mary?" LuAnna was looking in the wrong place for support.

Mary busied herself shooing a little boy and a girl outside away from the window, and didn't meet LuAnna's eyes. Sonny studied his fingernails like a hand model before a photo shoot, and said not a word.

"Everybody's right," said Ellis after a few more awkward moments. That earned him some attention. "We call this mess in, and we've done the right thing. LuAnna's right, too. Nobody's going to come out here for a couple-two-three days. Not with the weather that's coming in. So, we can learn what we might in the meantime."

Blackshaw said, "Didn't you just say we should leave her be?"

"And I meant it, Ben. Your lives are different now you've got a little one. Neither you nor LuAnna should be ripping and running all over the place, killing assholes that need it, saving the day. Folks who do that end up in jail, or dead, or on the news. You've been lucky so far on those counts."

"You're talking in circles, Ellis. Say what you mean." LuAnna asked.

"We thought she was a drowner. Victim of a terrible accident. Now, I'm not so sure." Ellis nodded toward the body, which so far had offered no opinion in the matter.

"Lordy go to fire," Blackshaw said, once he noticed where Ellis was looking.

The warming corpse was bleeding from somewhere on her left side. A dull red stain was spreading, but it was still sealed in beneath the icy glaze, and pooling at a low place near the small of her back.

"See?" said LuAnna in a sad sort of triumph.

Ellis said, "So call it in, Ben. It's completely up to you whether you tell them she was drowned, shanked, or shot."

CHAPTER 6

A FAST RHIB bore LaGleet's remaining team and Bonamy Screed away from Santander's beach toward an old fishing boat waiting in deeper water in the Bay of Biscay. Most of the oncoming traffic during the drive from the operation to the shore had been emergency vehicles headed for the site of the twin explosions. LaGleet's team van was not hindered other than pulling over to the curb a few times so fire trucks, police cars, and ambulances could yip, flash, yodel, and just barely squeeze past on the narrow streets. With any luck, the Centro Nacional de Inteligencia would accuse Basque Separatists of cutting up rough before anybody started riding hard on LaGleet's backtrail. He thought the NSA would realize exactly what happened much faster, but they would have a hell of a time explaining things to the dons if their support in any kind of investigation were needed. An international incident would take time to sort out, and that would suit Choad LaGleet and Faction just fine.

The rigid hulled inflatable boat caromed off wave after wave. It wasn't long before Screed puked. LaGleet had positioned his rescued operative in the stern on the downwind side of the boat for just such a moment, so his team would not be coated with vomitous blow-back.

LaGleet broached Screed's debrief as gently as he could on the way. He knew Screed had been one tough sharp-shooting bastard in the Army, but that was long ago. He'd softened as an upper echelon wonk, first at the NSA, then later at the FBI. Those white-collar billets were poor preparation for the questioning he had endured over the last few months.

"What's going on with your mitts?" LaGleet asked.

"They cut off my fingers to get me to talk."

"Who did?" Krill asked. "Those frat boys back there?"

"Before that," Screed said. "Some bastard. I don't know who he was working for. A former SEAL, and some rednecks. Now they're infected."

"Your file said you were eight weeks on Smith Island. You held up for two months of hostile interrogation?" LaGleet wondered how much bullcrap Screed was going to toss out before he got to the truth.

Screed looked ashamed. The relief of being rescued soon gave way to the fear of where he was headed next. He asked, "You're Faction, right?"

"Choad LaGleet at your service."

"Thanks for busting me out," said Screed. "Truth is, I held out as long as I could, but there were the stress positions, full blast country music twenty-four/seven in earbuds they duct-taped to my head, sleep deprivation, and then ..." LaGleet held up his hands.

LaGleet *tsk-tsk*ed as if he had a heart full of empathy for Screed's troubles. "And then?"

Screed dry-heaved over the side. Though his stomach was empty by now, he still looked green and sheened with cold sweat when he spoke again.

"I was turned back over to the FBI. Or I thought it was the FBI. I saw Pershing Lowry for five seconds during the hand-over."

"A Fed?" LaGleet asked.

"Big-time. FBI Executive Assistant Director for Counterterrorism and Counterintelligence," Screed said. "They took it pretty easy on me."

Because they had your full confession already, LaGleet thought to himself.

Screed went on, "My best guess, it wasn't twenty-four more hours stateside after I was handed off—"

"No pun intended," interrupted LaGleet trying to lighten the mood.

Screed missed or ignored the gallows humor, and said, "Anyway, I was on the road again. Bound. Blindfolded. A car. Then a plane. Then a car again. Where the hell did you find me? Mexico? I heard a lot of Spanish."

"Close. You got renditioned to a black site in Santander, Spain," LaGleet said.

"American?" Screed was trying to figure out how much trouble he was in.

"Yup. Uncle Sam," LaGleet confirmed. "How'd they treat you there?"

"More questioning. Trying to see if my story changed. It was pretty intense."

LaGleet knew Screed was practically living in a hotel when they found him. No new, or even old bruises. He was being kept on ice until somebody way up high remembered he existed and decided what to do with him. Except for getting bounced around a bit during the rescue, Screed looked more media-deprived than anything.

"And did it?" LaGleet asked.

"Did it what?" asked Screed.

"Did your story change? Specifically, at any point did you mention anything about Faction?"

"No!" Screed said. "It looked homegrown. The whole thing."

"Except your original mission was based at the Russian retreat on the Eastern Shore of Maryland. And you clearly had enough reachback support to conduct an international operation on Alderney in the English Channel, and send three operators there to neutralize the one guy who took down your whole op."

"Hold on! That property was mothballed since the Russians got kicked out. My posting up there looked totally opportunistic, using available space. That was Faction's idea."

Screed was getting nervous. He was beginning to wonder why he was still alive if he were in such bad odor with Faction. Why all the effort to spring him? Granted he'd been crapping his pants during the rescue, but he'd also been heads-up enough to know LaGleet had lost at least two operatives bringing him out. That was a heavy butcher's bill if all they wanted to do was quiz him to find out how exposed Faction had become thanks to his failure.

Screed affected a fatalistic mien, and said, "So what's it going to be Choad? A bullet? A gulag someplace cold? I know I screwed the pooch. Level with me." He felt so sick on this damn boat ride that any respite, even death, was starting to appeal.

LaGleet's eyes went wide with surprise. "You kidding? We're sending you back in. Same theatre of operations. You're getting a second chance."

It was Screed's turn to register shock. "What? What the hell? I'm blown. They know me."

"But that's a two-way street, Bonamy. You don't mind my using your first name, do you?"

Screed was lost in troubling memories of his interrogation on Smith Island. The prospect of getting back in the field anywhere near those crazy hicks filled him with dread.

LaGleet prodded Screed. "You still with me, Bonamy? Opportunities like this don't come around too often. Not with Faction."

"No, I get it. I'm good. So what's happening? What're my orders?"

"You know the Chesapeake Bay terrain already," said LaGleet. "Would you recognize the guys who took you down?"

"Yes. They weren't too careful about blindfolds and head-bags. And the guy who killed my asset—"

"Faction's asset," corrected LaGleet.

"Right. *Faction's* asset. I'd know that bastard again."

"Perfect," LaGleet purred. "So here's the deal. Faction's next operation is right there in that guy's back yard. There's a small chance the op is already exposed. We're not a hundred percent sure. But we need it to go smoothly, and we don't need that same guy messing it up for us if he gets wind of what's going down."

"I'm your man," said Screed.

"Sure you are," said LaGleet, who was already questioning Faction's wisdom putting Screed back in the game. "In the last op, before things went tits-up, you did manage to snuff that SEAL with a sweet long-range shot. Problem is, that target happened to be pals with the guy who came after you. They were brothers in arms at one point. DEVGRU. That's why he took such a hard run at you. It was personal to him."

"I get it," said Screed. "Boo-hoo. So?"

LaGleet said, "On this new op, we need you to tool-up and cover things on overwatch. You're a wizard with a rifle."

"They took off my trigger fingers with a bolt cutter! I can't shoot anymore." Screed was almost whining.

LaGleet drew his pistol and chambered a bullet. "Up to you. I'd consider my options carefully. To be on the safe side, we'll need you to track and kill the same guy who fucked up your manicure. You can get a little of your own back. Won't that be nice? So that's it. We need you to kill Ben Blackshaw."

CHAPTER 7

BLACKSHAW NEVER MADE the call to the police. Instead, Sonny Wright dialed the furnace thermostat at Ruke's back to its lowest setting, and let winter creep back in the old building to slow the corpse's decomposition. A gust of wind shook the store. Blackshaw knew this crystalizing cold was a polar vortex, but he secretly thought it was from hell.

Kathy Taylor-Donaway stopped by to hang beautiful handmade quilts from her shop to block the windows and brighten the gloom. Everyone on Smith Island already knew what was going on at the old café. The problem was that the kids found sneaking peeks at the dead woman through the windows irresistible, even when threatened with the destruction of all their precious video games. Grounding children born and raised on a small island carried absolutely no weight of dread.

The makeshift mortuary secured, there was only one thing left to do.

Blackshaw said to LuAnna, "I feel funny taking that woman's clothes off her to get the smart of what-all happened."

"Can't say as I'd like to watch you do that," LuAnna admitted. "Mary, would you lend a hand?"

"Sure thing, Honeygirl."

Ellis gave a quiet snort of derision, and said, "And you a big bad SEAL? But I get it. *'That was in another country—'*"

"'*—and besides, the wench is dead',*" said Blackshaw finishing the grim line. He added, "Hey Joe College, we've all suffered T.S. Eliot, even on Smith

Island. And I resent the implication. There wasn't any fornicating when I fought over there. I knew LuAnna was waiting for me here."

"Of course," said Ellis. "But given what you've seen overseas, and even here, too—I mean, it looks like you'll kill man or woman if need be, but you won't lamp a dead woman's remains? You've got some damn funny scruples, my friend. And a kind of prudery that a shrink would need years to unravel."

"I heard it said 'foolish consistency is the hobgoblin of little minds,'" recited Blackshaw.

"Emerson!" said Ellis, grinning. "Touché. So you're not just a pretty face."

Blackshaw said, "It just feels wrong, Ellis. Especially with LuAnna looking on."

"And listening, too." As LuAnna gently began removing the cook's apron from the body, she continued, "Why don't you three squeamish types take a walk around the gas dock while Mary and I handle things?"

"Oh, I don't mind this," said Sonny.

"Yes, you do," said Mary as she shoved her man toward the door.

LuAnna unfolded her pocket knife to cut the apron's tie around the body's waist.

From the door, Blackshaw said, "Just untie it, Hon."

"I want to see the knot that was used. Intact. It could tell us something," said LuAnna.

When Blackshaw stood there mulling what she had said, LuAnna went on, "If the knot looks funny, maybe it was tied on her by somebody else before she went into the bay. Forensic knot and ligature analysis is a thing, doncha know."

"Department of Natural Resources taught you that," said Blackshaw, bemused.

"Smarts is a natural resource, too," said LuAnna. "All I mean is, maybe somebody wanted whoever found her to *think* she was a cook, and bent the apron to her body postmortem. I could be wrong about those burns."

"You don't have no suspicious mind," was all Blackshaw could say in the sideways manner of Smith Island. He followed Ellis and Sonny out the door.

Before leaving the worn-out building, the three men had grabbed enough layers for the cold temperature, but not enough for the wind; it was gusting up, and carving warmth away from their bodies like a sharp knife flensing fat off beef.

They walked toward the water in silence until Blackshaw said, "Ellis, don't you tell me what I've seen. Don't you tell me how to carry it. You can quote me up and down on that."

Ellis said nothing. Sonny secretly wished he were a million miles away. Two million for good measure.

CHAPTER 8

LUANNA AND MARY exposed the body one piece of clothing at a time. They were gentle and respectful about it, lifeless though the young woman was. There had to be a dignity to it. With death waiting around any and every corner, both women were thinking ahead to their own time for final rites and requiems.

With her background in police work, it fell naturally to LuAnna to examine the trauma to the dead woman's side. Though it was puckered and blanched, it was a gunshot wound plain and simple.

She said, "Single GSW. Fired at close range."

"By close you mean—" Mary had reassembled the pieces of clothing, laying them out on the next table over like parts of a crashed airplane, as close to their natural position as possible.

"Nigh on a point-blank contact wound. There's tattooing from particles of hot powder residue. Less than I'd expect for such a large caliber," said LuAnna. She spread a stack of paper napkins on the table below the wound to sop up the oozing blood.

"I couldn't see through the bloodstain and wet," said Mary, holding up a blue cotton shirt, "But is this what you're talking about? Them little black flecks and pits around the hole?"

"That's making more sense," LuAnna said.

Mary smiled, happy to be helping. "So, it wasn't any pump gun."

"We can rule that out for now," LuAnna said.

Mary observed, "What I don't get is how a cook's got your garden variety no-name clothes, but her little bra here is La Perla. Three hundred dollars for just that, minimum."

"For just a bra?" LuAnna was aghast.

"If that's not the English Rose Plunge with the underwire, I don't know what is," Mary averred. "Not that the poor thing needed an underwire. So pert and perky, even in death." She lay the bra back on the table in its place, then covered the body's small bosom with a red and white checkered table cloth folded narrow like a bandeau top. "Good thing Sonny's not here. Take all damn day to get his jaw up off the floor."

"Her knickers—what about them?"

Mary examined the black lace panties. "English Rose again. A matched set. A buck eighty-five."

"So she's wearing near to five hundred dollars of matched underwear, but her shirt and jeans—" LuAnna mused.

"Maybe ten bucks all in at the Dollar General," said Mary. "The tag in the jeans is snipped up the middle."

"Aren't all tags cut like that?"

Mary shook her head. "Miss Thing, I need to take you shopping for real. No, a cut tag means they're factory seconds. Damaged crap."

"And she's rocking a little landing strip," said LuAnna, glancing at body's pubis.

"I think they call that one a martini glass," said Mary. "The upside-down pyramid thingy? As much as a hundred twenty dollars for that, depending on the neighborhood."

"Mary Wright, you are a font of interesting information."

"What did you think of her shoes?" Mary asked.

LuAnna ran her eyes along the body, then looked over at Mary's eerie assemblage of clothing on the next table. "Oh I get it. There aren't any. Just those little ped socks. Not much cushion to them for a gal who's on her feet in a kitchen all day."

"But you could slip those things right into a nice pump. A sneaker or even heels, if you were desperate." said Mary.

"And we've got neither of those. No shoes. I suppose they could've come off in the water," said LuAnna.

"If she was wearing shoes at all when she went swimming."

"So we got a gal who dresses like she's blue collar on the outside, but underneath, she's pretty high-end. Any papers or a wallet?" LuAnna asked her friend.

"No wallet. Some paper here. Still too wet to unfold without ripping it to shreds." Mary held up a damp fuzzy block, at least one letter-sized sheet creased into quarters.

LuAnna suggested, "Set it a couple feet from the radiator, would you kindly? It's still a bit warm. But the water's made the paper like pulp again. Too close to the heat, it'll harden into a wad."

Mary complied while LuAnna picked up the apron. She noted a small patch pocket in the center, about sternum-high with a Velcro flap securing the mouth. LuAnna thought Heaven only knew what the designers had in mind to put in that silly thing. Expecting little, she pressed the pocket between her thumbs and forefingers. There was something in it. But something else bothered LuAnna.

Then it hit her. From the way Mary carefully laid the apron on the other clothes, which together looked like an unstuffed scarecrow on the table, LuAnna realized the pocket was located on the back of the apron, next to the victim's shirt as if to hide things. Her excitement grew as she gently worked the sodden cloth. The object inside was thin and rectangular, shaped like a piece of Wrigley's gum the way it used to be wrapped in flat, oblong sticks. LuAnna carefully peeled the Velcro to gain access to the pocket. Finally, she had it.

"Oh my blessing," said LuAnna. "Look at this!"

LuAnna held the fragile item to the light. Mary peered at it over her shoulder.

"Haven't seen one of those in a couple days and more," said Mary.

"Not since college?" LuAnna said.

The translucent microscope slide had a shallow, circular depression at its center, and a whisper-thin glass plate covering some kind of sample that was tinted blue.

"No, I really mean *a couple days*," said Mary. "Pliny-Robert, my fourth grandson, he's been on us to get him a microscope, so we did. Thank the

Lord we ordered it before the bay iced over, or Christmas would surely disappoint."

LuAnna studied the slide, angling it this way and that. "Can't see anything."

"Guess that's where the microscope comes in," said Mary as tactfully as she could.

"Okay, smarty-pants. Can we get one out of the school?"

"I'll get Pliny-Robert's," said Mary. "Doubt he'd mind too much if Christmas comes early this year. Save me the wrapping of it."

CHAPTER 9

THE FREEZE RUINED the schedule for the event. Captain Abel Varna knew to expect delays from dockworker strikes, and weather. Setbacks came with the territory. It was why ship captains of old wrote in their logbooks that they were bound *toward* a given harbor, not *to* it, so as not to tempt Fate with the hubris of certainty. Every voyage was a gamble. There was plenty of room at the bottom of the sea for more unlucky ships.

The irony, in Captain Varna's view, was that the *Penelope*, an eleven-hundred-foot Q-Max Liquid Natural Gas transporter, had an appointment with catastrophe. The misadventure was not planned for the open ocean, but in the Chesapeake Bay.

The captain trained his binoculars from the ship's broad bridge forward toward the bow. When everything on the gargantuan deck seemed in order, he resorted to the on-board CCTV to make sure the crew, his *new* crew, was in position below decks, despite the wait for a thaw to melt the ice. He had to maintain discipline in a group of bastards used to regular adrenal saturation during firefights. There was none of that right now, no excitement at the moment, no damn fun at all. They had already been aboard for nearly two weeks, and that was thirteen days longer than anyone ever intended.

The *Penelope* was no longer under the control of the Transoceanic Vessel Group which operated the ship on behalf of a Qatari LNG shipping line. The new crew, Captain Varna's elite strike force, had arrived by parachute in the dead of night, landing on *Penelope*'s expansive deck, which was painted green to evoke thoughts of clean energy efficiency. Of necessity, the new crew had daubed the deck blood red here and there when a few of the onboard security team resisted sensible advice to stand down in the face of superior forces. The old crew had left the ship soon after the insertion.

And now Varna waited. For the tenth time in an hour, the captain checked the weather forecast looking for a break in the cold that would melt the ice and let this great ship move closer to its destiny.

CHAPTER 10

THE POUNDING RIDE to the old fishing boat in the Bay of Biscay finally ended, and Bonamy Screed thought he would come back to life. Unfortunately the larger boat was subject to a longer rolling swell that turned Screed's relief into silent prayers for Choad LaGleet to finish him off after all, he was so damn seasick.

One of the fishing boat's scruffy mates changed the soggy dressings on Screed's hands. LaGleet watched the process to get a better sense of his new operator's readiness for the job ahead.

The mate unwrapped Screed's left hand first. The patient flinched several times. There was a small nub of flesh where the index finger had been. LaGleet approved of the way the skin had been stitched together to form a stump. But the seams were swollen and angry, suppurating, and lines of infection trailed toward the wrist on the palm with more lines on the back of his hand. Screed looked away quickly, his guts flip-flopping. He could witness other squad mates injured on a mission, render first aid, and not feel a single twinge. This was not the case if he himself took a hit. The sight of his own maiming made him almost pass out.

LaGleet dropped the pharmacy bag in Screed's lap and said, "Take a few of those pills. Should help the infection. Hate to send you into the field with gangrene." LaGleet grabbed Screed's wrist, and sniffed the wound for the stink of rot. "So far, so good."

"How the hell am I supposed to go active?" Screed said. "I've never shot a gun like this."

The mate finished with the left hand. The bandaging was thick and bulbous, but it was clean and dry. He started on the dressing of Screed's right index finger amputation, which looked just as infected as the left.

"We have lots of pain killers," offered LaGleet. "And you should know there's a weather factor holding the operation up. You might have caught a break. Maybe a day or two extra to let those antibiotics go to work."

LaGleet sniffed closely at the wound on Screed's right hand. After a pause, as though he were nosing the bouquet of a fine wine, he sniffed a second time. Then he left the compartment without saying anything more.

CHAPTER 11

BLACKSHAW, ELLIS, AND Sonny returned to the store like mourners to a wake after a smoke outdoors. They brought Coleman lanterns to beat back the darkness. There was no hiding the cadaverous funk that was winning over the musty scent of the building's long disuse. LuAnna and Mary were taking turns staring down into a shiny new microscope bright with its own battery-powered light source.

"It's looking all *Quincy M.E.* in here," said Blackshaw recalling the early television drama about post-mortem examinations.

Mary Wright said, "Patricia Cornwell would know what's what. She really knows her forensicals. I love her thrillers."

Blackshaw glanced at the deceased. She now wore two table cloths, one each draped crossways over her pelvis and breasts.

"Men," was all LuAnna said.

"What's wrong?" said Sonny.

"You could have found us all some food," Mary said.

Sonny held a small Igloo cooler aloft and said, "Just as soon as I get the gas turned back on at the griddle, I'll knock some burgers together like to make your heart sing for joy."

Mary kissed Sonny by way of apology for her lack of faith. He went behind the counter looking for the propane gas valve.

"You found something," Blackshaw said.

LuAnna said, "A microscope slide with a sample of something on it. It looks all blue, like—"

"Horseshoe crab blood," said Blackshaw leaning down and peering at the slide with his naked eye.

LuAnna stared at him. "How'd you figure that?"

Blackshaw said, "Well I highly doubt it's Gatorade or Smurf piss. Where was it?"

"In a pocket on the inside of her apron," Mary said.

Ellis asked, "Was there anything off about that apron string knot?"

LuAnna said, "Oh my blessing, I found that slide and clean forgot to check."

LuAnna studied the knot, turning it over in her hands. She set it down on a table, and mimed tying a knot at her waist. "Nope. A bow, just like I'd tie. But her underthings are very spendy. Her jeans and shirt are factory seconds."

"Maybe one or the other is some kind of cover," said Sonny warming to his idea. "Like she's a secret spy, all bedraggled by day, and Miss Jaimie-Lu Bond by night. But which is her real identity?"

Ellis said, "It pains me to say Sonny's got a point. You think she was hiding the slide."

LuAnna passed the apron to Ellis and pointed. "The pocket's on the inside. See there? Good for keeping small things out of sight. Custom-made. Sewn in behind the apron's label so no one would see the stitching."

Ellis nodded. "So it is." He handed the apron to Mary who was conscientious about maintaining all of the dead woman's clothing in its proper configuration.

"Was she tampered with?" said Sonny.

"Like assaulted somehow?" LuAnna asked.

Sonny nodded, a bit too interested in the answer.

"You unrepentant, perverted ghoul," Mary declared. Sonny ducked back behind the counter to fire up the griddle.

"Again, it's an awful question," said Ellis, "but a fair one."

LuAnna said, "We don't have rape kits or any of that kind of gear here, but there wasn't anything obvious like a tear or trauma. But what the hell do I know about what it would look like after a rinse in the bay and a good while frozen. You want a Y incision and a look at her last meal? You think we need to go that far?"

"Lord no, don't do that," warned Mary. "We start cutting on her, then we'll have a hell of a time explaining it to the police."

"The horseshoe crab blood is a real mystery," Blackshaw said.

"See what I mean?" said Mary. "We got plenty to work on with that slide."

"Did they dye it blue like that?" Ellis was looking down through the microscope with a 600X magnification.

"No," said LuAnna. "Our oxygen gets shunted around inside with iron, which makes our blood red. A horseshoe crab sticks the oxygen onto copper for the ride. There's the blue."

"Be damned," said Ellis. "Still and all, why would she bother to make a slide of it? The things are so ugly. Like that face-hugger from *Alien*, but with a shell."

"She might not have made it herself," Blackshaw said. "She might have had it on her to put someplace. She might have stolen it from somewhere. No telling what direction it was going when the lady went into the bay."

"To the bottom," said Mary.

"Except it didn't," said LuAnna. "It didn't go to the bottom of the bay, and neither did she."

They all heard the hiss, followed by the *whump* of propane gas igniting.

Sonny said, "Burgers in ten minutes."

CHAPTER 12

THE *PENELOPE'S* BRIDGE was quiet tonight, but Captain Varna felt anger festering in his gut as he kept the middle watch there alone. The anchor biting into the Chesapeake's bottom eighty feet below was little more than a backstop for the job the surface ice was already doing locking the ship in place. The few fissures in the vast frozen sheet resulting from natural tidal action still left great slabs the size of city blocks stopping the ship's progress north toward the Dove Point Liquid Natural Gas terminal. To move the ship through this ice would rip the tanker's double steel hull like tin foil.

It could not be helped. He could not be blamed. This cock-up, scheduling a mission of this importance in winter, when the entire success or failure of the operation depended on favorable weather, or at least navigable waters, was a mistake made at the top. But Faction had its reasons, known only to the grand poohbahs and mucky-mucks on high.

Faction had either waited too long to pull the trigger, or scheduled the op too early in the season. The Chesapeake rarely iced up like this. In an ordinary year, the mission would have been over and done already, and the objective, whatever it was, achieved. He would have been paid by now. He would have his new identity. He would be living under his new alias in a warm and distant land where his wealth, his bribes, his generous tips, would wash away any curiosity about who he really was, or where he had come from.

His vision of a happy retirement dissolved when Silas Grodin stepped onto the bridge and cast a peevish eye over all the weather radar displays. His short-cropped red hair was barely visible beneath his watch cap. He let his FN SCAR 16 CQC dangle from its shoulder strap, and held a mug under the spout of the coffee urn. Only after his first sip did he speak to Varna. "No thaw in sight?"

Captain Varna said, "I'm working from the same data you are."

"I got a message from Faction. They're pissed."

"This is a tanker, not an ice breaker," said the beleaguered captain. He was in charge of the ship's operations, but Grodin was responsible for the overall success of the mission.

"They get that," Grodin said. He took a sip of coffee. "They're worried about the old crew. Want to be sure we got everybody."

"Which are they? Pissed, or worried? Jesus, you cross-referenced every wallet and passport with the crew manifest. There's nobody left aboard from before your arrival except me," said Varna.

Silas Grodin gave Varna a meaningful look.

"You can't be serious!" blustered the captain. "I've been with Faction longer than you! I've been in deep cover with this ship since her keel was laid!"

"Relax," Grodin said. "They're more worried about somebody extra, a stowaway hiding someplace. Somebody who could toss a monkey wrench in the works at just the wrong moment."

"Based on what? Your team swept the ship within an hour after you got aboard."

"Twice," said Grodin. "But there's chatter. A Missing Person alert out of D.C., with some kind of connection to the op."

"You've been aboard ten days," the captain said. "I'm more worried about food and toilet paper than a fucking mole. Who's missing that Faction should care about? From Washington? Once a swamp, always a swamp!"

"A journalist—"

"You put everyone over the side! Who could hide for ten straight days, even on a ship this big?" Captain Varna was working himself into a rage.

"And a photographer," said Silas Grodin. "Doing a story on the largest LNG ship to ply the Chesapeake Bay. Neither one of them would have been listed as crew."

Varna fell silent. After a moment, he grabbed a tablet off the digital map table and brought its screen to life. After a few taps and swipes of the bezel, he handed the tablet to Grodin and said, "There. The same schematics you used when you boarded, stem to stern, every damn deck. The same you and I already know like the backs of our hands. Do another sweep. I think Faction's getting bored. Or worried for no reason. *Chatter*? *Journalists*? For Christ's sake! Even with our skeleton crew, I'll see this ship completes its mission the minute there's the least open water. If there's anybody hiding aboard this vessel, they're making a bloody good job of it. So good, that when the thaw comes, it won't matter a damn anyway, as you well know. But if Faction's got an issue with the head count right now, it's your problem, not mine."

Grodin said nothing. He took the tablet from Varna, put down his coffee cup, and left the bridge.

When he had closed the door of the small first mate's compartment that he had commandeered, he sat at the desk and pulled out the mission brief memory stick for another look. He knew its contents as thoroughly as the captain said he knew the ship's layout. It was the empty space that nagged at his confidence, the small sleeve attached to the little drive the where the microscope slide had been slotted, that is what made him grind his teeth.

Why had Faction included the damn thing? He did not need it to complete the mission, not operating this far forward. Yet someone in the home office had over-cooked their job, and fully doped out the entire operation top to bottom, when the data should have been compartmentalized in smaller need-to-know packets. Perhaps the wonk had done it to motivate Grodin to do his best, and make his percentage of the profit, projected at fifty times his base pay for the gig, seem more important. The memory stick had already erased itself. That was not the problem.

He trusted his own men. Captain Varna was not imaginative or brave enough to rifle his kit and find the slide. Everyone had been too busy containing and liquidating the crew during that initial phase.

The problem was the time gap. He'd dropped his gear on deck the instant after he had touched down from his HALO jump. After disposing of the crew, he had taken over this compartment, and noticed the slide was gone. Forty-six minutes. That is the total time between infiltration and discovering the problem. Someone with a keen eye had gone through his pack. Someone with sharp eyes like a spook, or a cop.

CHAPTER 13

SENIOR RESIDENT AGENT Molly Wilde was trying to dig into her backlog of emails when the call came in to her Calverton Office. She had been on an extended maternity leave since the birth of her daughter, Ella Grace, and was not handling this first workday of separation from the baby at all well. This came on top of acute pain she had suffered anytime she attempted to nurse her colicky newborn, who seemed to have the bite force of a honey badger. Now the breast pump lay in its component pieces on the table across the room, and the special bottles in her small office refrigerator were all but empty of milk. The guilt she felt at being unable to feed Ella Grace naturally lay like a weight on her heart. What bonds between herself and her daughter were going unformed? Baby formula, and Wilde's visiting mom, were the only things keeping her child alive. Motherhood, more specifically, Wilde's feeling of inadequacy as a new mother, was destroying her sense of competence at anything.

With loving hands on deck at home, both Wilde's mom, and her husband, FBI Executive Assistant Director for Counterterrorism and Counterintelligence, Pershing Lowry had subtly suggested she take a break and regroup. They had meant her to go for a drive, or for a quiet winter walk through a park. For Wilde, it meant an early return to the distractions of work. When she arrived, surprised colleagues had dropped everything and taken interest, some genuine, some polite, in her baby pictures, which she scrupulously kept off all forms of social media. But soon, barely soon enough for Wilde's liking, the demands of heavy caseloads quickly drew her team back to their stations, to appointments, and to interviews, leaving her alone. In her first hour at work, she had called home only once to say where she was. Her mother's consternation crackled down the quiet phone line until finally she said, "You do what you think's best. Everything's fine here."

Wilde had resisted reaching out via a FaceTime call. There had to be some kind of baby monitor she could download to her computer from the nursery camera. She would research that later, after she decided whether to chew the last piece of Nicorette in her desk drawer (dating from a successful smoking cessation effort before her pregnancy.) Putting nicotine back into her bloodstream would signal complete defeat in breast feeding. For now, the gum stayed in the drawer, but it was whispering to her.

Until the phone call came, her slew of emails remained an indistinct blur. Wilde answered the phone, desperate for some fresh distraction, but praying it was not her mother calling with catastrophic news about the baby.

"Molly, it's Marla-Jo Carter. I was fixin' to leave a message." Years in Maryland at the bureau's field office in Salisbury had done nothing to change how Carter still drawled out her Deep South origins.

"Agent Carter, how tricks?" said Wilde.

"Fine, just fine. You call-forwarding, or something?"

Wilde said, "No, I'm in the shop for now. Some things can't be done well from home." She wanted no more questions along these lines. Adding a tone of impatience to her voice, she went on, "So, what's up, Marla-Jo?"

Carter took a breath and said, "Nothing, like as not. But our office got a call from a guy. Ham radio buff."

"We don't handle aliens. That's Air Force," said Wilde.

"Hah-hah, Molly. This guy's itch is ship-to-shore coms. Radio operators can get bored on watch all those weeks at sea, and my caller chats with them. Said these days, most of the data about the ships' status on speed, engines, water, oil, fuel, position, and such like gets telemetered automatically to home base via satellites, and that doesn't leave the radio operator with much to do on watch I guess."

"Now you're making me sad," said Molly, running her finger through the dust on top of a small filing cabinet. Wilde maintained a locked office with a strict No Housekeeping policy when she was absent. She did not want strangers in her space regardless of how extensive the surety bonding or how deep the security clearance vetting a janitorial company might have received.

"I know," said Carter. "But check this out. The guy says one of his regular contacts, a radio operator aboard a ship in the Chesapeake, just up and quit talking to him."

Wilde's impatience was growing more genuine by the minute. "If they've had a misunderstanding, it's really not your problem or the bureau's."

"He doesn't think that at all," said Carter. "See, after a couple tries to raise his pal, some new guy came on the radio acting all hard, talking military, saying any chat with my amateur ham guy was illegal or against company regs. And then the new guy said the actual radio operator, ham guy's friend, went on medical leave, and so he couldn't talk anyway, so clear the freq' and stay off it."

"It's a new world out there Marla-Jo. Everybody's tightening up security."

"Molly, the ham radio fella's been talking to his operator buddy on the *Penelope* for years. Guy's never been sick one day. And there's no way he's on leave."

"How so?" Molly asked.

"Ham guy was in touch with his pal since before this freeze dropped in a couple weeks back. The ship, *Penelope*, hasn't made port yet."

This confused Molly, and anything that seemed the least bit confusing got her full attention. "Can you clarify the time-line for me Marla-Jo? I think I'm missing something."

"Oh no, you've got it right. How'd this radio operator guy go on leave if his ship is stuck fast in ice in the Chesapeake Bay?"

"Does *Penelope's* management company use helicopters for crew transfers? I mean, like oil rigs. For their harbor pilots and the like?"

Marla-Jo said, "No uh-uh. Harbor authorities decide how harbor pilots get on and off. And Transoceanic Vessel Group handles its crew transfers by small boat in port. For medical emergencies, they rely on fancy on-board sick-bays and medical personnel, and if it's critical, and they're close to shore, they kick the patient to local medivac services for treatment ashore. That's State Police flying in Maryland, but you knew that. And no such sorties have launched."

"And what's Washington Center say?"

"Washington Center verifies it. Says no helicopter's been cleared through to any vessel in the Chesapeake. They've had plenty fixed-wing flights in the vicinity of *Penelope*. Tons of those. But that's regular arrival traffic through STARS and departures via SIDs to Dulles, National, and BWI. It's D.C. airspace, girlfriend. Third busiest in the country, and it's tighter than a rat's ass."

"So we've got a ham radio guy who thinks something's wrong on his friend's ship," summed Molly. "But somebody, who's a stranger, said his buddy went on leave. But the ship's been frozen in the Chesapeake since *before* the regular radio operator went silent two weeks back."

"Pretty much," said Agent Carter.

"Could be the military-sounding guy is bullshitting about the leave?" asked Wilde. "Like when somebody in a retail store says 'We're out of that', when they really just don't want to check the stock room."

"Okay," said Agent Carter in that drawn out way that means *maybe but I don't think so or I wouldn't have bothered you with this.*

Wilde asked, "Assuming the regular radio op really isn't on board *Penelope* anymore, how'd he leave the ship?"

"No idea," said Agent Carter.

"What kind of ship is *Penelope*?" asked Wilde.

"She's one of those Q-Max Liquid Natural Gas ships. Gi-normous. Over a thousand-footer. And yes, she's full up and topped off with LNG. So says my caller."

Wilde's hackles went up, but she kept her voice very calm. "Okay, Marla-Jo. Probably nothing, but if something doesn't smell right to you, I trust your nose. Please get on the horn with Transoceanic, and find out if the company thinks everything is hunky-dory on their ship. Keep it casual. Like random spot checks are a new protocol for the bureau. You're checking up on all the ships frozen in the Chesapeake right now as a courtesy. Or blame Homeland. Or say we're backstopping the Coast Guard for now while they ramp back up after this last government shutdown. And give me your ham radio guy's info. Probably nothing."

Agent Carter paused a moment. "You've said it's *probably nothing* twice."

CHAPTER 14

"GET THE BULLET," said Blackshaw, staring at the wound in the cadaver on the dining table.

Everyone else in Ruke's felt a chill descend, and turned toward Blackshaw as if he had suggested some kind of pagan defilement of the remains. Even baby Callum, held snug in Mary Wright's arms, opened his eyes and looked over at his father.

As if to explain, Blackshaw said, "There's no exit wound. It's still in there, right?"

LuAnna said, "I thought we were going to keep the tampering down to a minimum for when the authorities came to collect her. Remember? No Y incision? Anybody?"

Sonny chimed in. "What do you want to know so bad it's worth getting the cops up our noses with questions about what we done with her?"

"Let's say you pull out a nine-mike slug," said Ellis. "What's that tell you?"

LuAnna confirmed, "Everybody and their dog's got a nine millimeter these days."

"If we're careful," said Blackshaw, "we pull the bullet out the way it went in. We check it out, and pop it right back where we found it."

Sounds of disgust rose from everyone who heard that.

"That's just wrong, Ben," said Mary.

LuAnna said, "Hold on. Have to admit, Ben's got me curious. If we do it right, nobody's the wiser."

"What if we don't put it back just so?" Mary asked. Like any Smith Islander, she was much more familiar with shotguns and their work than bullets.

"Bullets do tumble, and ricochet off bones and such," said Ellis. "But saying we follow the bullet hole in, how do we get at the slug without adding obvious trauma to the wound?"

LuAnna said, "You're right, Ellis. If we aren't careful, it's easy for some medical examiner with a sharp eye to tell between antemortem and postmortem tissue damage."

Mary said, "And it's not like things aren't suspicious enough with how we cut her out of the ice, drug her indoors, thawed her out, stripped her bare, and ate juicy delicious burgers while we done it. Ain't lost your touch, Sonny."

Sonny beamed love at his wife who was admiring her half-eaten burger with appreciation.

Ellis said, "I for one don't have any surgical tools layin' around. And that's what it's going to take."

Blackshaw was quiet. Then he gave Sonny a hard look, and asked, "How's your *Winnie Estelle* model coming along?"

The *Winnie Estelle* was a big oyster buyboat owned by LuAnna's Uncle Conrad. The wealth of gold Blackshaw's father had brought to Smith Island had afforded Sonny free time he used to fill by oystering on the bay. Now he whiled away the dark of winter crafting ships in bottles. The *Winnie Estelle* was Sonny's fourth effort. He was getting much better with details, and had even sold a pretty little draketail deadrise in a Jack Daniels bottle for sale at Kathy Taylor-Donaway's Smith Island Quilting shop for five hundred dollars. Nobody asked Sonny where the empty Jack Daniels bottle had come from, and he hadn't offered to tell.

Sonny answered modestly in the sideways manner of Smith Islanders, "She's looking ugly enough, but stepping her mast is going to be a grunt and a half. I figure to hit the decaf a couple days before I give her a go, so my hand's nice and steady. I hate to give up Aram Polster's high-test coffee even for one day, but I will suffer for my art, yes sir."

Sonny appreciated the kind inquiry until he realized everyone was staring at him. "What? What'd I say?"

CHAPTER 15

CHOAD LAGLEET LOOKED in on Bonamy Screed in his small cabin on the fishing boat. The rust bucket was twisting through ever-steepening waves; Screed was still green with seasickness.

"How you feeling cowboy?"

In answer, Screed rolled toward the small sink next to his berth and dry-heaved for the hundredth time.

LaGleet ignored the vomiting. "Another hour, it'll be dark, and we're going to put in shore by inflatable on the beach at Arcachon."

"France?" was all Screed could manage.

LaGleet leaned away from Screed's rancid breath. "Right you are. A pretty little tourist town, but this time of year, most everything's closed. They named its four districts after the seasons. Quaint, right? Not that you'll have a hot minute for souvenirs. A chopper takes us off the beach to a strip where we've got a Faction aircraft waiting. You'll be stateside by tomorrow night."

Screed looked morose at the prospect.

LaGleet offered a pep talk. "Look, you dumb fuck. Jesus got a second chance at a comeback and still hasn't cashed it in. You should be a little more grateful. How're your mitts?"

"Hurt like hell. Like the fingers are still there," Screed mumbled.

"Phantom limb," said LaGleet. "I heard it's a thing, and now we know it's true."

"You're all heart, Choad," said Screed. "I'll need gear. Weapons."

"Already on the plane, big man," said LaGleet.

Looking at Screed, LaGleet was becoming even less sure his recruit was up to the job. LaGleet drew his pistol, racked a round into the chamber, and jammed the barrel to Screed's head. Screed pulled away, and put up a hand in defense. LaGleet grabbed Screed's hand, dug his fingers deep into the thick bandage, and wrenched hard. Screed's mouth opened wide as his face blanched in a rictus of agony, but no sound came out but a wheeze from deep in his chest.

"Are we good, my man?" snarled LaGleet. "Do we have an understanding of expectations, and of consequences if they're not met?"

Screed nodded, his eyes wet with tears.

LaGleet shoved Screed back down onto the berth with disgust. He thought Screed bore watching. Maybe on this gig, LaGleet and Krill would tag along.

CHAPTER 16

PENELOPE'S NEW RADIO operator, Castor, rushed onto the bridge. Grodin looked up from his study of the weather services displaying the same old bad news. Captain Varna was just stepping in from the port bridge wing where he had retreated for fresh air and healthy distance from the dour operative squatting on his command. Varna found that some men of action often made poor company when they were mired in stasis. And unit cohesion among the crew was deteriorating. Varna guessed they too were working on commission, and were fantasizing about the cash jobs they were missing out on while they were cooling their heels in the icy wastes of the Chesapeake Bay.

Castor said, "Remember that ham radio guy who was trying to get in touch with the old radio op?"

Grodin said, "What about him?"

"He stopped."

Captain Varna, "So?"

Castor went on, "Stopped a couple days ago."

Grodin and the captain exchanged tired looks. Grodin said, "You told him to fuck off, so that's a good thing, right?"

Castor said, "I don't know. See, the telemetry transmissions ramped up."

Grodin looked at Captain Varna to see if Castor's words meant anything to him.

Varna said, "The ship automatically sends data back to Transoceanic every day. Like sending a report from an autonomous ship's steward, quartermaster, and engineer all rolled into one system."

"Data on what exactly?" said Grodin. "We killed the uplink for the whole CCTV system and the crew's Wi-Fi. Transoceanic's not peeping us are they?"

"True, but they still get all engine functions," Varna said. "Cylinder head temps, oil levels and temps. Same for fuel, ballast, fresh water, generators, food. I mean everything, including the temperature of the liquid natural gas cargo. That's kept at its boiling point of negative 260°, and you can bet—"

"Hold it! Food?" Grodin stood and paced the width of the bridge. "How?"

Captain Varna said, "Like in a hotel room, when you take a coke out of the fridge, they know it down at the desk right away, and it automatically goes on your bill. Transoceanic provisions these ships like a space shot. So much fresh water per person per day. So many ounces of meat and slices of bread and eggs per day. Even veggies, but those are canned after the first week."

Silas Grodin stopped pacing and turned to the captain. "Walk it back. We boarded two weeks ago and liquidated the crew."

"Yes. I remember," said Captain Varna. He had allowed himself to form no deep personal attachments with his crew knowing a Faction mission like this would come one day, but still, some good sailors had died in the attack. Some lazy, querulous bastards had died too, for whom Varna felt not a pang.

Grodin continued, "We thought we were going to be aboard three days, max'."

"But the weather put a kink in the plan, I know," said the captain. "Where exactly do you think I've been this entire time?"

"We brought our own rations. For three days we ate those," said Grodin, looking more nervous by the minute. "What kind of picture does that paint in this telemetry thing?"

"Oh," said Varna, realizing where Grodin was going with this.

Castor said, "It looks like everybody stopped eating for three days."

"But then the freeze, the delay, and we started helping ourselves to ship's stores," said Grodin.

"Shit. The original crew was twenty-six. Your team plus me make a total of nine," said the captain, realizing the issue.

"They'll think part of the crew started fasting," said Castor.

"Okay, that's stupid—or maybe not," said Grodin, thinking on his feet. "Will they buy it that the freeze prompted you and the crew to cut rations?"

"And water?" Captain Varna shook his head. "*Penelope* was provisioned for one year. We're twenty-seven weeks into this cruise, and this is the Chesapeake Bay, not the Northwest Passage. No freeze in these latitudes would last long enough to starve us. No credible reason to stretch rations. Unless we claim a freezer failure, which won't work, because that would be transmitted, and because we could just stow the provisions outside on deck in the cold. No, your best bet is that nobody ever checks the telemetry data past the top sheet of the report on the ship herself, and the cargo."

Castor said, "That's what I'm trying to tell you. The telemetry bursts have been going out every day. But as of today, it looks like Transoceanic is querying the telemetry every eight bells."

"From once a day to four times a day. Shit!" said Grodin. "The main engines are shut down. Why do they care what's going on with them?"

Castor said, "So what we know is the home office has ramped up the queries, and that guy quit calling his pal on the radio."

"You're bored," said Grodin. "The ship's in unusual circumstances, and they're just checking up on the cargo."

Captain Varna said, "Then why haven't they bothered to speak with me?"

The three men were quiet, taking in the sound of the freshening wind rushing around the bridge, and the hum, beeps, and soft chimes of various systems. Slowly, they turned their attention to the forward-facing windscreen looking for the source of the alien sound intruding on the quiet. The beat of an approaching helicopter.

Grodin said, "What the hell? In this weather?"

Captain Varna said, "Castor, your eyes are sharp. Grab those binoculars. I want the N number off that chopper. I'll copy down what you read."

Castor did as ordered.

CHAPTER 17

MOLLY WILDE HATED flying, but she hated being a passenger in helicopters most of all. Birds have wings. Planes have wings. She could see that even without engine power a plane might return to earth in a glide. Wilde understood in a cerebral way that when a helicopter lost power, autorotation and a skilled pilot could bring the craft to the ground safely, but this seemed counterintuitive. Those thin blades whipping around, and all those other fragile-looking parts clattering somewhere above her head, they seemed in need of a functioning engine, the grace of a merciful God, and strength of her will to stay airborne.

Her regular pilot, McCourt, was usually unbothered by nervous passengers. Outwardly, Wilde remained calm enough, but she still made McCourt apprehensive. Wilde tended to attract as much gunfire stateside as he had taken in his Apache in Iraq, particularly when he flew her around Smith Island in the lower Chesapeake Bay. He remembered their first visit to the island by air, after which Wilde discovered a pumpkin ball shotgun slug embedded near one of the doors of his bird. He did not make a big deal about it with Wilde, but at the moment, he was sitting on his folded old ballistic vest as well as wearing his new one. McCourt was a careful pilot, and a wary one.

Wilde marveled at the Arctic white view spread below her. Recent snow covered the land, making it gleam behind black trees in in the sunlight. The frozen Chesapeake Bay was a blinding flatness stretching to an indeterminate horizon to the south, and bounded by built-up shorelines on the east and west.

"Where to, again?" McCourt asked. Wilde had requisitioned the bird, but had worded the case ticket in vague terms like reconnaissance, and observation.

Wilde pulled the mic of her David Clark headset close to her lips, and said, "Take a slow pass south of the Chesapeake Bay Bridge along the shipping channel. We're looking for a big LNG transporter."

"For landing?" McCourt asked, hoping for some precision flying at least.

"Negative," Molly directed. "And don't circle it. Don't slow down. Don't divert or descend toward it. But get us down to five hundred feet now, and seventy-five percent cruise. Copy?"

This did not surprise McCourt, since Wilde had requested an unmarked Bell 206 Jet Ranger without the blue DOJ/FBI roundels plastered behind the rear doors. She wanted to observe the target without stirring up a fuss.

McCourt complied with a gentle descent and reduction of power. In just under ten minutes, he said, "That must be her. Christ, what a whale."

Wilde already had a pair of high-powered binoculars aimed forward. She was grateful the binoculars were electronically stabilized. The turbulence would have made focusing difficult.

The *Penelope* was indeed a beast. She lay frozen at an angle to the channel, with her bow toward north northeast, and stern south southwest.

McCourt asked, "How much LNG is she carrying?"

"Could be as much as two hundred sixty-six thousand cubic meters," said Wilde.

"Is that as big a bang as it sounds?"

"If it's contained, or around ten percent mix with ambient air," said Molly. "Still, it would need a source of ignition."

McCourt kept flying straight and level. Wilde swapped the binoculars for a long lens camera, and triggered burst after burst of pictures as the helicopter flew past.

McCourt asked, "Do you think there's some kind of source of ignition down there?"

Wilde rested the camera in her lap as the tanker disappeared astern. "It's a distinct possibility. I don't want to tip the crew by giving them a second look at us. Stay on course a few more miles, then hang a right and take us back home over land."

CHAPTER 18

"HAND 'EM OVER," said Blackshaw to Sonny.

For a moment, the model ship builder clasped the rolled leather kit of tools to his chest. Then he said, "I'll never use them again. Not after this."

"Come on, Sonny. I'll spring for a new set," LuAnna said. "It's Christmastime."

Sonny parted with the kit. Blackshaw unknotted the thin canvas ties and unrolled the partitioned pouches and sleeves flat on the table next to the corpse. While Sonny had been fetching his model ship making tools, Mary had accompanied him to collect work lights, and run extension cords to the Methodist church a little way down Caleb Jones Road. She and LuAnna had arranged the lights next to the corpse so Blackshaw could see what he was doing.

Blackshaw chose the wire rig hook and long, finely pointed tweezers from Sonny's tool kit, and said, "Here goes."

LuAnna said, "I feel like we should say a prayer or something first."

Blackshaw said, "Don't let me stop you, but for my money, faith without works is dead. Like this here lady."

LuAnna and Mary bowed their heads in silence. So did Sonny. Blackshaw and Ellis remained quiet.

After several respectful, if not pious moments, Blackshaw began to slide the long tweezers into the cadaver's wound. He was surprised and how tough the tissue was, and wondered if the deep interior of the cadaver was still frozen.

There was a gentle knock at the door of the old store.

LuAnna peeked past the quilt hung there to block the view of the curious. There stood the Reverend Mosby, his hat in his hand in spite of the cold, his short gray hair flicking in the wind.

LuAnna said, "Speak of the Devil," and opened the door.

"Hey Rev'," said Blackshaw. "Wondered when you'd stop by."

"In the nick of time by the looks of things," said the preacher. He nodded to all present, but quick as a fox he set his gaze on the cadaver and the tool in Blackshaw's hand.

CHAPTER 19

THE FACTION HELICOPTER ride from the Arcachon beach to the disused airstrip was brief, but did nothing to quell Bonamy Screed's nausea. The same winds that made his life a living hell on the fishing boat kicked up turbulence bordering on windshear aloft. When the chopper landed near the runway of the airport, the four propellers of Faction's exhaust-stained, crumple-skinned C-130 were already turning.

"Christ, is this the best you got? I thought Faction had money," complained Screed. He had flown crammed into these transports while he was in the military. He remembered they were unpressurized, noisy barns in which one either froze or roasted, depending how close one sat to the heaters. And they were excruciatingly slow beasts, more like reliable workhorses bouncing through turbulence at three hundred twenty knots, not sleek thoroughbreds like Gulfstream business jets that could hurtle through the smoother Flight Levels above eighteen thousand feet nudging the speed of sound.

LaGleet stifled the urge to cuff Screed's head. He and Krill frog-marched their ailing operator toward steps reaching up to the aft side door into the cargo hold.

Screed was puzzled by what he saw inside. There, belayed to the deck, lay a large palletized box looking for all the world like a battered, rusty shipping container. Loadmasters were checking the box's moorings and attach points. At a door in the rear of the container stood a middle-aged man of Asian heritage in a white lab coat.

"Yo, Doc. Here's the patient," said LaGleet.

"Allow me," said Doc in a broad Downeast Maine accent.

LaGleet and Krill stepped aside, and it was Doc who supported Screed across the threshold into the container. In contrast to the worn utilitarian exterior of the plane, the inside of the container was appointed like a luxury VIP aircraft, with soft lighting, lie-flat club seating, a gourmet galley, two comm/work stations, and at least two lavatories with showers. Fully one-third of this space was devoted to sophisticated mobile medical care, including an examination table with brilliant overhead lights and a full complement of diagnostic equipment. A male flight attendant and a female physician's assistant rounded out the staff.

While LaGleet and Krill helped themselves to coffee in the galley, Doc eased Screed gently toward the table, and said, "You've been through a lot, sir. Before we take off, I want to do a quick examination and start working up a blood panel. Looks like your bandages could use a change. And I'd like to start you on an IV for hydration, an antibiotic cocktail that would make drug-resistant TB run for the hills, and maybe a little something for the pain. Sound okay, sir?"

Screed studied Doc to be sure all this respectful attention wasn't a joke. Still unsure, but with little to lose, he nodded and said, "Sure. Please. Thanks."

"Don't spoil him, Doc," said LaGleet, belting himself into a seat. "He's got hard work to do. In twenty-four hours, I need a soldier, not a basket case."

Doc smiled. "Not to worry, Choad. I've got a pick-me-up that'll have him charging up San Juan Hill like Teddy Roosevelt himself, and carrying the horse on his back while he's at it. We can flow that into the IV—" Here Doc checked an array of clocks from different time zones. "—Let's say after our last in-flight refueling."

LaGleet grinned. "Maybe you can hook Krill and me up with some of that, too."

"No problem," said Doc. "One bolus of this stuff I've developed, and you could cage fight for a solid week without a wink of sleep."

CHAPTER 20

REVEREND MOSBY STUDIED the cadaver with a look of sadness in his eyes. He asked no questions of the other attending Smith Islanders. After the death of Lorton Dyze the year before, Ben Blackshaw was head man hereabouts, especially in darker, blood-spattered doings. Mosby was still the man who received word of his flock's day-to-day worries, and a good measure of the gossip as well. He had heard all about the dead woman.

Blackshaw respected Reverend Mosby both as a man, and as a man of God. Whatever Blackshaw's personal crisis of faith, the waterman knew the preacher never stood in the way of necessary actions that helped neighbors survive any kind of hardship. His ancestors were Smith Islanders. Before the call to Methodism, they had harvested the Chesapeake's natural bounty; they had often plundered the seaborne goods of man as well. So fierce was their reputation that during the American Revolution, King George III had given Letters of Marque to Smith Island captains to burn, sink, capture, or otherwise destroy Colonial ships. Smith Islanders had been doing that anyway. To them, a document with a royal seal was a more a gaudy formality than a license. Recently, when Blackshaw's father had brought home stolen gold bullion with a pack of bloodthirsty government operatives hard on his tail, Reverend Mosby had stood with other Smith Islanders, gun in hand, and driven the invaders back into the Chesapeake. Mosby's burnt offerings to the Lord had a strong whiff of gunpowder about them.

Reverend Mosby walked slowly around the dining table-cum-catafalque supporting the dead woman. When he reached her head, he kneeled and placed his hands gently over her temples. He bent low, and whispered something into her ear. After another moment of quiet, he stood, his knees popping with age, and said, "Go on Ben. See if you can fetch that slug out into the light."

Blackshaw slowly pressed the tweezers further into the wound. About eleven inches of the tool disappeared into the flesh before Blackshaw heard the scrape of metal on metal. He said, "I think that's it."

Like a burglar working a difficult lock with multiple picks, Blackshaw followed the tweezers into the wound with Sonny's rig hook. LuAnna saw Blackshaw wince as if he were inflicting pain when the rig hook touched the bullet. Then he turned the hook ninety degrees and pressed it further into the channel past the slug. He twisted the rig hook's handle again, lowering the hook in place behind the bullet. With a good purchase on both tweezer and hook, he gently pulled.

Blackshaw was surprised at the amount of effort needed to start the slug moving. The body jiggled as he tugged. The slug moved a little more than an inch before the tweezers and rig hook slipped loose. The wound oozed gore. Everyone in the room released breath with the tension of the moment.

"That's okay, Ben," said Reverend Mosby. "You got to try again."

Blackshaw's tools slipped twice more before the slug clinked into an enameled tin mug LuAnna held under the wound.

As Blackshaw retrieved the slug from the cup, Sonny asked, "What ye got?"

"As ugly a thing as ever I've seen," Blackshaw answered. He held up the tweezers. Clasped at their tip was a small metal flower. The slug had not mushroomed. It had bloomed six sharp petals. "Black Talon."

Ellis said, "Naw, they don't make Black Talon anymore. Not since 2000."

"Ellis's got the smart of it," said Sonny. "Winchester replaced Black Talon with Ranger SXT, or *Same Exact Thing*, but no black Lubalox coating."

"Telling you, this is the old stuff," Blackshaw insisted. "Look. The black coating's still on it. Ten millimeter round, by the looks."

"Armor piercing?" asked LuAnna. "The cop-killer stuff?"

"No, that was media bull," said Blackshaw. "They also said it was Teflon coated. The Lubalox was to keep the barrel clean, not to butter the slug through Kevlar. Anyway, it was no worse nor better than other hollow points for wound path trauma. But it still says a lot."

Mary asked, "What-all does it say?"

"Killing this woman was special to the shooter," said Blackshaw, turning the bullet in the light. "This is the chosen ammo of a mean-spirited individual, a sadist who wanted to feel he—or she, to be fair—was doing this woman worse damage than an ordinary jacketed or hollow point bullet would do. The mystique of the Black Talon was it slashed up the insides along the wound path. And like Ellis said, this is old ammo, which means the shooter hoarded it up. Saved it for an occasion."

Ellis said, "Your psychologizing is nice, but it's still a hollow point round. You think about that, Ben?"

"I'm listening."

Ellis went on. "It's meant to stop inside the body and not ricochet out and hit others, or smash into other stuff. Air marshals use it to take down hijackers without bringing down the plane. Nasty as it looks, and I agree it's ugly, it's the bullet of a controlled attack. Not like a fifty-caliber exploding Raufoss round blowing holes in brick walls and such. Hollow point is about lethality *and* damage containment in situ."

"So this is a working man's load. A crazy, angry, sadistic working man," said LuAnna. "I get it. We all get it. What's your point?"

Ellis looked each person in the eye for a moment before he answered. "Is there anything around here somebody wants bad enough to kill for it, but he wants it undamaged?"

"You must have a thought on the matter, Ellis," said Blackshaw.

"Mayhaps I do. But I'm keeping it to myself for a time. Don't want to seem hysterical."

There was sharp knock on the door that startled everyone. Without waiting, Mary Wright's grandson, Pliny-Robert, burst in carrying a big eight-motor drone with a substantial camera slung below it. He stopped in his tracks staring at the nearly naked woman on the table. "Lordy-go-to-fire," whispered Pliny.

Mary snapped as she rushed at the boy, "You best turn right around and scoot out of here now, or the fire's gonna be on your behind!"

"Wait!" Pliny-Robert said, ignoring his grandmother's fury. "You got to see this!" He held his precious drone up in front of him like a shield.

Mary spun Pliny-Robert around until his back was to the corpse. "I told you to steer clear. Now what's all the fuss?"

"Look!" said Pliny-Robert, turning the drone's camera on. Everyone gathered around the boy as best they could to see. "I took her up for fun, and got these shots."

The picture thumbnails were small, and detail was hard to see.

Pliny said, "That's where you found the lady. See the dark spot you got her from? It's re-froze already. And that's the trail on the ice where you drug her back on the hard. The wind's almost wiped it away."

"We were there, Pliny-Bob. What's the point?" Mary asked.

Pliny-Robert scrolled ahead through the thumbnails. "I took this drone up real high. Wanted to see how far up she'd go. Its GPS held it on station, but I goosed the throttle and up she went like a spooked wood duck."

Pliny-Robert enlarged one thumbnail to fill the camera's small monitor. "See that? See them to the west? There. And there—"

LuAnna was the first to speak. "Looks like one, two—" she fell quiet counting the dark forms in the ice. "This lady didn't travel alone. That looks like there's eight more of these snow angels still out there."

CHAPTER 21

BONAMY SCREED'S PLANE was refueled in the air twice on its way across the Atlantic from France to the States.

Doc had been as good as his word, piping in antibiotics for the entire flight, and adding his personal blend of stimulants through a separate line in his other arm. Screed's heart was beginning to accelerate, and his mind was clearer than it had been in many days. Despite the amping of all his senses, the cocktail seemed to infuse Screed with an underlying calm that made him feel invincible.

Choad LaGleet glanced up at the IV bag suspended by his chair, and the line leading to his own left accessory cephalic vein in his arm. "My God, Doc! What's in this stuff?"

Doc grinned with pride. "It's a distillation of guarana, caffeine, cocaine, vitamin B complex, a dash of Phenylcyclohexyl piperidine, and a tiny bit of Klonopin to take the edge off a firefight and keep heads cool."

"Phency—what?" LaGleet asked.

"Slightly denatured angel dust would be the best way to describe it," said Doc.

Krill's nostrils were flared, and her eyes were wide as she sucked air deep into her lungs. She said, "Jesus! I think I'm going ovulate on the spot!"

Doc went on, "The beauty of the stuff is my proprietary sustained release formula that works with your natural metabolism in four successive phases. Usually, big pharma can only swing that through an active line or in multiple-pill dosing. But you'll get three more hits without going near a needle or a pill. Perfect for the soldier on the go."

LaGleet motioned for Doc to approach for a confidential chat out of Screed's hearing.

When Doc took a knee, LaGleet leaned over and asked, "Straight up. How's our boy doing? Think he's good to go?"

Doc answered, "He's got a severe infection that could devolve into sepsis. He should be in a hospital ICU, but he'll be on his feet and working hard for at least thirty-six hours. All the test subjects for my Sustained Forward Operations Protocol, S-FOP for short, they lasted forty-eight hours before crashing."

LaGleet asked, "So his infection will cut his effective time short, you think?"

Doc looked embarrassed. "I guess you didn't get the communique from Faction."

LaGleet shook his head.

Doc whispered, "You and Krill are getting the full four S-FOP phases in your IVs. When the last phase is metabolized, you'll feel tired, and likely sleep for twenty hours straight, if my test subjects are any indication. But Faction radioed with special instructions. Screed's fourth phase is a little different. It's a cloaked, bonded bolus of hydrogen cyanide. If he survives whatever his assignment is, he'll metabolize the end of phase three, and then lights out. Forever."

LaGleet studied Screed feverishly reassembling his rifle for the sixth time, and tapped his own IV bag. "I sure as hell hope you didn't mix up our IVs."

Doc smiled. "Not to worry. But if I did, there isn't a damn thing you can do about it now."

LaGleet had a lot on his mind as the pilot descended through the darkness and set the big transport down at Wilmington Airport, in Delaware.

CHAPTER 22

PLINY-ROBERT HAD LOGGED the GPS position of each of the eight new shadowy ice graves. The debate his discovery sparked was over quickly.

"It's dark enough," Blackshaw said. "If we hustle, we could cut them all out of the ice and bring them in before sun-up."

This raised protests from LuAnna, Mary, and Sonny, who said, "Bring them in? We shouldn't ought've brung *her* in. Bad enough we got her, and now what do we tell the police? 'We was out proggin' and got us these cadavers all in a bunch and decided let's bring them home like knickknacks?"

LuAnna said, "One corpse is a problem for us. Nine corpses, and the FBI will open a field office right here in Ewell next to Smith Island Quilting, doncha know."

Ellis took a Socratic tack. "LuAnna, if it were you chilling out there in the dark and cold, and if somebody found you, would you want to be left there for the fish and crabs and tide and current to take you away from anybody knowing what finally happened to you?"

"You had to go and make it personal," said LuAnna.

"Death is the most personal thing of all, Honeygirl," said Reverend Mosby. "We come into the world with our mamas. But we, many of us, go out of it alone—well, just ourselves and the Lord."

Mary Wright said, "Ben, you've left a corpse or two behind in your day. Even one cadaver you thought was your Pappy."

Blackshaw said, "Mistaken identity."

"You sure didn't know it at the time," observed Sonny.

"There was other urgent matter," said Blackshaw. "If it'd make you feel better, Sonny, we can go out and get that fellow come spring, though he's naught but soup bones by now, if there's aught left of him at all. Burial at sea didn't bother you when our fortunes were on the line."

"No thank you," said Sonny. "He was part of that crew that wished us all dead and done. He can stay where he is. And these ones out there got no claim on us," Sonny said.

Blackshaw said, "Even in Iraq, nine dead was a bad day. But this is home. Nine dead here is mass murder. Death is creeping close to all we care about. We need to know what's going on, and put a stop to it. I'm going to collect some gear and head out. Any and all of you are welcome to join, but I'm not waiting around for a head count."

CHAPTER 23

EXECUTIVE ASSISTANT DIRECTOR for Counterterrorism and Counterintelligence Pershing Lowry welcomed his wife home with their baby in his arms. Molly Wilde kissed Lowry, and clasped Ella Grace to her chest.

"I missed you both so much!" Wilde said. Ella Grace smiled, and farted gently.

Wilde's mother, Patience, tall, angular, and lovely with shoulder length gray hair in a ponytail, joined them in the foyer, "Was it a good day, Mol'? Feeling better?"

Wilde visited with her mother for a few minutes, expressing genuine gratitude for Patience's care several times.

Patience knew her daughter, shushed her, and said, "You went to work. Why?"

"Mom, it's a good way to clear my head and my desk at the same time," said Wilde. "I've been out of the office a while."

Patience gazed at her daughter and granddaughter with love, and said, "Something's come up. I can tell. Give me that baby, and you and Pershing go talk in the office."

"It can wait," said Wilde, who loved her mother, and never wanted to treat her like just a babysitter for hire.

Patience took Ella Grace in her arms and said, "I think a bath and a fresh diaper would be just the thing for the little miss right now. Dinner at eight."

Lowry took his wife's hand and led her into the home office they shared, though rarely occupied together. Their kiss took a few moments, but that was all.

"You need to see this," said Wilde, as she started her computer.

Lowry studied his wife, waiting for her to tell him what was on her mind.

"Marla-Jo called from Salisbury," said Wilde.

"I asked her to call you," Lowry confessed. "Her suspicions were reasonable. Calling my office wasn't wrong. But she had to develop her evidence beyond a hunch."

"You mean I had to develop it," said Wilde, feeling manipulated. "So you know I talked to her ham radio buff."

"Not specifically, but I figured you might," said Lowry, grinning. "What surprised me was your chopper ride."

"McCourt ratted me out," said Wilde.

"He was almost clever about it," said Lowry. "He called to ask if I'd need him today, and mentioned your flight plan."

Lips pressed tight in anger, Wilde made the old computer keyboard rattle loud as she banged her password into the FBI site to access her files. "Everybody's keeping tabs on the little woman."

"It's not like that at all," said Lowry. "Everyone cares about you."

"And knows I'm fucking up as a mother, or I'm depressed, or crazy. I'm surprised you haven't relieved me of my weapon."

"Should I?"

"You're welcome to try," said Wilde, looking hard into Lowry's brown eyes. She added, "Oh, and that's where you should've said I have it all together."

"I've never lied to you," said Lowry.

Wilde turned from the computer again to face Lowry.

He said, "The big lie is the well-packaged idea that motherhood is smooth sailing from the jump. We all get sold that by the good folks who make the baby food, the diapers, the car seats, the creams and lotions, you know—the subtle message that you're not doing it right unless you have all that stuff. You won't get the perfect Instagram images of your life unless you're teaching Ella Grace sign language, and reading her this book or that book, or playing the right music that'll make her an Einstein, or waving toys of this color or that pattern in front of her face twenty-four seven. You never fell for the hard-sell, Molly. But it's harder to toss out the soft soap meta-message of screwing up. We know the truth, don't we? Whatever things are like at the moment, it's okay. And it's going to be okay. And it's not you by yourself. It's us, Molly. And we've got this."

Wilde's eyes were moist.

Lowry said, "I'm sorry, Molly. I guess I'm not sure how to comfort you."

Wilde smeared away her tears and kissed Lowry. "You just did. But I'm going to need to hear that speech of yours every five minutes until further notice."

"I can do that. Now, was your mother right? Something happened at work?"

Wilde faced the computer once again, and clicked on a series of images she had snapped from the helicopter. The *Penelope* loomed large at first from bow to stern. Then Wilde scrolled through the digital contact sheet of thumbnails until she came to close-up images of *Penelope*'s bridge superstructure.

"There," she said. "What do you see?"

"The ship in question. Red hull. Green deck surfaces, where you can see through the snow. White tower structure."

Wilde spun the little wheel on her elderly mouse, zooming the image into a close-up of one particular porthole on the third level above the deck. "And now?"

Lowry leaned close to the screen. "That's odd. On the entire ship, that seems to be the only streak of rust in an otherwise pristine paint job."

"Keep looking," Wilde said.

In a moment of chagrin, Lowry reached into his breast pocket for a pair of reading glasses. They were a new addition to his personal effects, a reminder that he would never see his thirties again; from time to time, he still forgot he needed them.

Lowry's mouth fell open. Then he frowned. "Someone seriously injured came through that porthole from inside to outside. That's not a streak of rust—that's a hand-print. It's dried blood."

CHAPTER 24

ELLIS, BLACKSHAW, SONNY, Reverend Mosby, and LuAnna traversed the nighttime ice on the Wright's Gator equipped with rubber Prowler tracks. Though his wife had preferred the golf cart for spinning donuts on the ice the day before, tonight the Gator put paid to Mary's accusation that he had spent his money on it like a damn fool.

The breeze whirled fallen snow up into the air as they crept along slowly. They stopped from time to time to check the thickness of the ice, and to listen for sounds of it cracking.

LuAnna kept a close eye on the handheld GPS, which issued the only light. Everyone else wore Night Vision Goggles from Ellis's arcane store of tactical gear. Using Pliny-Robert's coordinates, LuAnna had attempted to create a circuit of lines and waypoints for each frozen cadaver for retrieval. They had plastic sleds, toboggans, and even a couple of old Flexible Flyers in tow for the recovery mission.

Sometimes a rough patch of ice meant they had to diverge from the straightest route, detour to smoother ice, and resume a new course toward the first body.

At last, LuAnna said, "Keep your eyes sharp, boys. The GPS says we're within a hundred feet."

Sonny slowed the Gator down. "Nothing yet."

He dropped the Gator's speed down to a crawl.

It was Reverend Mosby who alerted them to what lay ahead when he muttered, "Dear Lord. Cut her left a little, Sonny."

Sonny obliged, turning the Gator to the left.

"Oh my blessing," LuAnna said.

The Gator drew forward until Sonny stopped it ten feet from their macabre target.

They could only guess the cadaver was male, judging by the mass, the short hair. It sat upright, head and broad shoulders projecting from the ice thanks to a life preserver. Blackshaw leaned down and brushed hoarfrost from the saddle of the life jacket. He read, "*Penelope.*"

Ellis said, "That's a Type I commercial life jacket. Like a vest."

Sonny said, "Don't they abandon ship in those freefall lifeboats?"

"Especially in weather like this," averred Reverend Mosby.

Blackshaw looked at the front of the remains. The body had no face. Most of the features were torn away.

"Handsome devil," said Sonny, who had followed Blackshaw around the corpse.

Blackshaw removed the glove of one hand and felt through the corpse's stiff hair at the back of its head. "That's an exit wound up front there."

"How do you know?" Sonny asked.

"Because I got my pinkie finger deep in the entry wound," said Blackshaw.

LuAnna held up her pinkie and said, "Like a fancy tea party with brains instead of shortcake."

"That's not disgusting at all," said Ellis.

Blackshaw said, "Sonny's right. Those freefall lifeboats are usually the thing, especially in bad weather, but they'd come down kinda hard on this ice even if it were slush."

Ellis said, "Bet somebody faked a catastrophic emergency on this *Penelope*. They mustered the crew at the embarkation points to abandon ship. Then pop-pop-pop—back of the head, and they topple into the Chesapeake Bay."

LuAnna stared at Ellis, who finished, "That's how *I'd* do it."

Sonny returned to the Gator and retrieved a pick axe. "Let's get at it. Feels like a fuzzcod blowing in, and we shouldn't be out here when it does."

Blackshaw touched Reverend Mosby on the sleeve and asked, "What was the prayer you knelt to say over the lady back at Ruke's?"

Reverend Mosby was slow to answer. "It wasn't a prayer, Ben. It was a promise. A promise you'd find who killed her, and blow their shit to Kingdom Come. Don't make a liar out of me."

CHAPTER 25

BONAMY SCREED SURVEYED the storm-white town of Crisfield, Maryland, and added it to the list of places where he could never live. He allowed for the fact that it was the dead of night and blowing a hard blizzard. He took into consideration what he knew well, that like much of the Eastern Shore of Maryland, there was a summer seasonal aspect to the bustle and business of this place. It was charming enough.

The main avenue was broad and terminated at the waters of Tangier Sound in the Chesapeake. That was the problem. The scent of the water and mud teeming with life would not be suppressed even under a foot of ice. And that scent was a curse to Bonamy Screed. With the power of an H.G. Wells time machine, the aromas, subtle as they were in the cold, dragged Screed back just a few months to the hell of his captivity on Smith Island at the hands of Ben Blackshaw and his friends.

The removal of one of his index fingers with a bolt cutter haunted him. He could remember the shed—a shanty they'd called it. Even today he could feel them tightening the vise hard on his hand while several men had sat on his legs, chest, and hips to keep him from bucking during the amputation.

As Screed suffocated from the weight, Blackshaw had explained that the disgraced FBI director-cum-prisoner had killed his friend, Travis Cynter, a good man, a good soldier; Now they wanted to take the trigger finger that had sent the lethal round down range. There was no talking his way out of this. They did not want intel. They wanted revenge. They gagged him.

The bolt cutters were not new. Blackshaw closed the jaws around the offending finger, twisting and wrenching the blades through skin, flesh, and cracking bone until the digit came free.

Screed had howled, all dignity swept away in a cascade of pain and humiliation. How it burned, and ached. Then, the woman stitching the skin flaps over the stump was neither quick nor gentle.

Screed's fear ramped to horror as his captors began chatting among themselves as if he were not there.

"You ain't done a clean nor pretty job of it," said the man on Screed's legs.

Blackshaw, as the others called him, answered, "Thank you kindly. Good enough for government work. LuAnna's a dab hand with the needle, though."

The woman said, "I watched while Mary stitched up my hip that one time."

The man straddling Screed's chest slapped his pinioned, squawking captive hard in the face, and said, "You hush up now. You still got nine fingers left to scratch your butt and pick your nose."

The man crushing Screed's pelvis said, "Uh-oh."

All his captors turned their eyes to pelvis man, who said, "We got his right pointer finger sure enough, but odds-on, this chuckle-headed fool is a lefty!"

The men looked at one another, while Screed struggled and twisted and shook his head, screaming through the gag that he was indeed right-handed. It didn't matter. No one could make out the lie through the gag.

The woman said, "I've got thread aplenty for all his fingers and his toes to boot if you like. Needle's a tad dull, but I have a fine sailmaker's palm my momma gave me. I could push a phone pole up a frog's ass with that thing. Say the word."

And so Blackshaw had indeed spoken, as Screed recalled on that frigid boat landing in Crisfield. Then the woman had looked down and noticed damp patches on her shirt front. She said, "Dammit I'm leaking like a sieve. Let me nurse the boy before I burst, and then we can finish up, okay?"

The men all nodded. The woman left the shanty. Screed passed out.

He woke to the Smith Islanders wrestling his left hand into the vise while the woman, now returned, cranked the handle round, closing the jaws. Somehow Screed noticed she had changed her shirt. This could not be happening! Screed had read the macabre stories of Edgar Alan Poe, but this was worse. This was real!

It seemed the second amputation and stitching took longer than the first. He felt the bolt cutter's blades biting through skin and gristle, and finally cracking the bone. Again, Screed bellowed, but the gag was so thick and tight he was convinced no one could hear him past the shanty walls. He was also certain anyone who did hear him would never come to his aid.

Chest man asked, "What you gonna do with them fingers Ben?"

"Shame to waste them," said the man on Screed's legs.

Blackshaw mused a moment, then said, "Figure I'll freeze them until next spring, and bait me a crab pot or two."

The woman chided Screed's assailant in her infuriating, practical way, "Ben, you wrap them digits up tight and keep them away from my chicken tenders and ice cubes or I'll come after you with the bolt cutter."

When Screed smelled the waters of the Chesapeake, however faint the scents, he smelled that shanty ten miles to the west on Smith Island. To Screed it was the reek of Hell's brimstone. It made him remember the casual voices of his captors, and what they did to him there. It made his hands hurt, and his guts bubble.

Choad LaGleet roused Screed from his morose remembrances. "Yo Screed! We're done our reccy here. The bay's frozen. Back in the car. Faction's got a chopper meeting us at the Crisfield airstrip. We launch from there tonight. Unless you want to walk to Smith Island."

CHAPTER 26

WILDE AND LOWRY were quietly suffering in a state of stunned disbelief. They were alone in their home office on his speakerphone in a rare nighttime conference call with Special Agent Marla-Jo Carter in Salisbury, and Sid Hornsby himself, who was Director of the FBI.

Hornsby was saying, "You want the Joint Terrorism Task Force to muster out in this crap weather, for a lot of circumstantial evidence, that's what I'm hearing."

Wilde glanced at Lowry, who replied, "Yes, that's what we're saying. Something strange is happening on aboard *Penelope*, and it's precisely the deteriorating weather that's bought us any time at all to investigate whatever's going on."

Wilde said, "Sir, it's one of the largest LNG ships in the world."

"And it's exactly where one would expect it to be, waiting for a thaw at Dove Point Terminal, now that the place has finally been recommissioned," said Hornsby. He was referring to an explosion at the LNG terminal on the west side of the Chesapeake that was so fiery and devastating it made the FBI's troubles with the Branch Davidians in Texas seem like a noise complaint.

From Salisbury, Agent Carter took a stab. "Director Hornsby, as you know, I interviewed the ham radio operator from Agent Wilde's report. He was a credible witness in every respect. His concern was genuine, and well-founded; Agent Wilde, who also interviewed him, concurs. Somehow, there's been a change in personnel aboard that ship. A change that, under ordinary circumstances, could not be accomplished in this Polar Vortex with the bay completely frozen solid."

Hornsby asked, "What's the ship's operating company say?"

"On page twelve of the report, paraphrasing here," said Wilde, "Transoceanic says that the ship-board Wi-Fi is down. The radio antennae are damaged from severe weather and icing. Only the maintenance telemetry was functioning up until yesterday, but it has since also crashed."

"But the telemetry was nominal, wasn't it," Hornsby said.

"On page nineteen, you'll see that the systems were in fact nominal, except for a gap in food and water consumption two weeks ago. For three days, the telemetry noted no consumption. Then after three days, food consumption resumed, but at a greatly attenuated rate compared to average rates of consumption prior to the lapse."

Lowry said, "Sir, something definitely seems odd about that."

Hornsby said, "Maybe it was a telemetry glitch. Maybe they got tired of the chow. Maybe they went on a hunger strike and then woosied-out because they couldn't take it."

Agent Carter said, "With respect, it's not like they're fed salt-pork, ship's biscuit, and grog these days. Only our Navy submariners eat better than commercial tanker crews."

Hornsby was quiet at his end of the line, but Wilde and Lowry knew the telltale rasp of the director rubbing his hand through his buzz cut as he thought the matter over.

Hornsby said, "Norovirus. That bug goes through cruise ships like wildfire. The crew got sick, and they can't touch the food however fine it is because they're laid up in their racks when they aren't firing at both ends. Then some, but not all, got better and have started eating again."

Wilde asked, "How do we account for the bloody handprint on the superstructure—Appendix B, Image four."

Hornsby shot back, "You got a sample? Ran it through the lab? Didn't think so. To me, it looks like Rust-Oleum. The original reddish-brown color. And chasing rust is a full-time job on a ship."

Agent Carter in Salisbury said, "Director Hornsby, taken together—"

Hornsby interrupted, "We have bad comms on a ship in terrible weather. We have a radio guy on board who might be sick along with a substantial number of his messmates, and a brief period of anomalous but non-critical ship-to-shore telemetry at a time when other comms on board are crapping out right and left. We have a smear of indeterminate material, blood, paint, feces, rust, who knows! Not to mention you, Wilde—you've taken a joyride in a bureau helo, at no small government expense, at the same time as we have you down for maternity leave. So, taken together, or separately, in small groups, or in Venn diagrams, I do not have enough to marshal a task force in weather that's trying to be the mother of all nor'easters. Agent Carter, I appreciate your time, interest, your theories, but if you could leave the call, I need to speak privately to your superiors."

Carter knew the strength of her feelings had failed to translate strength to her argument. "Yes sir. Thank you, sir."

Before anyone spoke, Wilde, Lowry, and Hornsby all did their silent count to five to be sure Carter had rung off, and that the connection had well and truly broken.

Then Wilde said, "Sir, this isn't some kind of hype-creep up the chain of command. We have the utmost respect for Agent Carter and her powers of observation, her instincts, and intuitions—"

"As do I," said Hornsby.

Lowry said, "Then help us understand—"

Hornsby said, "Forgive me, but I need to bring in Special Agent Vine. She's been made head of the National Joint Terrorism Task Force. When I read the report, I copied her on it right away, and she asked to audit this call, and has been from the top. Now you know why I hate Skype and FaceTime."

A strong, warm alto voice said, "Wilde. Lowry. How's Ella Grace doing?"

"She's well, thank you," said Wilde, hiding her frustration at Director Hornsby's subterfuge. She and Lowry had met Sheila Vine several times at counterterrorism symposiums, and respected her, but they were in no mood for chummy badinage at the moment.

Hornsby said, "I want you both to know that even with a case as undeveloped as you've brought to us, we take it seriously. But our response has to be made with great care. Agent Vine?"

Vine said, "The two of you, better than anyone, understand the situation."

Lowry asked, "Is this a new situation, or a continuation of a pre-existing situation?"

"The mole," said Vine. "Former Deputy Director Bonamy Screed."

"He's been exposed," said Wilde.

"And detained," said Lowry.

Hornsby said, "But we're still trying to suss out the extent of his network within the bureau."

"We thought we were making progress," said Vine. "We were interviewing his office support staff, as well as probing his overseas contacts with the CIA's assistance. Then Screed got renditioned out of our hands by the NSA."

"Where to?" asked Wilde.

"*Out of our hands,*" repeated Vine. "Precisely where doesn't usually matter, does it?"

Director Hornsby said, "Which is a nice way of saying the NSA makes folks they're interested in go *poof*, no forwarding address, at least not for us at the bureau."

Vine said, "But NJTTF has resources in place all over, and without going into that any further, not long after Screed was captured and returned to bureau custody, a contact informed me Screed was renditioned to a black site in Spain."

"So the NSA is sweating him now," said Wilde. "But we've lost a key potential source of intel on the extent of his network within the bureau."

"Exactly," said Vine. "Hence the care in how we proceed with your intel. Geographically, this business with the *Penelope* is too close to Screed's former theatre of operations to discount his involvement."

Lowry said, "But the NSA's got him bailed up in Spain."

Hornsby cleared his throat and said, "Not exactly."

Wilde and Lowry exchanged a glance that meant *now what?* They kept silent.

Vine stepped in. "The NSA's black site in Santander was taken down thirty-six hours ago. There were casualties on both sides, but it was pretty clearly a snatch-and-grab of the guest of honor."

"Screed," said Lowry.

"Screed," Vine confirmed. She continued, "Both the black site and a foreign overwatch position in an apartment across the street were compromised, with losses on both sides."

"By compromised, she means blown to smithereens," said Hornsby. "It was covered in the media as a gas leak, of course."

"Who did it?" asked Wilde. "Any ID on casualties?"

Vine said, "We're hearing chatter about a group we're not familiar with. Something called Faction. We had some inkling of it through an operative in contact with Screed. Someone named Maynard Chalk."

"Chalk was killed in an op in Bermuda this year," said Lowry. "Molly and I were there."

Agent Vine said, "I read that report. Chalk was a bad egg. Good work."

Director Hornsby said, "Chalk was either associated with, or at least tracking, Screed's last op at the time of his death. But it was a Confidential Informant of yours who put Chalk down, correct?"

"Yes," said Wilde.

"A—let's see—a Ben Blackshaw, isn't that correct Agent Wilde," said Vine.

"Are you putting this together the way we are?" asked Hornsby.

"I think so," said Wilde. "Chalk was linked to Screed on his last op. Screed is linked to Faction on that op as well. Now you have linkage between Screed and Faction on this snatch-and-grab in Santander, which makes that either a rescue, or Faction took him to get a sense of their exposure through Screed. In addition to killing Chalk, it was Blackshaw who also detained Screed in the end, and supported our completion of that mission."

"So far, so good," said Vine.

Lowry said, "And you've got linkage between Screed and Faction again now, but only through proximity, that is, possible trouble aboard *Penelope* in the Chesapeake, and Blackshaw, of Smith Island, also in the Chesapeake."

Director Hornsby said, "Blackshaw is a person of interest."

"Because of where he lives?" asked Wilde.

"With his training and experience, he's like Sergeant York and Audie Murphy rolled into one," said Agent Vine. "He's pitched in on difficult cases in the past."

"At his sole discretion," said Lowry. "And on our side. He's an interesting type. His motivations aren't what one might call patriotic. He self-deploys on a purely personal basis when the spirit, so to speak, moves him. It's about right and wrong, and justice for those he cares about. We've attempted to leverage some of his questionable activities we're aware of to gain his compliance on our terms, but he doesn't care."

"That's when he negotiated for immunity," said Wilde.

"Come again?" said Vine.

Hornsby confirmed, "He wouldn't turn Screed over to us without an exculpatory document holding him and his group of irregulars harmless for anything they might have done to bring Screed in."

"Jesus!" said Vine. "That's not immunity. That's *impunity*. That's the Wild West! Who the hell signed off on that?"

Director Hornsby cleared his throat again. "The President."

Lowry and Wilde waited for Vine to digest this. "Well then," Vine finally said. "Patriotism won't work. Arm-twisting won't work."

Wilde offered, "His wife and I were pregnant at the same time."

"So you're buddies from Lamaze class?" asked Agent Vine.

"I wouldn't say that," Wilde admitted.

PART II
WISHBONE DEEP

CHAPTER 27

LUANNA, REVEREND MOSBY, and Mary Wright surveyed the macabre dining room-turned-morgue. Now nine tables each had their own cadaver freshly pulled from the ice and covered by red and white checked tablecloths.

LuAnna hadn't seen this many dead since a duck tour boat had swamped and sunk in a microburst storm on the Potomac, trapping and drowning an entire extended family beneath the amphibious craft's canvas awning. LuAnna remembered it had remained eerily quiet at that scene for the longest time; no one was left alive to keen and grieve. She wished Blackshaw and Ellis were back from Ellis's saltbox. They'd gone to gear up from Ellis's unusually well-stocked private armory.

LuAnna lifted back one of the table cloths, and bent low with a flashlight. Rolling the body onto its side, she said, "Dead Dude Number 6: Entry wound in the upper back just left of center. Center body mass. Going for a heart shot." She lowered the body onto its back and lifted the stiff life preserver to peer between the flotation device and the front of the man's foul weather jacket. "No exit wound that I can see. Maybe we can look a little closer when they really thaw out."

Mary Wright jotted down notes on an old green server's pad. In a wry mood she asked, "You want fries with that?"

"Guess we'll have ketchup aplenty when they warm up," LuAnna said.

"Ladies, show some respect," said Reverend Mosby.

He examined the body closest to him, and said, "Number 7 here: Male. I got an exit wound I could put a fist in over here on this one. On his front. From this other hole, I reckon the slug is caught in the padding of his life preserver but it's waterlogged and frozen solid. Still too cold to get at it."

Mary said, "Lest we turn up the heat in here, they'll never thaw 'til springtime."

LuAnna said, "Mary's got a point. We have to figure whether we want them warming up for a closer look, or if we think we know enough, and just want the chill to preserve them without a bunch of decomp'."

"Preserve them until when, LuAnna?" Reverend Mosby had once boiled the care of his flock down to *hatch*, *match*, and *dispatch*. When it came to the latter, he was very much in the business of burying the dead, or otherwise disposing of troublesome remains, depending on the nature of the death. Man of God though he was, like many of his neighbors, he honored the ways of the dark path, and the black flag of his Smith Island ancestors.

"Until it's revealed what-all we should do with nine frozen dead people," said LuAnna.

"They had folks, like as not," said Mary. "Relations who'll miss them, and wonder what happened."

"Compromise," said LuAnna. "Let's turn up the thermostat up a notch, and see if we can't pull some identification off them. Their pockets are still frozen solid. Maybe get a better look at who they are. See where that leaves us. Meantime, us, and the Lord above knows exactly where they are, and for now, that'll have to do."

Mary nodded. Reverend Mosby did, too, but more slowly.

LuAnna folded back another table cloth. "Interesting."

"You were bored before?" said Mary.

"I've got some defensive lacerations on the hands, wrists, and forearms, but the throat is also cut," said LuAnna.

"What's that tell you?" Mary asked.

The reverend answered. "Somebody attacked that fellow from the front. He lifted his hands to ward off the knife. Got cut up. But while he was doing that, somebody caught this poor fool from behind and slashed his throat."

LuAnna said, "A knife is quiet. This guy might've been the first take-down, so's not to alert the others, who look kinda executed. It also means more than one attacker. And where there's more than one, there might-could be more than two. Wonder if Ben knows what he's getting into."

Blackshaw and Ellis pushed through the door of the old restaurant, and stomped snow off their boots. They wore thick, white, cold weather gear, and carried white rucksacks, skis, and snowshoes. Blackshaw was toting a Cobalt Kinetics Winter 2019 Edge rifle furnished in white. Ellis carried his favorite CheyTac sniper rifle, a skeletal weapon chambered for the big .408 anti-personnel/anti-materiel bullet. The minimalist gun was black, not colored white for work in snow, but Ellis didn't care. With an effective range of two thousand meters, he would likely be invisible to his targets. They wouldn't know what hit them, let alone who, or from where, or what color the weapon was. He also toted his SRM Arms Model 1216 combat shotgun which had a short barrel, and four short magazine tubes, each holding four shells. Ellis had double-aught shells in two of the tubes, and pumpkin ball loads in the remaining tubes. He liked the magazines' total capacity, and the short gun's maneuverability in the tight companionways common in maritime architecture.

Ellis said, "That flaw, as you all call it, it's blowing up into a right proper fuzzcod." He used the arcane Smith Island word for a nor'easter, knowing full well he was too old to ever live long enough to blend in as a native.

Blackshaw looked at his wife, who stared at him with a worried look in her eye. "What's happened?"

CHAPTER 28

KRILL STUDIED LAGLEET and Screed on the brief van ride from the Crisfield quay to the little airport just outside of town. She was glad LaGleet had kept her on for this next phase of the mission. Even more than the lavish paycheck, she liked the adrenal, bloody missions LaGleet tended to draw. She was not clear why LaGleet had retained Bonamy Screed. After all the effort that had gone into taking him in Spain, wouldn't he be better off in a Faction safe house? Was his local knowledge so valuable?

To Krill, Screed seemed shattered by his stay on Smith Island; his state was not improved by the prospect of going back there. Prolonged captivity, the amputations, and the roaring infection had unmanned the former soldier, left him a quivering mess. He was a walking case of Post Traumatic Stress, on the verge of decompensating into a bucket of puke any minute. Yes, the Doc's S-FOP bolus IV made Screed open his eyes a little wider, but Krill knew the difference between a man who was ready to throw down in a fight, and a patient propped up on his last legs with dope.

So, what the hell did LaGleet really want with Screed? He was a liability more than anything. Maybe LaGleet kept him around to sponge up stray rounds in a firefight. Perhaps Screed could be traded back to the Feds for something important. Feds probably thought Screed was a leak that needed to be plugged. Even if his intel had no value anymore, his rendition and subsequent snatch-and-grab was an enormous embarrassment to both the bureau and the NSA. Regaining control of even a spent asset would at least save face on an interagency basis, if not in the eye of the general public.

Tactically, God only knew what Screed could do with a weapon with his mangled hands bandaged liked cartoonish mittens. He'd been a great sniper in his time not so long ago. Now, the first shot, the first recoil would likely hurt like hell.

Maybe the Doc's dope would desensitize Screed, and make a proper Berserker out of him. Krill had once seen a soldier fighting under the effects of angel dust. At Falluja, a man she had screwed the night before had suffered a head wound early in an ambush the next day. Under the influence of angel dust, the bastard just kept advancing and shooting with his gray matter hanging out over his ear. Then someone had opened up on him with a Russian PK machine gun. Half the ammo box must've flown down range at them. The guy didn't blink, not even when his right arm was sawn off above the elbow by the stream of bullets. Krill had watched in utter amazement as this crazy son-of-a-bitch bent down, stood on his own severed arm, pried his rifle loose with his good hand, and start shooting again. He was like a fighting golem. Unstoppable. For six more seconds. Until the other half of that PK ammo box lit him up liver and lights. Dating in the service was a bitch.

No, Krill didn't think Screed had that kind of balls-out fighting fury, even if he was doped to the gills. Not by a long shot.

CHAPTER 29

BLACKSHAW BRIEFED LUANNA on what he and Ellis hoped to do out there in the blowing snow.

The former SEAL unfolded a paper chart of the Chesapeake and said, "We checked the AIS on Ellis's computer. There's only one *Penelope* identified in the bay, and she lies right there." He pointed to a spot in the main channel east of Wishbone Deep. "That's where a ship stages once it's taken on a load of liquid natural gas, but before it heads south out of the bay. Why it stayed there long enough to get frozen in, I don't know."

"They have all sorts of weather products," said Ellis. "They could've seen the cold snap coming in plenty of time to get went."

"Instead, they stuck around and started dying," said Blackshaw.

LuAnna peered over Blackshaw's shoulder. "That's seven miles from here. Really? In this mess of a storm?"

"Nothing I'd like better than to be home with you by the fire, Hon, but—"

"Lord, don't start lying to me now, Ben," LuAnna said. "I just thought maybe with baby Cal in the picture, you wouldn't be in such a rush to lark around evil bastards n'mare."

Blackshaw asked, "Where is Cal, speaking of?"

Mary Wright spoke up. "Kathy Taylor-Donaway has him. You know there's a line of gals around the block who can't wait to look after that child."

LuAnna said, "Kathy loves him like her own dear heart."

"And I thought Sonny was with you, too," said Blackshaw.

LuAnna knew this wasn't good. Blackshaw hated when things were out of place. It dashed his powers of concentration. LuAnna knew he could compartmentalize, and not fret about her too much when he was out stalking trouble. Things were different now. Blackshaw had never deployed with a baby back home. Wondering if Cal were safe might tug at his mind in a way he had never had to deal with before. LuAnna worried it might prove a fatal distraction.

Sonny Wright stepped in through the door with half a blizzard swirling in behind. He was dressed in his Autumn Breakup camouflage coat, toting a small rucksack over his shoulder, along with his Remington twelve gauge pump gun with the extended ammo tube. An open pocket of his coat bulged with extra shells, or *hulls* as they were called on Smith Island.

Ellis eyed Sonny's kit, shook his head, and said, "Okay folks. We need to get a few things straight on what's about to happen."

CHAPTER 30

"IT'S RECON', ELLIS," said Blackshaw as the two men slid one foot, then the next foot forward on long, narrow cross-country skis. There were moments in the dark when even Blackshaw's night vision goggles were overwhelmed with snowfall to the point that the tips of his skis sometimes disappeared. Not for the first time, he wondered if the wind had whipped his words away into the darkness without Ellis hearing them.

"There's shooting on recons," said Ellis, whose breathing, despite his exertions, was as steady and relaxed as a man at home in bed. Blackshaw wondered how his friend found time in his globetrotting sybaritic lifestyle for any kind of cardio training.

"Not if you don't pull the trigger," said Blackshaw.

"Where's the fun in that?"

There was no use. His vision obscured, Blackshaw halted and pulled off his NVGs. Ellis followed suit. They took turns stowing the goggles in each other's rucksacks and pressed on in the dark. From time to time, Blackshaw shielded his compass, and lit its face with a small red-lensed flashlight.

"We still headed the wrong way?" Ellis asked.

"I'm an A-Number 1 navigator, and you know it," said Blackshaw.

Ellis did not comment.

Exertion kept the cold from creeping in to Blackshaw's core, but it still bit at his face and wrists.

Ellis said, "Sonny sure is pissed when we leave him behind."

"He kept his cool well enough."

"There's been times," observed Ellis, "when he's the only neighbor that's stood by you, not counting myself of course."

"It's no good paying him back by getting him killed. And him and Mary practically newlyweds," said Blackshaw.

He noticed that most of the time, there was still sufficient snow between the skis and the ice. Where the wind blasted patches of the ice clean, it was rough, and steeply rippled, and made for heavier going.

Their skis hissed forward in unison.

"You really just want to take a look at *Penelope*?" asked Ellis. "That's all?"

"That's all."

They pressed onward into the storm.

Ellis said, "Weather's so bad, you're going to break your skis off on her side before you see her."

"It's why we're looping southwest," said Blackshaw. "Soon, we'll cut back northwest, and if this fuzzcod lifts, we'll have the looms of Annapolis, Baltimore, and maybe Washington showing in the clouds to make a silhouette of the ship."

"If it lifts," said Ellis. "And when it doesn't?"

"Got a feeling we're going to be on snowshoes soon. We won't be breaking any skis."

"To your point," said Ellis, "ships have lights."

"The ones that want to be seen," said Blackshaw. "The *Penelope* is something different."

Ellis glided to a stop, reached for his insulated canteen, and took a long drink of warm water. Blackshaw did not drink. Instead, he rechecked his compass, and replanted his skis in line with his planned course. Ellis aligned his own skis with Blackshaw's, capped the bottle and stowed it low on his H harness. Then he made sure the Ops Inc noise suppressor of his CheyTac rifle was still capped with electrical tape to keep the snow out.

"There's more than nine crew on one of those tankers," said Ellis pushing off into the stormy black.

Blackshaw was a moment behind his friend, but within a few steps they were once again skiing in unison.

"Reckon so," said Blackshaw.

"So we're figuring there's others out here," said Ellis.

"Makes you wonder, doesn't it," Blackshaw said.

"I wonder about a lot of things. What's on your mind?"

"Why they left life jackets on some of the bodies."

"Rookie move," said Ellis.

"Or they figured to be long gone before anybody found what they've done," said Blackshaw.

"But a ship can be traced," Ellis said.

"True," said Blackshaw. "There's all kinds of ways a ship can be *long gone*. Some ways it won't ever be seen again. So maybe finding life preservers with a ship's name wasn't seen as a big deal."

After a few more sliding steps, Blackshaw went on. "We shouldn't have brought our guns inside again after we took them from your house," said Blackshaw. "Condensation."

"I wasn't going to say anything," said Ellis. "The oil in these weapons is good down to negative 120 degrees. It's experimental, so we should be okay. Meaning, you'll freeze to death before the gun locks up."

"Where do you get hold of this stuff, Ellis?"

Ellis kept his skis hissing forward through the storm.

"You can tell me," Blackshaw pressed.

"Sure I could."

"But then you'd have to kill me," said Blackshaw.

"I can neither confirm nor deny—"

They continued through the frigid dark through seven more stops to check their course, and make sure they were lined up on the lights of the right ship. At the last stop, they found the ice was shattered into plates canted at steep angles.

Blackshaw said, "Northwest now. And we're done with the skis. From here, snowshoes."

Without warning, the wind twisted another fifty knots into a brutal gust. Blackshaw bent low to keep from getting knocked on his butt. Falling snow mixed with whole upwind drifts lifted back into the air. He could not see anything. Total whiteout.

After a few moments enduring this Arctic wind tunnel, the gust abated.

Blackshaw said, "That wasn't too bad," in the sideways manner of Smith Islanders.

Ellis did not answer. Blackshaw turned toward his friend to be sure he was okay. He did not see Ellis. Blackshaw kept turning a full circle. Ellis was gone.

CHAPTER 31

ABOARD THE *PENELOPE*, Captain Varna and Silas Grodin peered forward through the heated sections of the bridge's windscreen. Both men knew an entire floodlit ship stretched away over a thousand feet toward the bow, mounded with the tops of six enormous spheres filled with liquid natural gas, but they could only see a white glow streaked with gray as snowflakes stuck to the screen and melted.

The closed-circuit monitors showed close-ups of icicles forming on the many exterior camera housings and nothing more.

"Can't see a damn thing," said Grodin. "Should get the guys in off the deck. There's no standing watch in this crap."

Captain Varna gently cleared his throat.

Grodin caught Varna's subtle note of disagreement. "What?"

Varna stood taller. "I'm not running the tactical side of this op, but if I still had my own crew, they'd stay put. In these conditions, I'd shorten the watches. Change them more often. But at no time would the deck go unmanned."

Grodin squared to Captain Varna. Though he was a few feet away, there was menace in the posture. "They're not your men."

"It's still my goddamn ship until the mission's complete."

Grodin said, "Nobody's coming at us in this weather."

"But we're iced in," said the captain. "It's not a boat ride to reach us, or even a swim anymore. It's a fucking stroll. Use your head."

"Who said anybody's coming out here anyway? It's the dead of night in a blizzard," said Grodin.

"That chopper yesterday. Castor pulled the N number off it."

Grodin tried to mask his concern. "So?"

"He checked, and it came up registered to an unspecified government agency," said Varna.

Grodin sputtered, "What the hell does that even mean? Law enforcement aircraft are marked up plain as day as exactly what they are. News choppers, too. Same with Army, Navy, Marines, and you can't miss that Coast Guard orange. We should kill the exterior lights. All of them. Mooring lights, or anchor lights. Black out the ports. Go dark. Make us tougher to be seen."

Captain Varna tried to push the anger down and stay civil, but failed. "That won't be suspicious at all. We still reflect a radar signature the size of a small town. Look, Grodin, I don't give a damn what's on the outside of the helicopter, do you hear me? It's who is riding inside it that I care about, and you should, too. It wasn't a civilian. Why the hell would anyone go up with this kind of weather coming in? Somebody thought it was important enough to risk his hide. And anyone interested in Faction or our mission doesn't need visible light to find us."

"Whatever. The chopper made one pass down the bay," said Grodin. "Some big-wig had to get from here to there. That was it. It wasn't a patrol. Castor's been on the radios. Did anyone try to hail us?"

Varna was slow to reply, but he admitted, "Except for a few pings from Transoceanic to reset the telemetry, no."

"See? Our cover's still good, and for all the delay this weather's causing the mission, it's also making radio silence totally believable, and keeping nosy neighbors indoors, exactly where my men should be."

The captain shook his head. "No. It's forty years since I was in the Army, but I remember well enough. You act like the enemy is ten feet from your perimeter at all times. You keep your eyes wide open. Wide open like there's a high voltage cattle prod shoved straight up your ass."

A low groan they had not heard before welled up from the guts of the ship, like enormous metal members of the hull wringing out of shape.

"Christ!" said Varna. "The ice is shifting. Any thicker, any more wind, and it could mash us flat."

"We need a thaw," said Grodin. "We've had no word from Faction."

"Which means we're still a *go*," said the captain. "We see this through. Then we get paid. Then we get lost."

Silas Grodin chafed mightily with all the waiting for this mission to go off. Captain Varna's macho harping about the bad old days was only adding to the annoyance of the entire situation; part of Grodin's discontent had set in because deep down, he knew Varna was right. It was no time to drop their guard, no matter how improbable outside interference might be.

Grodin capitulated, if only to make Varna pipe down. "Okay. Relax. We'll set thirty-minute watches, but not a minute longer."

Captain Varna nodded.

Grodin zipped his parka, pulled on his gloves, and yanked the cords drawing his hood tight. Without another word, he jerked the starboard door of the bridge open and went out on the wing. In a petulant gesture, Grodin left the door open. Snow blew across the bridge tossing paper charts into the air. The temperature inside the bridge dropped thirty degrees in half as many seconds as Varna wrestled the door closed again.

Watching from outside, Grodin raised his middle finger.

Varna locked the door, stepped over to a computer touch screen and keyed in a sequence. All the ship's exterior lights shut down. The outside CCTV camera lights now transmitted only black to his monitors. A few infrared emergency navigation cameras showed a narrow range of grays and blacks. *Grodin has what he wanted,* Varna thought. *He can get back inside from the main deck. Maybe he'll fall and snap his neck climbing down the icy steps.*

CHAPTER 32

BLACKSHAW TRUDGED A tight circle around the place where he had first discovered that Ellis was gone. Looking for tracks in the snow was pointless. The frigid wind obliterated his own snowshoe prints the moment he lifted his foot to take the next step.

He called, "Ellis!"

Only the wind howled in reply.

Blackshaw risked starting up his encrypted comms, hoping that no one would be monitoring the thousands of micro frequencies his radio traversed in every second of transmission. He offered a silent thank you to Hedy Lamarr, the actress-scientist who had invented unjammable frequency hopping. Then he keyed the mic, and said, "Ellis!"

He listened, but heard nothing but a hum and the static hash of snow and sleet rattling off his hood.

Ellis was gone.

This had happened more often of late, that Blackshaw would find Ellis gone, his saltbox home locked, the place quiet. It was a reminder in contrasts of the times when they worked together on Blackshaw's deadrise workboat, *Miss Dotsy*. Blackshaw most always knew where Ellis was, and relied upon him, especially when his friend was tending the air compressor pumping air down to his helmet on the bottom while he gathered oysters. Time apart on days off was normal, but Ellis was never far away.

There were even moments during their first sortie-at-arms when Blackshaw had not precisely known Ellis's whereabouts. Back then,

Blackshaw had barely been aware that there was trouble simmering on Smith Island, and that LuAnna was in grave jeopardy, let alone that he needed his friend to see the mission through.

Blackshaw took a fresh bearing from his compass.

Somehow, this disappearance was different. Blackshaw knew Ellis had the courage of a lion; a coward's retreat could not have drawn Ellis away. Something in this oppressive frozen waste gave Ellis's sudden absence a feeling of permanent and unnatural loss. The ice had opened and taken his friend. Or the darkness had got him. Or some other force that caused one man to part ways with another at the most crucial juncture where life and death lay in the balance.

Blackshaw bent low, and with the wind howling full in his right ear, he crunched off again toward the *Penelope*.

Why kill the crew of a ship that could not be moved once it was taken? The Chesapeake Bay had a special way of foiling the most carefully laid designs of any who dared go near it, or venture out on it, especially in foul weather like this. Maybe *Penelope* was never meant to sail far from where she lay locked in the ice. Blackshaw tried to forget about Ellis, and focused on lifting one snowshoe past the other.

His mind drifted back to the first body he had found. What on earth would that woman have needed with a slide smeared with horseshoe crab blood? He wondered if that small specimen on the microscope slide was the key to everything that had led him out into this hoary, unending storm.

The blue horseshoe crab blood on the glass slide yielded nothing to Blackshaw's musing on it, and his thoughts returned to his vanished friend. Perhaps Ellis had a sudden change of heart, and no longer believed in the mission. Maybe risking his life for a room full of corpses no longer held charm or excitement. Ellis was the most wealthy man on Smith Island. At a whim he could experience anything that life offered; all he needed to do was stay alive, and no corner of the earth was barred to him, no luxury would be withheld, no subject of study would deny Ellis its deepest truths. Maybe testing his mettle against the world's most deadly adversary was too shallow a thrill when his formerly narrow existence had broadened into a universe of possibility.

Blackshaw climbed over plates of ice and slid with care down the other side, hoping not to bottom out in an open crevasse of brackish slush and drown before he could shed his pack.

It began as a suspicion, a creeping sensation that something was out of sync. After several more steps, Blackshaw realized all his existential thoughts about whether Ellis had suddenly moved off-mission to some higher calling had more to do Blackshaw's own state of mind. He was now scrambling over treacherous ice in a blizzard—to do what? To stare up at the cliff-like side of a death ship, powerless to bring back the lives of the murdered crew?

Blackshaw's thoughts moved on to something his wife had said. LuAnna was his life's dearest heart. He had worked so hard to become the man she could finally accept as a true partner. He had nearly lost her forever more than once. How close she had come to death just to stay by his side and take up arms and make his battles into theirs. He was repaying her shabbily. He should not be here. He should be with her.

Blackshaw had an infant child now, a boy who would need a father for many years to come. True, Blackshaw admitted to himself that he was not as well off financially as Ellis, but his modest fortune matched his more humble tastes. He could show this boy the great wide world in reasonable comfort and safety. A full life, unimaginable just two years before, was his for the living. What was he doing here? What could this trek through storm and dark toward a death ship ever offer him in comparison?

The only answer that came down to him through the sleet was justice. Maybe all this risk, this stroll with mortality, maybe it would make sense if he could bring a righteous justice to the killers of the *Penelope*'s crew. Even then, Blackshaw wondered if that would be enough. If he were to die tonight, in the instant before he closed his eyes, could he be sure his wife and son would look upon his legacy and believe he'd done the right thing?

He stopped walking. Another gust of black wind shot ice into his face. No, Ellis did not come back, stepping out of this gale of cold the way he had disappeared into the blow before. Blackshaw was still alone.

He banished his questions about the mission and his purpose. He interred those thoughts in a deep, thick-walled crypt in his mind where doubts could scream full-throated but unheard during the hours to come.

Peering ahead into the frigid, stinging darkness, he thought he could see the lights of a great ship. The *Penelope*.

And then the ship went dark. All exterior lights were extinguished. Rather, the loom of the ship melted into the midnight black of the storm.

Blackshaw marched on.

CHAPTER 33

LUANNA BLACKSHAW GAVE a last forensic once-over to all the corpses laid out in the old restaurant. She sat with Mary Wright and Reverend Mosby, and accepted a steaming cup of coffee from a pot that Sonny had thrown together on the gas stovetop. It was a powerful, redolent brew. Smith Islanders customarily added cheese to their coffee. Since the cheese Sonny found in the defunct refrigerator was a gangrenous block of mold, tonight they all drank their coffee black but for a dash of sugar.

Reverend Mosby asked LuAnna, "You were a cop. What's all this horrible business mean?"

LuAnna did not answer him right away. She sipped her coffee three times, then finally said, "Department of Natural Resources Police isn't a hotbed of homicide cases. Anything that looked like a corpse out on the water, we usually looked to the Maryland State Police Marine Unit to claim their rightful jurisdiction."

Mary said, "You must have some idea."

After another pause, she said, "Mass murder. Grant you it's a civilian vessel, the *Penelope* is, so there's no crack security team on overwatch, or if there is, it's small. They maybe have a high-pressure water spray system to repel pirates trying to board from small boats. But most of that stuff goes on around the Gulf of Aden, or the Strait of Malacca, not Tangier Sound for goodness sake."

"No. Not here. Not these days, I reckon," said Sonny, alluding to Smith Island's pirate heritage dating to American Colonial times, and a good bit after. Sonny went on, "You've heard the awful rumor about us out here?"

"There's more than one salacious lie told about us," said Mary. "Which one you thinking of."

Sonny said, "They don't kill you—"

"They *keep* you," finished Reverend Mosby.

"Oh. That one's true," said Mary.

Sonny said, "Our ancestors filled out a crew one way or another if hands came up short."

"How does that apply here?" asked LuAnna.

"It does, and it doesn't," Sonny said.

Sonny rose, and topped off the coffee cups. He talked as he poured. "Pretty clear keeping a crew wasn't part of the plan."

"On the contrary," said Reverend Mosby. "Putting them folks over the side was step one. And I bet we didn't find everyone who was killed on that *Penelope*."

"'Twas done so's they could keep the ship," said Mary. "That's what you think they want, LuAnna?"

"Can't get much ransom from a corpse," said LuAnna.

"Amen to that," affirmed Reverend Mosby, as if that lesson hit home painfully hard with him.

LuAnna did not ask the man of God to clarify what dark business he was thinking of. She tried instead to focus on matters at hand, saying, "So they want the ship. To keep the ship."

"What for?" asked Mary, stating the question that must lie at the root of the all the brutal murders.

"Keep the ship for how long?" asked Sonny. "Answer me that. There can't be too many of those big LNG tankers in the world. So they're too awkward big to hang onto for more than a day or two, especially here, where there's cops and Coast Guard all over the place. Johnny Law's got—what is it? Territory?"

"*Territorial imperative*," said Reverend Mosby.

"That," said Sonny. "And the Law has the firepower here, a spritely step. Except for in this weather."

"So taking the ship here flies in the face of common sense," said LuAnna.

"Like a scalded bat," said Mary. "Makes no sense at all. And less than none when you take the weather into account."

"Ellis figured the ship had been loaded up with LNG at Dove Point," said Reverend Mosby. "In three years, America went from no gas exports, to being number three in the world. And still the price of it isn't like gold."

LuAnna sipped her coffee again. "So the ship is full of LNG. If the hijacking was found out, the ship could be recaptured, especially around here. So moving the ship is possible, but impractical."

"Impossible to move it in this freeze-up, not to mention this little fuzzcod," said Mary.

"So the weather likely wasn't part of the plan," said LuAnna. "And so far, we're the only ones who know something's wrong."

"Those dead people surely know. And God," observed Reverend Mosby.

Sonny said, "You think they're trying to move that ship up the Potomac to blow up Washington? If that's the case, maybe we should lend a hand."

Mary Wright rolled her eyes at her husband's loose, seditious talk, but in her deeps, she understood what he meant. Like all their neighbors, Sonny was a Smith Islander first, and an American patriot a close second.

LuAnna considered Sonny's words. "The Potomac's still frozen. And up river where an explosion could do damage to the city, a big ship like *Penelope* draws too much to get close enough, especially fully laden like she is."

LuAnna rose and crossed to the table where the first snow angel's few effects lay, including the folded sheets of wet paper, and the glass microscope slide with the pale blue horseshoe crab blood sample.

LuAnna said, "This little thing, and that big ship. What the heck connects them?"

Reverend Mosby said, "We can't eat horseshoe crabs. Taste awful. Used to be folks would catch them and grind them up for feed and fertilizer. Not now though. Artificial fertilizer does fine. Not worth it for feed these days, either."

Mary was poking and swiping at her Smartphone. "The food wasn't always great here, but now I remember. When it's all No Signal in every room of my house, I could always get more bars right here than anyplace except the church steeple."

"There's always a signal where the Lord's concerned," averred Reverend Mosby. "Just call on Him."

Sonny laughed. "Lord's blocked my number."

"Now I know why I never could stand the site of those horseshoe crabs," said Mary swiping to a fresh page on her phone. "They're related to spiders and scorpions! And I cannot for the life of me figure what drug companies wants with those nasty things."

"What was that?" asked LuAnna. At that moment, her own smart phone rang. The screen said, UKNOWN NUMBER. Since telemarketers had not yet discovered her phone number to plague with robocalls, a guileless LuAnna answered.

The caller said, "It's Molly Wilde. Remember me?"

LuAnna's eyes widened. The bottom dropped out of her gut, but she stayed calm. "Kinda late for the Sisterhood of Cracked Nipples. And no, I got no recipe for homemade, organic, gluten-free stewed prunes. Gerber's is good enough for—"

Wilde was exasperated when she answered, "I'm not—don't you remember? Dove Point? Bermuda? It's Molly—"

"I know damn well who you are. You're a Feeb, and every time you show up, you're trying to strong-arm my husband into doing your dirty work or bust him and put him in jail," LuAnna said. "And after all he's done for you and God and country."

"Given what's happening around you right now, jail might be the safest place for him," said Wilde.

CHAPTER 34

BLACKSHAW STARED UP toward where he believed the *Penelope* should have given way to the sky, but the weather made even that gross level of discernment impossible. He nearly walked into the floating duck blind. It had broken loose from its moorings somewhere up-current or upwind, and drifted in the Chesapeake until the freeze anchored it, like all things waterborne, rigidly in place.

He skirted its exterior once, determining that the walls and roof of the blind had been built onto an aluminum skiff some eighteen feet in length. The shooter's loop, which was partially open to the sky, ran the length of the structure's starboard side, but it seemed to be covered in dark, heavy canvas that could be drawn back when hunters were using the blind. The wind was so strong that the three of the brass grommets holding the canvas in place had torn loose, and the material flapped and cracked like a whip over and over.

Blackshaw shone his red-lensed flashlight inside. A bench ran along the port side of the skiff, its only occupant a dead gull frozen toward the bow.

"Beggin' your pardon for barging in," said Blackshaw as he crawled inside through the low doorway. The gull did not reply.

The roar and howl of the storm was muffled only slightly inside the blind. Blackshaw bent the loose canvas back in place over the shooter's loop, and bound it down with double-strap disposable wrist cuffs. The icy draft subsided, but a little snow still blew in from the doorway. It didn't matter. Blackshaw would be here only for a moment.

He pulled his radio from his jacket's pocket, and powered it up. "Ellis!" was all he said. He waited a moment, listening with the radio pressed against his ear. Just the hiss of static. Ellis was as quiet as the gull. Blackshaw shut the radio down and stowed it.

He sipped water as he thought through his options. Without Ellis, Blackshaw estimated that the likelihood of this operation's success dropped from fifty percent closer to ten. His odds of survival plunged even lower. Every factor including weather, mobility, likely enemy strength, and mission objective militated toward an honorable and intelligent decision to abort. Blackshaw dismissed that option immediately.

Blackshaw had another resource available to him, one he loathed to exploit. He pulled out his encrypted satellite phone again and speed-dialed a number.

The outbound hailing signal burred three times before it was interrupted by a groggy voice demanding if Blackshaw knew what time it was.

Blackshaw countered, "Do you know who this is?"

Michael Craig, weather guru, and tactical overwatch expert answered from a New England mountain cavern in which he maintained his proprietary server farm. "Mr. President, I already told you there is no way for me to remotely corrupt a video file that exists on a physical video cassette tape. Short of dropping a junkyard electro-magnet directly onto the original tape in Russia with pinpoint accuracy, which will likely create an international incident, possibly a war, or worse for you, trigger the release of this video through multiple social media outlets, you are asking the impossible. For the twenty million dollars you're offering me, can't you find some diplomat to walk into the Kremlin and snatch it, or buy it back? And count me out. My passport's expired. My advice, next time beware of hookers who arrive at your hotel room with nanny-cam teddy bears."

Blackshaw said, "Bet I could handle that gig."

Craig was quiet for so long, Blackshaw wondered if he had broken the line.

The hermit genius finally said, "So could I, Ben. I'm just not in the mood help that guy out. And you don't need the money. Why are you bothering me?"

Michael Craig had once used hijacked satellites and his own predictive weather software to guide Blackshaw's exfiltration through seven miles of oil rig fires in Iraq. Craig had kept Blackshaw one step ahead of fourteen pursuing insurgents for hours until he reached safety. One by one, the insurgents had all died of smoke inhalation. The grudging partnership had continued after Blackshaw and Craig had both left the service. World leaders, would-be dictators, generals, and intelligence agencies of every nationality often made Craig's work-ups an integral part of any planned operation. Craig's brilliance lay in the fact that his weather outlooks could accurately endure for days, even weeks. His hacking work was the stuff of legend. Not even an air-gapped computer was safe if Craig wanted in badly enough.

"Need some intel," said Blackshaw.

"You didn't say *please*."

"Do I ever?"

"Point taken."

Blackshaw heard Craig groan and cough as he cleared sleep away from his mind on the short walk from bed to his array of monitors. With every step, Michael Craig was transitioning from foul-tempered troglodyte to keen-minded cybernetic creature connected to every corner of the earth, even to satellites.

As Craig focused his digital feelers on Blackshaw's position, he bragged. "I rebooted Opportunity."

The non sequitur derailed Blackshaw's thinking for a moment. Then he said, "The Mars rover? I thought that thing gave up the ghost a while back."

"I fixed it," said Craig.

"Did you tell NASA?"

"Better. I've programmed it to drive a pattern while dragging its sample collector. It's cutting a message through the topsoil into the rock substrate. Big letters. Should take a couple years, with the winds, and it's slow, but it's worth it."

Blackshaw knew Craig would not get down to business until he was asked, "What's the message, Mike?"

"*Welcome Comrade*. The first astronauts on the red planet are going to have a cow!"

"Glad to see you're putting the good of Humankind before all," said Blackshaw. "Can you help a fellow out?"

Craig said, "Is there going to be blowback?"

"Gee, Mike. Is there ever?"

"Every time, Ben. Will there be any cash on the other side of it at least; a little taste for your old pal who's saved your bacon more than once?"

"How many millions do you have stashed away by now?"

"Millions? Please. Make that a *B*," said Craig. "These days, I'm turning away business if it's not interesting." He paused for a moment, then said, "Oh."

Feeling like a patient visiting a doctor who had bad news to deliver, Blackshaw asked, "What's *oh* mean?"

"It's snowing there."

"Check," said Blackshaw, listening to the gusts of wind thrumming the blind's canvas cover.

Michael Craig said, "I've got a few Man Overboard beacons transmitting from northwest of you. The frequency's used for commercial life vests, but the signals are weak. I'm spoofing a weather buoy to repeat and augment the signals to me."

"How many?" asked Blackshaw.

Craig took a moment. "Seven, by my count. Let me check back on—wow. Okay, looking back, the life jackets have been overboard and activated for over a week. Now the batteries are shitting the bed. You think somebody tossed a bunch of life vests over the side for a goof? Maybe where they were stowed on a ship and got blown loose during that storm."

Blackshaw took off a glove and rubbed his rough-whiskered jaw. "No Mike. I don't think either of those options is what's going on. It's why I'm calling you. What ship are those signals near?"

"Randomness prefers clusters, and the AIS says the signal sources are spread out, but closest to one ship. *Penelope*. That's where you're headed, no surprise. But there are two MOB signals coming from Smith Island. You collected life jackets with Man Overboard transmitters? Brought them home?"

Blackshaw said, "There were bodies in them. Murdered. We've pulled nine likely crew of the *Penelope* out of the ice."

"Bury the lede, why don't you. Jesus! *Penelope* is a big LNG container. A Q-Max. The biggest. That's why you're out there. Ben, you and liquid natural gas are a terrible mix. The ship's fully loaded."

"That's bad news. Got a line on when she was topped off?" asked Blackshaw.

"Eleven days back," said Mike Craig. Then after a moment of soft taps on touchscreens, Blackshaw heard him ask, "Why didn't it head for open sea before the Chesapeake froze?"

"We think somebody wanted it to stay in the bay for some reason. Where was it supposed to go?"

"China," said Craig. "They're addressing their pollution problem in the near-term by switching from coal to LNG which burns cleaner. Why should it stay in the bay?"

"Part or all the crew might've been hijacked and killed. If it's detonated just right, that ship's a big ol' bomb," said Blackshaw. "More like a big torch. The core meltdown at Chernobyl was easier to put out than *Penelope* would be."

Mike said, "And if whatever LNG didn't burn flowed into the bay as a liquid, it would do a boil-and-freeze-at-the-same-time thing like that grade school science experiment. You know what would happen to the bay."

"Mess it all up something awful," said Blackshaw. "But it seems a lot of trouble to go to just to pollute the Chesapeake. The Conowingo Dam is doing that just fine in dribs and drabs with every rainstorm, and for free."

Mike Craig said, "Affirmative. There are decades of pretty nasty pollutants trapped behind that dam. Pesticides. Chemical plant run-off. Manure. It would kill the bay if that dam came down all at once."

That made Blackshaw stop and think hard before he suddenly said, "Horseshoe crabs."

"What? I think the cold's getting to you, Ben."

"What's the deal on horseshoe crabs?" Blackshaw asked. "Why are they important?"

Craig dived in to the internet through his proprietary search engine. "Checking here—stand by—okay, Big Pharma uses their blood to make a chemical that verifies drug purity. The industry would be destroyed without it. They bleed the crabs a little bit in laboratories, and then put them back in the water. Lots of them die. Some don't. There are synthesized chemicals in use that can do the same thing, but way too expensive compared to the blue blood product. On the other hand, the blood LAL is worth sixty thousand bucks a gallon because of the clotting agent you can make from it. LAL, or limulus amebocyte lysate. Again, there's a synthetic agent in development, but it's even more pricy."

"Who makes the synthetic?" Blackshaw asked.

"One company. FerdeLance. They make CoproLite, which is a pesticide terrorists are using as a chemical weapon. FerdeLance used to be run by one John Turner Frost until—"

"Until what, Mike?"

"Frost was married to Department of Homeland Security Secretary Lily Morgan. They both died when you attacked—"

Blackshaw interrupted, "That was a while back, and I did not pull the trigger on them. Those two were hanging out where no decent people should be, and they burned."

"Sure about that? I'm accessing their covert, unredacted autopsies now, and yes, they both were shot first, then burned."

"I'm not saying I didn't pull the trigger once or twice in that fight, but I'm pretty sure I didn't smoke a cabinet secretary and her kinked-out husband."

"If you say so," replied Craig. "Anyway, they're still dead. And FerdeLance almost is. After Turner's death—by whatever cause—the company invested massively in developing the synthetic clotting factor, but so far, with horseshoe crab blood still being available, even expensive as it is, FerdeLance has been laying off staff, wonks, and eggheads in droves."

"And just to circle back, the Chesapeake is a big breeding ground for horseshoe crabs," said Blackshaw.

"You know it is. There are other places, but they're smaller, and none as productive as the Chesapeake far as the vampires draining the blood are concerned," Craig replied.

"So if the Chesapeake breeding ground is ruined—" Blackshaw began.

"—the synthetic LAL starts looking pretty good. Production would scale up, and there's the money." finished Craig.

"And anyone invested in FerdeLance scores big. Does FerdeLance have a parent company?" asked Blackshaw.

"Get back to you," said Michael Craig. After a moment, he went on, "I see you already called in the cavalry."

"I'm not following you," said Blackshaw. "Ellis was out here with me. You got a line on his comms?"

"Is Ellis flying a Black Hawk these days? Because one's coming west over Tangier Sound toward Smith Island."

"Dammit!" said Blackshaw. He felt like an idiot straying so far from LuAnna and his son.

"Oh," said Michael Craig in his doctor-with-bad-news way.

"What!"

"Not a friendly. At least it's not registered to law enforcement," said Craig. "I'm running my shell company application. It's chain of ownership runs back ten companies. FerdeLance is one. Right Way Moving and Storage is also in the bunch. There are rumors they're linked to an international syndicate called Faction. Bad people."

"Right Way was Maynard Chalk's shell company. Now him I definitely notched up. And a Black Hawk. Deep pockets. Mike, do you think you could—"

Craig broke in. "Checking the registry—now the build history—tons of mods, but this bird still doesn't have the crashworthy external fuel tanks on its stub wings. Cool. Gotta go."

Blackshaw shouted, "Do you have a line on Ellis? Is he—?"

The line was dead.

CHAPTER 35

CHOAD LAGLEET DIRECTED the pilot to approach Smith Island from north. The Black Hawk helicopter had state of the art hush-kits retrofitted onto the rotors, engine intakes and exhausts, but a UH-60 was still a great thumping, clattering beast. The modifications meant that it would first be heard over level clear ground from two miles away, instead of four. He recalled that it was often said a helicopter did not actually fly; it beat the air into submission. In this hellacious storm, with its neck-snapping turbulence and impossible visibility, perhaps the storm would get the upper hand in the end.

The helicopter had arrived at the Crisfield airport with seven additional Faction operators to support LaGleet, Screed, and Krill on the mission. The five men and two women were quickly briefed as soon as LaGleet and his team boarded.

LaGleet knew that if it weren't for the latest tech, the pilot would be flying blind in this lethal combination of darkness, wind shear, and snow. Even the pilot's onboard synthetic vision displayed on the glass instrument panel was not giving him the full picture of the world outside. Instead, this bird was equipped with Orbital Environment Telemetry. With just groundspeed, altitude, and heading data burped up to a satellite ten thousand times per second, the helicopter's entire surroundings were transmitted back to the pilot's headset complete with VR depth perception. The pilot's exterior sight picture was surrounded by key heads-up navigational instrumentation and radar displays, no matter what direction the pilot looked. There was no onboard database for all this magic. The pilot's entire world was beamed down to him from the satellite at that blistering refresh rate. This was a video game in which actual lives could be lost. The chopper's OET magic box was armor-plated to make it survivable in all weather and combat conditions; it was tougher than an airliner's flight data recorder. But it was refreshed by satellite, and that meant it could be hacked.

Faction pilots who trained on the OET were drilled to trust the sight picture the system provided implicitly, and not deviate from the flight envelope in which it centered the aircraft. Orbital Environment Telemetry was the perfect AI copilot. It never lied. Short of a complete satellite outage, which never happened, the OET was more reliable than human eyesight in broad daylight in severe-clear weather.

Knowing this, Choad LaGleet was wondering—according to the glass multifunction displays, which served as the backup instruments to the OET—why the hell the pilot was pointing the Black Hawk's nose at the earth at 190 knots, the aircraft's VNE, or Velocity Never Exceed. This was crazy.

LaGleet pounded the pilot on the shoulder, a shoulder which to LaGleet felt like rocks with the aviator's tension.

LaGleet shouted, "Pull up you fucking idiot!"

The pilot turned his head which was encased in the bulbous visor and helmet, and said, "Chill out! I'm on the Owet!" which was how OET was pronounced by flyers in the know.

LaGleet smacked the side of the pilot's helmet. "Something's wrong!"

The copilot, a woman who was also using the OET system, had the good sense not to waste time arguing once she heard LaGleet's panicked tone. She raised her helmet's goggle visor, scanned the less sophisticated backup instruments on the Black Hawk's actual panel, and shouted, "My aircraft!"

The pilot, in the right seat barked, "Your aircraft!" reflexively, but it took him a catastrophic additional second to fully relinquish his grip on the cyclic and collective controls, though the copilot was already doing her best yanking and banking to arrest the rapid descent.

Bonamy Screed's eyes widened in terror, though he did not have headset patched into the crew intercom to hear what was wrong. His stomach felt shoved toward his ankles as the copilot, now with the pilot's help, pulled serious g's to slow the Black Hawk down. The helicopter shuddered as its structure was overstressed.

LaGleet, a guy with barely a hundred hours in a Cessna two-seater, noticed something the flight crew did not. Like the OET, the glass panel was also out of sync with the mechanical steam gauges. The crew was still responding to crap data.

LaGleet was about to shout, "You're going to kill us all!" but could not get out a single word of his prediction because the chopper slammed into the ice, and the fuselage disintegrated around him in a whirlwind of jagged shrapnel parts and fire. The noise was explosive, shrieking metal, tearing carbon fiber, turbine engines eating their own fan blades, and Bonamy Screed screaming like he was being devoured by a shark.

Krill held on until a secondary impact threw her so hard against her harness that she grayed out. The fuselage broke in two. What was left of LaGleet's forward section of the chopper scraped spinning along the ice. Gaping holes scooped snow into the cabin with the force of highway plow trucks going a hundred miles an hour.

After what seemed like an eternity, the Black Hawk stopped moving.

LaGleet croaked, "Everybody out!"

In addition to Krill and Screed, two men and one of the female operators slowly unclasped their seat harnesses and crawled out through the mangled wreckage onto the ice. LaGleet stayed behind for a moment, shoving at the pilot and copilot to rouse them. They were either unconscious, or dead. LaGleet drew his pistol and with two shots, made certain it was the latter. On his precarious way out to the ice, he killed an operator who was convulsing from an open head injury. LaGleet scavenged the man's magazines and weapon, a Hechler & Koch MP-5 submachine gun.

Krill had found one operator limping, and the other female agent making her way out of the other large section of the fuselage. They did not share in the bounty of Doc's energizing S-FOP concoction. To LaGleet, Krill appeared only slightly shaken, but still amped and ready for mayhem.

Screed still looked sick, but thanks to the S-FOP, in the firelight, he looked like a dying man experiencing that last day or two of youthful energy before the end; that odd flaring up of life force that makes relatives who have traveled to a deathbed wonder if they should rebook their flights home until later, or scram now while the false good mood has everyone convinced no one will ever die.

LaGleet said, "That wasn't exactly what we had in mind, boys and girls, but here we are."

He cast a critical eye over the survivors to make sure they would be up to the job. Then he consulted a tablet with a moving map, turning three hundred sixty degrees in place to be sure it was orienting properly despite its cracked screen.

LaGleet announced, "There's a wildlife refuge a quarter mile that way. Then we cross Goat Island, and that's right across this little frozen waterway from Smith Island. That's where we'll find him. That's where we take Blackshaw down."

One of the Black Hawk's fuel tanks exploded, casting a ruddy glow into the snow-lashed night.

CHAPTER 36

BLACKSHAW WRESTLED WITH an urge to pray. He was too far from Smith Island to protect his family and friends from the occupants of the helicopter Michael Craig had spotted. It would require a monumental faith in something other than himself to trust that his neighbors were prepared to defend themselves against violence they had no reason to anticipate. He wondered if his need to believe that his people could survive without him was born of this crushing sense of helplessness. He had allowed himself, sword and shield, to be drawn away from everything he treasured. LuAnna. Baby Callum. His friends. His home. He was an abject fool, or worse, a deserter. Was he a greater fool, or a soldier, or ultimately a believer, if he compartmentalized the survival of Smith Island into a box labeled *Thy Will Be Done*?

"If I had to die, I'm glad it was you who finished me off," said a voice in the stormy darkness. It went on, "But for God's sake don't turn into a chump on me now."

Blackshaw peered toward the bow of the frozen duck blind. The dead gull was gone. In its place sat Maynard Chalk decked in yellow shorts, brown huarache sandals, a blue guayabera shirt, and smoking what smelled like a very expensive Cuban cigar. He was grinning like a gargoyle, and when he puffed the cigar, smoke leaked from the bleeding bullet hole at the base of his throat.

Chalk, a psychotic black bag operative for the former Secretary of Homeland Security, Lily Morgan, had crossed paths with Blackshaw several times, always resulting in grievous harm to LuAnna and other loved-ones. Blackshaw was puzzled now, because he distinctly remembered firing that neck shot killing Chalk in Bermuda months before.

"Yeah, boyo, I'd hate to think you were getting soft," said Chalk. "All the danger you went through while you were a SEAL, and never a prayer. Not even a foxhole prayer. No bargaining. *If you get me out of this spot, I'll—* whatever. Nothing."

"I'd kill you all over again if I had the chance," said Blackshaw.

"There he is! Consistency! That's what I'm talking about! Imagine how I'd have to hang my head in shame if you started clutching your prayer beads and walking everywhere on your knees spouting mumbo-jumbo to the void. I'd never live it down, if you'll pardon the expression. I could never brag again that I was finally taken out by the Mighty Ben Blackshaw."

The thought that Blackshaw might suffer badly from Post-Traumatic Stress tickled the back of his mind. LuAnna had encouraged him to seek help, but Veteran's Affairs had failed him at every turn. Delayed and postponed appointments. Incompetent counselors. In the end, he believed that marching back into combat in civilian life now and again was the better salve to his moral injuries—until this moment. He'd often been tormented by the specters of enemy targets he had eliminated. He had thought that the hauntings were over; he had rediscovered the spirit of Christmas, and bought the prize turkey, *God bless us, every one.*

"That's right," said Chalk, after another puff on his cigar. "Things are different now. You've got the brat. You're life isn't your own, if it ever was. Your wings are clipped, and you don't even know it."

"Hard truths, and a bunch of psycho-malarky, from you of all people," said Blackshaw.

"Yet here I am. What's waiting for you out there? Little man gonna take down the big ship? You could seriously freeze to death this time. Somebody could cut your throat and dump your body someplace they'll never find it. Bad enough you could die. Imagine what hell your kin would go through if you disappeared without a word, never to be seen again. That's some righteous torture as a legacy for a kid who's still too small to know you even exist. Not even Ellis is out here with you. What the hell is *that* about, *Ben*? What does he know that you don't?"

Blackshaw inspected his Cobalt Kinetics rifle for any signs the cold was hampering its action. He took a sip of water, and zipped his coat. He knew Ellis was no skitterbrook.

Chalk laughed. "That's right. Pretend I'm not here. What's the matter? You used to have more to say." He drew on his cigar and popped three smoke rings out through his collar.

"Innocent people are dead," said Blackshaw.

"Okay. Good," said Chalk. "That's life. What else is new? A bunch more deaths will even things out? I got no problem with that. You won't dare quit, because that means every death that came before would be pointless. Feed the war beast, Ben! It demands more and more blood all the time. I did my level best to slake that monster every chance I got with the lives of foe and friend alike as it suited me. It was a calling."

"You were a zookeeper."

Chalk squinted at Blackshaw. "Hell no. I ran a slaughterhouse. It pleased me to serve The Brute, and it loved me for every offering I sacrificed before it."

Blackshaw smiled. "That's a glamorous way of seeing it. You, the acolyte of war. Making the sacrifices, until the damn beast ate you right up, too. I might be talking to a vapor, but you are well and truly dead. I'm still alive. Change that if you can."

Chalk frowned. "You're right. I can't change it. But I can wait. One of these days, boyo, you'll be sitting right here next to me, and there'll be no turning back."

Blackshaw shouldered his pack, and stepped out of the blind into the teeth of the storm. He remained unsure if he was staying the course for the *Penelope*, and justice for the dead, or turning back for Smith Island, family, and home.

CHAPTER 37

LUANNA LOOKED UP from trying to unfold the wet paper from the first snow angel's pocket. The shadows in restaurant-cum-mortuary were deep in these dark hours. The wind blew through the building's wood trim in a way that surrounded the occupants with eerie moans and slurred words of warning just beyond human understanding.

Sonny and Mary Wright were working with the model ship-building tools trying to extract bullets from wounds that were clearly not through-and-through.

LuAnna asked, "Anyone else hear that?"

Mary said, "Do not start fooling and pranking us now, Honeygirl. I've had the creeps since we found the first one and drug her in here, poor lost thing."

"I don't mean the wind," LuAnna said. "A thump. Thought I felt it through my boots as much as heard it."

"Might be thunder," suggested Mary. "Thunder snow's a thing. Or Aberdeen Proving Ground."

Sonny said, "Not this time of night. Might be some plywood coming loose from someplace. I know Aram's got a few four-by-eights delivered to fix up his crab shanty. He had them vanged down good enough for an everyday flaw, but Lord knows where they might've blown to in this fuzzcod."

LuAnna did not speculate further. She threw her parka over her shoulders, and stepped nimbly through the door into the storm. She did not have to leave the old porch. Through the flailing ragged screens torn from the porch windows, away to the northeast, past the Bayside Inn, past the Big Thorofare, and maybe even farther out past the Martin National Wildlife Refuge, she beheld a glow pulsing low into the sky. It was not the pink-white loom of a city like Baltimore. Wrong direction for that anyway. It was dark orange, like oil or some other petrochemical burning dirty.

Another *thump* rolled through the storm from the northeast, and resonated through LuAnna's chest like a marching band's bass drum. The far-off greasy orange glow brightened.

LuAnna retreated inside.

She took up Sonny's shotgun, and said, "Give me some extra hulls."

"Hold on, LuAnna. What happened?" Sonny was loathe to let his pump gun go without explanation.

LuAnna answered, "That Feeb, Molly Wilde. She said there might be trouble coming our way."

Mary Wright, her fingers bloody from bullet removal, said, "We kinda had an idea about that already—"

"You heard me talking to her. I didn't tell her about all these folks dead in here. But stupid me, I thought that's what she was talking about."

Reverend Mosby asked, "What do you mean?"

"She implied Ben had a reputation, and because of that some ornery types were tolling in on us here. I look outside, and there's a big fire. Something's burning out at the refuge. Or something out past there. I'm going to see what it is," said LuAnna.

"Not by yourself, you're not," said Reverend Mosby. "Sonny, Mary, you two fetch some extra guns and hulls and warm coats. We're all going hunting."

Sonny grinned. "Thank the Lord there's no bag limit on confounded assholes."

LuAnna smiled at her friends with thanks that they understood her, and wanted to join the fun.

CHAPTER 38

BONAMY SCREED TRUDGED through the blizzard, staying as close to Krill and LaGleet as he could to avoid getting lost in the whiteout. The S-FOP drug that Doc had dripped into his arm on the airplane was amazing. His index finger stumps, which had throbbed without mercy since the amputations, barely ached. He sensed a bit of his old spirit returning. He might enjoy getting a little of his own back once he had centered his crosshairs on Blackshaw.

"How much farther?" Screed asked.

Krill spoke over her shoulder to Screed, "My God, you're like a two-year-old on a car trip!"

Screed bleated, "I'll need to get rid of these bandages before we make contact."

LaGleet unslung the dead operator's MP-5 and tossed it to Screed who bobbled the weapon with his bandaged hands before clasping it awkwardly to his body.

"What's this?" asked Screed.

"Your girlfriend for the next few hours," said LaGleet.

"No. Choad, I'm a sniper."

LaGleet cast a withering look at Screed through the snow. "We don't have the gear or the weather for you to stand off on overwatch while we get mano-a-mano for the wet work. From here on out, you'll be as close to me as you are now."

"I thought you wanted me here to put eyes on Blackshaw," whined Screed.

"Yes. And then you clip him," said LaGleet.

"I've never shot without a trigger finger," said Screed.

"You've got eight digits left, and two of them are opposable thumbs, right?" said Krill.

LaGleet barked, "Fingers, hell! Does he have the balls? Look Screed, I've seen a guy with his whole arm gone. Nothing but carbon fiber and steel hooks from the shoulder down, and at three hundred yards that gimp can shoot a group so tight you could cover it with a fifty-cent piece. There's another guy, no arms at all. He shoots with his fucking bare feet! For close work, all you have to do is identify your target, jam that gun in his face, and pull the trigger with whatever you've got. Use your pecker for all I care."

Screed managed to loop the strap of the deadly little MP-5 across his body. The snow drifted deeper here and there, giving him plenty of other things to feel sorry about besides close quarters combat and shooting with maimed hands. The helicopter had been the planned infiltration vehicle. There were no snowshoes as part of the gear LaGleet provided. Screed felt his feet getting wet and cold. He slogged on, his eyes fixed dead center on Krill's back.

"What are we getting into? Anybody sized them up over there?" Screed asked.

"You were there," said LaGleet. "You tell us."

"It's been a few months. Never got the lay of the place; only met a few of those people," Screed said. He held up his bandaged hands. "Mean. Vengeful."

Krill said, "Jesus, Screed. Sack up. It's a couple villages of fishermen and their wives, all snug in their beds."

Screed was by no means as confident as Krill. He had once been a hostage on Smith Island. He bore the scars of his imprisonment there. Screed broke out in a cold sweat. He felt the bolt cutters gashing through his phantom fingers. The crunch of his boots reminding him of the sound flesh, tendon, and bone make as dull steel blades bite down. Being well-armed in the company of stone killers with the element of surprise improved his mood, but only a little.

"Let's get this over with," said Screed. He slogged on.

CHAPTER 39

THE ICE SHATTERED into plate-size shards along the shoreline; it cracked like thick glass panes where the tidewater thrust it up coming in and dropped away again casting it down. The sleety snow welded sections back together, but not enough to make the footing less treacherous.

Choad LaGleet loved an infiltration in bad weather. The worse, the better. Despite the most rigorous training, and the highest pitch of vigilance, there was always a part of an enemy sentry's mind that said *nobody's out in this mess*. It was a projection of course; the best sentry could only guess at his attacker's mindset. A guard could only be certain that he wished he were indoors, warm, and dry. To be a good sentinel, you had to be like a hunter hunkered in a blind, desiring the prey to walk in close. The only difference between a dumb animal getting popped going about its business, and a human attacker was that the man was looking for the blind.

All that vigilance notwithstanding, LaGleet believed civilians by any standard were an easy take-down. They lived in a good world, and were always horribly surprised to see him appear on their doorstep, or better, to discover he was already indoors waiting like a spider for the fly to stroll downstairs in the wee hours, eyes full of sleep, thinking only of that last piece of cake in the refrigerator and a cool glass of milk. And then the sudden assault and beat-down. The binding. The torture that went on until safe combinations are revealed, passwords disclosed, hard drives handed over, secrets told. That moment of conquest gave LaGleet a sensation of genuine power that he rarely found anywhere else in life, except the kill, which was orgasmic, and just as fleeting. Yes, watching the subject's lights go out held a certain fascination, but there was no way around the truth that the split second after death, the fun was over. The target no longer feared him or felt the pain he inflicted. They simply ceased to be.

Blackshaw was tough. Breaking him would be a blast. LaGleet had no idea how it would feel to destroy his special target in the name of protecting the operation on *Penelope*, but if the sensations disappointed, or fell short in any way, there would still be plenty of neighbors to play with.

CHAPTER 40

MOLLY WILDE FELT responsible now. She had tried to warn LuAnna Blackshaw of impending trouble, without going into detail that would embarrass the bureau. The Smith Islander had been angry, as if Wilde was trying to coopt LuAnna's husband into something dangerous and illegal. LuAnna was right on that count, but in Wilde's defense, Blackshaw had been willing to lend a hand on three operations in the past. This time, an FBI response to the machinations around a disgraced, renditioned former bureau director, Screed, had to be handled with sensitivity, with deft surgical care; it required complete deniability for the bureau. And that meant Blackshaw.

Wilde sat up in bed. The clock reported that sunrise was many hours off. Pershing Lowry slept on, his snoring more like the purrs of a large, handsome, sexy cat. She crept out of bed, determined to do something normal, instead of following instincts that might lead directly to trouble. These days, Wilde wondered if she were really cut out for anything she was supposed to be doing, including marriage, motherhood, and supervising an FBI office.

She put her head in the nursery. Her mother was dozing in the big comfortable chair, the one in which Wilde was supposed to be keeping the night watch over Ella Grace. The baby was zonked, clasped to her grandmother's shoulder, and completely contented. An emptied bottle of breast milk stood on the table beside the chair.

Wilde had some sense of accountability. From the kitchen drainboard, she assembled the drip-drying parts of the breast pump like a seasoned soldier putting her .50 cal' back together in a drill.

With freshly filled bottles stocked in the refrigerator, she threw on her cold weather gear, including hat, insulated pants, turtleneck, fleece vest, and parka. She grabbed two thick but dirty socks from the laundry basket. In the dim light, she pulled on her boots wondering if the socks matched.

She jammed protein bars and water bottles into a bag, collected her weapon, and placed every spare magazine she could find downstairs in the pockets of her coat. An extra box of bullets also went into the bag.

Molly Wilde looked around the kitchen, then with no small amount of surprise, saw her mother watching her through the window in the doorway to the hall.

"Jesus, Ma!" said Wilde in an angry stage whisper, trying not to awaken Lowry or Ella Grace. "So creepy—"

Patience pushed gently through the door, holding a pair of waterproof mittens. She said, "You might need these."

"You aren't going to talk me out of this?" said Wilde.

"I raised you. I know how bullheaded you are. And you're still not feeling settled. Not yet."

"Will I ever?" asked Wilde, not sure what answer would make her happiest.

"How should I know?" said Patience. "I went on walkabout three months after you were born. Left you with your father."

"You're kidding!" This was a piece of family history Wilde had never heard.

"Not a bit. Why do you think you and your dad bonded so well? I was gone. I bought a *motorcycle*," confessed Patience, reminiscing. "An old Honda 175. It was all I could afford. And off I went. From Virginia to the Pacific. I met other bikers. Drifters. Camped out." Patience became wistful, stopped talking.

Wilde digested this divulged secret. "But you came back."

"Obviously. But not until I'd been out on the road for five months," said Wilde's mother. "Hey, it's not like I disappeared. I called home. I sent postcards. Your dad was so angry at first. Then he figured it out. But yes, when I came back, I was home for good. You. Molly, you haven't seemed so—engaged—in quite a while as when you got back from your check-in at the office. And your helicopter ride. You were glowing, dear."

"I can't sleep. I'm going out for a drive is all," said Wilde.

"With enough bullets for a brigade action. Don't worry. *Out for a drive.* That's what I'll tell Persh', of course," Patience said, kissing her daughter. "He'll be fine. Don't come back too soon. Not until you're ready."

"Will Ella Grace be okay if I bug out like this? Even going for a few hours, I feel terrible."

Wilde's mother smiled, "You turned out just fine. In fact, I'm proud of you. And I take absolutely no credit for who you are. You're an amazing daughter. A smart, brave, accomplished woman. You'll be a great mom. But not until you're ready."

Wilde hugged her mother, grabbed up the bag, and left through the side door into the garage. She tossed the bag into her Jeep and climbed in after it. The garage door opener would resonate through the house, but it might not wake Lowry. He slept heavily. If he woke, it would be too late. Wilde would be gone. *Gone.* Why did Wilde feel like an escapee?

She topped off the Jeep's fuel tank at the one gas station she found open despite the storm. From there, she took main roads from Alexandria into southern Maryland, where back roads led to Lexington Park on the Chesapeake Bay. The barricade at the park entrance was lowered in place for the winter, but the aggressive off-road tread on her tires made skirting the gate area and the ranger station easy. No one saw. No one would man that station until springtime.

Wilde drove through the snow-swept woods on ever narrowing tracks until the road opened at a picnic area, and her goal, the boat ramp where she and her father had put their fishing skiff in the water when she was a girl. What would her father think of what she was about to do? Though he was dead for eleven years, she still often wondered what he'd think of her.

She slowed the Jeep at the top of the decline between two cement walls where, usually, a fisherman would prepare to back a trailer down into the water until it submerged and the boat could float free.

The snowfall was so thick that Wilde could not see the Chesapeake ice only thirty feet ahead and six feet below. It was lost in the crystalline whiteness thrown back from the Jeep's fog lights mounted at the bumper.

Could she really drive into this mess? This was the moment. This was her last chance to turn around, drive home, and be right there next to Pershing when he woke. She could hold her beautiful child to her breast, and let her try to latch, painful as it was. That thought made her wince. It was all she needed.

Wilde shifted the Jeep into low, and eased it forward down the ramp at a snail's crawl. If the tires broke loose, the Jeep might slide too quickly down the slope and crash through the ice. Worse, the four-wheeler might skew to one side as it slid, and get wedged between the cement walls. Either scenario was fraught with more embarrassment than danger.

Thanks to Wilde's careful driving, the Jeep did not skid. Moments later, the front tires crunched across the cracked ice at the bottom of the ramp, but did not break through. Then, the rear tires crossed onto the ice. With the Jeep back in neutral, Wilde sat quiet for a moment, listening for telltale groans or pops from the thick ice below. She heard none.

Again, Wilde put the Jeep in gear and eased forward. With a keen eye watching the digital compass on the dashboard, she turned east southeast toward Smith Island and pressed the gas pedal down.

CHAPTER 41

KNOCKER ELLIS FELT a twinge of regret marching off and leaving Blackshaw alone in the midst of the frozen Chesapeake wastes, but he did it with the best of intentions. With any luck, he could press ahead, survey the battlespace at the *Penelope*, and pick up Blackshaw again on the homeward trek, mission accomplished.

Ellis had two reasons for breaking up the customary sniper-spotter team. The first reason: his wealth weighed upon him. He and Blackshaw had pulled down a king's ransom on a recent mission, so neither of them was short of cash. Their first mission had yielded a fortune in sunken bullion. Blackshaw, as captain and owner of *Miss Dotsy*, the deadrise workboat used in the gold's salvage, could have claimed the lion's share of the treasure. Yet Blackshaw had split the money right down the middle with Ellis. Then Blackshaw had further divided his share among all the other families of Smith Island, without any pressure or suggestion that Ellis do likewise. As much as he liked his neighbors, Ellis had not followed suit. That said, until the two men had liberated additional fortunes in subsequent missions, Blackshaw's decision had made Ellis the wealthiest man on Smith Island by far. And it left Ellis with an insupportable sense of debt, of oppressive obligation, though Blackshaw's largesse had been freely bestowed.

Ellis's second reason for pressing ahead of Blackshaw into the storm had to do with fatherhood. Ellis had no children, but his own father had been loving and generous, and raised Ellis alone since his mother's early death from cancer. Somehow, his father had seen him through tuition at

Morehouse on a plumber's savings and earnings. At college, Ellis had been a good student. He had maintained a grade point average high enough to avert being drafted into the Army to serve in Vietnam. Ellis's father was not simply educating his only child. He was trying to keep him alive and safe from a war that was killing off a generation of young, poor, Black men.

Then, Ellis had fallen in love for the first time. Rowena was beautiful, and wild. She demanded Ellis's full attention, and he gave her his heart completely. His grades suffered, plunging his class ranking dangerously close to the threshold below which the Army would end his S-2 deferment, and come calling to draft him.

It was a moment of terror when Ellis learned too late that Rowena's father was a Morehouse dean. Rowena lived alone in a small apartment, but one evening, her old man had dropped in and caught the passionate couple *in flagrante*. By semester's end, the dean had flunked Ellis out of Morehouse to protect his daughter. Four months later, Ellis was in Da Nang. His father died of a heart attack during that first tour overseas.

So, Ellis knew how important having a father was to a young man, even if he had broken his own dad's heart. Now Blackshaw had a son, and he and LuAnna had informally made Ellis the boy's godfather. Ellis took the responsibility seriously. He would do anything he could to ensure Callum had a living, breathing father for as long as possible; to that end, Ellis would ensure Blackshaw did not throw himself away on a mission before he discovered how crucial he was to that boy's life.

Ellis picked up his pace. The snowshoes were gripping well, helping his progress. Ahead lay the *Penelope*. On Smith Island slept an infant who felt like a nephew. Yes, little Cal was family. Ellis would not let him down.

CHAPTER 42

BLACKSHAW'S SEAL TRAINING had included a module on interdicting, repelling, and neutralizing pirates on vessels of all sizes, including large tankers and cargo ships. And that meant understanding how pirates boarded their fat, sluggish, valuable quarries in the first place.

If the target ship had few, or no security forces aboard, the attacker merely had to climb the pilot's ladder. In more innocent times, these ladders had been constructed permanently on the side of the ship. Ordinarily, when that ship was going into port, the pilot boat would pull alongside the larger vessel for the transfer. The pilot had knowledge of local currents, depths, and tides, and a working rapport with the local tugboat captains who could help maneuver the ship. He would gauge the waves, and with the agility of a circus acrobat, leap across the gap between vessels to the ladder. One misstep, and he could fall into frigid water and drown, or be crushed between the pilot boat and the tanker. Once he grasped the ladder, from there he would climb to an open doorway in the ship's side, or all the way up to the main deck, and make his way to the bridge. There he took over the helm of the vessel to bring it safely to its mooring, or to an offshore loading facility in deeper water in the case of tankers. Upon guiding a newly loaded ship away from the port, the pilot would disembark the same way he had arrived.

That ladder was often little more than a series of D-shaped lengths of steel bar stock welded directly to the hull. When incidents of piracy worsened around the world, those built-in steps and handholds had been cut away, and a temporary ladder that could be raised and stowed became the only way for the pilot to board and disembark from another boat.

Busier ports, like Durban or the Columbia River Bar, required split-second efficiency in the movement of the great ships through the facility; they might deliver the pilot via helicopter to open deck space, or to a dedicated helipad. Sometimes the chopper crew lowered the pilot from a cable and hoist to the deck. Either way, Blackshaw mused, it was one hell of a commute for the harbor pilot. So far, pirates were not boarding via choppers.

In the latest cargo ship designs, the pilot ladder had been done away with at the blueprint stage of construction. Sometimes a pirate could shinny up a pipe retrofitted outside the hull. Hollywood often directed attackers up the ship's anchor line, but that left the infiltrator exposed, hanging back-toward-water like a sloth, and vulnerable for too much of the climb. Blackshaw was in a strange position. To neutralize the pirates that he believed were aboard the *Penelope*, he had to think like a pirate. He had hundreds of years of ancestral buccaneering to draw upon in his Smith Island DNA, but his Cornish forebears never had to tackle a ship this big.

After what felt like hours of trudging across the uneven ice, the goliath *Penelope* loomed in front of Blackshaw, a vast dark cliff appearing from the oppressive swirl of numbing snow and ice. He approached her from the stern, and with quiet care, glanced up toward the deck whenever his footing allowed. He stole beneath the fantail overhang, and made his way along the port side of the vessel toward the bow. To see him, someone on that ship would have to be out on deck facing straight into the weather, and then they would have to look down. There was no pilot ladder. No lines or painter's gear dangled forgotten within sight, let alone within reach. At least no one raised the alarm.

After a hike along the side of *Penelope*, Blackshaw posted up beneath the bow's projection. He removed his pack and dug into it. He snatched out coils of lightweight rope, a collapsible titanium grappling hook, and other gear suited to ice climbing. Line and hook in hand he stepped back from the ship fifteen paces, aimed at the bow high overhead, and heaved. The grappling hook pinged off *Penelope*'s side. As best he could judge in the weather, it had struck just a few feet below the lip of the bow bulwarks. Blackshaw danced aside as the line descended in a snarl of crazed coils. After whistling down passed his head, the hook rattled off the ice. He stood still, waiting to see if he'd attracted attention from above.

When he was certain he was still undiscovered, Blackshaw faked the line down so it would pay out cleanly. With the hook in hand again, he adjusted his aim point, taking into account that the line would get heavier with every foot that lifted into the air. Blackshaw lofted the hook again. This time, the line disappeared up and out of sight into the white gale above. This time, the hook did not fall back to the ice.

Blackshaw gently pulled on the line, recovering a good fifteen feet before he met with any resistance. He increased his downhaul slowly, checking the grappling hook's purchase. Blackshaw's heart sank when the line went slack in his hands. Poised to dive out of the way of the falling hook, he watched. The line did not drop in a mess. The hook was still on deck. There was still a chance it might catch hold of something that could bear his weight. Slowly, Blackshaw began taking in the line. After recovering five more feet, the hook caught once again. Blackshaw pulled harder and harder. The line stretched a foot, but the hook did not budge. He looped the line through a strap on his pack so the wind would not whip it away into the night.

Blackshaw prepared his right- and left-handed Black Diamond ascenders, the handles that slid along the rope and bit down on it so he could pull himself upward. When the foot loops were ready, he put on his pack and rifle. Sliding one hand, then other up the line, using the ascenders' clamping grip, he kicked off the ice. Six such steps into the climb, he attained that peculiar point in the stormy space where he could no longer see the ice below, nor the ship's massive hull somewhere beside him, nor anything above. He felt the wind sway and turn him, eradicating what little grasp of his orientation to the ship he'd maintained since starting the climb. He was a soul suspended in snow, wind, and darkness, disconnected from everything except cold and exhaustion.

Blackshaw stopped climbing to listen, thinking he had heard a shout from above. His heart pounded. Next would come the bullet, or a sickening drop before being smashed on the ice below if a sentry had discovered his line and slashed it. None of that happened. He calmed his breathing. His heart slowed.

His hands grew numb. His back and shoulders were aflame with fatigue. His biceps shuddered as muscle failure drew closer. He reached upward with the ascenders, more slowly now, amazed at how his exposure to the foul weather, together with the wearying march, and a lack of recent training had ground his stamina away. And with the onset of this wintry weakness he became inexplicably drowsy. Hypothermia wanted him to drift off, to let go, to die hanging upside down from the foot loops. What a picture his corpse would make. That thought spurred him.

Blackshaw resumed cycling the ascenders ever upward. Slide, grip, pull. Slide, grip, pull. Had he always been climbing? Would it ever end? He bore down with an effort to concentrate, to hang on a little longer, and not surrender to frigid oblivion.

His left ascender clacked into something solid and would go upward no farther. Blackshaw gathered his forces, and heaved himself over the *Penelope*'s bow caprail, uncaring if he were seen, he was so tired. As he caught his breath on deck, he surveyed what he could of his surroundings.

He sensed, rather than saw the great hemisphere of the forward-most liquid natural gas storage tank rising into the storm. He knew five more lay along the keel behind it like a cargo of planets.

On his feet now, Blackshaw eased aft through the snow toward the superstructure topped by the bridge. Then he circled around the outer insulating cover of the spherical aluminum Kvaerner-Moss tanks within. If the destruction of the *Penelope* were the eventual goal, as Blackshaw's brief confab with Michael Craig suggested, there might likely be demolition charges set close to the individual LNG Type B tanks.

It took twenty minutes in the storm, but Blackshaw managed to make a full circle around the foremost tank using the dim glow from his red-lensed flashlight. He found nothing that looked out of place, as best he could determine beneath the blowing snow. And he discovered no sentries. Overlooking explosives, and missing patrols in this weather might mean anything. It seemed that no guards had been posted. Everyone was sensibly below decks. And the ordnance might be below as well where it could be monitored until it was needed. Blackshaw knew there was no insulating cover down there obstructing access to the inch-and-a-half thick aluminum walls of the tank. Charges could be placed closer to the skin with more devastating effect.

Then Blackshaw recalled from his training that each sphere on an LNG carrier had an enormous drip tray beneath it, complete with temperature sensors, to detect leaks from cracks well before a catastrophic tank failure. Even a shaped charge set off against a sphere resulting in a tank rupture would still void the LNG into that drip tray. After that, an explosion or fire would still have to breach the ship's double hull to create the holocaust Blackshaw thought the saboteurs hoped to achieve. Without a fire, an entire cargo of liquid methane instantaneously re-gasifying to six hundred times its chilled volume was a daunting prospect, even without the cloud's potential to suffocate every living thing within miles.

Once again, Blackshaw adopted the thought process of an attacking saboteur seeking catastrophic environmental destruction. He decided that there were too many passive boundaries and obstructions to breaching the tanks below decks. That left one place to search.

Recalling the narrow stairway he had passed on his initial circuit, the one ascending from the main deck in a helix around the Number 1 tank to the sphere's top, Blackshaw gauged that he could reach it by turning around and retracing his steps. He was barely three paces along when he walked straight into another man decked in winter gear including goggles. The sentry's surprise meant his death, delaying him that crucial instant before he could raise and aim his weapon. But Blackshaw was hunting. He was ready. He drew his knife and slashed out in a single movement, the scalpel-sharp blade slicing through collar and hood into flesh. The sentry staggered backward clutching his throat. Blackshaw stepped in closer with two centerline up-thrusts into the area of the man's abdominal aorta. No ballistic rifle plate turned Blackshaw's blade aside. The sentry collapsed writhing onto the deck, his wounds gushing a black cherry slurpy across the snow.

Assured the sentry was down for good, Blackshaw scavenged the dead man's radio, dragged the body to the side, and heaved it overboard. He barely heard the crack as it struck the ice. He continued on his way to the foot of helical stair. A quick inspection with his light revealed boot prints with the toes pointing to the edge of the treads. Though snowy gusts were quickly obliterating the signs, the man Blackshaw had just killed must have come down those stairs. Blackshaw climbed. Something up there was an important part of the sentry's tour of inspection.

The wind became more violent the higher he got, pushing, shoving, threatening to blow him off the stair. He stooped low and clutched the grab rail, which felt too small in his gloved hands to stop him from going airborne.

At the tank's equator, its southern hemisphere curved and fell away. Without the tank's overhang above, the wind blasted and buffeted him even more. That sentry must have had a good reason to risk patrolling up there, especially without any kind of jackline belaying him to the railing from a safety harness. Not for the first time, the thought welled up in Blackshaw's mind that this weather was not part of the saboteurs' plan.

That is when he heard the engine growling through the wind. A car in low gear but driven fast, Blackshaw guessed by the gearbox's whine. He looked down from the stair toward the bow. With the ship's exterior lighting dark, Blackshaw could see a vehicle in the distance; two snow-blurred headlights moving from northwest to east, maybe toward the south. Was there a road out there? If Blackshaw had boarded the wrong ship, a tanker lying closer to shore than *Penelope*, then he had killed an innocent man. The car or truck, whatever it was, passed in the distance off the starboard side of the ship.

After a difficult climb, Blackshaw reached the apex of the sphere: the tank dome. Below this cover, a structural support cylinder descended to the bottom of the tank. The cylinder was a conduit for pressurization sensors and refrigeration gear, which helped maintain the LNG at its 162 °C temperature. The tank dome also housed plumbing that bled, collected and conveyed boiled-off LNG to fuel the ship's engines and other utilities. A narrow catwalk surrounded by a complex of pipes ran aft from this dome to the five others topping the remaining spheres.

Blackshaw heard a gunshot and looked aft, certain he had been spotted. The catwalk was swallowed by the storm. He crouched low by the tank dome. No more shots. Then Blackshaw knew he had boarded the right ship. Kneeling in the snow, he noticed the small case strapped to the tank dome. An antenna projected from the case six inches. A single green light glowed on the side of the box. Blackshaw did not need a diagram to know a sophisticated demolition charge when he saw it. This charge was designed to be triggered via a radio signal. There were no wires leading to a detonator that could come loose. Blackshaw thought it was a good choice of load-out for the mission, considering the storm. If this charge went off, the tank would breach, exposing a tremendous volume of LNG to open air at atmospheric pressure. The liquid methane gas would vaporize, at first like a geyser, then with Vesuvian ferocity. If all six tanks were destroyed at once, the cataclysm would devastate the Chesapeake, its shoreline, and spread for many miles inland. It would be hellfire.

Blackshaw had no idea if the radio triggers fed telemetry warnings back to the transmitters if they were deactivated. Blackshaw's fingers had gone numb as he tried to leave the trigger mechanism intact, while still isolating them from the explosives. Fortunately, the person who rigged the devices had no expectation that there'd be any attempt to disarm them before they were set off, and had built no failsafe into the simple design. *It'll never happen* were the last words of many a lazy soldier.

Worst case, the trigger's telemetry would alert the saboteurs at the switch that there was a problem with the mechanism. That would bring an inspection party forward from the living quarters. He could not very well sit there and pick them off one by one as they came out. How could he spoof their radio contact protocols? So far, with no alarms raised on the scavenged radio, Blackshaw knew the dead sentry had still not missed a scheduled check-in.

With a tight grip on the catwalk railing, Blackshaw leaned into the wind and crept aft toward the next sphere, the next tank dome, and in all likelihood, the next bomb.

CHAPTER 43

SCREED WAS GLAD to be off the ice, as thick as it was. His relief at being on land was short-lived. Choad LaGleet had reported that they had come ashore on some kind of marshy wildlife refuge. They had to march nearly a mile from the north side, where they had crashed, to the southern boundary. Then they would have to negotiate a broader frozen channel, then cross another small island, and finally another frozen river.

This refuge seemed to be a mass of hummocks topped with dense, frozen reeds, with streamlets carving the land up every ten to twenty feet. There was an ungodly hiss and crackle as the squad pushed through the vegetation.

Fortunately, the target area of Smith Island was far enough away that the howl of the wind would blot the noise of their progress beyond a few feet. They moved single-file through the reeds, with LaGleet and Krill on point crushing a path through snow and vegetation for everyone behind them.

Step by step through the cold and treacherous footing, Screed regretted the loss of the helicopter. He could have done without the trauma of the crash, of course, but that bird would have saved them hours of humping through the unfriendly terrain and weather. They could have been standing over Blackshaw's corpse by now.

There was a sudden squalling of shrill honking sounds to the right of the path. Screed leapt out of his skin, and shied to the left while LaGleet and Krill brought their weapons to bear to the right. Then the air all around them was filled with gray and tan and black demons beating at the night with heavy wings.

"What the hell!" shouted Screed, loosing an aimless, fumbling burst from his MP-5 across the sky. His hands sent electric waves of pain to his shoulders from the recoil.

All the other operatives dove for cover, or at least for a point in space below Screed's angle of fire. Only LaGleet remained standing. He stepped off their path into the snow and dark. They saw a glimmer of his flashlight, which quickly winked out again.

"For Christ's sake," they heard him swear in the dark.

A moment later, LaGleet rejoined the group. He threw the bleeding carcass of a Canada goose at Screed's feet. "You're an idiot."

They walked on, Screed feeling a complete fool as LaGleet suggested.

Ten minutes later, Screed said, "We need to get out of this wind."

Krill had the tablet with the moving map. She stopped, and Screed and LaGleet instinctively formed a huddle with a few of the closest operatives to create a human windbreak in which they might hear one another.

She wiped snow from screen with the edge of her glove and said, "This is us," as she pointed to the central dot on the screen. "Half a klick west, it looks like there's a ridge. It's topped with trees. Wind is out of the west, for now anyway. We could move south in the lee of the ridge almost to the water. We might not be so beat up before the fight if we go that way."

LaGleet considered the idea, but not for very long. "You want to haul it half a click west straight into the teeth of this storm, so we can cover another klick or two south with less wind. Not *no* wind. Just *less*. If the wind doesn't round out of the east during that time, and hit us in the face again. No, Cupcake. We keep going straight toward the objective. We get there, do the thing, and we'll post up in Blackshaw's house all cozy as can be. We eat his food. We drink his blood."

Screed angled the screen toward himself. "What about that stream up ahead? It's frozen. It's headed roughly the way we want to go. It's clear of these reeds and bushes."

"Okay," said LaGleet. "That's half a fucking good idea. We'll do that."

CHAPTER 44

SILAS GRODIN STOMPED into *Penelope*'s bridge. It had been an hour since Captain Varna had closed the door, locking Grodin in the weather on the port bridge wing.

"That was a dick move," said Grodin.

"That was a reminder you're on my ship, sailor," said Varna, "even if you do plan to blow it to hell."

Grodin's attention was caught by something on the radar. "You see that?"

Captain Varna stepped over to the screen. Something small was moving less than a kilometer off *Penelope*'s bow. It had been so long since he had seen anything on that screen in motion. He was transfixed.

Grodin said, "An ice breaker. There must be a thaw we didn't notice."

Varna scoffed, "Nothing has changed in the weather. Absolutely nothing."

"But it's something. An ice boat? Some idiot on a snowmobile?"

"I seriously doubt it," said Varna. "The radar signature is bigger than either of those. It's going roughly northwest to southeast."

Grodin and Varna watched in silence for a few moments. Varna threw on his foul weather jacket. "It's going to pass us to starboard."

Grodin snatched up a pair of conventional binoculars, and a rifle. The captain grabbed an infrared monocular and pressed the initializing button. The two men slid the starboard door to the bridge wing open against the wind, and rushed across the bridge wing through the snow.

Grodin looked out into the storm. "There. See? A light!"

Captain Varna glanced through the infrared monocular, but it was still warming up. "Shit, this damn thing!"

"No, there're two lights. Yellowish." said Grodin, focusing the big field glasses. "Parking lights! It's a damn car. All the way out here."

Grodin chambered a round in the rifle, and aimed at the glow of the lights.

The captain batted the muzzle up just as Grodin fired, and said, "Safe that weapon, cowboy! Are you *trying* to draw attention?"

Grodin said, "Why are they out here? Doesn't feel right. Somebody's scoping this ship out—"

"It's some knucklehead on a bender," said Varna. At last, he got an image in varying shades of gray in the reticle of the monocular. "I'll be damned. It's a Jeep! And it's stopping!"

CHAPTER 45

MOLLY WILDE WONDERED what she was really running from, as much as she contemplated the deadly trouble ahead. The Jeep was performing well in the subfreezing cold. The headlights and fog lights were all working, but she preferred driving with the parking lights alone. The snow threw all the other lights directly back into her eyes. The ice was rougher out in the channel. She slowed down, but still the wind thrummed the Jeep's soft top as though she were going a hundred miles an hour.

It struck her that she was desperately far away from shore. For a moment, she chastised herself for not bringing some kind of life jacket with her. Then she realized that if the ice gave way, and the Jeep plunged into the Chesapeake, it would be fairly even odds as to whether she would succumb to hypothermia or drowning, life vest or not.

Wilde checked the moving map on which she had marked the position of the *Penelope*. The LNG carrier lay somewhere in the storm-thrashed darkness to her right. For some reason, innocent or nefarious she couldn't say, all the ship's exterior illumination was dark. Or she had driven way off course. She resisted the urge to turn and shine her headlights on the Leviathan, since that would achieve nothing except possibly attracting attention. She kept her heading toward Smith Island.

The *ping* of metal striking metal startled Wilde. The wind sounds in the Jeep changed, and now had a dissonant whistle along with the roar. Wilde slowed as she fished a flashlight out of the glove compartment. The flashlight's batteries were old, and further fatigued with chill. In the dim beam, she inspected the soft top in small sections as she drove. Then she saw them. Two small holes in the top, and between them, a small shiny groove in the frame. Someone, likely from *Penelope*, had shot at her, the bullet making an entry hole, and an exit tear in the cover, with a glancing impact on the frame in transit.

Wilde's anger erupted white-hot behind her eyes. Against all training, and counter to her objective, she slammed on the brakes. The Jeep skewed across the ice to a stop. She shut off all the lights, threw herself out of the Jeep, and drew her weapon, aiming it somewhere high into the snowy void roughly parallel to the angle of a line drawn between the two bullet holes. She chambered a round from the gun's magazine into the receiver, and waited. Waited as if she were studying a stranger instead of herself, to see what the hell she was going to do next.

CHAPTER 46

CAPTAIN VARNA DRAGGED Silas Grodin off the bridge wing before he could fire again, and threw the door closed behind them.

"Are you absolutely insane!" cried Varna. "What if you hit somebody?"

Grodin paced the bridge, rifle still in hand. "I can't sit here like this. My men are going crazy. I'm going crazy! We should have been done and gone by now."

"Christ man, this is the mission! These are the circumstances! If you want to fuck everything up, then take your bunch of tweaked-out hotheads, get down on the ice and walk away! Don't murder some stranger, somebody who might be missed. This is about containment until the job's done. Low profile. Heads down."

Captain Varna grabbed Grodin's H harness and shook the soldier, wobbling the grenades stowed there. "Pull your shit together!"

Silas Grodin took a slow deep breath. Captain Varna believed Grodin was cooling off. The soldier appeared to look up at the ceiling, but then he slammed his forehead into the captain's nose. Varna staggered backwards, dazed, hands to his face, blood seeping between his fingers.

With veins cording in his neck and temples, Grodin shouted, "You will never, ever put your hands on me again, or I will end you!" Grodin drew his Beretta, cocked it, and aimed at the captain who propped himself against the bulkhead, eyes wide with terror. "I will fucking end you!"

In his heightened state of stress, it was a wonder Grodin saw anything other than the captain who for the moment appeared to be the root of all that was wrong with the mission. But in of the corner of his eye, something registered outside in the cold, dark, and wet of night.

Grodin keyed his mic and said, "Collins, I want you on the catwalk. Start at the aft-most tank and move forward. Eyes open. Somebody's out there."

Collins replied on the radio. "I'm on it. Drake should be forward already."

Grodin keyed the mic again. "Drake! Report!"

There was no reply.

"Drake! You check in or I'll hunt you down and kill you myself!"

Radio silence.

"Shit!" shouted Grodin.

"You're out of your mind," said Captain Varna.

"I saw a light. A red light," said Grodin. "I know it."

"Oh sure. Tinkerbell?" sneered Captain Varna.

Silas Grodin raised his pistol and shot the captain twice in the face.

CHAPTER 47

LUANNA FOUND THIS interesting. Here she was dressed in her warmest foul weather gear, packing a 12 gauge shotgun, and easing herself down off the fuel dock onto the ice sheet that was the Big Thorofare. Across the ice to the north lay Goat Island only yards away, but invisible in the darkness and storm. The real curiosity lay just behind her. Reverend Mosby, Sonny Wright, and Mary Wright were with her. Sonny and Mary were helping Mosby move down from pier to ice without sacrificing a hip. It might be nothing, but LuAnna noted that without any discussion, she had been designated the leader of this expedition.

Good for you, Honeygirl, she thought to herself, and high time.

Perhaps it was her service as a Corporal in the Maryland Natural Resources Police that conferred a mantle of authority on her shoulders even in this less formal mission. That part of her résumé had not always worked in her favor on Smith Island. Carrying an NRP badge with so many neighbors and relatives earning a living following the water had won her no admiration at the time, even though monitoring catch limits, as well as crab and oyster sizes actually protected the Chesapeake fishery from the predations of super-efficient watermen, many of whom believed the bay was inexhaustible. It was not until she had quit the NRP in a moment of desperation that the warm esteem she had enjoyed as a youth was finally returned to her again. When she was welcomed back into the fold, she realized that as a cop, she had been held at arm's length as a traitor.

Sonny studied the distant fiery glow through the storm. "That's t'other side of the refuge. A long half step, there to here."

Mary asked, "That's what your Feeb friend said? They were coming this way?"

LuAnna said, "She wasn't long on specifics. You heard my end of the chat. She happened to indicate there might be trouble on a certain ship called *Penelope*."

Sonny chuckled, "She ain't long on stuff we don't already know."

"I didn't want to let on we were wise to it," LuAnna said. "I mean, one or two dead bodies can roll down on anyone's doorstep. Nine corpses might take some explaining."

"Did she have aught to add to the situation at hand?" asked Reverend Mosby.

"In a manner of speaking," said LuAnna as she led off walking across the frozen Big Thorofare. "Said whatever was brewing on the ship was connected back to the eight-fingered fopdoodle we had to visiting this summer."

"That Screed article. Now that one was a patriot," said Mary in her sideways Smith Island way, and meaning the precise opposite of her words.

"What's the problem now?" groused Sonny. "We gave most of him back!"

"But another bunch of government types got custody of the leftovers," LuAnna explained. "Then he got kidnapped by some others."

"Dumbass should put *kidnap victim* on his next job application. Seems all he's good for," said Sonny.

"And now he's back around here?" Reverend Mosby asked.

"But not all by his onesy," said LuAnna. "Miss Molly Wilde thinks Screed's whole job now is bird-dogging Ben so a team of cutthroats can notch him up and take him off the board—so he doesn't interfere with the deeds and doings of shit-heels the way he likes to do."

"Was a time, Ben would be the one trying to head off trouble," said Sonny, as they mounted the bluff shoreline of Goat Island. "Now, them fonnyboys are heading off Ben before they even start trouble."

"Preempting Ben," said Mary. "He's getting a reputation."

"He came by it honestly," said LuAnna. She kept the pride out of her voice, but despite the blizzard, it warmed her heart all the same.

CHAPTER 48

KNOCKER ELLIS MISJUDGED Blackshaw. Ellis had hoped Blackshaw would not press on alone without his spotter. To Ellis's great chagrin, he observed Blackshaw's approach to *Penelope*, and his ascent up the ship's side. It gave Ellis fits when, through his FLIR LSX night vision spotting scope, he observed the sentry moving slowly forward toward the bow on the catwalk, then descending the helical stair around the forward sphere toward the deck and Blackshaw.

Nothing happened for nearly a half an hour, but Ellis did not budge from his post at the top of the old decommissioned Misty Shoal lighthouse fifteen hundred yards away from *Penelope*. Then his worst dread was realized. A body toppled over *Penelope*'s bow, smacking onto the ice sheet below. Was it his friend? Had he failed Blackshaw and the child Callum despite his most noble intentions? Why hadn't Blackshaw turned back for Smith Island like any well-trained operative? Blackshaw should not have been out there alone. Ellis should not have left Blackshaw to make poor life choices by himself.

Ellis powered up the CheyTac rifle's night scope and removed the cover from the muzzle. There would be payback if his friend had just died before his eyes. He switched from the spotting scope to the rifle's sight. The image was fuzzed by snow, but Ellis could see well enough to shoot.

He saw a figure climbing the helical stair. If it were the sentry returning along his own backtrail, that would be unusual, but not unheard of. If it were the sentry, that would mean Blackshaw was now dead and cooling on the ice below.

Ellis's hopes began to rise the higher the distant figure climbed up and around the spherical tank. There was something familiar with the gait; the unidentified man was so careful. This was not a sentry moving like he knew the layout and the footing of the ship at all well. *And he had a pack on his shoulders.* The sentry didn't. Ben was alive!

Ellis watched as his friend bent low to examine something on the catwalk next to the tank dome. Then Blackshaw rose and moved aft, continuing his reconnaissance.

Ellis snapped into overwatch mode, and scanned the main deck, returning to pass the cross-hairs of his scope along the catwalk. Another sentry was moving forward, still two hundred meters aft of Blackshaw's position. But Blackshaw was heading directly toward his unseen enemy. Blackshaw appeared fixated on the object by the tank dome. Why wasn't Blackshaw using his NVGs?

Ellis willed Blackshaw to look up, to descend the helical tank stair, and get out of the sentry's path. Instead, as if in mule-headed defiance, Blackshaw rose and edged aft along the catwalk. Ellis watched the distance between his friend and the sentry close with every second. Too late Ellis wondered if Blackshaw was monitoring his radio. Ellis turned his own radio on, waiting the few seconds for it to boot up in an agony of worry. As Ellis watched his friend walk into danger, he knew there was no time left for warnings. He had to act.

The blizzard's ever-shifting wind shear would play hell with Ellis's shot. He had the range doped. The shot would be taken CCB, and CBM, a clean, cold barrel, for center body mass of the enemy. No trick headshots. A clear path and a neutralized target were all Ellis wanted for his friend.

CHAPTER 49

BLACKSHAW ADVANCED ALONG the catwalk toward the stern. He kept his head low as much to avoid being buffeted off the narrow grating by a gust of wind as to avoid detection. He arrived at that point where the driving snow and dark swallowed the catwalk both in front of him, as well as behind. He stood in a featureless void. It could be someone's idea of hell. To Blackshaw, it was another day at the office.

When he sensed the curve of the second tank rising up to meet the catwalk, it was no real comfort or security. If he toppled over the side for any reason, he might drop onto the sphere after a survivable fall; with nothing to grab on the tank's smooth surface, he would slide helpless down to the deck, or perhaps to the helical stair before that. Either way, there would likely be some kind of hobbling fracture.

Though the storm was still pelting down thick torrents of icy snow, Blackshaw maintained a watchful eye on the walkway ahead, as well as behind him. When he was searching the storm toward the stern of the ship, he saw two muzzle flashes define the windows of the ship's bridge, which Blackshaw realized was at his eye level several stories above the deck. In those two instants of illumination, he spied the silhouettes of a pair of men, one clearly doing the other a mischief.

Blackshaw wondered if Ellis would have gotten here ahead of time, and started mixing it up without him. It could be that authorities of some sort had nosed the troubles brewing on the *Penelope*, and come calling in a nighttime incursion. Blackshaw had a passing respect for government operatives, many of whom had fought bravely in the military beside him before retiring from the service, but he knew a few of the gung-ho types could only hold off and sneak around perimeters for just so long before announcing their arrival with gunplay and flash-crash grenades. *No*, reasoned Blackshaw, *a couple of shots did not make a raid.*

That left two possibilities. The first, the one Blackshaw preferred, was simple dissent in the ranks of the hijackers. There had been a falling out amongst the fonnyboys. Unexpected circumstances, for which there was no established contingency action, had caused men of small brain and large gun to have to think on their feet, leading to disagreement on how to proceed. Blackshaw thought he could exploit a mutiny right well given the chance. The other possibility was that the shooting was some sort of undefined action Blackshaw could not understand based on the intel at his disposal.

Blackshaw pressed on to the tank dome of the second sphere. He crouched and saw the small case, with its antenna and power-on indicator light. Another bomb. Again, he was tempted to disable it in some way. Ideally, he would disconnect the primer cap from the explosive material, but leave the radio telemetry intact. The bomb would be harmless, but the person with his hand on the switch would not know that. There was no time to figure the weapon out to that extent. He carefully disconnected two visible wires even though Blackshaw felt his best bet was to find the master trigger and disable the entire explosive matrix from there, killing anyone he discovered along the way who was associated with the devices and the diabolical plan.

Blackshaw left this bomb in place, but disabled, as he had the first, and picked his way farther aft. In spite of his vigilance, he was surprised to hear a human grunt up ahead in the dark blizzard. A moment after that, he was sure he heard the report of a large and distant rifle away to the west. That gunshot was followed by a cracking thud of a tumbling body somewhere down on the main deck.

Blackshaw held still for two minutes, awaiting any fallout, any alarms, or unwanted attention resulting from the odd trio of sounds. Then there was a new sound. The tinny, small voice of a very angry man rose up from below. *Collins!* It seemed to call, at least twice. Blackshaw realized it was the radio of someone down on the main deck. Couldn't be anything else; he had turned off the unit he had salvaged from the sentry he had killed at the bow.

Blackshaw moved on, keeping his pistol trained over the edge of the catwalk and down toward the deck. After five meters' travel like this, his left glove, which had been sliding over the ice-slick railing was gummed to a sticky stop. He examined the glove, and the railing. He knew the texture, the coppery scent. It was blood congealing in the cold. Someone had died here moments before; an enemy, for Blackshaw had no friends aboard. That disembodied voice must have been someone calling on a radio for a second sentry, now killed and fallen, observing radio silence forevermore. Blackshaw believed he knew who to thank for notching up this unlucky guard. He turned toward the port side of *Penelope*, gave a small wave, and pushed on.

CHAPTER 50

GRODIN SURPRISED HIMSELF, killing Captain Varna. In that moment, he did not want to be alone with a corpse. He radioed for a two-man team to hit the bridge double-time.

Carter, a husky redheaded cowboy with a bottomless Adderall prescription, and Munson, a small-framed Black man, had caught the CO's tone over the radio, and materialized in under twenty seconds. Munson was still buckling his belt on arrival following his interrupted visit to the head.

Carter glanced between Varna's corpse and Grodin's livid kabuki war-face. Grodin realized he was freaking his man out, and holstered his weapon.

Grodin said, "He had it coming. No respect for the chain of command. Ditch him. Over the side."

Munson, the cooler head, said, "All due respect, sir. If we put him over, and he's kinda laying there on the ice in broad daylight, and the blizzard clears before the thaw we need—well somebody might notice is all."

Grodin took a deep cleansing breath though he felt his hand moving back toward the butt of his holstered pistol. He spoke slowly, seething with the mission stress that Varna's murder had compounded rather than cathartically relieved. "There is a body on my bridge. I do not want that body on my bridge. I want you two to fucking handle it!"

"No problem," said Munson.

As Grodin's temper cooled, he realized it was in fact a huge ass-ache cleaning up after his own rashness. Grodin went on, "And double up the guard around all the forward companionways. We've been boarded."

CHAPTER 51

LUANNA TURNED NORTHEAST to cross Goat Island. And still Sonny and Mary Wright, and Reverend Mosby followed her close behind, their shotguns in the low-ready position; the barrels angled downward just enough to allow seeing the hands of a potential target in close quarters. The thick weather meant an enemy would be standing practically on one's boots before making a firing decision, but LuAnna and her party had sharp eyes in rotten weather going back generations. Anybody who missed a trick out on the Chesapeake, where flaws and fuzzcods breezed up quick as quick, had paltry odds of survival.

"How come we're still tromping on these hummocks and reeds," asked Reverend Mosby. This was as close to grousing as the man of God might ever get, but LuAnna knew his arthritic knees might be paining him.

She said, "If there's others coming at us, how do you think they'll go about it?"

Mary Wright answered, "If they have a decent map, with all the streams and guts laid out plain, they'll follow those because the footing's clearer on ice."

"Amateurs," said Sonny.

"But what if they know their stuff?" LuAnna asked.

"They stay on dry land. Come in straight no matter the ground," said Mary.

"But if that was a crash, they're shook up," said Reverend Mosby.

Sonny said, "And if your pal at the FBI says they're looking for Ben, does that mean they ain't looking at us expecting trouble?"

"Screed's the wildcard," said LuAnna. "He knows Ben has skills. If he's part of this, maybe he'll extrapolate and figure out that the rest of our heads don't button up the back."

"Lord, what if that's a crash of innocents?" said Mary. "What if a helping hand of kindness is what they're needing?"

"Whatever they need or want," declared LuAnna, "they come through us."

Reverend Mosby said, "If we were out to hunting geese, I'd be overjoyed about all our gum-flapping and stomping about."

"And rightly so, for geese are smart," LuAnna said. "But those who lift a hand in anger against Smith Island will get the usual, paid in full."

"A moment of dread—a long time dead," said Mary.

Sonny said, "I think I know where you're taking us, because we're there."

LuAnna smiled in appreciation of Sonny's knowledge of Goat Island. Before them stretched a clear frozen expanse ringed with reeds. Lorton's Pond. LuAnna halted in the largest frozen stream that in warmer weather would flow out of the pond to the south toward the Big Thorofare and Ewell on Smith Island.

LuAnna said, "Whatever kind of map they're using, marine, aviation, or Geological Survey, they'll either walk the frozen guts to the pond, or tramp overland. They're tired. They might be banged up. There's only one obvious way out, and that's this gut. And the fire tower is—"

"Fifteen yards west," said Mary. "My first three hulls in this gun are pumpkin ball slugs. What do you say, Honeygirl?"

LuAnna dug into her coat pocket and pulled out four shotgun shells. "Ben passed these to me before he went. Dragon's Breath."

Mary Wright grinned through the storm. "Goody gumdrops! Christmas's came early, and the Fourth of July to boot! Always wanted to shoot some of these hunting, but Spoilsport here said no." She nodded at Sonny. "I say, kill a goose and cook it, too! All in one go."

"You get to the tower, and reload with those to fire first, Mary," said LuAnna. "You know the signal. Now let's deploy like we know what we're doing."

Mary kissed Sonny good-bye long enough to make Reverend Mosby blush, then crouched to make her way toward the long-abandoned fire tower. In an instant, she was lost in the weather.

LuAnna, Sonny, and the reverend took positions around the frozen gut, and crouched behind marshy hummocks, hoping dark and storm would offer what cover the low landscape denied them.

Reverend Mosby grinned at LuAnna, and took out his favorite duck call. His voice cut through the wind, "We must all watch out for Beelzebub tonight."

CHAPTER 52

KRILL TOOK POINT as the team crossed the frozen stretch between the Martin Wildlife Refuge and the chunk of land called Goat Island; beyond that lay Smith Island. LaGleet was directly behind Krill, watching the left flank. The other operators scanned sectors to the left and right. Though Bonamy Screed was last, he was nut-to-butt with the man ahead so he wouldn't lose him in the weather. With no obstacles, man-made or natural, the wind seemed to double in speed on the open ice, stripping off warmth like a North Pole gale.

LaGleet fell back to Screed's tail-end position, and asked, "What's the layout?"

"It was a hostage situation. I'm not your Michelin Guide," said Screed. The Doc's S-FOP drug bolus might have been keeping Screed vertical, but it did nothing for his mood.

LaGleet pressed, "Single family houses? Apartment blocks? Is this going to be FIBUA all night until we burn them out?"

"Fighting In Built Up Areas? Hardly. Houses. One and two story is all I saw when my blindfold slipped. I was stashed in a shack by some water. I could hear that. Krill was on target when she said this is a sleepy vil' full of sleepy people," said Screed.

"Except for the ones who nipped off your digits," LaGleet reminded. "They have battery acid for blood."

Screed shivered from memory more than cold. "You all've got my back, right? I'll eat a round before I let them take me alive again."

"Good attitude," said LaGleet, knowing the lethal phase of the Doc's medication was swirling in Screed's bloodstream poised to finish him. "But sure, teamwork makes the dream work. You've got my word."

CHAPTER 53

BLACKSHAW CREPT AFT toward the tanker's superstructure. With the exterior deck lights doused, through the snow and sleet, he could barely make out the reddish loom of the bridge's night lighting at the level of the tank catwalk.

He had passed three of six spheres, and dismantled each of the three of the demolition charges fixed to the tank domes. Thirty feet from the fourth tank dome, Blackshaw stopped, and slowly lowered himself until he was prone on the catwalk, his weapon aimed forward. He had seen movement ahead. The next tank dome was still difficult to make out, but something seemed different about it. The silhouette against the bloodshot bridge lighting was misshapen, more organic than mechanical.

Blackshaw sighted along the barrel and flipped off the safety. He had just crossed a line. He had a cocked weapon aimed toward the plumbing of an enormous liquid natural gas tank, which had a demolition charge strapped to it. There was every chance of this ending poorly.

A dark shape separated itself from the tank dome ahead. Definitely a man, probably armed. Blackshaw gauged where the center of the soldier's body mass was, and began to squeeze the trigger.

He felt a cold, hard pressure on the back of his neck. A voice in the storm said, "I want to see your hand come away from that trigger. Slow."

With a sickening realization that the man in front of him had been a decoy, while another operator had stalked in on his six, Blackshaw opened his grip on the rifle. The hardness at the back of his neck lifted for a moment, and then someone smashed Blackshaw's lights out.

CHAPTER 54

CHOAD LAGLEET HEARD the clack of hooves on ice, the thump of impact, and turned in time to see Bonamy Screed launch through the air from off of the biggest pair of curved horns he had ever seen. Screed howled, his arms and legs flailing, and landed in a heap out of sight in the dark.

Krill whirled, raising her weapon, hollering, "What the fuck!" as she loosed a three-shot burst of gunfire into the night.

LaGleet peered through the storm in the direction of a plaintive moan from Screed, who lay somewhere off their path across the icy pond. The other operators dropped into a crouch, weapons raised, covering their sectors. The beast was gone.

"Screed!" called LaGleet. He got another moan in reply.

After a moment, Screed said, "Over here. Don't shoot! Coming in. Jesus, I think my ribs are broken."

An operator asked, "What was that—" just as a clatter of hooves ratcheted in through the wind from another direction, louder and louder.

Screed begged, "No! Get away! Get—" and there was another crunch of horns against gear, another wail. Screed crashed back onto the ice and slid to a stop at Krill's feet.

LaGleet said, "I saw it! It's—it's a goddamn billy goat!"

"It's trying to kill me!" Screed shouted as he attempted to stand. His feet kept slipping out from under him.

All LaGleet's operators were scanning and panning left and right, sighting along their weapons, covering their zones.

Distant hooves rattled hard off the ice again. All the operators turned to face the staccato hoof beats of the onrushing enemy.

LaGleet bellowed, "Shoot! Open fucking fire!"

All the operators except Screed fired at the implacable goat, which startled at the noise, and leapt to one side. Some of the bullets found their mark, and the beast, nearly two hundred pounds of ornery meat, fur, stench, and horn dropped dead on top of Screed, bowling him down onto the ice for the third time.

"Get this damn thing off me!" Screed yelled from somewhere beneath the carcass.

The operators rolled the big beast off Screed, who lay twisted on the ice covered in goat blood. Then they helped him to his feet. He was shaky.

Screed bleated, "Jesus! What is that smell!"

"It's you," said Krill.

"Where's your weapon?" LaGleet asked.

"Hell if I know," said Screed. "Out there somewhere. That—thing knocked it out of my hands."

"Go find it," said LaGleet. "We'll wait. But not forever. Chop-chop!"

"Shhh!" Krill was listening to something on the wind.

"What do you hear?" said LaGleet.

Krill listened for a moment more. "Nothing. Thought I heard somebody laughing."

CHAPTER 55

BLACKSHAW ROSE FROM a dark world of nothing, to a gray world of racking migrainous pain in the back of his head. His hands and ankles were zip-tied. He lay on his left side, a thoughtful gesture by his captor in case he puked from a concussion. He was on the floor in a small utility compartment that smelled of heavy lubricating oil and cleaning products.

Blackshaw heard the rasp of a Zippo lighter struck to life nearby, followed by the small crackling burn of deep drawn cigarette tobacco. Then he heard the Zippo flipped shut with its telltale metallic ring-and-snap.

"I know you're coming to. You stopped snoring. Your breathing went shallow. I saw you test your restraints. Nice try though."

Blackshaw rolled slowly onto his back, then onto his right side. Lightning bolts of pain shot around his skull and down his neck. A soldier squatted a wary ten feet away outside the compartment door. He was smoking an unfiltered cigarette, and staring at Blackshaw.

"I'm Grodin. You patrolled in without ID."

"Blackshaw. You're not *Lieutenant* Grodin? *Captain*, maybe?"

"Paying me the compliment of a leadership position as a sign of respect, to build rapport, and reduce the harshness of your confinement. Except it means you really think I'm a grunt. You've been trained pretty well. Force Recon?"

"You guessed it in one," said Blackshaw.

"You're a goddamn liar. We saw your tattoo. Eagle. Anchor. Pistol. Trident. You're a shit-hot U.S. Navy SEAL. Or you were. Not so much now."

Blackshaw glanced down and realized he was no longer wearing the clothes in which he had deployed from Smith Island. While he was unconscious, he had been stripped so his gear could be studied, and dressed in blaze orange coveralls, likely pulled from ship's stores. The biggest size available, perhaps, but still too small for his frame.

"How'd you get aboard?" Grodin asked.

"Same as you," ventured Blackshaw.

"Bullshit," said Grodin. "No HALOs in this weather."

That was useful intel. A HALO meant Grodin had access to gear, an aircraft and crew, and an arrival before the freeze and this storm.

Blackshaw changed the subject. "You put a lot of crew over the side of this ship, Grodin. Too bad about the freeze."

"A good plan is still good regardless of timing," said Grodin.

"Like Gallipoli, right?"

"Exactly," said Grodin, failing to cover his grossly inadequate grasp of military history. "Who clued you in?"

Blackshaw didn't wait for Grodin to brag he was once a door gunner on the space shuttle. Instead, he offered a shred of intel to bait Grodin into revealing something, anything more. "You clued me in yourself. Ice. Bodies. Some of the dead crew were wearing life jackets marked *Penelope*. Not that hard to figure. You expected to be long gone before anyone found out what you'd done to them."

Grodin masked his worry. "I guess the feds are on their way."

"Sure. With the likes of me on point. Like I have the Feebs on speed dial," said Blackshaw.

"You some kind of ronin? A vigilante?" Grodin asked.

"Not hardly. Just like to know what's going on around home," said Blackshaw.

"You killed one of my men," said Grodin.

"*Two*. The first guy patrolling all the way forward. Second guy up on the catwalk. I'm not bragging, mind. But they wished me ill."

Grodin's momentary consternation shifted to triumph. He swelled. "Didn't make a bit of difference. We got your handiwork on those charges repaired. They're good to go. But you'll get to see that first hand. Super up-close."

Grodin stood, dropped his cigarette butt, ground it out on the deck with his heel, and left. Another sentry, who had been standing by the door just out of view, reached in and slammed the compartment door shut.

CHAPTER 56

LUANNA WATCHED THE enemy encounter with Beelzebub the Billy Goat with a mix of wonder and sadness. The beast was so territorial that it was a rite of passage among Smith Island kids to venture onto its island and escape with one's life, along with some bruises, and maybe a fracture. And now the legendary guardian of Goat Island was dead, but not in vain. In dying, it had let her know with the certain evidence of gunfire that the interlopers were armed, and prepared to shoot at anything and anyone strange.

It took nine minutes for one of the invading party to discover where the weapon had skidded out of sight across the pond ice to lodge beneath a low drift of snow. It took another three minutes before the operators reformed their line and set off toward Smith Island. LuAnna counted six troops in all, all of them spooked and moving carefully. The one that had borne the brunt Beelzebub's wrath, taking three solid hits from the big, foul-tempered animal, limped in the middle of the line where his teammates could watch and keep him out of more mischief.

Beelzebub's selfless attack against overwhelming odds also revealed to LuAnna that this was a skittish bunch of shitbirds come to make trouble. The crash, the fires, which still burned, had softened them up, likely thinning their ranks. That was good. The rampaging goat had further terrorized them, and injured one more operator. They still marched on, though it was likely they expected no human conflict until they reached Smith Island proper. Oh they were keyed-up all right, but for four-legged relatives of Beelzebub out for revenge.

LuAnna glanced toward Reverend Mosby's position. She couldn't see him, but she knew he was hunkered down twenty feet to her left somewhere in the blowing snow.

Peering to her right, she knew Sonny was holding a flank position. She knew by now that Mary was aloft in the old fire tower, maybe not all the way up in the watch room at the top, but high enough on the open metal stairway to hold a commanding firing position.

Still the enemy approached. LuAnna began to worry that Reverend Mosby's vision was bad, and he just wasn't realizing how close those six operators had tolled in. If he was waiting to see the whites of their eyes in this dark and weather, they'd all be nose to nose before the shooting started. She needn't have worried.

From her left she heard the reverend's duck call quacking like a pissed off mallard. The signal. She fired her Remington pump gun three times at the intruders, catching one in the leg with a pumpkin ball, maybe snapping a femur, and with luck rupturing the femoral artery and many of its branches. He dropped as his leg bent the wrong way.

Reverend Mosby let fly on the left. A blistering din of cussing burst from the invaders, as well as a few common-sense orders like *take* cover, and *get down*, and *return fire*. Then Mary illuminated the scene with blasts of the incendiary Dragon's Breath shotgun shells. Her first shot caught one of the operators full on. It was a lightning strike, with Olympian gouts of sparks that ignited the operator's uniform. The operator screamed, slapping at the flames consuming her. She dropped and rolled, but the fire wouldn't go out. Worse for the enemy, the flames backlit all her squaddies who dashed away from her to any shadow that would hide them. Just their luck they vaulted away from Mary's gunfire toward Sonny's. Screams and the scent of burning meat whirled through the air with the snow.

Those intruders who were able to returned fire blindly. Mary shot her last Dragon's Breath shell. White hot sparks danced on the ice, and another invader burst into flames. Sonny let that bastard burn alive, instead zeroing in on soldiers who could still charge a weapon and pull a trigger.

In less than twenty seconds, it was over.

LuAnna yelled, "Reload!"

Rather than moving straight across the ice into the open from their cover, Reverend Mosby, LuAnna, and Sonny shifted to their right through narrow frozen streamlets, some only as wide as their boots. They were going to sweep up anybody who had gained cover, but who lay in wait instead of retreating.

Ahead of LuAnna, Sonny called, "Got one here." When LuAnna reached his position, she saw the operator she had struck in the leg. He had dragged himself into the reeds, but could go no farther. Sonny was standing on the man's gun.

The stricken operator's eyes were open. LuAnna stripped off his black balaclava. He was White, looked to be in his thirties, a mix of anger and fear vying for position on his pockmarked face.

LuAnna was matter of fact. "What've you got to say for yourself? Leg looks pretty bad. You're bleeding. Reckon you're bleeding out."

She gave the man's injured thigh a firm nudge with the toe of her boot.

The wounded man hissed "Fuck you!" through gritted teeth.

LuAnna didn't flinch. "Purty talk. Tell me who you are. We've got QuikClot, trauma dressings, pain killers. Might could save your miserable life."

"You're dead. You're all dead! Nothing's going to save you," the soldier raged, though his conviction was ebbing as fast as his lifeblood.

LuAnna ratcheted a shell into her shotgun's chamber, and jammed the gun barrel up under the fallen man's ballistic vest. Sonny stepped back.

LuAnna cocked an eyebrow. *Last chance.*

The fighter spat at her. She pulled the trigger. The soldier convulsed, and blood belched from his mouth.

Sonny said, "You weren't really going to sew him up if he talked."

"We've been friends too long for me to lie to you," said LuAnna. "Of course not."

Reverend Mosby called from the pond. "You are not going to believe this. Look who's here."

LuAnna and Sonny joined the reverend next to another soldier who lay on his side curled into a fetal ball.

Reverend Mosby struck the man in the ear with his shotgun butt. "Hey! You best speak your name, or it's going to be one loud *bang*. *Whimper* ain't on the menu."

The man slowly uncurled and looked up at his captors.

LuAnna was surprised. "Lordy go to fire. Bonamy Screed. Is that you come back to say hello?"

Mary joined the party, kicking and nudging the two smoldering victims of her hellish shotgun loads along the way. "Look smart everybody. Two out of six got away. LuAnna, you got any more of those fireworks? I may never go back to double-ought—" Mary stared and said, "What in the name of our dear Lord Jesus H. Christ is *he* doing here?"

"Language," scolded the reverend.

LuAnna said, "Reckon I'm not sure, Mary, but we're going to find out."

"Best hurry up," said Mary. "Those human tiki torches layin' over there got grenades that still might cook off."

In the bloody gloom of LuAnna's red-lensed penlight, Screed's face was a rictus of terror.

Sonny muttered, "Been meaning to return Ben's bolt cutters."

At that, Bonamy Screed fainted dead away.

"Oh no," said Mary as she slumped against her husband.

Sonny said, "Easy there, Honeygirl. He'll come around."

"Not him I'm worried for," Mary said, her words slurred. "I think they winged me." She touched her left shoulder and pulled blood-stained fingers away. "So much excitement. Shit. Reckon this is me going into shock—"

Sonny got both hands on her before she slipped to the ice.

CHAPTER 57

KNOCKER ELLIS HOGAN cursed himself roundly for a few
moments before he quit his position at the Misty Shoal Lighthouse for the
barren icy wastes. He had witnessed Blackshaw's takedown, unable because
of the proximity of the liquid natural gas tank domes to fire even a single
killing shot. The sentry he had notched up before had been out in the open
on the catwalk, almost midway between two tanks; it had been a clean kill,
with less possible brisant collateral damage.

Ellis stalked in toward *Penelope* on his snow shoes with little idea of what
he would do once he reached the ship. The mission objective was uncertain.
Would he be avenging Blackshaw's death and recovering his remains? Jesus,
LuAnna would kill him a hundred times over if he didn't die in the effort.
Perhaps it would be a rescue after all, but Ellis was not an optimist.

He trudged to the tanker amidships, port side, craning his neck up to
the deck and superstructure levels in case he could glimpse a sentry through
the weather. He had not been spotted by anyone so far as he knew, but guards
could be lying in wait for him anywhere. For the moment, it seemed the
Arctic weather was good for keeping hostile heads down, and maybe even
below decks. It could be that these pirates were lapsing into dangerous
indolence as their mission dragged on, but Ellis was not counting on this. It
was more likely that Blackshaw's capture as well as significant losses had
prompted a spike in the enemy's vigilance.

Ellis hugged the port side, and advanced toward the bow as Blackshaw
had done just over ninety minutes before. Where the hull began curving to

the right toward the bow, he found the body of the sentry Blackshaw had killed. Blood had pooled and frozen on the ice revealing how Blackshaw had dispatched the hapless operator. Even if Blackshaw hadn't wielded his knife to lethal effect, the crazy angle of the spine told Ellis the operator's neck had snapped on impact. Blackshaw was nothing if not thorough. Usually. Ellis wondered how his friend had let the decoy sentry fixate his attention to the point that he'd forgotten to check his six. Ellis should have seen them, too. Should have dealt with them to protect his friend.

Ellis stuffed his beloved CheyTac rifle into the snow drifting by the ship's hull. He then rigged his own set of mountaineering ascenders to Blackshaw's ropes which he found billowing in the wind. With his Model 1216 shotgun secured on his back, he began the long climb up toward a hell he could not foresee.

CHAPTER 58

REVEREND MOSBY PRODDED Bonamy Screed forward with his shotgun across the frozen Big Thorofare between Goat Island and the hamlet of Ewell on Smith Island. Sonny followed supporting his wife who was walking as if exhausted. An application of hemostatic QuikClot and a trauma dressing were hard-pressed to staunch the wound. Mary had a Warfarin prescription that made her a bleeder even with minor household injuries. The groove of flesh the stray bullet had taken out of her deltoid still seeped. They would be able to do more for her with needle and suture once they were all indoors.

LuAnna brought up the rear, watching their backs for the two operators still at large, and keeping an eye out for any bereft nanny-goats wishing to avenge Beelzebub's murder.

Bonamy Screed whined, "My hands are infected. They never healed."

"We'll do better next time," LuAnna promised.

Reverend Mosby jabbed the captive in a kidney to encourage forward motion. Screed yelped and tried to hop out of Mosby's reach, but the elderly preacher kept up without missing a step.

By the time they gained the middle of the Big Thorofare, LuAnna was walking backwards, scanning the shoreline of Goat Island. A lighter band of precipitation was passing overhead now, and the visibility was better.

"See anything back there?" asked Sonny.

"It moves, it dies," LuAnna assured. "You keep watch ahead in case those fonnyboys got in front of us."

"Somebody got ahead of us," said Reverend Mosby. "Whose Jeep is that at the top of the boat ramp?"

CHAPTER 59

CHOAD LAGLEET MARVELED that this simple interdiction could go so completely sideways. The snatch and grab in Santander had gone smooth as silk, with acceptable casualties. The exfil to France by boat, and thence to Delaware, was a well-planned, perfectly executed operation where all moving parts meshed and hummed like a sewing machine. Faction was on the ball as ever.

But beginning with that snakebit helicopter ride, the crash, and the attrition of personnel, these were so uncharacteristic of both Faction and his own near-perfect record that his bewilderment bordered on denial.

LaGleet spoke to Krill as if she had been party to his thoughts for the last ten minutes' march through the storm-thrashed marsh. "Anybody could see Screed wasn't up to the task. When those bastards clipped his trigger fingers, it was like they nipped his nuts in the bargain."

Krill was limping behind LaGleet as he charged off aimlessly ranting like a mad Bible prophet in a snowy wilderness. His moving map tablet had a hole in it from a shotgun slug, and dead reckoning blind in the bad weather was going to be a problem. Krill was fairly certain she had at least one, and possibly three pieces of double-aught shot deep in the bones of her right ankle. Her boot squished with blood at every step. To keep pace with LaGleet, all she'd had time to do was tighten her bootlace until the leather was hard as a splint. She tried not to wince at every step. LaGleet was lethally intolerant of malingering slowpokes.

"Say Boss, maybe we should cut over toward those lights," said Krill. She broke a Fentanyl lollipop out of her IFAK and jammed it in her mouth hoping for some relief from the agony throbbing up her leg.

LaGleet adjusted his course toward the lights of what must have been a small village, but he kept ranting. "Who smashes up a helicopter on a ten-mile hop?"

"The weather—"

"Don't give me bullshit about weather! That bird was tricked out with more nav' gear than Air Force One, and still we lost half our crew. You're lucky to be alive!"

"A-firm." Krill was unsure if her current straits represented any kind of good fortune. She knew, even if LaGleet forgot, that he had executed as many stragglers and wounded as the crash had killed outright. She slurped harder on the lollipop, and an opioid warmth spread through her limbs, wrapping her mind in soothing lamb's wool. The ankle still hurt like fuck, but she didn't seem to care as much.

"You think Screed bought it back there?" LaGleet asked.

"If he's lucky."

"True. As a hostage, he's kinda pre-owned," said LaGleet.

They trudged on through the frozen marsh toward the street lights of the distant hamlet.

"He knows about Faction," said Krill.

LaGleet stopped so abruptly that Krill nearly walked into him. Her eyes were twitching left and right for menacing ungulates.

"He's always known about Faction," said LaGleet. "Faction signs his paycheck. And mine. And yours."

Krill said, "But Screed knows there's an op' in motion *now*."

A thoughtful LaGleet removed the Fentanyl lollipop from Krill's mouth, stuck it into his own, and began sucking it absently. "You're right. Even if he doesn't talk, Screed being back in-theatre means he's part of something going down."

Krill looked with longing at the lollipop stick poking from LaGleet's lips. She said, "Do you think they'll figure his part in it even if he doesn't talk?"

"To bird-dog and kill Blackshaw? They'd never think he was capable. He presents as a weak sister." After a moment, LaGleet continued, "But he has local knowledge. He ran that last op that went tits-up at the Russian retreat up the road in Centreville. Maybe these Island Yahoos will buy the local knowledge angle."

"If he doesn't blow the mission outright," said Krill.

"He was compartmentalized. He's not going to tell them he's in town to take in the sights, eat some oysters, and kill Blackshaw. He's not a total idiot. Is he?"

In answer, Krill said, "So now we've got to kill Blackshaw and Screed."

LaGleet was thinking of the final phase of the Doc's S-FOP jump juice, and how Screed's customized cocktail would likely put him down—here LaGleet checked his watch—in less than fifty hours.

All he said was, "No, don't you worry. Ultimately, Screed's not going to be a problem. Blackshaw remains the target. Maybe the crash and the dust-up at that pond will work for us. We're the chaff and flares to keep the rubes focused on us instead of where the real action is."

"They put up a lot of resistance," said Krill. "It's just you and me, Boss."

"We'll reconnoiter and do whatever needs to be done," blustered LaGleet. He took the Fentanyl lollipop out of his mouth and jammed it so hard into Krill's it clicked off her teeth and made her gag. "Just you wait and see, Pussycat."

CHAPTER 60

BLACKSHAW HAD DOZED in the makeshift brig deep inside *Penelope*'s lower decks. His infiltration had been exhausting, but as a SEAL he could utilize rest like a rifle or any other vital matériel.

He heard bootsteps coming down the companionway. The guard threw open the door.

Grodin told the guard, "Take a break, Munson."

The other man said, "How long—"

"A break!" snapped Grodin.

Yes, Blackshaw felt certain that morale and unit cohesion among the pirates were suffering.

After Munson's bootfalls retreated down the companionway, Grodin squatted and lit another cigarette. He took two puffs. Then he took a third before he said, "I got a problem with you."

"Not a big problem, though, am I right?"

Grodin ignored Blackshaw's remark. "You haven't asked what's going on."

Blackshaw waited a full thirty count before saying anything. Grodin covered his increasing discomfort pulling deeply on the cigarette. Blackshaw observed that Grodin left the paper on the end wet with saliva, and had to tongue a small sprig of tobacco forward in his mouth to spit it out. The unfiltered affectation wasn't working for Grodin.

Blackshaw finally said, "You don't care if I've seen your faces. You've said the charges are all armed again. So I have a fair idea what's to happen to me, and how."

Grodin narrowed his eyes. "But you haven't asked *why*."

Blackshaw said, "Wow. So we're at that part of the movie where you're a hundred percent certain you've got me dead to rights, and you go on and on about your cause, or your pain, or your cleverness until I get so bored I wish you'd shut up and get it over with. I could do with some water."

"Good to know," said Grodin.

Blackshaw had slapped at Grodin, then given him a way to save face through refusing a simple request. He went on, "You're holding a ship full of LNG ransom. If the ransom's not paid, you destroy the cargo and ship."

Believing this was Blackshaw's genuine assessment, Grodin got comfortable, dropped his ass on the deck, with his legs straight, boot soles toward his prisoner in a way that the people of many traditional cultures would find offensive. He settled back against the bulkhead.

Blackshaw said, "How does it feel to be running Plan B?"

Grodin was robbed of speech.

Blackshaw went on. "You know the ship and the cargo are insured. The owner might just let you do your worst, blow it all up. They'd suffer a few weeks or months of bad press for the pollution, and they'd have trouble hiring a crew that believes the company is looking out for them, maybe they have to hire security details for their ships to boost confidence—"

Grodin looked impatient, made the cigarette ember glow bright orange with a deep, nervous drag.

Blackshaw continued. "This isn't a cargo ransom, or you wouldn't have murdered the crew. You're eco-terrorists trying to use this ship to destroy a natural resource for Big Pharma, so they can corner the market with their much more expensive synthetic product. But the ice has locked you out of position. You're still too far south of your target."

"What?" Grodin squirmed. Suddenly he didn't want to be sitting flat on his ass at eye level with Blackshaw, but he didn't want to twitch a muscle and show Blackshaw was right.

"You're Plan B, Grodin. Second string. Junior varsity. You think you've got the only transmitter to trigger those demolition charges? Your bosses at

Faction are really controlling when the fireworks go off, and believe me, they'll be sipping their whisky at a safe distance when they press the button. You're in play only if Faction can't blow the real target: the Conowingo Dam. Tons of silt behind that dam would do the job. But like I said, thanks to the ice, you're stuck. So I guess you're not even Plan B after all. You're a loose end."

Blackshaw had a millisecond; Grodin would be shocked that his mission was exposed and so trivial. A millisecond later, maybe he'd realize he was about to die.

His ankles and wrists still zip-tied, Blackshaw pivoted onto his feet, grabbed Grodin's boots, stood to his full height, and deadlifted the shorter man straight up. Grodin flailed, reaching for the pistol in his belt holster instead of protecting his neck. Blackshaw slammed Grodin's head into the deck like a pile driver. Grodin went limp. Blackshaw dropped him in a heap. Raising his wrists high again, he brought his elbows down fast past his flanks. The wrist tie bit into his flesh for a painful instant before it snapped. He grabbed Grodin's knife and slashed through the ankle tie. He gave a barefoot finishing stomp on Grodin's throat.

Blackshaw was now loose on a ship full of armed men, but he had Grodin's pistol and knife in hand. Bootfalls echoed down the companionway. Munson was coming back. Blackshaw dragged Grodin's corpse into the utility compartment, closed the door, and sprinted silently away.

CHAPTER 61

MARY WRIGHT'S HEAD swam on the verge of shock. Her thoughts weren't coming together with any kind of ease. Might be the crashing adrenaline after the gunfight. Might be the long exposure to the cold. Might be the gunshot wound in her shoulder. She was tough. She had birthed two of her four children on Smith Island before she'd even heard about the marvels of epidural pain management. She could feel that Sonny as much carried as led her through the door into Ruke's Café and Mortuary.

Inside, through the wash of warmth and sudden quiet away from the gale, she was baffled to see Reverend Mosby as still as a stone, the muzzle of his Remington hovering behind Screed's left kidney. There was a woman poised among the corpse-topped tables. And damn if she didn't have a pistol, too. Damn if it wasn't pointed at Reverend Mosby. Had one of those poor cadavers resurrected?

The spectral woman barked, "FBI! Freeze!"

"I'm froze clean through already, Honeygirl," slurred Mary.

Sonny said, "Reckon I know who you are," as he ignored the order and helped Mary to a chair.

LuAnna backed into the space, her shotgun aimed out the door; she was still wary of the operators who had escaped the ambush. With Reverend Mosby leading the way into the café, she'd given little thought to hostiles getting the drop on them there. She should have. Someone had driven that Jeep across the ice to Smith Island from the mainland.

The stranger with the pistol said, "Special Agent Molly Wilde. Put your weapons on the floor!"

LuAnna turned, squinted at Wilde and said, "You might clip a couple of us, Molly, but if you don't drop yours, you'll learn the hard way there's a table with your name on it. How's your little baby girl?"

Pretty much none of this made sense to Mary Wright.

CHAPTER 62

KNOCKER ELLIS CREPT aft on *Penelope* at the deck level. Things hadn't worked out so well for Blackshaw up on the catwalk. If the storm weren't enough, there was more cover on deck than there would be if he were exposed on the high walkway.

By the time he reached the aft superstructure topped by *Penelope*'s bridge, Ellis had seen no one. Not surprising. The ship's exterior lights were still completely blacked out.

The CCTV camera lens angled toward the door into the superstructure was encased in ice. No reason for Ellis to say *cheese*. There were two levers dogging the heavy steel door shut. Ellis slung the shotgun onto his back. It took both hands to dislodge the rime ice welding the dogs in position. He pulled on the door. It opened slowly, with shards of ice cracking and falling to the deck. He could imagine there was a security panel somewhere indicating the door was open. With the cameras blinded by ice, Ellis wondered if anyone was still on duty watching the security warnings. He hoped there was. It would save him time.

Finally, he was below deck in the sudden warmth and light. Ellis drew the door closed behind him and refastened the dogs. The quiet hum and distant throb of machinery was a stark contrast to the roaring storm. Next step, get to know anyone investigating the Door Open signal.

CHAPTER 63

MOLLY WILDE NOTED an earnest gleam in LuAnna's eye as more and more gun-toting Smith Islanders pushed inside Ruke's from the storm. Wilde's eyes widened when she saw Bonamy Screed stumble through the door.

"Director Screed," said Wilde. "We've been wondering where you were."

Screed begged, "Special Agent Wilde, you've got to save me from these animals! Arrest them! They're—"

Screed was cut short with a blow to the head from the butt of Reverend Mosby's shotgun. Screed folded to the floor in a heap.

Reassessing the odds, Wilde slowly rested her pistol on the nearest table without a cadaver. "Ella Grace is fine, thanks for asking. How's your son doing?"

"He's a biter," answered LuAnna grimly.

With sympathetic pangs in her bra, Wilde understood what LuAnna meant.

LuAnna said, "We have coffee. And Sonny here knocks together a mean burger if you're staying. But I don't think you should stay."

Wilde looked around the room at the bodies. "*Yes* to coffee. But *God no* on the burger. Thanks."

Sonny hid his disappointment, and continued gently peeling his wife out of her coat so he could better dress her wound.

"How was traffic?" LuAnna asked.

"Light," said Wilde. "Someone took a shot at me."

"Warn't none of us," said Mary. "Least-wise, not this time."

"Mary's hurt," said LuAnna. "Shocky. Doesn't know what she's saying."

Wilde lifted a life jacket that had been removed from a cadaver. The jacket was marked *Penelope*. "I was driving close by this very same ship when it happened. The gunshot. The top on my Jeep is brand new, and now there're two holes in it. What happened to these people?"

"Lead poisoning," said LuAnna. "What do you know about this, Molly? When you called, you said trouble might be coming our way. Was this what you meant?"

"Did I hear shooting a little while back?" Wilde countered. "When I drove in, it looked like there was a fire dying down off to the north. A big fire."

"You first," LuAnna insisted.

"I don't know anything more than when I called you. Except a large portion of the crew of that tanker are laid out here like the Blue Plate Special."

"More like catch of the day," said Mary. Nobody laughed. A gust of wind hurtled around the shuddering old building like a passing freight train.

LuAnna pressed Wilde, "So you don't know anything. But you haven't told us everything. Why'd you drive here from all the way across the Chesapeake? Bucket list? Just to keep us all in the dark a while longer? There's no percentage in that, Molly. You're wasting time we don't have."

Wilde considered for a moment how much to divulge. "Something's happening on that ship. It seems like a crew swap. Whatever the operation is, it kicked off about the time the bay froze."

Reverend Mosby said, "For once, the Chesapeake weather seems on our side, slowing up the big show."

LuAnna said to Wilde, "I can confirm the timeline. The bodies drifted within a mile of here before the bay froze. Are you thinking pirates were taking the ship and got locked in by the ice?"

Wilde said, "Then why are they keeping the low profile?"

"Except for shooting at you," said Sonny, finishing Mary's bandage.

"No ransom?" LuAnna asked.

"Not so far," said Wilde. "And usually ransom for the crew is part of the demand. Not just for the ship and cargo."

"What about ecoterrorism?" asked LuAnna. "Fouling the Chesapeake."

"Destroying the ship? What are they waiting for?" said Wilde. "As you put it, where's the percentage in that?"

"Tell her, LuAnna," said Reverend Mosby.

"Tell me what?"

LuAnna picked up the microscope slide with the blue sample. "What do you know about horseshoe crabs?"

Wilde answered honestly. "Kinda gross looking. Like a spider hiding under a Dough Boy's helmet."

"That's them to a T," said Mary.

LuAnna moved to the snow angel they had discovered first. "She had this slide sewn into her apron."

Wilde took the slide and turned it in the glare of Sonny's work light. "Blue?"

"That's horseshoe crab blood," said LuAnna.

"You think this woman was a mole," said Wilde.

"But she got killed along with the rest of the crew."

"Sounds like some deep cover," said Wilde. "Maybe a journalist."

"Oh? Not a spook?" asked LuAnna. "She had some papers on her, too, but they got so wet and stuck together. We've been trying to dry it out without turning it into a rock."

LuAnna picked at the folded papers. They were drier now, and with care, and with Wilde looking on, she slowly peeled them apart. "The ink or toner's run something bad from the water."

Reverend Mosby peered over Wilde's shoulder. "I can see L-A-L. What's that?"

"Lordy go to fire!" said Sonny looking up from his phone. "Sixty grand a gallon is what it is."

"What are you talking about?" Reverend Mosby looked at Sonny's phone.

"Limulus Amebocyte Lysate. Says here they check drug purity with the stuff," said Sonny. "They bleed the crabs, and make the LAL from it, and check vaccines and hospital equipment for e. coli and such like. They throw the crabs back after they bleed them, all humane-like, but a third of them die.

And the ones they throw back are sickly. They might-could-be running out of crabs to make the LAL stuff."

LuAnna mused, "Somebody wants to blow up an LNG ship and wreck the whole Chesapeake to protest animal cruelty? That's drastic. And backwards. You usually don't try to kill the critter you're trying to save."

"Terrorists do it all the time, killing people to make a statement, all in the name of making life for Humankind better," said Molly Wilde.

Reverend Mosby took the phone from Sonny, and said, "Don't worry about your flu shot, or pandemic vaccines. They're working on a synthetic version, but it's even more expensive than the crab stuff."

"That's it," said Wilde. "That's where the money is in all this."

LuAnna got the picture. "Kill off the crabs quicker, and the synthetic LAL starts looking pretty good at whatever the price. But there're horseshoe crabs here and there on the east coast, even the southern coast in the Gulf. One tanker going off here isn't going to kill them all."

Wilde said, "You don't have to kill all of them. All you need is to contaminate or destroy a productive horseshoe crab breeding ground, severely pinch the harvest, and you reach a tipping point where production of the synthetic alternative can be scaled up enough to make sense financially. It's a big play. Very big."

"Who stands to gain?" asked Sonny.

Wilde said, "I've got an idea about that."

"Care to share?" asked LuAnna.

"Gee I don't know girlfriend. It's so classified," said Wilde.

"Look around you, Molly. Corpses for days. Your former boss here on the floor. We're involved. Fill us in on the rest. You owe us that."

"Maybe," said Wilde, hedging. "The immediate problem is who's been sent into the field to pull this operation off."

LuAnna kicked the inert Screed. "Your own people, that's who. I know it's a hard swallow, Molly, but we're on your side. You're looking at the good guys."

The sound of Wilde's Jeep roaring to life outside made everyone snap into action. Molly snatched up her weapon and dashed for the door. LuAnna, who grabbed her shotgun on the way, was first outside. Together, they watched the tail lights of the Jeep race down the boat ramp, slew a wide left turn, and race west across the ice into the night blizzard.

"Shit! Who the hell is that?" shouted Wilde in the wind.

"I have an idea, but it's classified," said LuAnna. "Care to trade intel? For real this time."

"We should interrogate Screed," said Wilde.

"I've got bolt cutters," said Sonny.

"Sweet Jesus," said Wilde.

LuAnna said, "I've got me a Presidential pardon, Molly. Relax."

"Not that." Molly picked something up from a tire track. A crushed mobile phone held together only by its ballistic case. "Must've fallen out of my pocket when I got out. Got a phone I can borrow?"

"Plenty, but the Verizon tower blew down this afternoon," said LuAnna.

"How'd your friend search that LAL, then?"

"We've jerry built a work-around. Kind of off the books. It's a patchy satellite uplink, but it gets the job done. What do you have in mind?"

CHAPTER 64

KRILL WASN'T SURE how much farther she could patrol through this frozen stormy waste with LaGleet. Usually a gung-ho soldier, she could no longer predict what shape she'd be in when time came for a fight. Her fentanyl lollipop was having a weird interaction with Doc's S-FOP Keep-Em-Shooting IV cocktail from the plane. She kept glimpsing yellow-fanged goats with leathery bat wings out of the corners of her eyes, but when she turned to focus, she saw only darkness and weather. Though her energy level was nominal, and every step on her perforated ankle was a manageable throb with a crepitus scraping grind of bone on bone, it was Krill's mind that verged on freaking out.

She kept on, picking up and putting down, step by step. LaGleet was bent low as he stalked forward, peering ahead from time to time to make sure they were still on course for the nearest town on Smith Island.

"Hold up here," said LaGleet finally, with his fist upheld in the signal to stop. Krill gratefully sank to her knee, her weapon raised and angled forward across what appeared to be a frozen river. Beyond the featureless white ribbon, she could make out a few scattered lights in windows. Around the lights, her mind filled in the one- and two-story houses of the little village of Ewell which the darkness and howling weather concealed.

LaGleet went on, "That ice is open ground. Twenty meters. No cover."

"You think they've set out pickets?"

"Only one way to know," said LaGleet. "Move out, soldier. Signal if the coast is clear."

Krill grumbled inside, and stepped forward down the bank, and onto the ice. She could feel her shoulders rising as she braced herself to take a bullet fired from the opposite shore. Her rifle plate would protect her vitals, but that left a lot of vulnerable flesh, including her head. Crossing the ice took forever. She glanced over her shoulder and saw a Morse Code of bloody dots and dashes from her ankle trailing back toward LaGleet's position among the cattails. Tightening her bootlaces hadn't compressed the wound enough after all.

To Krill's surprise, she arrived at the bottom of a boat ramp without a shot fired. She ascended the slippery ramp, and found a Jeep tricked out with a bar of extra lights attached to the front bumper. A seductive warmth radiated from the engine compartment. She nestled in close to the heat. Double-checking, she noted boot tracks and tire ruts in the sheltered snow of the boat ramp. Someone had driven on the ice. *Ballsy*, she thought.

She drew out a small penlight with a red lens, and shined it three times toward LaGleet across the ice. He dashed down the bank, missed his footing, and slid ten feet facedown across the ice. He stood, brushed off the snow, and made a spectacle of himself zig-zagging to Krill's spot next to the Jeep.

"See? No sentries. Amateurs," LaGleet declared. "What've you got?"

"There's a building six meters that way," said Krill, pointing. "Lights in the windows, but they're covered on the inside. Looks like an old store or something. Not a house. There's a museum across the street. A church across the way there. I could establish a firing position up in the steeple."

"Did you peek in these windows?"

"Negative."

LaGleet frowned at Krill before he sprinted low to the side of the ramshackle building. He had to peer through several windows before he found one where the makeshift drape hung off to one side enough to let him see within. His eyes were wide and riveted for several moments. Then he pelted back to Krill, and slid to a stop beside her with a look of horror on his face.

"It's a slaughterhouse!" said LaGleet. "Corpses all over the damn place. They're mass murderers."

"Is Blackshaw in there?" For Krill, only Blackshaw's elimination would signal the end of this mission—and the prospect of medical care for her ankle.

"Naw. A couple geezers, a few frails. And Screed. They got him! Christ, no wonder these Yahoos spooked him so bad."

Krill took this in. "Is he talking?"

"Out cold." LaGleet glanced at his watch and calculated, "He's been AWOL fifty minutes since that firefight, at least. Figure most of that was in transit getting him back here. He could've been singing like a little bitch this whole time, or lying there on the floor like a lox. Krill, it's time for our secondary objective. We need transport."

"Keys are in this Jeep. Tire tracks lead down the ramp onto the ice," said Krill. "It might hold."

In an instant, LaGleet leapt behind the wheel and fired up the engine. Krill made an excruciating scramble on her shattered ankle around the front, and hurled her pack and weapon in through the passenger door. LaGleet threw the Jeep in gear, stomped the gas, and spun the tires carving a tight one-eighty, nearly ejecting Krill out into the snow before she could get a grip on the *oh-shit* handle on the dashboard.

CHAPTER 65

FBI EXECUTIVE ASSISTANT Director for Counterterrorism and Counterintelligence, Pershing Lowry, couldn't get through to his wife. This was a common complaint of husbands the world over, but Lowry and Molly Wilde had clear, open, affectionate lines of communication. They worked hard together to straighten out the ordinary misunderstandings of matrimony and new parenthood. Disagreements at work were more strenuous, because they each came at the question of what constituted the greater good for bureau and country from different perspectives. Tonight, Lowry couldn't get his wife to pick up her cell phone. After dialing her many times, he left a single dignified yet urgent message to get in touch with him as soon as possible. His discovery that Wilde was gone from their bed, and that her Jeep was gone from the garage had prompted the calls. Now he went to the kitchen.

Lowry's mother-in-law, Patience, was warming a bottle of milk for Ella Grace who bobbled close by in a springy baby seat. Lowry picked the baby up, and cuddled her close.

He said, "Everyone seems up early but me. Where's Molly?"

"Out for a drive, I imagine," said Patience.

"At this hour? In this weather? Where did she say she was going? I didn't find a note."

Patience said nothing.

Lowry went on, "She leaves a note if she doesn't speak with me before going out. Or with you."

"You know Molly."

"Yes, I do know her. Her weapon's gone. Her spare mags, too. Patience, what aren't you telling me?"

Ella Grace yawned. Patience took the baby, sat at the kitchen table, and offered her granddaughter the bottle, which was accepted with a slurp.

"Persh' I can't tell you what I don't know," said Patience.

Plausible deniability, thought Lowry. Smart.

Phone in hand, Lowry went into the home office he shared with his wife, and brought up the bureau's cellular phone tracking application. In seconds, he had her phone's location pinpointed on a map display.

"What in God's name—" he muttered.

After a particularly violent case months before in which Wilde had been held hostage, she had grudgingly allowed her Jeep to be fitted with a tracking device. To corroborate what the cellphone locator app was telling him, Lowry opened the tracking software for Wilde's Jeep. What he saw alarmed him even more.

He scrolled down to a phone number among his list of contacts and dialed. FBI Director Sid Hornsby growled into the phone. "What's up, Persh'?"

"I apologize for calling you at this hour," said Lowry.

"I was awake. Get to it."

"Molly—Senior Resident Agent Molly Wilde—"

"You mean your wife. What about her?"

"I'm worried, sir. She left the house in her Jeep sometime in the night."

"It's *still* night."

Lowry said, "True. She didn't tell me, though. She didn't say where she was going. Not even to her mother."

"The weather's crap. You said it was a Jeep, right?"

Lowry didn't want to put his discoveries into words, since this would somehow make them painfully real. He went ahead anyway. "I tracked her cellular phone to Smith Island. In Ewell. One of the towns there."

"Dammit! What's she doing? Did you tell her to go?"

"I think she's following a hunch, sir."

"What did she say when you called her?"

"She hasn't picked up. I made several tries."

Hornsby was quiet for a moment.

Lowry went on, "I also tracked her vehicle."

"Don't tell me," said Hornsby. "It's parked in Crisfield."

"No, sir. Her vehicle was actually on Smith Island as well."

"She drove across the ice? What do you mean, *was?*"

Lowry explained, "The tracker line shows her vehicle crossed the ice to Smith Island from Western Maryland. From a boat ramp in a park. But now it's moving again. It's back on the ice. It's headed straight up the Chesapeake."

Hornsby said, "Her phone, which she's not answering, is separated from her vehicle, which is in motion. And the phone is collocated with a bunch of folks who have a noted history of violence."

"And a history of aiding us in difficult cases," countered Lowry.

"Hold on. Another call coming in."

Lowry waited. Patience, carrying Ella Grace, stepped into to the doorway of the study with worry etched across her face.

Hornsby came back on the line. "Looks like Molly was right. Our acoustic gunshot sensors up and down the Chesapeake are picking up multiple shots around that tanker. *Penelope.*"

"Sir, we need to mobilize," Lowry said.

"Where the hell to?" said Hornsby. "The storm is messing with the detection gear, but there's more gunfire reported just north of Smith Island. The tech says it's like Fallujah out there."

CHAPTER 66

BLACKSHAW SEARCHED FOR the bombs' trigger aboard *Penelope*. The bridge seemed the most likely location. There, or the dead operator's cabin. He was several deck's below the bridge level. He figured senior officers' quarters would be close to the bridge; given the number of bodies laid out on Smith Island, there were ample vacant quarters aboard.

Blackshaw, still barefoot, moved toward the entry to the ship's crew mess. He heard voices, and pausing, made out three distinct men chatting over food. They seemed relaxed, confident that Blackshaw remained neutralized, and that he was no further threat.

To reach the bridge level, he first needed to get to a companionway stair just beyond the entryway to the mess. Then Blackshaw realized he was leaning against the frame of an elevator door. Times had changed. Serving aboard modern civilian shipping was not without its conveniences.

As appealing and direct as this elevator might prove to gaining his objective, Blackshaw didn't want to leave three known enemies to jump him from his backtrail.

He had already checked the load and readiness of his foraged pistol. Now he raised it, and stepped through the door and into the mess.

"Hey assholes. It's time." Blackshaw fired quickly, catching the armed operators mid-meal, with one in the act of biting into a corned beef sandwich. Meat, mustard, and rye bread surrounded the bullet hole in this operator's face, and coated the wall behind him, heavy on the gray matter. Blackshaw caught the next one under the arm as he raised a reflexive hand in defense.

By the time Blackshaw acquired the third man in his sights as he was struggling to rise from the table and clear his pistol. Blackshaw dropped his aim below his enemy's ballistic vest, firing a slug into the pelvis. Two more shots finished the job. Blackshaw foraged the operators' weapons to rearm and reload. He also scavenged the boots of the largest dead man. They were tight even without socks, but they'd do.

As Blackshaw was zipping the second boot, he heard the telltale ding of the elevator arriving on this deck. He bolted out of the mess and covered the single door an instant before it opened.

Inside the compartment, Knocker Ellis Hogan grinned at his friend and said, "Lido Deck. Shuffleboard, Over-50 Singles Mixer."

"Oh," said Blackshaw lowering his harvested MP-5. "Where'd you get to?"

Ellis lost the grin. "Took an overwatch position on the lighthouse away out to port. Notched a fellow up for you. You're welcome."

"Two others still got at me."

Ellis looked hurt. "Jesus Ben, it's a rifle, not a magic wand. They were so close to you, I couldn't be sure of my windage in this storm."

"Now answer the question. *Where'd you get to?*"

"I told you."

Blackshaw said, "You said *where*, sure. I'm really interested in *why*."

Ellis hesitated. "If I'd told you *stay home and look to your family*, would you have done it?"

"No," Blackshaw admitted, to himself as much as to Ellis.

"And maybe if I said that, you'd have thought I was shy of a proper fight," said Ellis.

"Never that."

"I figured if I checked out for a minute, you'd have the good sense to abort the mission on your own, and get back to LuAnna and Cal. You wouldn't be dumb enough to carry on solo. And we could all let the powers that be work this mess out in their own time, in their own way."

"Yet here we are," said Blackshaw. "You clean failed to save me from myself."

"You never were a fan of protocols."

"Less and less," said Blackshaw.

Another enemy operator, a woman with short-cropped red hair and a light step sprang from around the corner at the end of the corridor. She almost managed to say, *Freeze* before Ellis shotgunned her, and Blackshaw took her with a double-tap to her neck and chin. The operator twisted and dropped to the deck.

"Somebody might've heard that. Let's move out. They've got all those LNG tanks wired with demolition charges," said Blackshaw.

"What are we doing here?"

"Trying to find the trigger, reckon."

"We need to disarm the charges," said Ellis.

"After we clear the ship of anybody who might want to *rearm* them."

Ellis said, "Bet you there's more than one trigger. Maybe somebody could set things off from shore."

"That crossed my mind, too. The on-board trigger is likely a timer or cell phone activated," said Blackshaw. "Or it might be that a cell phone is the only way. Or a satellite phone, since cell coverage out here is spotty at best. No timer. Whatever it is, it's got to give these fonnyboys time to get clear."

"Clear how? They'd have to haul ass clear to Virginia to be safe if this boat goes up. No, I bet all these bastards are expendable," said Ellis. "From the beginning, only they didn't know it."

CHAPTER 67

SCREED WOKE TO find the old preacher covering him with a shotgun. His head throbbed from being knocked out. Through the pain, he discerned the woman who'd stitched up his index finger stumps months before in a close chat with Molly Wilde from the FBI. Screed tried to move, but his wrists, elbows, knees, and ankles were trussed to a stout wooden chair. To his horror, a further glance around the space revealed bodies. Dead bodies laid out everywhere. Screed had wakened into a nightmare.

"He's coming to," said the preacher.

Screed braced himself as the stump stitcher broke off her confab with Wilde and crossed over to him with a familiar pair of bolt cutters dangling from one hand.

"Molly!" Screed called. "You can't let her hurt me!"

"This is awkward," said Wilde. "LuAnna's our hostess. And she's got a Presidential pardon for whatever she did to you last time."

LuAnna pulled a chair over, and sat in front of Screed, with the bolt cutters across her lap. She said, "If you come back and stay here one more night, the next night's free."

"Stay the fuck away from me!" said Screed, with an embarrassing squeak in his voice.

"Language," said the preacher, aiming his shotgun at Screed's midsection.

"I'm surprised to see you again," said LuAnna.

"Jesus Christ, you think I want to be here?"

Wilde said, "You were in Spain, last I heard. Why'd you come back?"

"Fuck you!"

The preacher reversed his shotgun, and snapped the butt down quick and hard on Screed's injured hands, and said, "I won't tell you again."

Screed howled. The blow resurrected breakthrough pain that even the Doc's magic formula couldn't hold at bay.

"Who brought you back here?" LuAnna asked. "You're a long half step from useful in the field. Anybody can see that."

Screed wasn't sure he'd be able to take another hit and remain conscious. He said, "They wanted me to identify Ben Blackshaw."

"And put his lights out?" asked LuAnna, fingering the bolt cutters.

"Long overdue," said Screed. LuAnna swung the bolt cutters double handed. The heavy parrot beak of the tool bit into Screed's scalp, cutting a bloody runnel.

Wilde asked, "Why bother coming after Blackshaw? Your operation is on that tanker."

"What tanker?" Screed was baffled.

"You're looking at her crew all stretched out here," said LuAnna. "Finding these bodies, that's what set Ben going. None of us would've known Friday from Sunday if these poor folks had stayed aboard, alive or dead. Tossing them in the bay tipped your hand."

"I don't know a damn thing about any of that," said Screed. "My brief was Blackshaw, beginning, middle, and end. All I know is Faction didn't want him interfering with an op. They wanted him off the board."

Wilde looked Screed in the eye, and said, "Would've been luckier for you if you'd found Blackshaw. Instead, you found his wife. Poor bastard."

To Screed's horror, LuAnna Blackshaw drew a pistol and jammed the barrel hard against his forehead.

CHAPTER 68

BLACKSHAW ASKED ELLIS, "How was the weather when you came aboard?"

"Blowing like hell, but out of the south now."

Ellis opened the first in a row of utility closets in the next deck above the crew mess. Blackshaw turned on the interior light.

"Now we know how they got aboard, if there was any doubt," said Ellis as he poked the barrel of his weapon into deep silky sheaves of olive drab colored Terylene, and coils of nylon shrouds and parachute containers.

"The whole lot inserted via HALO jump," said Blackshaw.

Ellis opened the next utility closet and stepped back. "Here's somebody they didn't put over the side."

Blackshaw took a knee in front of a corpse jammed into the space, and read the nametag. "Varna. Captain of a ghost ship."

"Fresh. Why didn't they kill him weeks ago?" Ellis asked.

"Needed him to verify comms? Especially when the freeze stretched the mission."

"Or he was an insider, part of the plot," said Ellis. "And he had a little falling out with the new guys, captain to captain."

"These fonnyboys are a bunch of strapped-on hot-heads. Blackwater type contractors," said Blackshaw. "Wouldn't surprise me if they're fidgety waiting around."

"We've greased seven at least. Can't be too many more," Ellis said.

"Let's watch our step. Whoever's left knows were here."

They closed the utility closet doors, about to clear the next flight of stairs to the deck above.

An M67 fragmentation grenade clattered down the steps toward them, spinning and rolling along the deck, coming to a stop at their feet.

CHAPTER 69

THE ENGINE SPUTTERED, balked, and died. LaGleet dropped his hands from the steering wheel into his lap as the Jeep coasted to a stop, and said, "Well here's a howdy-do."

Krill pinched at the touchscreen of the navigation app on her phone, expanding the area the map displayed. "We're still hours out from the target. Maybe we should cut left to the tanker."

They had been driving north across the frozen Chesapeake, often at a dangerous clip risking damage to the Jeep or even drowning in an icy fissure. Sometimes their progress had to slow so LaGleet could negotiate his way around ice rucked high, one giant plate on top of the next.

Taking advantage of the stillness, Krill unlaced the boot on her injured ankle. Her sock was drenched in blood down to her toes. Pulling the sock back, she found a single piece of double-aught shot just below the skin. She drew her knife and levered the lead ball out into her hand. Then she packed the wound with a hemostatic BloodSTOP dressing. For a moment she wished the active ingredient was still old-school zeolite, which became very hot as it worked. Anything for more warmth at this point, even a second degree burn from a dressing.

"You want to walk to the tanker, Krill? We're out of gas."

Krill laced her boot tight again. "Yes sir, we're out of gas in the tank. There's a five-gallon jerry can hanging off the back."

"Good eye," said LaGleet. "If it's full, we can make it to the objective."

"Okay, but if it's full, it's north of forty pounds, sir," observed Krill as she wiped her blood from her hands on a silk scarf she found in the glove box. "Kinda heavy on this ankle."

LaGleet stared at Krill for a second, before he said, "So only pour a gallon at a time. Hurry the fuck up about it."

CHAPTER 70

THE GRENADE SPUN in place on the deck like a deadly top. Ellis opened the dead captain's metal utility closet door with one hand, grabbed Blackshaw with the other hand, and kicked the M67 down the corridor. The instant Ellis yanked the door closed, the grenade went off with an earsplitting *crack*.

Ellis put a finger to his lips to make sure Blackshaw didn't speak. Blackshaw nodded, understanding. They waited in absolute stillness. Whoever had thrown the grenade down the stairway had certainly not been peeking from cover to watch the result, or he would have caught a face full of shrapnel. Now the operator would want to verify that he had put Blackshaw and Ellis down. They heard a single quiet step on the stair above.

Whether it was decomposition or digestive gasses, they would never know. The tuba sound of flatulence and corrosive odor led to the unpleasant realization that in the confined closet space, they were both standing on the dead captain's torso; their combined weight was exerting considerable pressure. That pressure was now being relieved. The stench rivaled that of a wet dog rolling in Limburger cheese.

The metal door of the closet might have stopped a .22 magnum fired at an oblique angle, but it would barely slow higher caliber rounds shot straight at the door. The attacker, still on the nearby stairway, fired a pistol at the closet door, digging deep grooves in the metal, striking the knob, shattering the latch mechanism. By reflex, Blackshaw and Ellis crouched to become the smallest targets. That meant stooping deeper into the dead man's eyewatering reek. Blackshaw lost his footing, and rolled against the door which burst open. He sprawled out into the grenade smoke onto the corridor deck.

The operator, a tall Black man with a thick beard, froze in surprise on the stair for a moment, made sloppy, hurried aim, and pulled the trigger. The bullet slapped into the deck by Blackshaw's knee, and shattered. The spent casing pinged off the wall. The operator's pistol slide remained open, the magazine and chamber empty of anything but smoke. He fumbled for a fresh change of magazines. Ellis stepped into the corridor, his shotgun raised, and cut the operator down.

Blackshaw confiscated the dead man's coat. Blackshaw also grabbed the fallen man's mobile phone and examined it, looking for a number that might connect to the trigger mechanisms on the explosive charges.

As Ellis rotated a new magazine tube of shells into place in front of the shotgun's receiver, he said, "I can't wait to clear this scow and freeze to death outside."

CHAPTER 71

"WHAT THE HELL happened?" LuAnna asked in amazement. "I didn't even shoot him."

"That whack on his noggin was barely a tap," said Reverend Mosby.

Both Wilde and LuAnna stared down at the inert form of Bonamy Screed sagging against his bonds in the chair.

Wilde said, "It looked like he had trouble breathing, then all of a sudden, he shook like he seized."

LuAnna felt Screed's throat for a pulse. "I got nothing. This joker's dead."

"He can join the club," said Wilde.

Her pistol still loose in her hand, LuAnna asked, "This isn't going to be a problem, is it Molly?"

Wilde caught LuAnna's drift and wisely said, "You were interrogating a prisoner for critical, emergent intel under my supervision. Your interview techniques were well within bureau parameters. An unknown underlying medical cofactor must have contributed to his death. End of Screed. End of story, as far as I'm concerned."

"Thanks girlfriend."

"Don't push it."

Reverend Mosby approached the pair. "We got one last table. Let's get him on it." He pulled out his knife and sliced through Screed's restraints.

"We need to get after whoever took my Jeep," said Wilde, reaching for Screed's ankles.

LuAnna tucked the pistol in her belt, and grabbed Screed's wrists. "What harm can these fools do out in the middle of the ice in this weather?"

Together they shuffled to the remaining empty table and hoisted Screed on it, doing their best to lay him out in some semblance of funereal propriety.

Wilde said, "There's a tracker on my Jeep."

"Wow. Your man done pissed a circle around you, didn't he?" said LuAnna.

"I was on the wrong end of a hostage situation in the past," said Wilde. "Trackers on personal vehicles of bureau personnel are now recommended. It'll be required equipment pretty soon, I'm betting."

"If you say so."

"I'm worried my husband will go after the Jeep expecting me to be in it. He'll be in for a surprise."

"Lowry? He won't do anything stupid," said LuAnna. "And he won't go it alone, am I right? Not like you."

Wilde chafed. "How do we find them before Pershing does?"

LuAnna brightened. "We've got cars, Honeygirl. Junkers, most of them, but they move."

Reverend Mosby said, "We need to get after them before their tracks blow away."

Sonny Wright rushed through the door, stamping snow off his boots. "Got Mary situated over to the Donaways. Kathy's already sewing her shoulder up. Now who we getting after?"

LuAnna said, "Some of those fonnyboys got into Molly's Jeep and took it out on the ice. But we need to get ahead of them. Organize a reception, Smith Island style."

CHAPTER 72

BLACKSHAW AND ELLIS had cleared two decks immediately above the one where the dead captain was stashed. Checking the superstructure of the tanker was a room-by-room search of a multistory building. Meeting no more opposition since the guy with the grenade, they edged ever upward toward the bridge.

As Ellis carefully stepped along a corridor, his shotgun raised, he asked, "You know what a moral injury is?"

"Somebody might have mentioned something like that at the VA. I paid it no mind."

"Of course not." Ellis aimed his shotgun to cover the door into a crew berth. Blackshaw went in first, low and fast, followed by Ellis. No one there. Blackshaw searched the gear bags there for trigger devices, but came away with a large winter parka likely the property of a big man from the ship's original crew.

Ellis said, "It's something that happens to a person, like a soldier for instance, when they're forced to do something that's wrong, and they just can't abide it down in his soul. Even if he just sees something terrible, it sends him off. Guilt. Shame. Anger. PTSD."

Blackshaw glanced at Ellis. "LuAnna put you up to this?"

"I think you're a good person, Ben."

"Not now."

"Then when?"

Blackshaw checked his watch and said, "How about half-past never. Does never work for you?"

They climbed another open stairway, with Blackshaw walking backwards, sighting upward into ambush positions along his weapon.

Ellis said, "You might be too good a person to handle all that warfighting. I'm not saying you're weak, mind you. We both know better. But you pulled some tough missions in the service. Maybe even tougher ones since you got out. I was there for most of those. You said yourself you don't like wet work Stateside as a civilian."

"I recall," said Blackshaw. "Ellis, we're trying not to die while we're looking for a triggering device. You know what they look like."

"If it's milspec, sure. And if it's homegrown, it's likely a cell phone. Don't change the subject." Ellis edged forward with an eye cocked on their six o'clock. He went on, "Problem is, you always want to make things right."

Blackshaw didn't answer. He never let his objective of reaching the next staircase lure him past a compartment doorway without clearing it first.

Ellis continued, "You fight for the little guy. The helpless. And nobody's more helpless than the dead, God forgive me. But the guy who does that, he's a personality type. He's what's called a Moral Enforcer."

Blackshaw said, "That's the second time you've hitched me to the word *moral*. Injury. Enforcer."

Ellis said, "An injured enforcer. Well now who's more dangerous to a hunter than a wounded animal, Ben?"

"A spotter who won't clam up."

Ellis remained quiet as they searched the next deck for the trigger.

Finally reaching the bridge deck, they pushed into and cleared a First Mate's cabin. Blackshaw tore into a rucksack he found there looking for clues. He pulled out a file, and cracked it open while Ellis covered the door.

Blackshaw said, "Maybe the failsafe is that the call to the right trigger number has to come *from* the right number."

"Might could be," said Ellis. "Anything else in that file?"

"Let's forget the triggers and just disable the charges. We're falling behind. We've got to move out. It might be too late."

Ellis said, "We can't be in two places at once."

"Two places? Try *three*," said Blackshaw. He pulled a sheet of paper from the file, folded it, and jammed it in a pocket inside his coat.

Ellis said, "I need to make a call," as he pulled out his satellite phone.

"Really? Now?"

"You'll thank me," said Ellis.

"Somebody might be monitoring this barge for wonky signals," said Blackshaw. "We don't want to tip the fonnyboys on shore that we're here—"

Ellis held up an index finger signaling Blackshaw to pipe down as his call went through. "Mr. Harrier, we could use your assistance, my position." Ellis paused to listen, then said, "Weather permitting of course. That's fine. Just fine."

CHAPTER 73

KRILL'S ANKLE THROBBED without mercy. She had struggled in the blowing snow to wrench the jerry can off the side of the Jeep, her face going numb all the while. It had been difficult to manage her footing on the ice while she hoisted the can and tipped the fuel into the Jeep's tank. When the last of the gas went in, she tossed the can aside. The wind blew the container clanking into the night. LaGleet had hollered useless encouragement from the relative comfort of the cab.

Krill scooped up a handful of snow that had drifted against a tire while she refueled. Once back in the Jeep, she loosened her boot laces and packed snow around the wound. It wouldn't help for long, but maybe it would deaden her ankle the way it had stripped all sensation from her face. That would be welcome. The fentanyl lolly was fine, but too much of that stuff, and she would be in no shape to complete the mission.

"Took you long enough," said LaGleet as he started the Jeep and put it in drive.

"Could've done it faster yourself, sir?"

LaGleet said nothing. Only Krill's decision to phrase her rebuke as a question kept him from railing her for insubordination. That, and her bum ankle.

He tugged his glove off with his teeth, pulled his satellite phone from the depths of his parka and pressed a button. It buzzed only once before the call was answered and LaGleet started on his Situation Report. "Blackshaw's in the wind. Our squad is down to two." He paused a moment to listen.

"That's right, I said two, *including* me. Your chopper pilots were drunk. Crashed. Killed damn near everyone. Then we hit resistance. And Screed? Useless. We can't find him. KIA, most likely. We're rolling out on the ice right now. We'll get to the secondary target in under two hours. We'll need some extra hands there."

LaGleet listened for a few moments. Krill saw him blanch in the reflected headlights, then tuck the sat-phone away without another word. "There are three more targets. But buck up, Krill, because ours is the big one."

Krill leaned back on the headrest during a smooth stretch of ice. With the growl of the Jeep's motor and hum of the knobby tires, she had almost dozed off despite Doc's warfighter S-FOP power-drip, when LaGleet barked, "I need dry land! Point us to the closest northbound road on dry land. Now!"

CHAPTER 74

BLACKSHAW AND ELLIS had ascended to the bridge deck slow and easy. With weapons at the ready, they now advanced along a companionway bent low with a quick stealthy step toward the bridge itself. They took the bridge fast. With their eyes sighting along their gun barrels, they collapsed sectors left and right with speed and care. The place was empty.

"Looks like we're running the joint," said Ellis. "How do your picaroon genes feel, actually taking a ship? And a big one at that—"

In the dim red lighting of the space, Blackshaw scoured the chart screens and the helm position for any clue that would further explain what was happening.

Blackshaw said, "I feel like a damn fool. Nothing here we need or can use, but the whole ship could go up any second."

"Then let's get our butts out to those demolition charges and neutralize them," Ellis said, "before they neutralize us."

"Have a care in case somebody we missed creeps up on our back trail," said Blackshaw.

"Copy that."

They went out onto the port bridge wing, and made their way to the aft end of the catwalk.

"Here goes nothing," Blackshaw said.

CHAPTER 75

"PLEASE DUCK DOWN, or kindly move your head a bit, would you Molly?" suggested LuAnna. She was at the wheel of an ancient Ford minivan named *Mehitabel*, with a sliding side door that would not close. That was not the only issue from which the venerable rattletrap suffered.

In the middle bench, Wilde leaned against Reverend Mosby to give LuAnna a clear view as she drove the van across the Chesapeake ice. She nearly shoved the old man out the open door into the storm-racked night. How LuAnna was navigating in the white-out weather was anyone's guess.

The Special Agent complained, "Seriously, LuAnna?"

LuAnna was matter of fact. "Reckon we have other rides on Smith Island, but *Mehitabel's* the only one that'd start that wasn't buried in snow up to the roof and more. We had to get ghost quick, doncha know."

Wilde felt awkward that she was the only passenger to lodge a complaint. Sonny Wright and the reverend were complacent in the face of the van's most glaring quirk; its only working gear was *reverse*.

Sonny, who was both riding shotgun and toting one, said, "You're gonna want to come right ten degrees." He held up his pocket compass to double check.

"Hang on everybody," LuAnna advised as she turned the steering wheel clockwise taking the van in a tight curve as they traveled backwards, the bald tires slipping on the ice more than once.

Wilde said, "I know you all have some unique ways of phrasing things, LuAnna, but you're turning left."

"Now you're learning. *Mehitabel* won't go forward, and she won't turn left if she could go forward," LuAnna explained. "Her gearbox and steering shit the bed back in the Reagan administration. So if you want to turn right going backwards, you have to turn a full circle to the left going backwards, and roll out smartly on your heading. Overshoot your course, and you have to go all the way round again."

"Jesus," muttered Wilde. She realized that driving backwards on uncertain ice in a pitch-dark nor'easter blizzard was as terrifying to her as traveling by helicopter. Wheeling around in this big three-sixty spawned murder hornets in her stomach. She considered asking Reverend Mosby if she might sit by the open door in case she had to vomit. She hadn't felt this nauseated since the first trimester of her pregnancy. She tried a few deep calming breaths, and held her tongue for now.

"Speaking of headings—" advised Sonny.

LuAnna straightened out the wheel.

Sonny checked his compass and nodded, smiling. "That weren't too pretty," he said in the sideways manner of Smith Islanders, and meaning that LuAnna had hit the new heading just right.

"Don't you worry, Miss Molly," said LuAnna. "We got us a sweet ride waiting for us in a heated garage in Crisfield, courtesy of Knocker Ellis."

"If we get there," said Wilde.

"*Oh ye of little faith*," said Reverend Mosby, chuckling.

boss.

PART III
SUSQUEHANNA UNDAMMED

CHAPTER 76

BLACKSHAW AND ELLIS had welcomed that moment of stepping out of the tanker's closely heated super structure onto the catwalk and back into the blizzard. The renewed cold was enlivening. They had moved from tank dome to tank dome with electricity in their veins, and with eyes toward the many possible points from which they might be ambushed; death might come from forward, from their six, and from below. Neither man assumed their patrol through the ship had eliminated every enemy. With Ellis on overwatch, Blackshaw worked on each charge in hopes of rendering them harmless.

So far, he had managed to neutralize the demolition charges on the first five tank domes in a professional and businesslike manner working from aft toward the bow. It meant disconnecting the receiving unit from the smaller detonator charge before safely lifting all this away from the main demolition charge. It was major surgery with blunt instruments; they had only Ellis's SOG Multi-Tool to work with. Now they were working on the final, forward-most tank. The final explosive.

Ellis said, "Sun-up in a couple hours."

"I hope we live to see it."

"Then don't get all butterfingers on me, Ben. You've got aplenty to live for."

Blackshaw sighed at what he sensed was the resurrection of an earlier topic.

Ellis proved him right. Leaning close to be heard over the wind, Ellis said, "Is anything you do out here, anything we do, going to fix what drove you out here onto the ice in the first place? Away from LuAnna? Away from your son? Away from home!"

Blackshaw asked, "Why the hell are *you* here?"

"Me? I'm here for the fresh air. Don't change the subject."

Blackshaw said, "Aren't you the least bit eager for some wet work now and again?"

Ellis scanned the catwalk that stretched back toward the superstructure, then peered downward toward the unseen deck for any intruders. Then he did it again. "Saying I'm an adrenaline junkie?"

Blackshaw looked up from the bomb, the SOG wire nipper poised over the zip tie holding the receiver and detonator charge to the big packet of C4. "Did you ever come home from overseas, Ellis?"

"Shut the hell up! You know I did. Ben, we're all just waiting around for *you* to show."

In a surge of anger, Blackshaw squeezed the nippers closed with one hand snapping the zip tie. With the other hand he lifted the receiver and detonator away from the larger explosive.

A moment later, an indicator light on the receiver blazed bright in the darkness and buzzed like it was taking an incoming call. On instinct, Ellis snatched the gizmo from Blackshaw and hurled it downwind toward the starboard side of the ship. The small detonator charge exploded in mid-air like a flashing firework swaddled in distant cotton. The ragged echo of five more reports rose up from the ice where Ellis had tossed the previous five detonators.

A wide-eyed Blackshaw said, "Somebody actually made the call to blow up the ship."

"Good thing you finished when you did," said Ellis. "You shouldn't chat so much with our lives on the line like that. Stay focused, Ben."

"I'm plenty focused." Blackshaw was going to say more on the topic but refrained as he sat on the catwalk for a moment to uncoil his nerves. A few breaths later, he said, "You know where we're headed next. Any ideas on how we get there?"

Ellis said, "I got it. We launch one of those lifeboats over the side. We take a couple of those shitbirds' parachutes from that locker below, fix them to the boat, and let the wind blow the lifeboat north across the ice to the next objective. That's where we're going, right? North?"

"Have you lost your mind, Ellis?"

"Oh no Ben. I'm dead serious." Ellis grinned as he went on, "We could make an ice boat. Or we could take my chopper."

An instant later, Blackshaw heard the thrum of a helicopter's main rotor over the wind. It was approaching from the southwest. A few moments later, he saw navigation and landing lights, first as a glow. As the chopper drew closer, the lights quickly resolved as brighter pinpoints of light marking the aircraft's path through the air toward Ellis's and Blackshaw's position on the catwalk.

Ellis said, "Mr. Harrier. Right on time."

An instant later, the muffled pop of gunshots made Blackshaw and Ellis turn aft. Someone, an enemy operator who had remained hidden while they cleared the ship in search of the master detonator, stood near the superstructure firing a submachine gun at the chopper. There were no tracers in the attacker's magazine. Only little glints of muzzle flash gave away his position.

"Oh shit," said Ellis. "This won't go well for that bastard."

Blackshaw watched as the side door of the helicopter was wrenched open and flung back on its stops. Almost simultaneously, a GE M134 electric six-barreled minigun was lowered on a mount from the chopper's cabin roof and fixed facing athwartship. The helicopter pilot, Mr. Harrier, made a quick tail rotor adjustment bringing the gun to bear.

"Stay low. Mr. Merlin's about to work his black magic," Ellis said.

The six gun barrels spun up into a steel cyclone, and a beam of buzzing tracers flew forth and down. Spent cartridges poured out of the gun's delinker like little brass meteors. Mr. Merlin walked the torrent of bullets toward the attacker on deck and cut him in half as near-misses ricocheted everywhere like sparks from hot iron hammered on an anvil.

"Tracers and Liquid Natural Gas don't mix, Ellis," said Blackshaw.

"Nor did they," said Ellis, absolutely confident in Mr. Merlin's aim.

The deadly work complete, Mr. Harrier brought the chopper down until it hovered just straddling the catwalk.

Blackshaw shouted over the thwop-thwop of the main rotor and the scream of the turbine engines, "You couldn't whistle up this bird to save us some of that walk before?"

Ellis hollered, "The boys were tinkering with the Jesus nut, and what not. And I really hoped the long infil' would give you time to rethink this whole thing."

Ellis stooped and dashed toward the side door of the chopper, where Mr. Merlin waited, his pencil thin cheroot clamped in his insane buccaneer's grin. Ellis looked back at an astounded Blackshaw and yelled, "Come on! Let's get this over with!"

CHAPTER 77

NARROW CRISFIELD STREETS prevented LuAnna from any
kind of big circular steering swings in the old van. Once she and Sonny had
navigated the rust bucket up a boat ramp, an act that to Molly Wilde required
the precision of threading a needle in the dark, they gathered their weapons
and ammunition and struck out on foot through the storm. Bitter cold as it
was, the fresh air went a long way to quell Wilde's queasy stomach.

LuAnna led the frigid march through the snow. Wilde understood why
so few of Napoleon's troops made it back from their stroll to Moscow. After
only twenty minutes, they fetched up at an older shoreline condominium,
where LuAnna punched in a code on a keypad by a garage. The big door
hummed like an electric motor that was jammed into useless stillness.

Reverend Mosby said, "Must be froze," as he kicked the bottom of the
door with his boot several times, and slammed the side of the door with the
butt of his shotgun. Sonny followed suit on the other side of the door, which
popped loose and slowly rose after a few raps. Inside lay a black Cadillac
Escalade shoehorned tight into a garage bay meant for a much smaller
vehicle.

LuAnna passed her shotgun to Molly and squeezed down between the
SUV and the garage wall muttering imprecations about baby weight until she
passed the door, and tapped in a code on a key pad that Knocker Ellis Hogan
had had custom-installed. The Escalade came to life with convenience lights
outside, and overhead cabin lights within. LuAnna contorted through the
narrow door, wrenched herself behind the wheel, and grabbed the key tucked

above the driver side sun visor. The 6.2 liter V-8 rumbled to life. LuAnna threw the shifter into low and eased the truck out of the garage. A minute later, with everyone aboard, they were rolling along Crisfield Highway toward Ocean Highway, and north.

LuAnna brought the navigation system up on the dashboard screen.

"Where are we going, exactly?" asked Wilde.

For a moment, LuAnna took her eye off the near white-out conditions ahead and glanced hard at Wilde in the seat beside her. "You got the intel', Honeygirl. Why don't you say?"

"It's just a guess."

"An educated guess," said LuAnna.

"If that ship had blown up according to plan, we'd have heard about that."

"No denying," said a rueful Sonny, who had close-up experience with large scale detonations in the past, and whose hearing in one ear had suffered for it, not to mention a significant amount of body hair that had never grown back.

Wilde went on, "Which means to me that this group, this Faction, has backup plans, like coming for Ben, just to make sure he didn't disturb the operation."

"Though he must've tossed a monkey wrench in things, we agree," said LuAnna. "Him and Ellis."

"So how do you wreck a Chesapeake breeding ground, when your Big Bang has fizzled? They like blowing things up," said Wilde. "That's their modus operandi."

Reverend Mosby asked, "So what's next on the hit list?"

Molly Wilde said, "The bureau keeps tabs on vulnerable infrastructure. The electrical grid is part of our purview."

Sonny said, "We aren't trailing folks who're trying to do a blackout in a whiteout, are we?"

"If I'm right," said Wilde, "a blackout could be a side effect."

"Dam!" said LuAnna.

"LuAnna!" scolded Reverend Mosby.

"Not *that* kind, Rev'! I mean the Conowingo Dam. Is that what you mean, Molly?"

"I don't follow," said Sonny.

LuAnna said, "The Conowingo Dam sits a few miles up the Susquehanna from the Chesapeake."

Sonny said, "Nigh on ten miles upstream. I'm confused, not stupid."

Reverend Mosby said, "I get it. There're hundreds of tons of pollution, farm runoff, nitrogen, phosphorus, and silt built up behind that dam. *Nutrients*, they call the manure. Since nobody's stepping up to dredge it, not the state, the Feds, not even the company that owns it, anytime it rains heavy, water comes down the Susquehanna River, they release overflow. Nobody can swim or fish at the top of the Chesapeake for days and weeks from bacteria and chemicals. And snags run in so bad, you even get small craft advisories so folks don't bend their props and snap their rudders hitting sunk tree trunks in what looks like free and open water."

Sonny said, "So if the dam came down all at once, and all the sludge ran into the Chesapeake, you're saying that'd do it for the horseshoe crabs."

LuAnna said, "Right when pandemic vaccines will need purity checks by the billions. Though there're other breeding grounds around the Eastern Seaboard and the Gulf of Mexico, the Chesapeake's the biggest. Destroying it, or even putting a dent in it for a few years, could tip the scale enough to make a synthetic LAL supply seem more reliable to Big Pharma and hang the expense, which they'd just pass on to us anyway."

"They weaponized pollution, for profit" said Molly Wilde. "That's fresh."

"It's disgusting," said Reverend Mosby.

LuAnna said, "True. The trouble is, our bench isn't so deep when it comes to defusing large scale demolition charges."

Sonny leered as he said, "Naw, all you do is shoot the bastard with his finger on the button, and we're good to go."

Molly Wilde was quiet as the windshield wipers swished back and forth a few times. Then she said, "I'm not sure what Faction calls Plan A or Plan B in all this, but what has me worried is whether there are back-ups to their back-ups."

LuAnna asked, "What's on your mind, Honeygirl?"

Wilde said, "There's more than one dam on the Susquehanna River."

CHAPTER 78

LAGLEET'S SAT-PHONE chirped. Two near misses with open water fissures on the ice had instilled an unusual sense of caution in LaGleet which still jangled his nerves even though they had transitioned to terra firma two hours before. Keeping his eyes riveted on the unplowed road ahead, he said, "Grab that, will you?"

Through the haze induced by her Fentanyl lollipop, Krill extracted the sat-phone from a holster on LaGleet's H-gear, glanced at the small screen and said, "It's Doc. From the plane?"

"You answer," ordered LaGleet.

Krill pressed a button on the phone and groaning inside, said, "T-Rex's line."

Despite the roar of the Jeep's engine and the storm's thrum on the poly-cotton soft top, Krill could hear tension in Doc's usually laconic Downeast Maine accent when he said, "Morning. How's everybody feeling?"

Krill said, "He wants to know—"

"Put him on speaker," said LaGleet.

Krill complied, and held the phone near LaGleet.

LaGleet barked, "T-Rex Actual. You want to know what, exactly, Doc? You're not my direct report. You work for me!"

Doc replied, "Sure enough, T-Rex. I'm not asking about the mission, Heaven forfend. Doubtless you have that well in hand. No, I'm checking on you and the team, just to see how the S-FOP is treating you all."

Until that moment, LaGleet had been pretty jazzed about how Doc's Sustained Forward Operations Protocol had kept him and Krill on their toes, but inquiries like this were suspect. He said, "It didn't make the team crash-proof. Certainly not fireproof, and not bulletproof, if that's what you're asking."

The Doc digested the implications of LaGleet's answer for a moment, then said, "My-my. Well, the rest of the team got hot coffee, not what you received. How about my other subject?"

LaGleet was growing impatient, and that made him more candid than usual. "We got separated from Weak Sister. At last contact, he seemed vertical and compos mentis."

"Interesting," said Doc.

"Not to me," said LaGleet. "You know I'm in the middle of an op' here, don't you, Doc? Get to the goddamn point! Or put Sneezy on. Somebody who can talk sense."

Doc said, "There's been a recall of sorts. On the S-FOP."

LaGleet stared into the snow ahead. His eyes grew even wider than the weather demanded. In a quiet fury that penetrated Krill's Fentanyl fog and made her nervous, he said, "*A recall. Of sorts.* Care to fucking elaborate?"

"In the batching," said Doc. "All the ingredients were present, yes, but not exactly correct."

Krill pulled the phone close to her mouth and said, "What the hell does that even mean? In plain English!"

Doc said, "I was concerned when telemetry from Weak Sister's chip recently flatlined. I wanted to confirm whether that was from action on your end, or from this little mix-up on our end."

LaGleet stomped on the brake, sending the Jeep into fishtailing swerves that almost plowed them sideways into the snowdrifts choking the highway median. When the Jeep finally stopped rocking on the shoulder, LaGleet said, "Chip! What the hell kind of chip?"

Doc said, "Oh boy howdy, I can see your heartrate is jumping up a tick, T-Rex. Your breaths per minute are elevated. And your pal's there, too."

Krill growled, "You chipped us?"

"Just the three of you," said Doc. "You two, and Weak Sister. It's standard. Harmless, microscopic nano stuff through the IV. S-FOP is new, and we like to monitor test subjects' progress."

"Test subject!" said Krill.

"Everyone's a test subject in this man's army," said Doc. "It was in your Faction Hiring Documents, Agent Krill. I'm looking right at your initials on the page in question."

"What page?" shouted Krill.

"Page 83, Section 15, Part 42, Subpart LXXIV, Clause xxxvii," said Doc. "You didn't just initial and sign everything without reading it, did you?"

"Everybody does," said Krill in a quiet voice.

Doc admonished, "This isn't Facebook's Terms of Service, you know. Just scroll to the end and click *Accept.*"

"Hold it, we're chipped, so do you know our 20?" LaGleet asked.

Doc rattled off, "Maryland. Route 301 northbound, mile marker 36.8. A long way from your insertion point—"

"Where are you, Doc?" demanded LaGleet.

Doc hesitated, "Um, whatcha going to do with that information, Buddy?"

"I think Krill here is going to find *your* insertion point, shove her Beretta in it up to the trigger guard, and empty her mag. Right Krill?"

"A-fucking-firmative, boss," seethed Krill.

"And when she's done," said LaGleet, "I just might park a Mike Six-Seven in there for good measure, pull the pin, and watch your sorry corpse go all to pieces. You feel me, Doc?"

"Now hold on, Pal—"

"No, *you* hold on. What the hell are you doing on this line anyway? What's all this about Weak Sister flatlining, and batches, and mix-ups? You make me tired, Doc. What's your purpose? Why are you breathing?"

Doc had finally wended his way to the point, and wanted to end the call as soon as practicable. "Weak Sister's chip indicated that he didn't expire from injuries. His special formula, which you and I discussed on the plane, it seems to have moved into its final phase sooner than intended."

"Too fucking bad for him," said LaGleet. "He was a complete and utter waste of skin if you ask me. Go back to bartending school, fix your mix for the next go-round, and I'll be first in line for more. I feel like a million bucks."

Doc said, "That's nice, but this is where the batching mix-up comes in. I regret to inform you that, because of my poor handwriting on the order, it's possible you three all received the same special formula as Weak Sister."

Krill eyed LaGleet, "What special formula?"

LaGleet snatched the sat-phone out of Krill's hand, opened the Jeep's door, and lobbed the phone high into the storm. An instant later, he drew his pistol, aimed, and fired three times. He hit the phone twice as it fell, blowing it to pieces.

He holstered his weapon, slammed the door, and pulled back onto the highway. Only then did he glance at Krill and say, "Kiddo, I have absolutely no idea what he's talking about."

CHAPTER 79

SPECIAL AGENT VINE, head of the National Joint Terrorism Task Force, breezed into FBI Director Hornsby's office with a briefcase under her arm. Without waiting for an invitation, she sat in the only remaining open chair. She said, "Sid. Pershing," and with that, greetings were done.

Lowry said, "We're sure on the count. Six detonations."

Vine said, "A muffled detonation with the signature of a fragmentation grenade was detected forty-three minutes prior to the tight group of six which were exterior to the Penelope. Sporadic gunfire as well."

Sid Hornsby asked, "Who's shooting at whom? Do we have any assets whatsoever in play?"

Both Hornsby and Vine looked directly at Pershing Lowry for his answer. "Not to my knowledge. My wife was in the area of Smith Island, but isn't any longer. At least her vehicle isn't."

"What the hell was she doing there?" Vine asked.

"She felt like going a drive," said Lowry.

"On Smith Island," pressed Vine. "Which is an *island.*"

"The ice is quite thick."

"But I'm not. What's going on? Is your Blackshaw guy in play?" Vine asked. "We really need to know."

Lowry said, "Short of an armed mutiny aboard *Penelope*, the gunfire might indicate that the enemy operators met with some form of resistance.

More than that, I can't say with any degree of certainty. What about *Penelope's* cargo?"

Vine said, "I authorized a sortie, a flyby with some very sensitive detection equipment aboard—"

"Aboard what?" Hornsby asked.

"It's a loaner from the Navy," said Vine. "I need to leave it at that."

Hornsby was not happy about being kept in the dark by an underling, but he had learned that whenever he noticed non-critical information being withheld by someone he respected, it was best to let it go. Plausible deniability was much better for his blood pressure than having a control freak's exhaustive understanding of every detail.

Lowry was not so sanguine about Need To Know intel. He said, "All due respect, Sheila, we're trying to gauge a threat, and that means we need a clear picture of all the assets in play. Even the ones you'd prefer not to discuss."

Vine was quiet for a moment. Then all she said was, "TACAMO."

"Dear God," said Hornsby.

Lowry said, "Take Charge And Move Out. You've got an E-6B buzzing a Q-Max supertanker in this weather? A Boeing 707."

"It was specially equipped with sensors to detect whether it's safe to land after an engagement," said Vine. "Things like radiation, bioweapons, low-tech explosives, and off-gassing energy sources like LNG. The point is, for now *Penelope's* tanks are sound."

"Hold it," said Hornsby. "An E-6B is primarily an airborne communications platform for talking to the fleet's boomers for nuclear launch control."

Vine said, "And Minuteman missiles. Yes. And nuclear cruise missiles. I'm aware of this, of course."

Lowry said, "But this operation is on American soil. The idea of nukes—"

Vine said, "If that LNG cargo were released all at once, just its expansion would send suffocating shock waves all over the Chesapeake Bay watershed, and that includes Washington. And that's even if it's not ignited."

Hornsby's eyes were wide as he said, "Okay, So what's a nuclear warhead—"

"A *tactical* nuclear warhead," corrected Vine. "A little one."

Lowry caught Hornsby's urgency. "Little! Didn't we learn anything from that dirty bomb that was detonated in the Chesapeake?"

"Of course. We learned it's manageable," said Vine. "The idea is to destroy the natural gas at a molecular level in situ, in its remote location, minimizing the destructive firestorm the LNG would present if it flashed conventionally. It's like backburning to remove brush and other fuel during a wildfire. Keeps things under control."

"With a nuke," said Lowry. "Am I'm hearing you correctly?"

"On American soil," said Hornsby in disbelief.

"A little one," Vine repeated. "Or two."

"The president has to authorize deployment—"

Vine sounded smug when she said, "Honcho has been read in on the situation. He's got the nuclear football within arm's reach. He's standing by."

Hornsby said, "But we're pretty sure those six larger explosions near the *Penelope* were detonation charges being neutralized. The tanks, the hull, you said it yourself, they weren't compromised. So you can get that loaner E-6B back on the ground, and out of the equation."

"*Pretty sure* doesn't cut it, Sid," said Vine. "Neutralized—maybe—by some as-yet undetermined asset? You mean, like the threat just went away, and everything's hunky-dory? Like a miracle?" said Vine. "No boys, we're keeping that plane loitering on station until we know without a doubt that the threat posed by that tanker, which has already been weaponized once, has been eliminated, one way or another."

CHAPTER 80

THEY PREFERED TO call themselves The Mechanics. *Operators* sounded too much like they worked for the phone company. Faction didn't care if they called themselves the Mickey Mouse Club, since they were brutally efficient, and effective, if not entirely discrete when fixing setbacks on a mission.

Nose Bone was a tall, sinewy brunette, and a sadist, pure and simple. A jab to her face in a bar fight had snapped her nose, and finding the break to be a foil to her beauty, which had always drawn unwanted attention from men including her father and two of her uncles when she was little, she canceled the surgery to have the injury set, and never looked back.

Nose Bone had found that work as a correctional officer at Louisiana's Angola Prison Plantation too dull for her liking. Though she had learned where all the surveillance camera dead zones were where she could have her fun with inmates too elderly or fearful to resist, after five years, she had turned herself out as a mercenary. Via a Reddit page, she met and signed on with two Louisiana mounted correctional officers, Belly Boy and Tripod Rick, who were tired of riding horses for a living; their hard-mouthed steeds were damn sure tired of them. The trio hired themselves out as a team to Faction and other clients as The Mechanics who repaired gigs that were broken.

Belly Boy definitely had unearthly appetites that included a gargantuan capacity for food. Contrary to what his name implied, there was no fat on his six foot, five inch frame. His metabolism incinerated food calories, converting them to muscle, which he honed with long daily training sessions in hand-to-hand combat.

Tripod Rick's side hustle while working as a mounted gun bull had been working as a photographer specializing in high-end children's portraiture, birthday parties, bar and bat mitzvahs, and graduations until his collection of child pornography came to light. A close relative in the Louisiana state legislature had afforded Tripod Rick an excellent lawyer, who managed to help him cop to a lesser plea resulting in house arrest. Some dedicated work with a Stryker saw followed, the ankle monitor came off. Before anyone wondered why the pornographer hadn't moved from his bathroom in twenty-four hours, he disappeared. The Mechanics all had new identities now.

"Tell me," said Belly Boy, in a voice that rumbled up from the floorboards of their armored Suburban.

"You sure?" said Nose Bone. "I'm showing thirty minutes until we get there."

Belly Boy said, "No, I can't stand it anymore. Tell me."

Belly Boy delighted in knowing nothing about an upcoming mission until the last possible moment. Like a child, he relished surprise. Like a storybook warrior, he prided himself on being able to deploy in seconds, quickly assess his orders and circumstances, and get cracking on the mission without hesitation. His concession to his own lack of planning was allowing Nose Bone and Tripod Rick to prep his rucksack and loadout with all the necessary gear and weapons that the mission, which his comrades made a point to understand in exhaustive detail, would require. For Belly Boy, opening his pack just before the mission insertion felt like Christmas morning.

"No, not yet." said Nose Bone, her sadism rearing upon her own comrade.

Belly Boy pounded his thighs. "Dammit! I hate you so much!"

"You're welcome," said Nose Bone, grinning. "I could give you a hint—"

"No! I'll break your neck!" said Belly Boy, with a bloody look in his eye.

Nose Bone pulled a can of Red Bull energy drink from a cold pack at her feet, opened it, and passed it to Tripod Rick in the driver's seat. She opened another for herself and took a long pull from it. None for Belly Boy. Not yet.

Nose Bone's eyes traveled from the speedometer to the snow that was now blowing horizontally across the windshield. She asked, "How's the traction in this mess?"

Tripod Rick said, "The truck's good. The—package—is catching these gusts pretty bad." He had said *package* instead of trailer, not wanting to tip Belly Boy too early to clues about the mission, such as the three supercharged snowmobiles on the small flatbed swaying on the Suburban's hitch.

Nose Bone said, "Don't slow down unless you absolutely have to. Our timetable's tighter than a rat's ass."

"We'll get there."

"No doubt," said Nose Bone. *It's more about getting home in one piece*, she thought.

Tripod Rick said, "One of these days, Belly Boy, you're going to have to brief a mission in advance like the rest of us. Like a fucking grown-up."

Tripod Rick felt the cool itch of a sharp combat knife blade pressed against the skin of his throat. From the back seat, Belly Boy said, "Okay. My plan, my grown-up mission, is to cut your fucking head off."

Nose Bone said, "Then we crash. Then we don't get paid for the gig. Then Faction docks us for getting blood out of the upholstery, which is a bitch. Ease the fuck up, Belly Boy. And for the record, I think Tripod Rick has a valid point. If you don't help with the plan, you can't gripe if things go sideways. For all that muscle, tactically, you're dead weight because you don't know shit from Shinola."

Belly Boy removed the blade from Tripod Rick's throat, sheathed it, and sat back staring into the snowflakes beating at the window like an endless swarm of moths.

CHAPTER 81

MR. HARRIER DROPPED Ellis and Blackshaw a mile to the north of the Conowingo Dam on the frozen Susquehanna River, and flew the helicopter away into the storm to the west. Ellis examined the small pile of gear on the ice next to him, then started pulling on his baggy cold water SCUBA diving drysuit. "You know I'm not much of one for swimming below, say ninety degrees."

Blackshaw checked the gauges on his rebreather, and said, "It'll be quick. Down to the sluicegate intake, and in we go. Fifty yards. Don't have to swim a stroke. Current will take you. But watch the ceiling. Don't go past the access tunnel in the ceiling. Then climb up and into the turbine room. Nobody's the wiser."

Ellis switched on the night scope on his rifle. "And if I float on past that access tunnel? What do I do then?"

Blackshaw considered. "In that case, you might as well just relax. You go into the turbine next. Spin around some, as you're torn to pieces. Pretty soon you'll be part of the 572 Megawatts of electricity brightening this dark and stormy night in a hundred and sixty-five thousand households. Imagine that."

Ellis peered through his spotting scope into the storm toward the ramparts of the Conowingo Dam to the south. He scanned slowly left, then to the right. Without another word, he set his scope down, picked up his SRM Arms Model 1216 combat shotgun, abandoning the rest of the weapons and diving equipment, and setting off toward the dam on foot.

"Ellis?"

When he received no reply, Blackshaw grabbed his rifle and caught up with his friend. "You going AWOL again? What's up?"

Ellis slid a tired glance toward Blackshaw, but kept walking as he said, "There's some debris gathered up against the dam. Logs. Bulky waste."

"Okay," said Blackshaw, not understanding. "So?"

"There's also a ladder from the dam's roadbed down to the water—the ice, I mean—you get me. I'm going in that way. So, I'm not going to swim in with you, even if you could find a hole in the ice."

"A couple charges, maybe grenades oughta—"

"That's very stealthy. Go ahead then. You can if you want. And which weapon is going to fire after a long immersion in cold water? Not what you brought. I sure didn't bring any Russian APS needle guns."

"Next time," said Blackshaw.

"What next time? You going to knife your way through this op?"

Blackshaw couldn't answer.

Ellis went on, "And that's if swimming into the intake of an active hydroelectric turbine doesn't turn us into chum."

Blackshaw kept pace with his friend, listening, but glancing from time to time at the cache of expensive gear receding in the snow behind them.

Ellis went on, "Ben, something's not right. You're self-deploying into conditions and circumstances that aren't survivable. Can't you smell a suicide mission when it's right under your snout? Are you a total NAFOD?"

Blackshaw ignored the acronym's significance; No Apparent Fear of Death. It was not a macho acronym; it was nothing to boast about. It meant Blackshaw would so disregard his own survival that he had become a menace to his team. "We can complete this. I know we can."

"There's a lot of ways to define complete. Could mean success. It could mean success at any cost."

Days of steady downstream wind had first rippled, then mounded the ice ahead of the two men. Then they came to the first of the detritus. They stepped over the tops of logs that had fallen or been tossed into the river; like so many discarded things, the logs had drifted until stopped by the outskirts of other interlaced flotsam and jetsam. Such was the accumulation of river junk, the Conowingo Dam itself was still two hundred feet ahead.

Ellis said, "Watch for planks. Rusty nails sticking up."

Blackshaw picked his way with care across the old tires, bleach bottles, blue plastic barrels, stained contractor's buckets, and even a shattered porta potty. Over his shoulder, he told Ellis, "I saw him."

"Who might that be?"

Blackshaw kept up his careful scramble over the river refuse, but said nothing more.

"Ben, who'd you see?"

"Chalk."

Ellis stopped mid-step and stared at Blackshaw's back as it faded into the snow squall ahead. "You mean you think you saw him? You saw somebody who looked like him?"

"It was definitely him."

"When?"

"While you were on walkabout. In an old duck blind. Before the whole business aboard *Penelope*. I took a rest inside the blind to get out of the wind for a minute. There he was."

"You dozed off from cold and fatigue. Had a bad dream." There was worry in Ellis's voice, with outright anxiety not far behind.

"I was as wide awake as I am now."

"But Chalk's dead! Dammit, *you* killed him. A bullet through his throat in Bermuda. In by the neck, out through his spine. Bam! Lights out!"

"True enough," said Blackshaw.

Against his better judgement, Ellis trod on a sensitive subject. "I know there was a time you used to see folks you'd killed in firefights overseas. Said they stared at you. Okay. Okay, so maybe it's a guilty conscience. Or PTSD. Let it go, Ben. At least for the next hour, please God, let it go."

"Sure. But this was different."

They scrambled carefully forward over plates of ice, and frozen floating discards of upstream humanity. With every second step, they stopped and scanned the parapet of the dam. They were approaching its center; it melded away a half mile to the left, and a half mile to the right—they glimpsed only the things that the wan street lights spaced along the top illuminated through the snowfall. They saw no one, but did not trust that the dam was unguarded.

Finally, Ellis asked, "Ben, is he here? You see him now?"

"Can't say as I do. He mostly wanted to say *hello*—in his way."

Between ice-crunching footsteps, Blackshaw heard Ellis cuss under his breath.

Ellis said, "They never talked to you before, the dead ones that came calling."

"Told you this was different. Maybe the others were at peace with their lot, dying righteous in battle."

"But not Chalk."

Blackshaw was smiling when he said, "That one never had a single thought he didn't say out loud."

Blackshaw held Ellis's shotgun while he crossed a wider lead in the ice.

"Well?"

"Well what, Ellis?"

"What'd Chalk say?"

"Nothing much."

"Ben."

"He told me he's waiting."

Ellis was stricken into silence pondering the ill-harbinger of Blackshaw's words. Or rather, of Chalk's words, if Blackshaw were to be believed. Ellis was about to offer advice, counsel, and comfort when he heard a distant buzz coming from up river. The single sound divided into the high RPM whine of three different engines being throttled and gunned. Blackshaw followed Ellis's gaze and saw three headlights moving fast downstream toward the dam. Three snowmobiles, and each one speeding up when the way ahead was clear and smooth, or slowing down when the ice got rough, or when detritus jutted up and required a change of course.

Blackshaw said, "Drunk joyriders."

First the glint, then the crack of gunfire broke out from the drivers of two of the machines. Their shots went wide, slapping into a sodden pull-out couch with its mattress half disgorged, and shattering an old Sony Trinitron TV.

Ellis said, "Hostiles, and they've got intel on us."

"They're coming at us the only way possible."

From the dam's street-level rampart behind Blackshaw and Ellis, a powerful handheld searchlight pierced the storm; it slowly played across the field of frozen junk seeking them with the patience of a calm, experienced operator. Pinched between the dam and the oncoming snowmobiles, Blackshaw and Ellis flattened themselves into the debris. Blackshaw lay in the shadow of a tattered, summery patio umbrella with a lead of slushy water just beneath him. Warmth radiating from the dam's powerplant did not allow the closest waters to freeze all the way.

Ellis hunkered low, but he was in the open. The searchlight passed across him. The snowfall and his white parka hid him at first, but something about Ellis's silhouette still looked just human enough to arrest the searcher's eye; the blinding pool of light stopped and slowly backtracked. Ellis played possum until a sub-machinegun opened up at him, gouging ice chips and splinters from a waterlogged phone pole near his head. Ellis tried to get as small as possible burrowing into a drift. To his horror, a hand burst up at him through the snow, grabbed his coat collar, and pulled down like a demon drawing him to Hell. Ellis sank through the drift, hung in space for an instant, and dropped into the icy slurry of the open lead next to Blackshaw.

CHAPTER 82

LUANNA STEERED THE Escalade through the storm with assurance. A few times, she hit patches of ice and felt the front tires come loose, but she held firm on the wheel without twisting it in a tizzy. Within a second or so the wheels bit into snow with enough grit and salt in the mix to keep them all out of the ditch.

Molly Wilde said, "Wasn't that the turn to the Conowingo?"

"That's right," said Reverend Mosby. "Headed to New York City to take in a show, Honeygirl?"

Sonny Wright piped up, "It might be enough to take down the Conowingo, but these fonnyboys like insurance."

"So?" said Wilde.

Finally, LuAnna said, "Sonny's got the smart of it. If you want to wreck a whole fishery, you need the all ick upstream behind a few dams to do the job, not just one dam, big as the Conowingo is, and deep as her silt goes. So you need to take down a dam or two upstream to be sure that last dam is totaled. You need the force of all that water released at once."

Sonny said, "I get it. We're going to the next dam up, see if we can save it. The Holtwood."

"Farther upstream," said LuAnna.

Reverend Mosby whistled. "Talking about the Safe Harbor Dam?"

LuAnna nodded. "My guess is this outfit has a lot of fingers in a lot of pies. Likely they've been buying up interests in nearby power grids for when these three hydroelectric dams go off-line. Not just one."

Wilde eyed LuAnna. "So, they make money selling emergency energy at a huge markup, as well as killing off enough horseshoe crabs to make the synthetic LAL look economical to Big Pharma. We've been over that much already."

LuAnna said, "But it's especially necessary during a pandemic, this one or the next one, to hog the market on LAL for vaccine purity testing," said LuAnna. "And a single pandemic has multiple waves. Waves mean booster shots. More shots need more LAL. Really, LAL is for anything injectable in humans and animals, even for making medical devices. But shorebirds eat the horseshoe crab eggs when they migrate. Fewer crab eggs, fewer birds. Everything's affected by this scheme. The LAL is worth fifteen thousand bucks a quart. Here's the thing, Girlfriend. Even at that price for the horseshoe crab stuff, the synthetic alternative has been around for twenty years; Big Pharma hasn't made the switch, because the old way still has all the regulatory standards in place. There's no risk it'll be outlawed or restricted like could happen with the synthetic. But see, the patent is about to run out on the synthetic, so when the patent lapses, anybody could come in and make it, and competition will drop the price. Corner the market from the annihilation of horseshoe crabs until the synthetic patent goes *phhht*, you get those emergency approvals from the FDA like with the COVID-19 vaccines, and you make a killing."

Wilde said, "How do you know about—"

LuAnna's smile was grim. "Ben and the boys have been harvesting the Chesapeake since way back in Bible times. But you know I was Natural Resources Police for a minute. I protected the Chesapeake. That was my jam."

Wilde said, "You and Ben were made for each other."

LuAnna sighed, and said, "True—since God was a bitty baby."

Wilde squinted at oncoming headlights. "First car in hours."

An instant later, two large, dark vehicles made the Escalade shudder as they rushed by, whipping up a brief whiteout in their wake.

Sonny Wright said, "Whoah! Blacked-out SUVs. Federales?"

Reverend Mosby asked, "Should we turn about and get after them?"

LuAnna said, "I don't think so. It's only a couple miles to the Safe Harbor Dam. We might be too late."

Looking over her shoulder at the receding SUVs, Wilde said, "It'll be too late if we don't chase them down right now."

LuAnna said, "We don't know who they are. Could be anybody. But if they're fonnyboys, I've got an idea how we can gain on them, maybe pass them. But we have to go forward. Not back."

CHAPTER 83

BELLY BOY SLOWED his snowmobile long enough to finger snow off the lens of his night vision goggles. Then he twisted the throttle open again like he was wringing the neck of a rat one-handed. Ahead he could see the beam of a searchlight angling down from the roadbed of the dam onto the ice. He could just make out the form of someone pinned by the light. He leaned just enough to the left in his snowmobile's saddle to get the business end of his FN P90 bullpup submachinegun around the windshield; he opened fire. He loosed short bursts to keep his targets low and bothered.

Nose Bone and Tripod Rick were also firing as they sped in toward the dam. Suppressing fire with a P90 was great fun at a rate of 850 rounds a minute. Of course, if he were using two hands, Belly Boy knew he could be more accurate. Shooting straight should have been a big deal. Nose Bone and Tripod Rick had finally briefed the mission with him, making it clear that there might be effective resistance at the dam. So far, Belly Boy was disappointed. There'd been no return fire at all.

Belly Boy heard Nose Bone's voice in his headset. She said, "Dismount! Dismount! We patrol in from here."

Belly Boy acknowledged as he throttled his machine down to a stop. Tripod Rick did the same. Belly Boy would really rather have stayed on his snowmobile to make their approach a high-speed mechanized cavalry charge, but Nose Bone would dock his pay if he went full berserker and disobeyed orders. She'd done it once before. Though Belly Boy rationally understood he could snap Nose Bone in two in the blink of an eye, the larger, less rational part of his mind was terrified of his partner.

He rolled off the snowmobile while it was still moving so it would coast to a stop ahead of his position. The machine's halogen headlight would distract an enemy looking for a target. Once again, Belly Boy wiped snow off his night vision goggle lens. He swapped his P90's empty magazine for a full one. Then he moved out toward the dam keeping his massive body as low as possible.

CHAPTER 84

ELLIS SPUTTERED AS if he were just back on dry land from near-drowning. Bobbing in the icy water in the air pocket beneath the surface trash cast up and frozen against the dam, he found his words quickly enough. "You trying to kill me?"

"Quiet, or you'll kill yourself and me. That fonnyboy with the spotlight's still up on the dam."

"I still hear engines," said Ellis.

"I hear *you*!" said Blackshaw.

"I'm serious! Listen!"

They clutched the yellow handle bars of a child's discarded Big Wheel tricycle, and listened to the whine of distant snowmobiles. One after another, the screaming engines dropped off to a purr, then went quiet.

"Same three as before," said Ellis.

"On foot now," said Blackshaw. "The noise, the shooting, they're trying to spook us, announcing their numbers and firepower."

Ellis said, "Ben, there's an undertow pulling at me."

"Thirty feet east, that bare patch in the ice—that's the sluice gate down into the turbines. Don't let go. You might get pulled in."

"Think my drysuit's sprung a leak," said Ellis. "Need to get out of this water. It's like a prison toilet Slurpee."

"Leaky suit—you hit?"

Ellis said, "Too numb to be sure. Like as not, something sharp in this junk pile—"

As Blackshaw listened to Ellis, he drew his pistol, drained the barrel, then shook water from the action through the ejection port, and peered up through the flotsam. He watched the searchlight play on the detritus above their position. The beam of light stabbed deep into the surrounding cover now and then, not quite reaching their hidey hole, nor marking the path of a clean shot for Blackshaw.

Three shots rang out from the rifle of the operative up on the dam. Blackshaw fired the pistol once up through the rubbish heap.

"Think I tagged him," said Blackshaw.

"Good enough for me." Without waiting a moment longer to verify that their enemy was in fact wounded, Ellis was scrambling up through the detritus. By the time Blackshaw reached the top of the frozen trash heap, Ellis was halfway up the ladder on the dam's upstream wall, and bee-lining for the top.

CHAPTER 85

ARLIS SPATCHCOCK SWEPT the floodlight slowly across the frozen flotsam heaped at the base of the Conowingo Dam's upstream side. Over the wind, he thought he had heard voices, two men arguing down in the debris. The voices had been drowned out during that fusillade of suppressing automatic fire from the three operators snarling in on their snowmobiles. Spatchcock had ducked behind the dam's parapet wall to avoid catching a round from the barrage. When the shooting stopped, he rose again and saw that the machines had halted, but all three headlights still blazed forth into the storm. *Idiots.* Now these dumbass operatives were backlit by the headlights as they crept in downstream toward the damn. Fine with Spatchcock.

He pulled off a glove with his teeth, and dug his nails into his scalp under the black balaclava. He had shaved his head a few days back. Big mistake. Just when he needed to focus, the new growth itched like hell.

Spatchcock checked his watch and stage-whispered into his headset. "The cavalry's here, and the Safe Harbor Dam goes up in two minutes, twenty-seven seconds."

The voice of Rupert Kläng, who oversaw the Conowingo demolition charges, crackled in Spatchcock's ear. "We're good here. When this goes up, the force will crack teeth for miles around. Add the water pressure of the two upstream dams bursting—"

Spatchcock interrupted Kläng. "The Holtwood Dam goes in seven minutes. If it fails, you don't get the wave pressure here—"

Kläng said, "I trust my teams. It'll be a tsunami down here. First Safe Harbor, then Holtwood, and last but not least, Conowingo. Wham! The Chesapeake Bay will be a cesspool. Job done."

"Then let's get moving!"

"Final checks. Two minutes, and we're out." Rupert Kläng fell silent.

Spatchcock stopped rasping his nails across his right temple and listened. The voices below again; it was definitely two guys arguing. He played the spotlight down to where he thought he heard the men, rested his FN SCAR 16S rifle on the parapet, and angled it down holding it one handed. It was already set to single shot. Spatchcock pulled the trigger three times.

Someone shouted in pain. Turns out it was Spatchcock himself. For a split second, he thought he'd gotten a lucky hit until he felt the hot poker agony in the muscle on the left side of his neck. Staggering back from the parapet, he released the spotlight, and let his rifle clatter to the deck like a rank noob. He sat down hard, yanked off his other glove, and probed the wound. Wounds, actually. *Shit!* A through-and-through shot. Warm arterial blood pulsed between his fingers from the small, round entry wound. The exit wound was a gaping mess; it was pulsing, but not spurting. He yanked the blowout kit from his thigh cargo pocket, and slapped a dressing impregnated with a clotting agent onto the wounds. Spatchcock knew he'd bought himself time, but not a cure. He needed a doctor. No, he needed a fully staffed surgical suite, and one hell of a lot of luck.

He heard footsteps at a run. Finally, Kläng was finished with the charges, and could help him.

"Kläng! I'm hit! Over here!"

Somebody loomed over Spatchcock. It was hard to recognize the guy through the weather; the roadbed streetlights were little better than glowing white clouds in the snow floating high above him. No, it wasn't Kläng after all. The man was dressed like a cosplayer from the movie *Tron*. Space Age stuff. Spatchcock wondered if blood loss was making him shocky. Then this bastard leveled a gun at Spatchcock's face. That's when it all went dark.

When black returned to gray, Spatchcock realized he was being carried on someone's shoulder along the dam's roadbed.

Then an older man asked, "This bare patch? That's the flume into the turbine?"

"Affirmative," came the distant reply.

Then Spatchcock was weightless, tumbling through space for a moment, until he hit the frigid water below. Jolted to consciousness, a part of his mind marveled that he had not landed on solid ice. Another shred of his psyche, the part most concerned with self-preservation, wondered why he was being pulled farther down in the water despite his best efforts to follow his bubbles up.

CHAPTER 86

LUANNA PULLED THE Escalade into the parking area of a small marina just upstream from the Safe Harbor Dam on the Susquehanna River. The marina actually served Lake Clarke, the long, shallow body of water formed when the dam was constructed in the early 1930s.

LuAnna stopped the big SUV and climbed out. She surveyed the dam and the large turbine hall where the dam's electricity was generated.

Reverend Mosby, Sonny Wright, and Molly Wilde stepped out of the Escalade, and peered into the weather trying to see what LuAnna was studying.

LuAnna said, "We're talking 1.1 million cubic feet per second going over that spillway."

"Let's get moving," said Molly Wilde. "If they blow that dam, a heck of a lot more water than that will head downstream right at the—"

"—at the Holtwood Dam," said LuAnna. "And if that dam goes, only the Conowingo Dam stands between all that contaminated silt and the Chesapeake Bay. But it's too late."

"There's always hope," stated Reverend Mosby.

Sonny Wright shook his head. "Anybody in that power plant has likely met their maker, courtesy of the folks in them SUVs."

"Big assumption," said Wilde. "We phone it in."

"And get a bunch of first responders out on the dam just in time for the fireworks?" said LuAnna. "We have to cut losses here."

"You didn't bring us up here to do nothing," said Reverend Mosby.

LuAnna had shifted her focus to a Sea Ray Sundancer 320 cruiser moored at the end of the marina's longest T-pier. "Reckon there's not much time. Let's get aboard."

The other's followed LuAnna to the chain link gate securing the T-pier where she drew her pistol, picked her angle, and shot the padlock to scraps.

Sunny Wright slashed an opening in the white plastic winterizing shrink wrap protecting the thirty-two-foot boat.

As they climbed aboard the Sundancer, LuAnna said, "Reverend Mosby, do you think you can hotwire the engine?"

The man of God saw the look on Molly Wilde's face and said, "The church lawn mower has a wortonoggled ignition. Needs must." Then he tipped down the sun visor over the helm, and caught the set of keys that slid off it. "But not tonight."

As Reverend Mosby brought the eight cylinders of the cold MerCruiser 6.2 Liter engine to life, LuAnna said, "Sonny, let's us cast off."

Puzzled, Sonny Wright said, "Fat lot of good that'll do. This boat's locked up solid in the ice. See? Even the bubbler gave up the ghost in this cold." Sonny pulled up the perforated hose that lay frozen atop the ice around the boat. Usually, compressed air leaving the hose would agitate the water enough in winter months to prevent its freezing and damaging the boat's hull.

"Are the mooring lines frozen?" LuAnna asked.

"Knots are hard as rebar," said Sonny. "But doncha know I got a fid on my knife," meaning the tapered steel awl for marlinspike work with maritime lines and cordage. Sonny drew his pocket knife again, flipped open the fid, and started jabbing and wheedling at the bow line's knot.

There was a deep rumble, followed by a series of earsplitting cracks, and all eyes turned toward the dam. The turbine hall walls were toppling inward, and the roof was collapsing. The dam itself was erupting at its center; explosions extended outward in sequence toward land on both ends. Shockwaves rolled across the ice and made everyone take a step to catch their balance. The lights on every street around them winked out.

"Cut 'em," said LuAnna.

"What?" asked Sonny.

"Cut the lines, Sonny. Now!"

Sonny slashed at the bow line, and then sawed through the bow spring line. Reverend Mosby went to work with his own knife on the stern line and then the spring line as well.

"The dam's just—gone," said Wilde. "Except for the ends. They blasted all the middle."

Though not as loud as the demolition charges, the groans of the Lake Clarke ice field reverberated like a monstrous banshee waking as water sluiced over the ruined dam and fell away from beneath frozen plates the size of city blocks. Then the ice sheet fragmented with reports like cannon fire. And the Sundancer started to move.

"I hate to ask, because I think I know," said Reverend Mosby, "but where to?"

"Follow these new leads in the ice down river," said LuAnna. "Them, and the pack ice coming down from up river, should shove us where the water's running fast."

"We're going over that damn dam—," said Sonny Wright, intending no pun.

"It's the quickest way to the Conowingo," said LuAnna.

"After the Holtwood Dam—," said Molly Wilde.

"Yes," said LuAnna, "Once they blast that one, which they'll surely do in a few minutes when this surge from the Safe Harbor Dam rolls down on it—it's my fault. I thought we could bust on up here and take these fonnyboys head on. Save everybody. Save this dam anyway. Reduce the upstream pressure on the Conowingo. Cut Ben's and Ellis's workload a bit. I surely messed up something awful."

Reverend Mosby guided the Sundancer as best he could. The leads and ice sometimes spun the boat so it rushed downstream stern first. At other times, the pack ice closed a lead around them, squeezing the boat, with its steep V deadrise hull, up onto the ice; there it lay careened hard over on its side, passengers flung in a heap for a moment until the boat's weight crushed down through the ice into the water again.

Before long, they approached the Safe Harbor dam where the water churned swiftly over the shattered center section.

Using flashlights and flood lights they discovered stowed below, LuAnna and Molly Wilde took lookout positions forward on the port and starboard sides trying to spot detritus from the ruined dam, including twisted rebar, shattered concrete, and other broken structural members that could rip the bottom out of the boat. They shouted alerts and course corrections to Reverend Mosby. Sonny Wright helped by pushing off from larger obstructions with the boat hook.

Then finally, "Brace!" shouted Wilde.

Everyone gripped a hand rail. The Sundancer dived through the ruined segment of the dam, and hung in mid-air for what seemed like an eternity. Then it crashed down into open water that had been freed of ice by the torrent from above.

Wilde clutched her left arm in her right hand. "I don't want to do that again."

"You hurt?" asked Sony Wright.

"Bruised, but I'll live."

"Everybody okay?" asked Sonny as he peered at Reverend Mosby and LuAnna, both of whom nodded.

LuAnna said, "About eight miles to the Holtwood Dam, Reverend. Let's see what she can do."

Reverend Mosby pressed the throttle forward. The engine RPMs climbed, but there was a new thumping shudder in the cockpit sole, like a ghoul beating its way up and out of a grave. The reverend observed in that sideways Smith Island manner, "The prop shaft's running smooth as silk."

Downstream, the sky lit up with the loom of a distant fireworks display that they all felt in their chests.

"There goes the Holtwood Dam," said Sonny.

LuAnna said, "We've got to reach the Conowingo in time to help Ben, or at least warn him."

The boat wallowed. Molly Wilde shined her spotlight through the companionway into the galley below. "I'm no sailor, but should all that water be sloshing around down there?"

"Nope," said LuAnna, looking over Wilde's shoulder. "We're sinking."

CHAPTER 87

KNOCKER ELLIS HEARD the second big blast of the night, and looked from the Conowingo Dam's roadbed upstream to the great dome of light illuminating the snow. The light was more pronounced as houses on the dam's electrical grid went dark. "That's not Aberdeen Proving Ground. Safe Harbor Dam's gone, and now the Holtwood, too."

Blackshaw said, "Then we don't have much time."

A bullet's worth of concrete splintered off the railing. Both men ducked and turned away as the gun's report reached their ears.

Ellis said, "If you think you can deal with the noisy stuff down below, I'll hang out up here to welcome those snowmobile nimrods."

"It's three against one."

Ellis smiled. "It's three against me."

Blackshaw dashed for the small structure covering the access stairway down to the dam's works.

"Hey Ben!"

Blackshaw turned, "Yeah?"

"When it comes to swimming around in ice—"

"Yes, Ellis?"

"I prefer when you leave me out of it."

"Copy." Blackshaw raised his gun and headed for the stairs.

Meeting no opposition on the steps, Blackshaw quickly surmised the attackers had viewed the dam as soft target. The only KIA Blackshaw saw was a tech wearing the dam's power company uniform: he lay shot, sprawled at the bottom of the steps.

Blackshaw still wasn't sure how many operators had been detailed to accompany the demolition specialists. The team hitting the ship had gone in heavy. So far, the only resistance here was one operator on top of the dam. Then there were the three operators on the snowmobiles who seemed like they were a rapid response contingent filling in for too light an insertion team. Perhaps someone had figured that the ship contingent had been neutralized, and the munitions were now off line. That would shift the Conowingo Dam from Plan B to the new Plan A in the mission to destroy the Chesapeake Bay fishery, and with it, the major source of horseshoe crab blood for Big Pharma.

The hum and whine from the distant turbine hall was so loud in this central stretch of the dam that only the most rudimentary thought was possible.

Then knifing through the din, Blackshaw heard someone shouting. "Spatchcock! Spatchcock, it's Kläng! It's all set! I'm coming up!"

As Blackshaw took cover behind a concrete pillar, he glimpsed an operative in head-to-toe white camo twisting at the volume knob on a handheld radio. Blackshaw switched on the radio that Ellis had taken from the operative atop the dam. Keying the transmit button, Blackshaw said, "Kläng, stay put! There's trouble up here. Stay put!"

"What? Hell no! The timer's running!" said Kläng. "We gotta boogie!"

The man called Kläng jogged toward the stairway, and Blackshaw's position in the shadow behind the pillar.

Kläng shouted at the radio in panic. "Spatchcock! I'm coming up! Don't fucking shoot!"

Blackshaw stood behind Kläng, rammed his pistol hard under the operator's jaw, and said, "Let's take a look at your work."

Kläng's yelp was cut short as Blackshaw's arm tightened across the trachea. When the operator realized that resisting was useless, and might cut his life short along with his ability to breathe, Blackshaw loosened his grip slightly.

Kläng said, "This whole place is going up!"

Blackshaw dragged Kläng a hundred feet back to where a nexus of five small radio triggers were plugged into a laptop on the floor. On the screen, a .gif of a nuclear mushroom cloud rose into the air over and over.

"Subtle," Blackshaw said. "Now defuse it."

"Okay! Just don't hurt me." Kläng knelt before the laptop.

Blackshaw mistook Kläng's craven tone for submission. While one of Kläng's hands played over the laptop's keyboard, his other withdrew a short-bladed knife. He slashed at Blackshaw's abdomen. The drysuit opened in a six-inch gash. Blackshaw stepped back, and before the laceration's sting could deepen to an all-consuming burn, his pistol was smoking, and Kläng lay bleeding out with three bullets placed for keeps.

Blackshaw grabbed the radio triggers in one massive hand, gripped the laptop in the other, and yanked. He froze, listening for the explosive roar, awaiting the crushing shockwave punch, bracing for the inrush of cold, lethal water. Nothing happened. Somehow, rotten with fear, Blackshaw had survived his ham-fisted attempt to downrig dam-busting explosives.

As he returned up the steps he'd descended moments ago, the hum of turbines gave way to the howl of the storm and sporadic gunfire. Peering over the top stair, Blackshaw saw Ellis crouched returning fire on what sounded like two shooters farther down the dam's roadbed hidden in the storm.

Ellis saw Blackshaw and said, "To the left, someplace under that watch tower."

The distant gunfire halted. Blackshaw said, "They're moving up on us. A rush."

"Might have night vision gear."

Ellis stood, perhaps to catch a glimpse of a target. Immediately the top of the dam wall erupted in a flurry of whining cement shards. Ellis crouched quickly, but then rolled back hard on his haunches as if in a daze, gripping at his upper arm.

Blackshaw crouch-crabbed to his friend. "Thought you took care of those fools on the ice."

"Me, too. One of them—must've been playing possum." Ellis grimaced with pain. "I'll be needing some medical attention pretty quick."

Blackshaw yanked a hemostatic dressing from a dryseal pocket on his thigh, and stuffed it down the sleeve in Ellis's tactical drysuit. Then Blackshaw yanked on one of the six tourniquets integrated at crucial joints throughout the suit.

The tourniquet cinched down on the arm just under Ellis's shoulder, slowing the pulse of his brachial artery, as well as a gooey veinous seep.

A roaring sound grew beneath the storm's shriek. Blackshaw peered over the dam wall. "Here comes the surge from the busted dams upstream!"

A torrent of water broke over the dam wall, drenching the roadway to the east and west. With no ordnance having weakened the dam, its hundred-year-old structure held. Blackshaw continued his examination of Ellis.

"Bullet's still in. Heads-up! Here we go!" said Blackshaw.

A small-framed operator lurched into view from the east, a decided limp slowing her progress; some injury made her crouching movement seem painful. The operator let off two shots toward Blackshaw and Ellis, then toppled over in the snow.

Blackshaw said, "You tag her? Because I didn't."

"Can't say as I did. Maybe she's playing possum, too."

A second operator, a man, his eyes ablaze with rage, rushed past the still form of the first, gun set on full auto, though he loosed only short bursts of suppressing fire. His berserker's scream was more fearsome than his shooting was straight.

From the upriver side of the dam came three shots that sent Blackshaw rolling for the deck next to Ellis. The second and third shots caught the bellowing operator in the legs, and sent him sprawling, his weapon disappearing into a snow drift.

An astonished Blackshaw watched a familiar-looking woman leap over the dam wall into the roadway and kneel low, covering the downed enemy who writhed in pain.

Blackshaw said, "LuAnna?"

Another woman, followed by Reverend Mosby and Sonny Wright, gained the roadway, smartly collapsing and covering sectors. Blackshaw and Ellis put up their hands.

"Nobody here but us chickens," said Blackshaw. "Hey Hon, I thought you were holding the fort on Smith Island."

LuAnna didn't look at Blackshaw. She had her weapon trained on the man she had shot as Reverend Mosby patted him down for weapons. She said, "This fonnyboy came calling. We had to thin his ranks. And that Bonamy Screed from the FBI even came back for seconds, doncha know."

Blackshaw paced in consternation, only managing to say, "There's another one down the road a piece. Is that—Molly Wilde? There's FBI all over you. Are we in trouble again?"

LuAnna said, "She's minding her p's and q's. Those other dams blew up. What about this one?"

"The charges are still down there, but the triggers are neutral."

Reverend Mosby said, "No weapons, but he's got a wicked look in his eye. Might put a couple in his noggin to be sure."

The wounded man found his voice. "You idiots! Do you know who I am?"

Wilde and Reverend Mosby strode off to check the other attacker.

Blackshaw said, "Any thought to who's minding the baby?"

LuAnna said, "Kathy's in her heaven looking after him."

Blackshaw stopped pacing next to LuAnna, but out of her line of fire. "What if we'd both been killed?"

LuAnna flared. "That's your hot take? What if even one of us were killed? You or me!"

"It takes a village—" Blackshaw said.

"It takes parents! Two parents if at all possible!" said LuAnna.

"The only reason I'm *here* is because I thought you were *there*!" Blackshaw said.

LuAnna's jaw dropped for a moment. "The only reason I'm here is saving your fool neck! Why the heck do you do everything you can to push away the folks you're closest to?"

Blackshaw raked his soul for a reply, but had none.

The crippled man on the road shouted, "You need to get me to a doctor, dammit! ASAP!"

Ellis said, "Me first. That shitbird can wait."

The snow was abating, and predawn light showed in the east.

Molly Wilde shouted from down the roadbed. "This one's dead. Hardly a mark on her, except her ankle looks FUBARed. Is that—that's my Jeep!" In a wave of distress she kicked the body at her feet. "You stole my Jeep!"

Several big SUVs, led by a Teradyne Gurkha armored personnel carrier roared onto the dam from the westerly approach. They braked, and Pershing Lowry dismounted from the Gurkha in full tactical kit at the head of a heavily armed team. "Everybody freeze!"

"Freeze yourself," said Blackshaw. "A little late to the party."

Wilde shouted at the new arrivals, "Persh? That you?"

"Molly! What are you doing here?"

There was an utter lack of tactical correctness as they ran to embrace each other.

After a kiss that made all onlookers glance at their boots, Lowry said, "When I saw you'd gone, I had no idea you were involved in this. Is—is that your Jeep?"

"These suspects stole it from Smith Island," Wilde said.

"How did it get to—you drove on the ice." Lowry was aghast. "You drove across Tangier Sound all the way from Crisfield?"

"That was later, and it was from Smith Island to Crisfield, not the other way, and not in the Jeep. By the way," said Wilde, "I think somebody took a shot at me as I went past that *Penelope* LNG carrier."

Lowry's consternation only deepened. "You drove across the entire Chesapeake Bay to Smith Island!"

Wilde said, "The shortest distance between—"

"What if you'd hit a fissure and gone in?" said Lowry. "We'd never know what happened to you!"

"I reserve the right to a little goddamn mystery, Pershing."

"That's exactly what I'm talking about," said Blackshaw to LuAnna. "Unnecessary risk for no reason."

Lowry ignored Blackshaw and went on, "The *Penelope's* secured now, thank goodness. But it was full of heavily armed operatives. All dead. It's a ghost ship. Blackshaw, you're usually at the center of these shit-shows. Do you have any idea what happened there?"

"Can't confirm or deny," said Blackshaw. "But we've got most of *Penelope's* original crew on Smith Island."

Lowry asked, "So who's behind all this? What's the crew telling you about the pirates?"

"Very little," Blackshaw said. "But we're thinking Big Pharma is in the running."

A fresh gale of wind whipped snow into the air. Ellis rose painfully as his helicopter set down on an empty stretch of the roadway. He said, "You all talk too much. I need a doctor, and that's my ride."

Lowry asserted his authority. "Ellis, you will make yourself available for debriefing as soon as possible. And you Blackshaws stay put right here to answer questions."

The rear door of the helicopter slid open; a nasty looking man unshipped a nastier looking minigun and aimed it casually toward Lowry and his team.

Ellis shook his head. "No, Agent Lowry. The Blackshaws are with me."

To ease the sting, Blackshaw told Lowry, "There's a couple KIA down those stairs. The demolition charges are neutralized. Have yourself a nice day."

As the helicopter roared away into the gray morning light, Pershing Lowry detailed his team leader to take over the scene. Then he said, "Molly, let's take my car home."

Wilde said, "Seriously? I've got my Jeep."

"But Molly—"

"Pershing, chill. I'm driving my Jeep home by myself."

Smarting from the gentle rebuke, Lowry made a study of his team assuming control of the scene, triaging the wounded, tagging the dead, applying first aide to those who could still benefit from it. Upstream, the world was dark from the loss of hydroelectric power. The bomb techs descended into the dam to secure the explosives. The Blackshaws had left an epic level of havoc in their wake, but in the mayhem, they had prevented so much more devastation. From the corner of his eye, Lowry watched Molly drive her Jeep away toward their home, the one place where his sense of utter dominion was happily, but absolutely undone.

BLACKSHAW SHORT FICTION

From time to time, I have the great privilege of working with extremely talented interns from several fine colleges and universities. Some interns come from business schools, and focus on marketing the Blackshaw books through various social media portals.

Other interns concentrate on illustration, and they are charged with reading the Ben Blackshaw novels and adapted screenplays, as well as other one-off scripts. I then ask them to choose pivotal beats of action and emotion in the stories and illustrate them for the marketing interns to use in their outreach.

Every intern earns an opportunity to collaborate with me on a Blackshaw short story to be published at the end of the next Blackshaw novel. Not every intern takes advantage of this offer of publication. For those who do, the work flow goes this way: First, we discuss a wide range of possible Blackshaw-adjacent plots together. When the idea is winnowed down to a story, the intern then creates the story outline. With the outline tweaked, then the intern roughs out the story itself. After we discuss refinements to that first draft, the intern follows up with a rewrite. I then undertake a final editorial pass.

While I was writing Blast, three interns, Erin Blake, Charles Ta, and Deana Reynolds stepped forward to collaborate on a trio of fascinating short stories which I am proud to include here.

AWOL

By

Robert Blake Whitehill
With
Erin Blake

Ms. Erin Blake is the longest-serving intern I have had the pleasure of working with thus far. She dived into all aspects of media, and publishing; between her master's degree in business from Montclair State University, and her extensive and diverse internship experience (which included social media strategizing and outreach, app development, and wicked-smart business presentations) she is qualified for a C-suite, though she is now earning her way up the ladder in management in the medical field.

AWOL is Blake's second short story. Her first, PARDON ME, was published with the Blackshaw novel DOG & BITCH ISLAND.

In AWOL, Blake chose to explore the prickly rapport between LuAnna Blackshaw and her reclusive sister-in-law, Annie Vo Blackshaw. Blake ably wove family and mystery together in a way that ever deepens fascination with the story page by page. This could be the start of a novella, but AWOL is tantalizing in what it leaves unresolved. Run-of-the-mill narrative closure is not Erin Blake's thing.

AWOL

CHAPTER 1

CALLUM GIGGLED AS Penelope chased after the soccer ball. He did his best to keep it away from her. Penelope, the speedy wisp of a preschooler, loved time outside playing with someone her age. And playing this childlike amalgam of keep-away, soccer, and tag helped young Callum burn off a bit of his pent-up energy. Back on Smith Island, Callum spent a large majority of his time outdoors with his mother, LuAnna Blackshaw. The pair were inseparable. Together mother and son enjoyed riding their bikes (or tricycle, in Callum's case) around the island, and progging for arrowheads on the beach.

Penelope finally caught up to the soccer ball as it came to a halt near the wood rail fence. Her straight black hair swished beside her pale face as she guarded the ball. A six-inch height difference did not blunt Penelope's competitive spirit. With swift, calculated movements she charged past Callum, knocking him out of the way.

"GOALLLLLL!" cheered Penelope as she extended her hand to Callum. In one quick motion Penelope yanked, and Callum was once again on his feet.

"My ball this time," commanded Penelope. The children reset the soccer ball to the middle of their makeshift field and resumed play. LuAnna watched her son with pride from the comfortable vantage of Annie Vo's front porch. Her effort to maintain a relationship with Ben's half-sister appeared to be paying off. The Blackshaw cousins seemed to enjoy their first playdate with one another. The future of such gatherings would now depend on LuAnna and Annie Vo's ability to remain amicable. *Mothers will do anything for their kids*, LuAnna thought.

"Peaceful out here," said LuAnna as she surveyed Annie Vo's property. The three-story Virginia farmhouse was a vision of luxury. Annie Vo and her wife Janie had spared no expense restoring the home to its original glory, then adding many modern amenities and grace notes. Gray bricks clad the exterior walls protecting both the structure of the building and its inhabitants. Decorative white wood trim and railings accented the porch. Fresh flowers and shrubs outlined the circular gravel driveway. From the outside, no one would know a retired sniper resided here with her little family.

"Just the way I like it," said Annie Vo. "Peaceful, quiet, and secluded. All I need is Janie and Penelope." After years as a professional sniper, Annie Vo had retired to a simpler life. She occupied her time with family and the restoration of her new home, uncovering ceiling beams, stripping paint from wainscoting, chair rails, crown molding, and removing ancient horsehair plaster to expose brick here and there.

"It's beautiful. Nice to finally see where my sister-in-law's been living."

"This was a one-time invitation. For the kids. Don't plan on coming over every Monday night for Chablis and The Bachelor."

"You Blackshaws all have one thing in common. You sure like to be alone."

"It's a family trait. You'll get used to it one day," smirked Annie Vo. "Speaking of family, how's Ben? What's he up to nowadays?"

"Ben's good. He and Ellis are off fishing. It's rockfish season. You'll have to come over and try some for yourself. All you have to do is cover the fillet with a bit of Panko and some Old Bay. It's a delicacy on Smith."

"Sounds like a new Smith Island classic. I'll consider it," said Annie Vo. Her lackluster interest in LuAnna's invitation was evident even without the barely concealed eyeroll. Even as sisters-in-law, Annie Vo and LuAnna never knew what to say to one another. Awkward silences often suffocated their conversations which otherwise consisted of passive aggressive sniping.

"Penelope! Where are you running off to? I asked you to stay closer to the house."

"Mom, Callum and I saw a car coming down the lane." replied Penelope.

In the distance the faint sound of a car engine roared closer to Annie Vo's secluded retreat.

"Are you expecting more company?" asked LuAnna.

"It was a stretch inviting you here. Let's not get carried away. Penelope, why don't you show Callum the chicken coop out back. Aunt LuAnna and I will be there in a minute."

Penelope grabbed Callum by the arm and dragged him to the backyard.

"Now let's see who we have here," said Annie Vo as she eased a curved karambit blade from a sheath inside her jacket.

A blacked-out Suburban crawled up in low gear stopping ten feet from the porch where LuAnna and Annie Vo sat. The passenger side door swung open; a pair of Louboutin heels showed first.

"Careful, those red bottoms may get scuffed on the gravel. I'm not paying for the damage," called Annie Vo.

The woman closed the car door behind her.

Molly Wilde stated, "Don't worry, I have a few other pairs. These are for field work."

Molly raised her left hand and gestured to the driver of the Suburban. The signal seemed to say, *this will only take a few minutes, keep the car running.* Turning back toward Annie Vo and LuAnna, Molly readjusted her velvet Saint Laurent suit jacket and brushed her brown bangs out of her eyes. Molly walked toward the porch and said, "Beautiful home. I'm Molly Wilde, Senior Resident Agent of Calverton, Maryland."

"I remember you. You're that feeb Ben saved at Dove Point," Annie Vo replied. "I've heard stories of you showing up looking for Ben to do your dirty work. Newsflash Sweet Pea, he ain't here. What do you want?"

Molly responded, "I see the Blackshaw family resemblance. But yes, I was hoping to have a conversation with Ben. Expecting him any time soon?"

"Not soon enough, Princess," smirked Annie Vo.

"What Annie Vo means to say is Ben's away on a fishing trip. He will be gone for a few more days. Can I take a message?"

"Rockfish season?" asked Molly.

LuAnna nodded.

"Wait, how did you know?" questioned LuAnna.

"Good guess," said Molly as she crossed her arms and smirked.

"Since she showed up here uninvited, I think it's safe to assume she paid a visit to Smith Island first," commented Annie Vo.

"I may have stopped by to see if anyone was home. I love what you did with the landscaping. The new flower bed is gorgeous," said Molly. "Ran into your friends Sonny and Mary Wright. Out for a stroll. Sonny sure takes his job looking after your saltbox seriously."

Of course Sonny told her where I am, thought LuAnna. "Stay far away from my home, Molly. We don't need Ella Grace to see her mommy tied to a chair again. Do we?"

"Relax ladies, I'm here on business. Not to audition for the real housewives of Darkest Nowhere, Maryland," said Molly.

"What business do you have with Ben?" asked LuAnna. "He's a family man now, Molly. Callum and I are his top priority. We don't need him running around the world for you, so your designer suits stay clean."

"You're right, I'm all for leaving Ben out of this. The question is, did he choose to leave himself out of the situation?"

"Are you implying that Ben's already involved in whatever case you're screwing up?" asked LuAnna.

"What I'm saying is Ben's involvement is being taken into consideration. If you'd like to keep your little family together, I'd advise you give Ben a call. Make sure he comes home ASAP and stays home," said Molly as she began to walk back toward the Suburban.

"You can't just walk up here, imply my husband is a person of interest and leave. What is the case?" asked LuAnna. "You clearly want the Blackshaws' help, so read me in."

Annie Vo added, "Send her a text. I don't need the feebs dragging me into this. You guys need to handle your business and leave me out of it."

"Too bad Annie Vo, consider yourself involved. I wanted to run some details regarding the missing head of the National Joint Terrorism Task Force past Ben," replied Molly.

"You lost Sheila Vine. Did you retrace your steps? A missing fed is kind-of a big deal," responded LuAnna.

"We're not sure what's going on," responded Molly. "Her protection detail gave her a moment of privacy to pay respects in the cemetery. When they went back, she was gone. Nowhere to be found. She's expected to attend an important conference in two days."

"Who'd want to kidnap an FBI Poobah?" Annie Vo asked. "Maybe she's on walkabout."

"Doubt it," said Molly. "Security cameras in Arlington captured footage of her disappearance. Looks like it was a one-man job. CCTV makes the abductor as a middle aged, physically fit, white male. He was wearing a black hoodie covering any distinguishing features." Molly surveyed LuAnna's reaction.

LuAnna became defensive. "Are you here to ask Ben for help or to ask if he's recently taken a trip to Washington D.C.?" Molly stayed silent.

Annie Vo erupted, "Okay Buttercup, you need to leave. You're not going to drive up on my property and accuse my family of jack shit. Ben saved your life. Don't make him regret it." Annie Vo pointed toward in the direction of the car. Molly gracefully turned toward the car, walking slowly.

"Sorry for the intrusion ladies. Please tell Ben I stopped by to say hello." Molly climbed into the passenger seat of the running car. The car rolled around the driveaway loop and left Annie Vo's property down the lane.

"She's got some balls. The car, the heels, the suit," commented Annie Vo. LuAnna's stare drifted toward the end of the driveway as she listened to Annie Vo's rant. "LuAnna, are you listening?"

LuAnna pulled out of her trance-like state. "I'm sorry. What did you say?"

"Get ready for dinner. Janie made softshell crabs and pasta salad."

LuAnna nodded and followed Annie Vo toward the chicken coop where Callum and Penelope chased the chickens. Something about Molly Wilde's visit bothered LuAnna.

CHAPTER 2

LUANNA WASHED HER hands in Annie Vo's guest bathroom, in preparation for dinner. She considered digging through her purse to find her sat phone to call Ben and tell him about the visit from the FBI agent. By asking where Ben was, Wilde implied he was a person of interest in the kidnapping of a high-ranking FBI administrator. That couldn't be Ben on the surveillance video. The description was too vague, perhaps intentionally so. Wilde was probing. Just kicking up dust. Wilde's insinuation was not worth overthinking. LuAnna talked herself out of contacting Ben. The phone call would ruin his fishing trip with Ellis.

"LuAnna, dinner's ready!" called Janie.

Some softshell crabs and company were surely what LuAnna needed to put her mind at ease. LuAnna dried her hands and passed from the bathroom into the adjoining guest bedroom. This one room was the size of the entire first floor of her saltbox home on Smith Island. LuAnna took a moment to look around at the space. Annie Vo and Janie had furnished the room to stay true to its original décor while offering more modern design elements. Two black and white photos of plows hung over the queen-sized bed. A tan quilt covered the guest bed, which was decorated with a bright red accent pillow.

How strange, thought LuAnna. Underneath the decorative pillow a piece of paper was hidden. *The kids must've made arts and crafts up here with Janie,* LuAnna realized.

LuAnna picked up the note for a closer look. Four words were printed on the cardstock. *Stay out of it.* The handwriting looked familiar, but she couldn't place it.

"Stay out of what?" questioned LuAnna as she flipped over the cardstock. "Oh my." The note appeared to be a homemade greeting card. The picture on the back was a cemetery. Only one gravestone, a cross, was in focus, but a line of other crosses stretched away behind it. The engraving on the cross read Daniel MacGlen.

LuAnna ran to the door of the guest bedroom, "Annie, can you please come here for a moment." A disgruntled Annie stomped up the steps.

"This better be good. I just sat down to eat." Annie explained. Without a word, LuAnna handed the card to Annie Vo.

Annie Vo read the note. "What the hell is this?" asked Annie. "Where did you get this?"

"Found it under the pillow," LuAnna answered as she pointed to the spot.

"Is this yours? It sure isn't mine," said Annie Vo. LuAnna shook her head. "Someone must've broken in!" Annie Vo scanned the room, looking for signs of a break in. "Well, I'll be—The window's unlatched! Did you open this when you came in?"

"No. I washed my hands and was about to come down for supper when I noticed the note," responded LuAnna.

"And you don't recognize the handwriting?"

"Seems familiar, but I can't place it. If it was from somebody on Smith Island, 'Stay out of it' would really mean—"

"'Dive right in,'" finished Annie Vo. "First the feeb shows up, and now a break in." Annie's face blanched with anger. "This obviously has to do with that missing fed."

"Look at the back of the card, Annie. It's a photo of a tombstone. 'Daniel MacGlen'. I think who ever left us this note is leaving us a clue."

"You think this Daniel MacGlen has something to do with the invasion of my privacy? All those crosses—"

"Why else would the note be here? Let's think about this for a minute." LuAnna began pacing the room. "I think Daniel has something to do with the case. Maybe him personally, or the location of where he is buried. Let's grab your laptop," ordered LuAnna.

LuAnna followed Annie Vo across the hall to the master bedroom and her custom-built laptop.

"What are you going to do? Become Facebook friends with Daniel's family and cyberstalk him?" teased Annie Vo.

"As much as I would love to, I am going to Google him. Let's see if we can find where he is buried." LuAnna aggressively typed away as Annie Vo scanned the room for any additional clues. "Check this out," LuAnna called to Annie Vo. The two women looked at the screen. "Daniel MacGlen is buried in Arlington National Cemetery." LuAnna continued to examine the photo of the grave.

"I thought those headstones looked familiar. Hour-thirty by car. Looks like we're going to pay our respects," Annie Vo said as she stood up to leave.

"Arlington's closed now. Won't open until nine tomorrow morning," advised LuAnna.

"Who said we need to wait? We're leaving right now. Someone broke into my home and that gets my undivided attention. Grab your stuff and let's go. I'll get a pistol for Janie. She'll secure the place after we're gone; keep the kids safe tonight. Hustle! We're ass-on-curb in five." Annie Vo strode out.

CHAPTER 3

THE CAR RIDE from Annie Vo's farmstead to Arlington had been
quiet. Annie Vo's anger only grew over the invasion of her home while
LuAnna pondered Ben's possible involvement in this case. In what little
conversation they had during the trip, the women discussed their plan to
scout the outside perimeter to find an unguarded location where they could
sneak in.

The women arrived at Arlington National Cemetery around midnight.
Annie Vo parked her Audi SUV near the Service Complex lot of the
cemetery, which was the closest lot to Daniel MacGlen's final resting place.
Before they left the car, LuAnna and Annie zipped up their sweatshirts and
pulled the hoods over their heads. If they were going to break into a National
Cemetery, they wanted to avoid a front-page news story.

The women headed through the Service Complex parking lot and
straight through to the Patton Drive gate. LuAnna and Annie Vo needed to
act quickly. They patrolled in on foot just off of Patton Drive, toward the
Coast Guard memorial and the location of Daniel's grave. Red-lensed
flashlights helped the women highlight the faces of the tombstones as they
searched the area for their target grave.

"I found it! Daniel MacGlen. Right there. Annie, come take a look,"
whispered LuAnna. The light of Annie Vo's flashlight grew brighter as she
walked toward LuAnna. "Interesting design for a tombstone," commented
LuAnna. "All of the others are solid stone. This one is stone with a gold grave
plate placed on top. Look at the dates."

"Daniel MacGlen, January 1956 – August 1909. Beloved father, son, and husband," read Annie Vo.

"Exactly! The dates are backwards! How could someone be born in 1956 and die in 1909," questioned LuAnna.

"It must've been a misprint, and they never fixed the issue," said Annie Vo.

"You're right but look at the postcard. If you look really close you can see the dates in the photo are in the correct order. Why would the physical tombstone be incorrect when the one in the photo is right?" LuAnna stared at the tombstone reviewing the details once more.

"The photo is older. The change to the stone is recent. Hold still, I need to get something out of the bag," asked Annie Vo. She dug through the small day-pack, and pulled out heavy sheets of paper and a crayon. Annie knelt in front of the grave and held a paper up to the stone.

"What on earth do you think you're doing?" asked LuAnna as she snatched the paper from Annie Vo's hand.

"Relax! You've never rubbed a tombstone during your eighth-grade trip to Washington D.C.?" asked Annie Vo. "You take a piece of paper and place it on the tombstone, then you gently rub the crayon over the text." Annie grabbed the paper from LuAnna. "It traces the words." Annie Vo began to rub over the tombstone lettering.

"Why are you doing that?" questioned LuAnna.

"Clearly something is wrong with the tombstone, so I can trace the lettering for us to review later. We can't stay here all night staring at it." Annie Vo continued to rub over the lettering.

LuAnna's flashlight dimmed. She flicked on her iPhone's flashlight screen. A sharp scraping noise occurred as if Annie had scratched the tombstone.

"Are you alright?" worried LuAnna as she aimed her light in the direction of the noise.

"Yeah, but what was that noise?" asked Annie Vo. She focused her attention on the rubbing for a moment, then said, "LuAnna, you're not going to believe this."

The grave plate which once covered the stone had shifted positions to reveal a hollow opening in the cross.

"What is that?" asked LuAnna.

"Not the usual headstone. It's a dead drop," replied Annie Vo. "Someone will hide an item in this tombstone. The tombstone blends in with its surroundings so it doesn't seem suspicious. Someone else will eventually pick up what's inside," explained Annie Vo.

"Is there anything in there?" asked LuAnna as she peered into the opening.

"Yes." Annie Vo removed a small oblong object from the void. "A thumb-drive."

"Hang on. It doesn't have a USB plug," observed LuAnna.

"It's Bluetooth."

"So, we can assume that whoever was meant to grab it hasn't done that yet."

Annie Vo said, "Not necessarily. This probably is encrypted to only two devices. First, the device from which this thing was loaded."

"And the second," said LuAnna, "is the device meant to read or receive the data."

"I was assigned a few of my gigs this way," said Annie Vo.

"You mean, sanctioned murders."

"Tomato, tomahto," said Annie Vo. "The beauty is, the recipient doesn't have to attach the drive to a device or even touch it. Just stroll by the drop with the right device, and the drive automatically handshakes with it, and burps the data to the device via the Bluetooth. But you have to be close. The transmission range is only a few feet so it can't be picked up and triangulated by a third party."

"Fancy-shmancy," said LuAnna. "So whatever is on this thing could already have been picked up."

"Right. Does Ben have something like that? A tablet? A laptop?"

"Why Ben?"

"Because of that notecard you found back at my place," said Annie Vo. "The words said, 'Stay away,' but the photo led us right here. Smith Islanders have a way of saying the opposite of what they mean."

"As a matter of fact," said LuAnna, "Ben does have a laptop."

"And here it's only the 21st century," said Annie Vo. "Quite the early adopter, by Smith Island standards."

"But his phone is barely more than a Jitterbug old-folks flip-phone."

"The phone you know about, that is," said Annie Vo, carefully.

"You think he's some kind of sneaky baw-bag with burners and such like?"

"You bought him a few burners yourself back when we all met up for the first time."

"That was totally different," said LuAnna. "We, emphasis on *we*, needed them to throw off a bunch of over-financed shit-heels." LuAnna went on, "And I happen to know Ben's laptop is back in our saltbox on the kitchen table. He doesn't take it fishing, doncha know. No, we need to figure out if this Daniel MacGlen fella is real. Luckily I know someone who may be able to help us out." She flicked off her phone's flashlight and dialed.

CHAPTER 4

THREE RINGS WERE all it took for Michael Craig to answer.

LuAnna said, "Do you know who this is?"

A drowsy Craig replied, "It's a pleasure to hear from you again, m'lady. I appreciate your generosity, but like I've said, I can't accept tickets to your next concert. I have a family commitment on the same day. I can't back out of it. The package you sent was more than enough. My wife and I loved the Oreos. Pink cookie with green filling, cool design."

"I imagine you have quite the poker face, Michael. Do you know who this *really* is?" chuckled LuAnna.

"Oh. Terrific. I can see your husband's charisma has rubbed off. Why are you calling? He's usually the one dragging me into some mess."

"The tables have turned today, Mike. My husband's on a fishing trip, and I was hoping you could give me some more information on a former soldier. Name's Daniel MacGlen. Buried in Arlington."

"Is Mr. MacGlen a family member, or ex-boyfriend?" asked Michael Craig as he got to work.

"No relation or old flame. I think he's is connected to the disappearance of the Sheila Vine. FBI," stated LuAnna.

The distant mouse clicking and typing coming from Michael Craig's end paused. "Oh. So you're following your husband's footsteps, inserting yourself into a situation where you don't belong."

"Can you help me or not? I don't have all day and I am sure you have other A-list gossip to attend to."

"The answer is no. I cannot help you. I actually advise you to stay out of this mess. I think you have more important matters on your hands."

LuAnna's patience was growing thin.

Then Craig asked, "Didn't you say your husband was away on a fishing trip?"

"Why does that matter?" LuAnna asked.

"Looks to me like he's kicked his feet up on the couch at home."

LuAnna hung up the phone.

LuAnna turned to Annie Vo who had finished the tombstone rubbing. "My friend was no help. I think we should head to Smith Island to see what Ben is up to."

CHAPTER 5

AFTER A LONG drive, and a midnight boat ride across Tangier Sound from a friendly Crisfield captain who was also an insomniac, LuAnna stood at the door of their saltbox. A brief inspection of the outside pointed to signs that Ben was in fact home.

Around back, LuAnna had seen Miss Dotsy docked and bobbing gently in small waves of their quiet gut that led out to the Chesapeake Bay.

Annie Vo told LuAnna she was going to take a stroll through the neighborhood, just to take a gander. LuAnna took a deep breath and opened her front door.

Inside, LuAnna heard the sound of pots and pans banging in the kitchen. The smell of warm food soon followed. LuAnna followed the sound and scent into the kitchen where Ben stood at the stove.

"That was a quick trip," greeted LuAnna. "Fish not biting?"

"I could say the same for you. You're back from Annie's awfully early," responded Blackshaw.

"What happened with fishing?" asked LuAnna. As she waited for Ben's response, she quickly examined him. No scratches, bruises, or marks. No signs of sleep deprivation. But blood stained his t-shirt. And there was his laptop on the table where she last saw it.

"Ellis had to come home and pick up some gear. He didn't pack enough. Figured I come home to cook up the catch before we head back out."

"Since when did Ellis not pack enough of anything? You'll have to change your shirt. It's got blood on it."

"From filleting the fish. Hope it washes out. It's my favorite," said Ben.

"A little soap and elbow grease will …" LuAnna was cut off by the ring of their house phone. LuAnna turned to leave the kitchen for the parlor. In the process of turning, LuAnna managed to stub her toe on the plastic garbage can near the end of the kitchen counter. Inside, LuAnna noticed white Styrofoam plate and cling wrap from grocery store packaging. *Ben could have at least tried to hide the evidence of store-bought fish*, she thought.

Closing the parlor door behind her, LuAnna lifted the phone from its cradle, "Hello?"

"LuAnna, it's Molly. I wanted to apologize for before. I shouldn't have stopped by Annie Vo's."

"You're definitely not welcome there anymore," said LuAnna. "Not that you ever were."

"I have good news. Vine arrived for her flight this evening. She's on her way to that conference," informed Molly.

"Any idea what happened to her?" asked LuAnna.

"No idea at all. She walked into the airport with her protection detail like nothing ever happened. She won't talk about why she dropped out like that."

"That's strange. Someone like her doesn't just up and disappear for two days."

"I agree. Uh, gotta go. Pershing is looking for me. Just wanted to apologize."

"Noted," said LuAnna as she hung up the phone.

So, Sheila Vine was safe, and Ben was home. But for some reason, her concern about his involvement only grew.

LuAnna left the parlor and headed for the kitchen. "Hey hon. I'll clean your shirt if you go change—" She entered an empty kitchen. The stovetop where Ben had just been frying rockfish was now turned off. The warm pan rested in the sink. The cooked rockfish lay on a serving plate on the kitchen table covered with aluminum foil. A folded piece of paper lay on the table next to the fish.

LuAnna could not believe her eyes. Ben was gone, but there was a note. She unfolded the note and read it aloud, "*I will be back soon and explain everything.*

Don't come looking for me, and leave Annie Vo and Michael Craig out of this. Trust me."

"Sounds like you just found out Ben ran out of here," Annie Vo commented from the living room and the waterside door. She entered the kitchen where LuAnna stood in disbelief.

"What did you see?" asked LuAnna.

"I was doing a recce around the neighborhood. I was near the church when I heard the motors from a go-fast boat. Idling. Took a detour to get a better view. I was right. A speedboat. Two men. One at the helm. Both wore suits. Maybe the FBI or Secret Service? Ben ran out the back door. He was carrying something. He boarded the boat. I came back to see what was up to send him hare-assing off like that."

"His laptop was here. Now it's gone. Must be what you saw him toting," said LuAnna. "Which way did they go?"

"Towards Crisfield. Headed to the mainland where a car's waiting, I bet. Or maybe to the west shore of the Chesapeake," answered Annie Vo.

LuAnna sat at the table and uncovered the rockfish. Ben was into something, and but once again, she'd been left on shore. "It's not softshell crabs, but might as well get it while it's hot. Oh and Molly called to say 'sorry' for taking a run at us like that."

Annie Vo collected plates and forks. "How nice. But we still have a dead drop, a missing feeb that's been found, and Ben's gone again—"

"And we're none the wiser," said LuAnna.

"Welcome to the world of Blackshaws," said Annie Vo. "We may never know what's going on."

"Oh, I'll find out from Ben. You can bet on that," said LuAnna. "Coffee?"

"Yes. Hold the cheese."

Annie Vo's attention was drawn to LuAnna's phone on the table. "Um LuAnna, when was the last time you looked at your phone?"

"Back at the cemetery, when you needed extra light for the rubbing." LuAnna checked her iPhone. The screen was strobing intermittently. Facial recognition unlocked the phone. "Look at this," LuAnna said.

Annie Vo leaned in close. "Now we know. The recipient device for that thumb drive was your own phone. Not Ben's laptop."

"But I didn't put any decrypting software on my phone," said LuAnna.

"Do you shower with your phone? Do you sleep with it?"

"No. And it's charging by the bed at night, but beyond that, who knows? I'm asleep, after all." LuAnna paused. "Oh. I see. Ben did it. Clever boy."

Annie Vo said, "So let's see what that thumb drive uploaded to your phone."

The two women read together in silence.

"That's it, then," said Annie Vo.

"Sheila Vine and Ben are working together on a mission."

"And they're not even close to done. It goes all the way to the top," said Annie Vo.

"Now I remember," said LuAnna removing the original card that had been left for her at Annie Vo's house. "It was nagging me all this while."

"What?" asked Annie Vo.

"The handwriting," said LuAnna, holding the note out to Annie Vo. "It's Dick Blackshaw's."

"Pap's? Really?"

"Hand to God," said LuAnna. "You don't recognize it? He's your own father after all."

"True, but I'll take your word for it on the handwriting," said Annie Vo. "He only reconnected with me in the digital age. I don't think I've ever seen him with a pencil in his hand unless he was sketching in a range card for a gig."

"You mean for a sanctioned—"

"Or unsanctioned, but highly paid, termination mission—"

"Tomato, tomahto—" said LuAnna. "Now the big question is, what are we going to do?"

Annie Vo said, "I don't know about you, but right now I'm going to eat this store-bought fish your man cooked for us." With her mouth full, she went on, "And it's delicious. Old Bay?"

"If Ben cooked it, it's Old Bay."

"So Pap dropped by and left you a note. I'm a little hurt," said Annie Vo. "We always teamed before."

"Maybe he doesn't know his way around your place," said LuAnna. "And he put it in the first bedroom he found."

Annie Vo said, "Maybe. But the software's on your phone."

"That so? You already checked your phone?"

Annie Vo took out her phone and observed the now familiar strobing screen. "Well I'll be dipped in a bucket. But how'd the decrypting software get loaded on my phone?"

"If it's as fancy as you say," said LuAnna, "it might just be able to leapfrog from one phone to another designated phone."

"I bet that's it."

LuAnna said, "So we've both been read-in to this mess. What are we going to do?"

"You're going to pass me more rockfish," said Annie Vo. "Then we'll see what it all looks like on a full stomach."

"Fair enough," said LuAnna, as she pushed the serving dish to Annie Vo. "You finish up, and I'll pull together my shooting iron, some ammo, and put on that coffee, no cheese. It's going to be a long night."

Annie Vo said, "If Dick Blackshaw's involved, it might be our last night. There's always a firefight around that one."

"The voice of experience," said LuAnna as she laid out her 9mm Glock, her little .25 Beretta 950 Jetfire for her ankle holster, spare magazines, and several boxes of ammunition. "Together, we'll get to the bottom of this."

TOUGH LUCK KID

By

Robert Blake Whitehill
With
Charles Ta

Mr. Charles Ta, alumnus of The New School, is the only illustration intern to accept the narrative writing challenge to date. His drawings are just as vivid, but far more dynamic and complex than the 1960s stylings of Peter Max. You will see what I mean when you check out Ta's Instagram page here. www.Instagram.com/CharlesTaArt

It will come as no surprise that Ta brings that same intensity to his narrative prose. After several conferences, he decided to write about the violent backstory of the Kid, and this character's eventual hiring as one of Maynard Chalk's most savage henchmen; all this takes place before their storyline picks up in the first Ben Blackshaw thriller, Deadrise.

Fair warning; there is a strong aroma of Edgar Allan Poe in this tale, suffused with an eye-watering smoke from another Charles: Bukowski. To any readers who might be triggered by references to child abuse, particularly the sort that takes place within a family, this story is not for you. Enough to say that the Kid did not become the feral golem we met in Deadrise on his own.

TOUGH LUCK KID

CHAPTER 1

THERE WERE FEW things that the Kid feared, and solitary confinement more so than death itself, was one of them. He'd become used to, even numbed to death by this point in his life, even though he was only twenty; he so often found himself with a gun or a knife in his hands, standing over the bleeding corpse of one of his many, many victims. To the Kid, there was a kind of thrill to be found in murder, arson, theft, any manner of crime, really. A bone-deep excitement in pursuit by cops while wilding with his gang, the Nevermore Boyz.

Little else (except maybe cocaine or crystal methamphetamine) could give him the euphoric highs he felt from hearing the screams of the innocent, or the wailing of police sirens. They got his heart pumping, his skin sweating, and his body coiled like nothing else. In those moments, in those days, the Kid remembered, he had fun. The twisted kind of fun one would expect from a guy who loved that game of cat-and-mouse in which he would toy with the law, with people's very lives. That's what all his nefarious doings were to him: games. Games that made him feel powerful and free. He felt like he could do anything he wanted. He felt like God.

Things were different now. The Kid was not having any fun where he was, because he had no people to play with, no drugs, none of his favorite thrills. There was nothing to do, no one to talk to. No light, except a dim bulb that flickered on and off from the ceiling. No sound, either, except the Kid's own breathing, and the occasional muffled noises behind the metal door of his cell. Sometimes fellow inmates down the hall screamed. At regular intervals known only in the world outside this time-crushed cell, a faceless prison guard slid him a tray of Nutraloaf through the door. Other inmates ate together in the dining room.

The Kid's cell, like all the others at the Maryland Correctional Adjustment Center, was bound on all sides by white concrete walls; it had almost nothing in it except a metal cot, a stinking toilet that hadn't been cleaned in years, and a grimy metal sink with a faucet from which the water trickled even when the tap was wide open.

No one had ever bothered to upgrade the prison's HVAC system. The Kid shivered in the dead of winter, curled up in his cot, or lay on the metal floor, drenched in sweat in the middle of summer. His thin jumpsuit certainly didn't make conditions any more tolerable. It wasn't enough to keep him warm when he needed it to, but when temperatures rose, he knew better than to take it off. He knew he was being watched from a security camera at the corner of his cell. The last time he stripped to be just a half degree cooler, four guards burst in on him; he was beaten into the floor, and tased over and over; the goons were looking for any excuse to abuse their petty authority. Sometimes, he wished he could smash that security camera to bits, but it was placed too high for him to grab, and protected by a heavy wire cage. Being short for his age had a lot of drawbacks.

For weeks, or was it really months on end (the Kid had long forgotten, just like he'd long forgotten his total body count) this was the reality that greeted him from the moment he stirred from his febrile nightmares to the hour he dropped into the rare moment of somnolent oblivion, day in, day out. To him, it was all a conspiracy to make him feel as powerless, as small, and as miserable as possible. It drove him mad, because there was little he hated more than not being in control, than being told what to do by bastards who treated him like a rabid beast, rather than with the respect he deserved.

When he wasn't clawing at his skin, or ramming his head on the white walls of his cell, or punching and kicking at his steel door, or howling like a banshee, or demanding to be released (only to be met with silence), the Kid spent his days pacing to and fro, yelling back at the voices in his head, and looking at the shadowy figures that often appeared in the corner of his eye— figures he could never quite see when he tried to mad-dog them straight on.

Sometimes he lunged for the figures like a tiger pouncing on its prey, but to no avail. They always disappeared, vanished just beyond his grasp, unlike the helpless people he murdered; this goaded him into rage. As time went on, their untouchable presence made the Kid attempt suicide, if not to grab the attention of the guards forced to restrain him, then merely to escape his daily hell.

The nights, however, were worse for the Kid than any torment the day could bring. Even in his sleep the voices in his head, and the shadowy beings from earlier did not spare his psyche. They penetrated his dreams to toy with his deteriorating mind, making him relive memory after memory from his tortured childhood, his amoral adolescence, and his depraved young adulthood. Memories full of violence, anguish, and finally betrayal.

Recent horrors of Morpheus, if they didn't jolt him awake in the early hours of the morning howling like a dog gone feral, they would make him toss and turn in his cot. Then he would wake and curse his cruel parents for ever bringing him into this world, recoiling from the headaches, stomachaches, or phantom childhood bruises throbbing across his body. And for good reason, too. He remembered the visceral images from those nightmares as if he had lived these worst days of his life on repeat, on a time loop, or as if he were trapped between two opposing mirrors in a hellish infinite regress.

In one dream, he was six years old again, back home in one of the poorest neighborhoods in Baltimore. There, in front of the Kid, was the shadowy figure from his hallucinations, taking the form of his old man drunk off his ass after being released from prison, kicking him in the head and in the stomach, and calling him a *stupid boy*, or a *good for nothin' kid* over and over. Behind the shadowy figure always stood the Kid's mother, callously ignoring the suffering of the son she never wanted, a cigarette screwed tight into the corner of her mouth, counting the bills she'd earned for whoring herself to dozens of men.

In another dream the Kid was twenty, and had managed to escape from the Correctional Adjustment Center after striking a deal with some of the convicts to help him break out. They all knew he had been a big shot, the head of the infamous Nevermore Boyz—the same gang responsible for terrorizing Baltimore with every crime from arson to human and drug trafficking, all the while taunting the cops and evading capture time and time again. That earned the Kid street cred, and made even the most death-hearted criminals fear him. Unsurprisingly, he liked the feeling of seeing people larger and taller than he was tremble and shrink into nothing when he stared them down. It was easy to get them to do what he wanted with his history of unbridled cruelty.

CHAPTER 2

THE END OF the Kid's torture in solitary confinement was anticlimactic. He had eaten his morning gruel, which looked like gray feces, hours before, and had launched into his usual daily lunatic routine. He figured it was just before noon when he heard the metal door to his cell open up with a groan and a creak.

Behind the door stood two armed guards with a restraining chair on wheels. They didn't say what they wanted, not that Kid gave them a second to explain. Without hesitation, he lunged from the corner of his cell at the guards, pouncing on them like a lion and frothing at the mouth. But the guards came prepared, brandishing their tasers and their batons, they shocked and beat the Kid down to get him onto the restraining chair.

Not wishing to squander this sudden chance at actual freedom, he kicked and screamed at the guards making their job of securing him nearly impossible. Two more guards rushed to help overpower the Kid's surprising strength; they all held him down with brute force, gradually managing to strap him onto his chair, pinning his legs down on the chair's foot rest, his wrists, arms, and shoulders on the chair's armrest, and his waist and neck on its sturdy frame. Even so, the Kid continued struggling to escape, no matter how ineffectual the effort was.

Fed up with the little shithead, one of the first two guards cracked the Kid in the head with his baton. The Kid reeled from the blow with stars flashing behind his eyes.

"Relax, Kid," he said. "There's someone here for you. You'd better shut up and sit tight."

The Kid decided to calm down. He grew curious as to the identity of his mysterious visitor. He mulled over the implications as the guards pushed his restraining chair down the hall, passing by the metal doors leading to the cells of other convicts shunted away in solitary confinement.

The Kid heard his fellow inmates' screams, yet they didn't faze him. He'd gotten used to the din over time. What did nearly send the young criminal over the edge, however, was when he saw, or *thought* he saw, a shadowy figure staring directly at him from behind the reinforced glass window of one of the cell doors. The Kid made a face at the figure as if to taunt it, but the figure laughed like a demon before vanishing, as if it had never been there. He could have sworn the shadow looked just like him, with its wild hair, jumpsuit, and a devilish leer that matched his own.

Seconds later, the Kid grew more uneasy when he heard voices in his head again, for the thousandth time this week. One of them sounded like the angry voice of his prostitute mother, always belittling him for torturing animals, setting fire to dumpsters, houses, cars, and homeless derelicts; harping on his lack of ambition and dropping out of school for a life of robbery and looting between stints in juvenile detention. She had once hoped the Kid would grow up and save her from herself.

You're a monster, a bastard son I shoulda never had, the gravelly whisky-and-cigarette voice said in unmistakable tones of disappointment and anguish.

Oh yeah? the Kid thought to himself, not wanting to incur the wrath of his guards again, *you're the same worthless bitch who let my piece of shit old man fuck you without a care in the world!* He was glad he had run away from that slut at the age of fourteen. It was *her* fault that the Kid endured misery every day, *her* fault the Kid came out of the womb so deformed of heart and soul.

The Kid shook his head trying to pull himself together. His hallucinations began to fade. Before long, he and his guards had left the solitary confinement wing. Traversing more empty gray hallways and steel doors, they arrived at the office of Dr. Maureen Wilson, the Kid's psychologist.

The Kid actually kind of liked Dr. Wilson, at least more than most people he'd met in life. While Dr. Wilson did ultimately have a job to do, she was the only person he'd ever known who actually treated the Kid with respect. Dr. Wilson understood the Kid better than anyone else, and this was something he had never felt before. The Kid never attacked the good old Doc during his psychotherapy sessions with her. After every infraction of the rules, Dr. Wilson barely masked a look of pain on her face that made the Kid feel something akin to remorse. Almost. But in his head he'd never felt guilty for any of his actions. He was a reactive creature of circumstance, with no baseline of morality or impulse control to govern his violent outbursts, except with Doc. Maybe she felt the Kid's pain. Maybe sensing that might have made a difference to the Kid, if he had worked with her longer. That was not to be.

The Kid worked hard to settle himself, to be on his best behavior as one of the guards knocked on the office door. When it opened, the Kid saw Dr. Wilson, sporting her classic brown wool suit and steel rimmed glasses. But he felt something was off. Dr. Wilson looked nervous, disturbed, as if she feared for her life.

It didn't take long for the Kid to see why. Behind the Doc, looming over her, were two others—a man and a woman—wearing coveralls and sporting buzz cuts, and armed with compact H&K MP5 submachine guns. The Kid got wistful at the sight of the guns. Oh, the mayhem he could have wrought with one of those, and a few magazines of 10mm Auto. He reigned in his bloodlust, and turning his eyes to the right as best he could with his head restrained, he saw a third person sitting next to Dr. Wilson's desk—the Kid didn't recognize him.

This guy looked to be in his 60s, with thinning gray-white hair. His face was like a middle-aged incubus straight out of hell; his unsettling appearance was offset by the stylish white suit and white pants he wore, almost for some special occasion, or a night at a disco decades ago. The man also held a folder containing a thick sheaf of papers which he had begun skimming at a leisurely pace. Leisurely, like his suit. From his half-smile, he liked what he was reading.

The Kid's eyes widened when he noticed that, peeking out from under the man's jacket was a Colt 1991 pistol, which was an updated version of the tried-and-true M1912. The Kid looked away, pretending not to see. Now he knew for certain there was something weird about this visit. Why would a well-, if oddly-dressed creep with a gun and two goons go to all the trouble of visiting the Kid's sorry ass?

"Hiya, Doc!" the Kid slurred through his bite mask and spit-shield, feigning a smile he hoped might reach his eyes. "It's been aaaages! I heard someone came to visit me in the zoo. Don't feed the animals, mister."

Dr. Wilson, who had sweat beading on her upper lip, said nothing. She turned her head and, clearing her throat, looked towards the man in the white suit. The stranger looked up from the file he was reading, tucked it under his left arm, smiled, and stood up from his seat.

"You're finally here!" the man said, a cordial expression on his face. "I was beginning to think something had happened to you back there in solitary." The man looked at the Kid's guards, noticing they were battered, with sleeves bloody from human bites.

Then he extended his hand towards the Kid. "I'm Maynard Chalk, the son of a bitch who's going to post bail to free you. And you must be Billy the Kid Kilgore, the famed Beast of Baltimore and boss of the Nevermore Boyz. It's a pleasure to meet *another* son of a bitch face-to-face!" Noting the Kid was still restrained, the visitor dropped his outstretched hand to his hip.

Despite the good news, the Kid flinched. He hated being called by his first name, because it reminded him of his scumbag father. His last name did suit his profession and employment history in a weird twist of fate. Appreciating Chalk's flattery, and the private joke of him being an *actual* son of a whore, he figured he'd let the disrespectful introduction slide. After all, Chalk *was* the Kid's benefactor; he was already starting to like the man— something previously reserved only for good old Dr. Wilson.

"Let's get these restraints off," Chalk went on, with unnerving assurance he would be obeyed. "He's a human being after all."

The guards cast a worried glanced at Dr. Wilson, who simply nodded.

"It's a pleasure to meet you too, mister," the Kid replied, smirking. "I'd shake your hand if I could—"

Chalk laughed a hoarse laugh, liking the Kid's sense of humor.

After the guards removed the Kid's bite mask and spit shield, they went to work unbuckling the heavy leather belts.

Suddenly the atmosphere in the office room went from jovially surreal, to unnerving, ominous, and tense to an oppressive degree.

"Well? Speed it up!" Chalk barked. His mood went from happy to impatient as if a switch had been flipped somewhere in his head. "I didn't pay you as much as I did for you to stand there like morons. Chop-chop!"

The Kid's guards picked up the pace. Just as they were about to finish freeing him from his restraints, however, Dr. Wilson mustered the courage to speak up.

"Mr. Chalk," she said, "I cannot with good conscience allow you to do this. This is simply madness. Don't you realize the Kid is a dangerous—"

So much for all the doctor's genuine empathy, the Kid thought. *Probably a sham the whole time.*

Dr. Wilson fell silent at the sight of Chalk pulling his jacket back and drawing his pistol, which he aimed at the psychologist's forehead. Then he looked at his own two guards.

"Bonnie! Clyde!" Chalk shouted.

The two guards immediately grabbed a terrified Dr. Wilson, and forced her to lie face down on her own wooden desk, MP5s jammed at the back of her neck. Clyde held both of the Dr. Wilson's arms together, while Bonnie brutally bounced her head off the desk. No matter how hard she struggled, Dr. Wilson couldn't escape the grip of the guards pinioning her.

A taste of her own medicine, thought the Kid. The psychologist simply could not match the physical ferocity of Chalk's team, who appeared to have been molded into cold-blooded brutes with years of training.

The Kid stared at this turn of events in shock, but he didn't smile as anyone who knew him might expect. Rather than make a scene, he decided to hang back and wait and see what would happen next. His heart pounded with both genuine fear and excitement. Just what was Chalk up to? Covering the guards that had wheeled the Kid into the office, that's what.

Chalk said, "You fellas are done here. You've got your pay, and by the looks of things you earned every penny. Now shove off."

All but one guard shuffled out of the office right away. "Mr. Chalk, sir?"

Chalk looked up, surprised anyone but his own crew was still in the room. "What is it?"

"You wouldn't be hiring anybody else, would you?"

The Kid was astounded by the balls of this guard who'd been particularly savage to him during the entire length of his imprisonment.

Chalk looked over at the Kid. "Do we need this cat?"

The Kid answered, "Please take him, so when he and I are away from here, I can cut him neck to nuts."

Chalk shrugged as he looked at the guard, "Sorry, Mack. Looks like you wouldn't survive too long on the team. Take what you've earned, be grateful, and didi mao to your happy place, most rikki-tik."

The guard scowled at the Kid as he slunk out of the room.

Chalk returned his attention to Dr. Wilson. "Listen to me very closely." Chalk put his angry scowl next to Dr. Wilson's ear, and forced his pistol barrel into the psychologist's jaw. "Do you remember who I am and who I work for, or have you already forgotten like the worthless shit stain you are?"

Dr. Wilson flinched from Chalk's breath, his flying spit, maybe both; she started tearing up, unable to speak coherently.

"In case you don't recall," Chalk continued, "I'm here because I work for Uncle Sam, alongside some very rich, and very powerful people who've got more money and influence than you could ever imagine. You saw my credentials, so you know *exactly* what's up. Tell me, do you know what happens when you get to work for Uncle Sam, when you're being backed by large multinational corporations, wealthy donors, Senators, and special interest groups, Dr. Wilson?"

"Please—let me go!" Dr. Wilson begged. She squirmed from the pain of her head on the desk, the gun barrel against her throat.

Chalk ignored the plea and cocked his gun. "Answer the fucking question!" Chalk ordered. "Or you get a bullet in that thick skull!"

"I don't know, Mr. Chalk. I don't know!" Dr. Wilson said, breathing heavily.

"I'm glad you so *politely* asked" Chalk responded sarcastically. "Well, when you work for Uncle Sam, and are being backed by those rich sons of bitches I mentioned, you get a shit ton of money and the highest-level security clearance possible, even above the goddamn *President of the United States*. And when you have that much authority, that much wealth, you can do whatever the hell you want, and that includes breaking the law with zero consequences. Lady Justice is my bitch. She likes the blindfold, let me tell you. How do you think I got here in your office without so much as a scratch on me, Doc? How was I able to wipe the Kid's criminal record clean, and grant him full immunity for all future crimes, and give him a new ID, new name, like he never existed before today? It's all very simple, Doc. I bribe the guards, the cops, the lawyers, this two-bit clink, the courts, the news media, and every last sucker you can think of, all so I could free Billy here and take him under my wing. You must understand, Doc, I need him precisely *because* he's dangerous, *because* he's a cold-blooded wingnut, a natural born killer!"

The Kid couldn't help but smile. He could barely contain his ecstasy hearing he was no longer deemed a criminal. He giggled at his stroke of luck—because now he was free. But one question remained on his mind: what did Chalk need him for?

"For heaven's sake, Doc," Chalk continued, "he's scored a 39 on the Hare Psychopathy Checklist—been murdering poor saps for years, and almost getting away with it too! He's a maniac! A tried-and-true ape-shit savage! Only an idiot wouldn't take advantage of what this gentleman has to offer."

"But I—" Dr. Wilson began. However, she was interrupted again by Chalk, who pressed his handgun onto the Doctor's head. Dr. Wilson cried out in fear.

"I wasn't done talking! We had a *deal* earlier, and you signed the contract on behalf of the US government, remember?" Chalk asked. "Or did you forget that too, birdbrain? You give me the Kid's personal files, and certify the Kid's sane, and I pay you five hundred grand, enough for you to pad your shitty IRA and retire and live out your years in something close to comfort. If you refuse or back out, you get the shaft. Those were the terms in black and white. Got me?"

Dr. Wilson slowly nodded. At this point, the Kid had had enough of what he was seeing. Chalk may have been on his level, but Dr. Wilson was innocent, a nice enough lady who never did the Kid or Chalk any wrong. He took a few steps forward and spoke up.

"Hey, Mr. Chalk, I don't mean to be a bother, but I think you should let the good old Doc go. Not because I don't like you, but because she and I go way back. She treated me with respect. So maybe let's beat feet out of here."

Silence filled the room before Chalk, seemingly deep in thought, slowly retracted his gun from Dr. Wilson's head, easing the tension. He *was* going to kill the doctor right there on his desk if she didn't comply, but changed his mind, not wanting to upset or distance himself from the Kid—his new asset. Chalk wasn't the type for mercy, but just this once he would allow it.

He motioned for his guards to let go of Dr. Wilson. Both Bonnie and Clyde complied, then took their places beside Chalk. Dr. Wilson stood up teary and coughing from her desk readjusting her bent glasses. Before she could speak, Chalk threw down the Kid's file, went around the desk to Dr. Wilson, and grabbed her by the lapels of her suit. Dr. Wilson sobbed, shaking her head back and forth, wondering what Chalk would do next. For a few moments Chalk did nothing. Then, upon surveying the doctor's desk, he noticed a few picture frames with members of the doctor's family: her husband, son, daughter, two sisters, and cousins. He decided to torture Dr. Wilson a little bit more just before leaving the prison, forcing her to look down at the picture frames of her loved ones, while waving his handgun around in a not-so-subtle fashion.

"Consider yourself lucky, Dr. Wilson, because you got me angry on a *good* day, and the Kid here wants me to save your skin. Before I go, there's something I want you to remember, something I hope you will never forget for as long as you live. Here it is: I can do a *lot worse* than threaten to kill you right here on the spot. I have a couple dozen private mercenaries, goons, ex-Navy SEALs, and hitmen at my disposal, and I can call them anytime, anywhere. When I do, I can order them to hunt down your family, your friends, and everyone you know and love. They get paid good money for this, and they're really good at covering their tracks, so no one will ever know whodunit. Plus, they're the best I could find from the world over, so you can bet your ass they'll gun down your loved ones before they even know what hit them."

Chalk then aimed his pistol at the picture frames on the Doctor's desk and, almost as a demonstration, shot all of them, one at a time. The frames, now with holes and broken glass, spun backwards across the room shattering on the floor. Dr. Wilson wept even harder, unable to bull her way through the horror Chalk had laid out.

Chalk concluded, "I'll make sure no one will investigate the murders, and the news media will never pick up the juicy story. Why? Because I'll have paid them all to keep their mouths shut and turn a blind eye to the massacre, or create cover-ups. You'll live with the pain of seeing all your people dead for the rest of your sad little life, and it'll be *all your fault*. So if you care about your momma and papa, your hubbin, your brats, I suggest you stay out of my way, and do as I say. Your money will be waiting for you in your account. *Capisce?*"

Dr. Wilson nodded furtively, her eyes wet with tears, her lungs heaving, and her heart racing. "Yes, Mr. Chalk. Now, for the love of God please go."

"Of course," Chalk replied with a grin, before uncocking his gun and putting away under his jacket. He picked up the Kid's file, turned to the Kid who had a wild look of triumph in his eye, and walked with him out of Dr. Wilson's office. Bonnie and Clyde followed close behind. Slamming the door to the office shut, the motley crew of murderers left Dr. Wilson a terrified mess inside, regret and primal fear swirling about in her mind for committing a grave moral wrong, and putting her family in danger, all for half a million bucks.

Dr. Wilson sat down at her desk and, burying her face in her hands, began to cry uncontrollably. In her current state, she was in no position to see any more patients, both now and for the next several months. She needed some time off. Or a new job, a new identity, and a new life somewhere far away.

As for Chalk and the Kid, their departure from the Maryland Correctional Adjustment Center was a piece of cake, free of any incident. There were very few guards patrolling the hallways, and when they came across Chalk, his goons, and the Kid, they ignored them, casually strolling away. They knew damn well what would happen if they tried to get in Chalk's way. Plus, for turning a blind eye, they were getting paid far more than they would otherwise make as correction officers in a given *year*.

The Kid stepped out of the prison with a huge smile on his face. It was early afternoon, and the sun shone bright between white clouds. The Kid hadn't felt the warmth of sunlight or a summer breeze in forever. He looked towards Chalk, who was also beaming as they walked to the parking lot. In Chalk the young criminal might have found a kindred spirit—a man as ruthless, as amoral, and as psychopathic as he was. Unlike the Kid, Chalk had real power, and looked like he was willing to share some of it with him, especially a life of violence without conventional consequences. And for that, the Kid was glad.

"Thanks for busting me out, mister," the Kid said. "I really appreciate it."

"Don't mention it, laddy-buck," Chalk replied.

A few moments passed before the reached his van parked in a corner of the lot away from other cars. The Kid immediately noticed the bold lettering on the side of the van, which said "RIGHT WAY MOVING AND STORAGE, INC" followed by the logo of the corporation.

Chalk went to the back of the van, opened it, and tossed the Kid a Right Way coverall and a new pair of tactical boots. He barely caught the clothes in time.

Chalk ordered, "Suit up."

The Kid hopped in the back of the van and changed. Everything fit perfectly. Chalk had done his homework on the Kid's sizes. He tossed his prison uniform and slip-on shoes into a nearby trash can.

The Kid realized his uniform was the same as those worn by Bonnie and Clyde. He began to suspect what this whole *moving company* business was all about. Perhaps the whole thing was a clever cover-up for more illegal operations. Furniture wasn't all that was being transported for Chalk's clients, but dirty money, drugs, weapons, sensitive cargo, contraband, and probably even bodies too, all under the guise of a legitimate enterprise.

Chalk pulled out a fake Maryland ID from his pocket, and gave it to the Kid. It was indistinguishable from a real ID in all respects, with a fake name, fake birthday, fake series of codes, and forged signature on it. ROBERT JOHNSON, the ID said. A common enough name to be believable, but not so common it would arouse suspicion from any cops.

"Keep the ID, *Bob*. Don't lose it. I paid a pretty penny to have that little card printed, but it'll keep you in the clear for the next three years," Chalk said. "Get in. We got things to do, and places to be!"

Bonnie and Clyde got in through the side door, and sat on the first bench.

The Kid was the last of the group to board, shoving his ID into his right pocket, and clambering up onto the passenger seat to Chalk's right. The van's wheels screeched against the asphalt, as Chalk tore out of the parking lot, and into the road.

For the next several minutes, both the Kid and Chalk said nothing, as Chalk hit the gas pedal and drove the van westward, then turned southward towards Baltimore's city limits.

"So," the Kid began, putting his hands behind his head as he leaned back in his seat, "now that you've freed me, care to tell me what's next?"

"Sure," Chalk replied. "As of today, you've been officially hired as an employee of Right Way. For your job orientation, I'm going to lay out some ground rules so you know what's up. From there, I'll show you around the Right Way HQ in Langley Park, and introduce you to the rest of my crew. You've already met Bonnie and Clyde—two of my best operators—and you've seen them in action. A hotspur like you should have no problem fitting in."

The Kid liked what he was hearing, so far. "Ok, cool. Give me a rundown. I'm all ears," he said, confident and self-assured. He detested rules, but that usually applied to the strictures of people who treated him like an inferior, like the cops or gangbangers who got in his way. Chalk wasn't like them—he had the smarts to see the Kid as an equal, and treat him with the respect he deserved. Plus, he was in Chalk's debt. If it weren't for Chalk, the Kid would still be suffering in solitary, trapped in his bare cell with crap food, a plaything of his demons. Now his life had veered for the better. So he'd give this bastard a pass. For now.

APACHE 8

By

Robert Blake Whitehill
With
Deanna Reynolds

Ms. Deanna Reynolds, of Montclair State University, interned extensively in the marketing area, with a focus on social media outreach. It's fitting that she chose to mirror her own rapid growth as a student and as an intern in the young character, Ela, who works on the all-female wildfire hotshot crew, the Apache 8.

Reynolds crafted a fine detective plot in which Ela thrives despite danger from Nature, from a murderer, and from being ignored by the police. Ela also faces a strong sense that her future does not lie with the Apache 8, though strong family tradition is leading her in that direction. Reynolds really captured the defining moment at which a young woman decides to chart her own path forward.

APACHE 8

"C'MON ELA, IT'S time to get up. We have to hit the hardware store first so we're leaving early," Kushala announced to her daughter. "Ela!"

Recently, Kushala felt a deepening concern for her only child. She would often observe Ela off in her own world, staring blankly toward the distant mountains with a slight frown set into her lips; sometimes friends would have to call her name several times before she responded.

"Almost done," Ela said. She scrutinized herself in the mirror. Her tan skin was graced with light freckles that would darken in the summer months. Her inky hair had a shine that her White friends at school envied. Her eyes were a warm, inviting brown. She was referred to as her mother's carbon copy, though her mother's eyes were accented with lines too fine to be called wrinkles. The two rushed through their morning routine, fired up the old truck, and made rounds picking up the other women.

Another day here, another day feeling out of place, Ela thought as she drove with her crew through town. Thanks to her mother, Ela had grown up around an all-women wildfire hotshot crew: The renowned Apache 8. They all lived with the rest of the White Mountain Apaches where they supported the community by fighting fires and maintaining the forest's health. The crew consisted of multiple generations of strong women who were proud of their work. It's not that Ela didn't like being a part of her hotshot crew; she had a gut feeling she was meant to be somewhere else. Where that was, she wasn't certain, but the more she thought about it, the more guilt consumed her. Shouldn't she be grateful she had a path laid out before her by family tradition?

"Here goes nothing," she sighed as she took her keys out of the ignition and began walking towards the store. Whiteriver, Arizona was a small, rural town but it was the largest settlement on the Fort Apache Indian Reservation.

Its people were surrounded by tall mountains where many hiked, skied, hunted, and camped; outsiders delighted in all four seasons here. For Ela, walking under the Arizona sun even this early in the day was no joke. She whipped her long black hair into a bun and beelined towards the door.

As the women made their way through the hardware store, in search of hand tools and ignition devices, Kushala was aware of the tense set of her daughter's shoulders.

Although firefighting wasn't Ela's passion, she loved the women on the Apache 8 crew like family. She cleared her mind and walked the single-bit ax towards the cash register. Immediately, she felt a chill skitter up her spine as she glanced at the young cashier. His dark brown eyes moved across her face in a deliberate manner followed by an eerie smile. The rest of his appearance didn't settle her fears, with his greasy blond hair and several gaps where teeth should be.

"Well, hello there, miss. Will that be all?" he murmured as he scanned her ax and safety glasses.

"Yes, that's it for today," she answered in a rush.

Ela silently begged for him to move faster when she noticed his freshly abraded knuckles and bandaged arm. To make matters worse, her eyes also spotted a custom Damascus steel blade tucked into his belt with no sheath.

"That's odd," she muttered as she took the bag from his grasp.

"Something wrong?" he challenged. She quickly shook her head and retreated outside where her aunt, Nalin, was holding her usual shopping bag jammed with granola bars. Nalin sensed Ela's discomfiture, but knew not to ask until they were out of earshot of strangers, and in the car.

"You okay, honey?" Nalin asked as they climbed into the truck. She was around her mom's age, but with pretty strands of gray hair showing around her temples.

"Yeah, but did anyone else think the cashier was off? The custom blade was way above his paygrade."

"He did look angry, I guess, but you know no one's as observant as you," Nalin winked.

Ela wondered if once again her aunt was chastising her for overthinking things.

They drove through town in quiet anticipation of the work ahead until they reached the staging area at the edge of the forest. Their plan was to work on the tribal lands from here, and inch their way towards Hawley Lake. The reservation was surrounded by towering mountain peaks covered with large, verdant spruce and pine trees. Its beautiful landscape bounced the sunlight back in a way that made the sandy valley floor gleam.

"Okay, ladies let's make this day successful and keep the forest and the critters safe," Kushala spoke with enthusiasm.

The women gathered at the back of the truck to grab their packs. Each one consisted of essential equipment including a canteen, sleeping bag, lunches, rations, a portable GPS, and a headlight. They took scraping tools like axes, shovels, and fire rakes for fighting grass fires.

The crew slung their heavy bags over their shoulders and began the trek into the wild. Indigo buntings whistled above them as if wishing good luck to all. Scrambling over boulders and logs, Ela was reminded of the beauty of Nature. It always calmed her no matter the circumstances. After several hours of thinning select pine trees, the smell of smoke began to waft toward them.

Mischievous fire was on a mission of chaos close by. It hadn't stretched its long legs in a while, and it itched to break free. It attacked tree trunks with a vengeance; they were hogging all of the space. Ambition grew within the greedy spirit, and it increased its pace reaching a larger open area of the reservation. A smile stretched across the inferno's face as its essence continued to spread a fiery red. All eyes filled with tears due to its smoke traveling on the breeze. Ela's throat turned scratchy and raw, a sign that trouble was near.

Nalin uttered her ritual old joke. "I know how this fire started."

Everyone obliged, and chorused, "How?"

"Small," Nalin said with a grin.

The women chuckled. Ela rolled her eyes.

Kushala said, "You guys know what to do. Let's put this fire out before it grows any bigger!"

The closer they drew to the fireline, the more apparent it became that fighting this wildfire was going to be strenuous. The wisps of silver smoke curled through the thick trees creating a haze. Nothing could be heard over the blazing fire steadily burning ancestral pine, spruce, and aspen to the ground. Their trunks loudly sizzled to ash. Leaves transformed into a dull brown. Home to so much wildlife was destroyed.

The crew leaped into action, tools ready for the madness. Some wielded their axes chopping stumps. Others used their shovels for smothering parts of the fire that advanced on the ground. Despite their efforts, the fire had grown so large they had to spread out to attack it.

Now Ela couldn't even see her crewmates because of a substantial hill obstructing her vision. Her mother would be angry she had strayed. Ela threw dirt on a pile of leaves that was developing into a ball of red-hot fire. Sweat started to bead on her lip and pool by the small of her back which grew tight with fatigue with each shovel of smothering earth. She knew she could hang in there. She had to. After many intense hours of wielding other tools, like her fire swatter, she was able to knock down the flames, turning them into mere dying puffs of smoke. She finally took a breath and squatted down on a row of logs with her canteen.

Wow, I haven't come across one this bad in a while, she thought. The sensation of icy water sliding down her throat satisfied her thirst. "I hope the others are okay," she whispered to the air, like a prayer.

Ela rose, stretched her back, and set off in the direction from which she believed she'd come. The absence of sound hung in the air reminding her of the recent destruction that had taken place. Something was wrong. Her heart kept up an unusual quick rhythm, with no sign of slowing. Ela took a deep breath to steady her nerves, but continued to feel on edge as though her body knew something was about to happen.

Unfortunately, as more time passed by, she recognized fallen wildlife that hadn't fled fast enough, or had gotten lost in the smoke. From elk, to coyote, to prairie dog, sadly it seemed that every species was hit.

"Oh, poor elk calf," she said, squinting in an attempt to distinguish its charred form. After a few steps, she paused and remembered it couldn't be a newborn because it was still too early in the season. She wondered as she advanced towards the carcass, careful to not stand too close and attract fleas departing the remains, fleas that could kill her with hantavirus. Her heart began to jump as she realized it wasn't a forest animal at all. It was a young woman, her features burned away, her dyed blonde hair singed mostly black.

Ela assumed they were a female's remains from the charred brassiere, bracelets on her blackened wrist, and tasteful hoops in her ears singed back almost to nubs. To an outsider, one would think she died trying to escape the fire, but Ela's eye read a different story from the scene.

Upon closer inspection, Ela discovered several puncture wounds along the victim's midsection and a long bloody scratch near her collarbone. *Who'd be this sick to do this?* she wondered as she looked around for additional clues. Five feet away lay a blackened leather knife sheath, and a phone that she worked fast to collect. Suddenly, a crow cawed close by, reminding her that she should get back to the crew before it turned to dusk. Stowing the evidence in her pack, Ela silently promised the woman she would come back soon.

She did her best to rid her mind of the strange smell; it was barbecue, with an acrid note of burned hair. It was an oddly appetizing odor that made her cringe with disgust. Ela hummed an old melody her mother sang to her as a child to compose herself, but as the sky cast over into an indigo blue, then the oncoming blue-black of night, her anxiety would not abate.

On the east side of the mountain, she found a nearly level place to unroll her sleeping bag.

"I guess the fire split us up more than I realized," she said to herself. Ela unpacked her rations for the night and decided against starting a fire. It would remind her too much of the disastrous events that had unfolded. Her dinner was sliced peaches, a protein bar, dehydrated potatoes, and mixed vegetables. After cleaning her space, she laid her lightweight goose-down sleeping bag on the forest floor. Although she was alone in the wild, it was her family's well-being she worried about. Ela assured herself that tomorrow she would find them unharmed. The last thing that entered her mind before her eyes fully closed was how grateful she was to be alive.

The sun warmed her face as it slowly climbed into the morning sky. The young woman secured her pack and set off. Eager to find everyone, she tripped over thick branches which slashed in a long scratch on her leg. Ela moved to brush herself off when a piece of metal sparkled under the sunlight. She snatched it up full of happiness recognizing it was a bracelet that belonged to another Apache 8 team member named Lenna. Her eyes filled with unshed tears.

"Mom? Mom! Are you here? Nalin? Lenna? I'm coming to you guys!" No one answered but something rustled behind her and she soon felt her body squeezed her in a hug.

"Mom!" Ela trembled, inhaling in her warm cinnamon scent. "Is everyone okay?"

"Yes, honey some minor bruises, but we all survived like I knew we would!"

"How did you find me," Ela asked as she embraced the other women.

"We were going the opposite direction, but turned around when we heard your footsteps."

"Lenna actually led me here with her bracelet." Ela looked affectionately at the piece of jewelry. "Even though it was unintentional, I appreciate it," she smiled as she placed it into the petite woman's hand. "It was meant to happen," she said.

Before Kushala could utter another word, Ela asked, "We need to stop at the Bureau of Indian Affairs Police station as soon as possible."

She told her crewmates what she had found.

The women swiftly buckled up for the long ride to the BIAP Station. From their location, the trip would take around three hours; with Ela's intensity of purpose, she knocked off thirty minutes.

The BIAP building was located in the heart of Phoenix and provided oversight to tribal law enforcement for 42 different tribes including the Apache. Its exterior was clad in mirror window films from top to bottom that reflected the faces of all who walked by.

"You guys can wait in the parking lot. Thank you for coming on the long ride, I appreciate all of you," Ela swiveled her body around to look at each of them.

"I'm going inside with you, I just got you back," Kushala squeezed her arm. Ela walked side by side with her mother through the doors.

Lenna said, "Wait in the parking lot?" The entire crew followed Ela and Kushala.

Ela's senses were flooded from the bustle of the people inside; phones blared, people spoke over each other, and the space was crowded. Taking a deep breath, Ela approached the front desk and filled out contact information.

A female officer finally called, "Ela Conrad?" Every step towards the counter made Ela's stomach tighten.

"So, you all found a body near the Fort Apache Historical Park?" the officer asked, indicating the Apache 8 women watching from a distance across the lobby.

"I did, Officer Alopay. They're here in support. We're the Apache 8." she responded reading the uniform nametag. "It looked like the victim was stabbed several times and tried to fight back."

"And you're sure they didn't die in the forest trying to escape the fire?"

"It's a she. I'm positive. I inspected the body very carefully, and also found a burnt knife sheath and cellphone a few feet away," Ela stated as she handed over the items. Then she gave a detailed description of where the body was located.

After all that, Officer Alopay frowned. "Miss, aren't you aware that you should never take evidence from a possible crime scene?"

Ela pushed back. "Yes, but with foraging animals, or a sticky-fingered passerby, you'd never have these things to help you identify her—"

"True," said Officer Alopay, appraising Ela afresh. "But now, there's a possibility that only your DNA will show up. I know you were trying to help but you might've made our job harder."

"Sorry, but without help, you wouldn't know there was a job in the first place," Ela said.

"We have your contact information, so I'll have my team work up the phone and see if we can find any other clues from the evidence."

"When will I hear back from you?"

The officer smiled. "Slow your roll, kiddo. Your work here is done. Watch the papers for an update. You're a minor, so we won't put your name out to the press."

"That's good," said Ella, but she didn't move.

Officer Alopay knew dogged persistence when she saw it. She produced a business card, wrote her cell phone number on the back, and handed it to Ela, saying. "Give us a week."

Ela nodded her head and was about to turn away but felt the need to say more. "I know maybe I acted impulsively, but this is serious. The murderer is still out there, and that woman is lying up there all alone."

Officer Alopay was a strong-willed woman who rarely changed her mind once her decision was set, but when she gazed into Ela's eyes, she saw her younger self shine back. She couldn't say no. After a long pause, she relented. "We could probably locate the remains without you, given your directions, but—my team and I will follow you back to the park and in to the scene. Save time."

None of the Apache 8 were the least put out that they had to drive all the way back to the scene. Though death was sad and murder was fraught with menace, they could not deny their excitement.

Ela felt tired, but the thought of giving the victim peace pushed her forward through the wilderness ahead of several BIAP officers, including Alopay.

Officer Alopay caught up to Ela, and said, "The digital unit was able to pull some pictures off the phone. We believe the victim owned the weapon she was killed with. Now, this can't be confirmed without inspecting the knife in person however, there are several pictures of the woman with a knife in a sheath on that phone. We assume it was a new purchase considering it was one of the last pictures the victim took."

Ten more minutes walking brought them to the remains. Officer Alopay said, "Impressive you were able to identify she died from something other than the fire. Unfortunately, if we can't find more evidence it'll be hard to track the person responsible. My team will keep searching and hopefully find something that connects her to a suspect."

Half of the crime scene unit was instructed to look for more clues and the other began recovering the body. These people were good at their craft, but Ela had a hunch they were looking in the wrong area. She worked alongside them turning over rocks and lifting up fallen branches to no avail. Her toes ached from squatting so often, but she pushed through the discomfort. Her eyes were drawn to something in an overlooked gopher hole in the ground ten feet away. She just knew something was there. Ela stuck her hand in the gopher hole, extracting a piece of the white paper. Her hands shook as she unraveled the ball to reveal a receipt from the store the dead woman had visited a few days ago. She cautiously examined the fragile paper. It was charred at the edges, but no one could deny the store's name in big bold letters on top. The transaction revealed basic snacks were paid for by credit card. Skimming over the paper she noticed the word 'Customer'.

"Huera Duncan," Ela said. "I found a receipt. It has a name," she yelled as she made her way to Officer Alopay. "It was away from the woman's body, in a small hole. Detective gopher might have saved it for us. This could be the woman's because the date on it is 2 days ago."

Officer Alopay gently took the paper from Ela's hand and inspected it.

"This has a high possibility of being hers considering its location." Then she said more loudly, as if she were making an announcement, "I'm surprised someone on my team didn't spot it. Good eye." After frowning at her unit for a second, she continued, "It's a good thing you were here because it may have never been found. I'll have our people check the store's surveillance footage."

Ela said, "The man working at that store the other day was extremely creepy. I feel like he's connected to—this." Ela spoke softly as they moved to a quieter location. "I completely forgot about him, but the more I think about it, the more it fits. The man's arm was bandaged. It looked like he recently fought someone. Can I see the pictures you found on the phone?"

Officer Alopay passed Ela her phone which now had the images salvaged from the victim's phone. The picture of the knife was all she needed to confirm her suspicion. She nearly dropped the phone from shock. "The man in the store had that exact same custom blade on him! That can't be a coincidence," she urged. "You've heard of Locard's Exchange Principle?"

Impressed, the officer nodded, "I see where you're going with this, but the evidence we have now can't exactly prove that the guy working there is the killer. Locard's Exchange Principle states that when objects come in contact a transfer of materials occurs, so that means that man had to have left blood, DNA, or even fibers that could trace back to him. I agree with your thought process, but if we find something on the blade, he could just say it's fish blood unless we test it." the officer let out a breath in disappointment.

"Correct. Fish DNA isn't people DNA," Ela said as she scratched the back of her neck.

"Seems you have a crazy idea about how big our budget is, but I'm listening."

"When I was younger, I would wrestle with my brother all the time. One day he hurt my neck putting me in a headlock. I chomped his forearm. Basically, if the woman bit his arm you could get evidence from her teeth."

A 'v' formed between the Officer's eyebrows "In this fire? Barely anything left of her own DNA let alone somebody else's."

"Her teeth would be protected from direct heat because that same heat would swell up her tongue. Same with foreign DNA between her teeth. And if he does have teeth marks on his arm, you could also compare them to her unique dental records to be sure. It might seem out there, but it's worth a shot," Ela stated.

"Forensic odontology is getting a bad rap these days," said Officer Alopay.

"By itself, yes. But it's still valid if it's used to corroborate other, stronger evidence—"

"—like DNA," finished Alopay. "Good idea. That's the kind of intelligence we need on this team."

2 Weeks Later

Ela sat in the kitchen with her mother mindlessly mixing her cereal around. She couldn't focus. The BIAP had yet to contact her. Each day she mulled over her actions, second-guessing herself, wondering if she did the right thing. Deep down inside herself, she knew she was onto something, but a small part of her wondered if she had accused an innocent man. Despite her curiosity, she dared not use Officer Alopay's cell number. She couldn't thrust herself forward more than she already had.

"Honey, you did everything you could. You were a big help. You can't mope around the house forever," Kushala sighed.

Ela jumped when her phone buzzed. It was Officer Alopay's call. Not wasting a moment, she pressed 'answer' and waited for the news.

Officer Alopay spoke in a rush without stopping. "Ela, first and foremost I want to apologize for the attitude I gave you when we met. I thought you were a curious kid looking to butt in, but I was wrong. You were right about everything. The victim was on the surveillance footage of the hardware store, and we even saw the man leaving a few minutes later. When we lifted his bandage there were bite marks and they did in fact match Huera's dentition. We talked to her dentist, and she was saving up for braces. Her angled front tooth put a unique bite mark on the suspect's skin. We found his DNA between two of Huera's back molars. For DNA to end up there, it must have been a hell of a fight. She did her best trying to survive. Gave everything. The fact that you knew her tongue would insulate and keep the teeth intact in the fire is impressive. And creepy. What I'm trying to say is you should consider police work. You've already shown you've got a feel for the job. I think you'd be helpful at completing other investigations. There's an academy that I recommend you go to that offers great training. When the time comes, I'll give you my personal recommendation."

Ela said, "I can't believe this, I'm truly speechless. I've wanted something like this for so long. I need to talk about it with my family." Ela did her best to avoid her mother's curious gaze.

Ela sat at the table with her hand covering her mouth. "Mom you might not like this but—"

"I'm proud of you," Kushala said with tears in her eyes. "I will miss you dearly on the fireline, but this could be your path."

Ela threw herself in her mom's arms and silently sobbed. Her next journey in life might be intimidating, and stressful at times, but she was ready for the challenge.

"Across the United States and Canada Native Women and Girls are being Taken or Murdered at an Unrelenting Rate."

Please give what you can to help bring these women home to their families and bring an end to this dehumanizing scourge.

Missing and Murdered Indigenous Women (MMIW)
(nativehope.org)

SPECIAL THANKS

Once again, I must offer my heartfelt thanks to the team at Telemachus Press, to Studio042, and to artist Buffalo Gouge for bringing this book to life. My family's patience with my writing this book is ever a source of strength as well as healthy distraction. I grieve the passing of my erstwhile editor, Richard Marek. To work with the person who has edited Thomas Harris and the Hannibal Lecter books, and Robert Ludlum and the Jason Bourne series, as well as Hemingway's final work, A Moveable Feast, will be one of the greatest honors of my writing life. He taught me lessons that live on in each title. Coming from a writing family as I do, it was an easy decision to entrust the editing of BLAST to a most able writer and editor, Cecily Sharp-Whitehill, who also answers to Mom. Thank you so much for jumping in!

ABOUT ROBERT BLAKE WHITEHILL

Robert Blake Whitehill is a Maryland Eastern Shore Native, and an award-winning, critically acclaimed author and screenwriter. In addition to the English editions, his Ben Blackshaw thrillers are also published in German by

www.Luzifer-Verlag.de

Whitehill is a member of International Thriller Writers, as well as a sometime contributor to *Chesapeake Bay Magazine* and *The Audiophile Voice*.

Find out more about the author, his blog, and the Chesapeake Bay at:

www.robertblakewhitehill.com